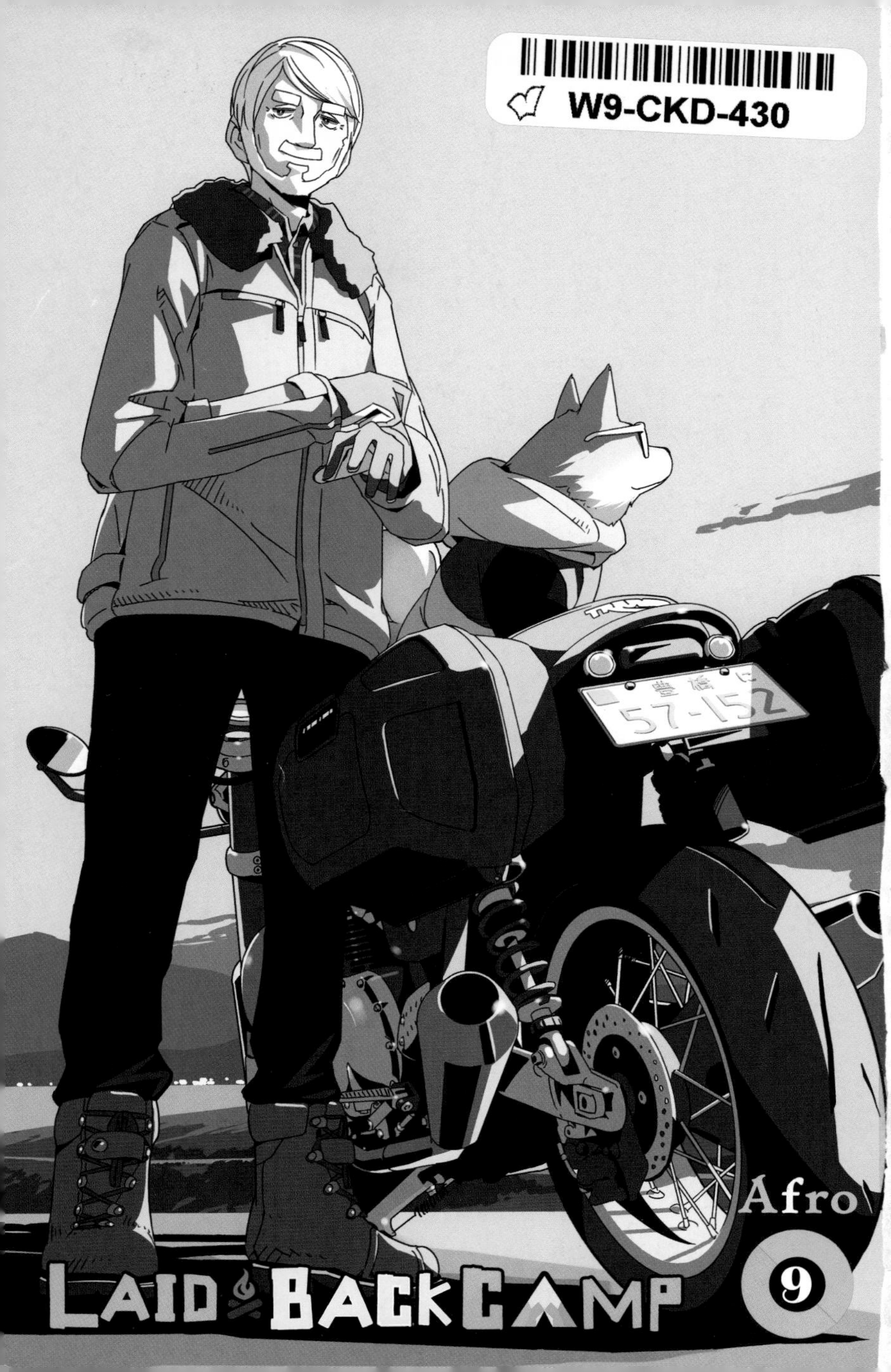
57-152
Afro
LAID BACK CAMP
9

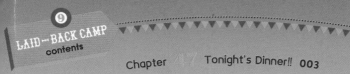

9

LAID-BACK CAMP
contents

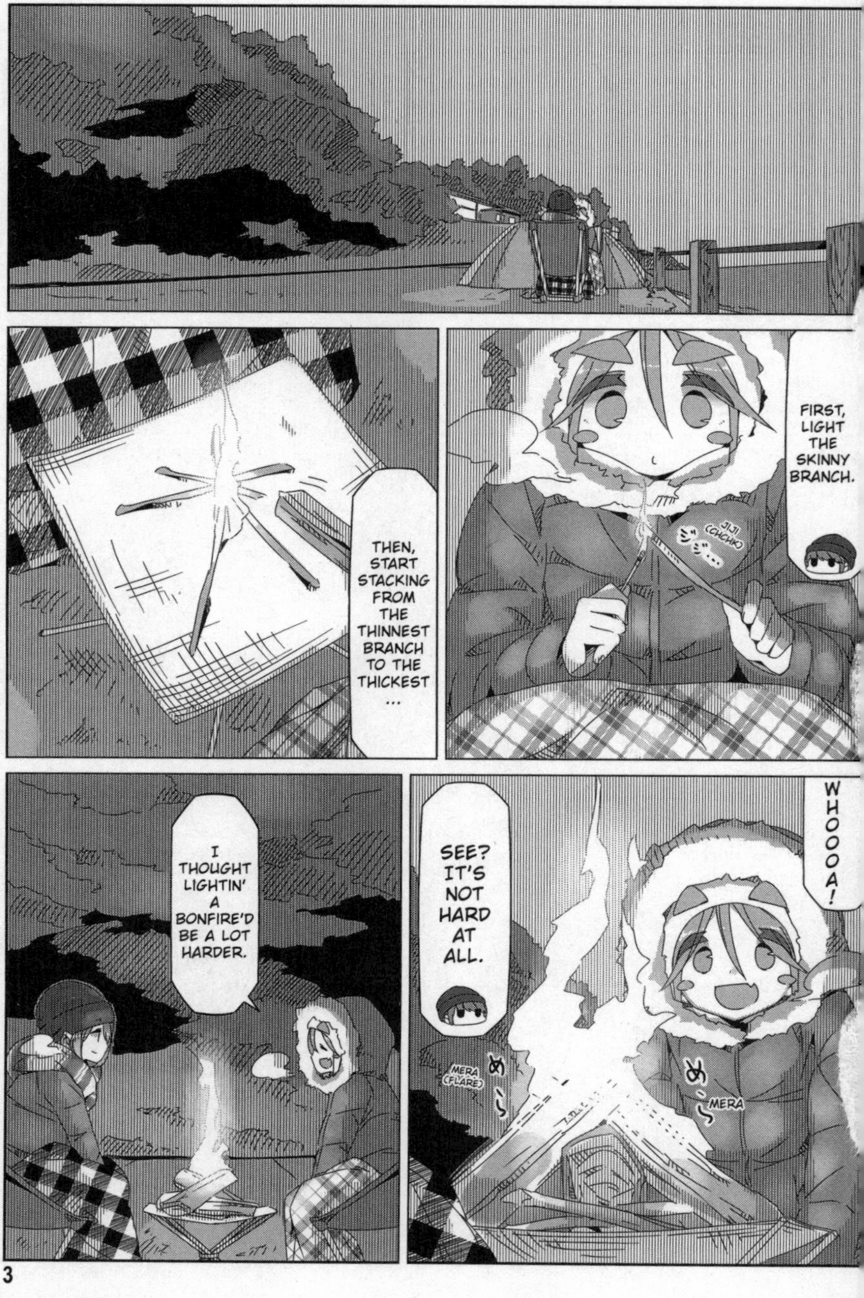

FIRST, LIGHT THE SKINNY BRANCH.
JIJI (CHCHK)
THEN, START STACKING FROM THE THINNEST BRANCH TO THE THICKEST ...
WHOOOOA!
SEE? IT'S NOT HARD AT ALL.
MERA
MERA (FLARE)
I THOUGHT LIGHTIN' A BONFIRE'D BE A LOT HARDER.

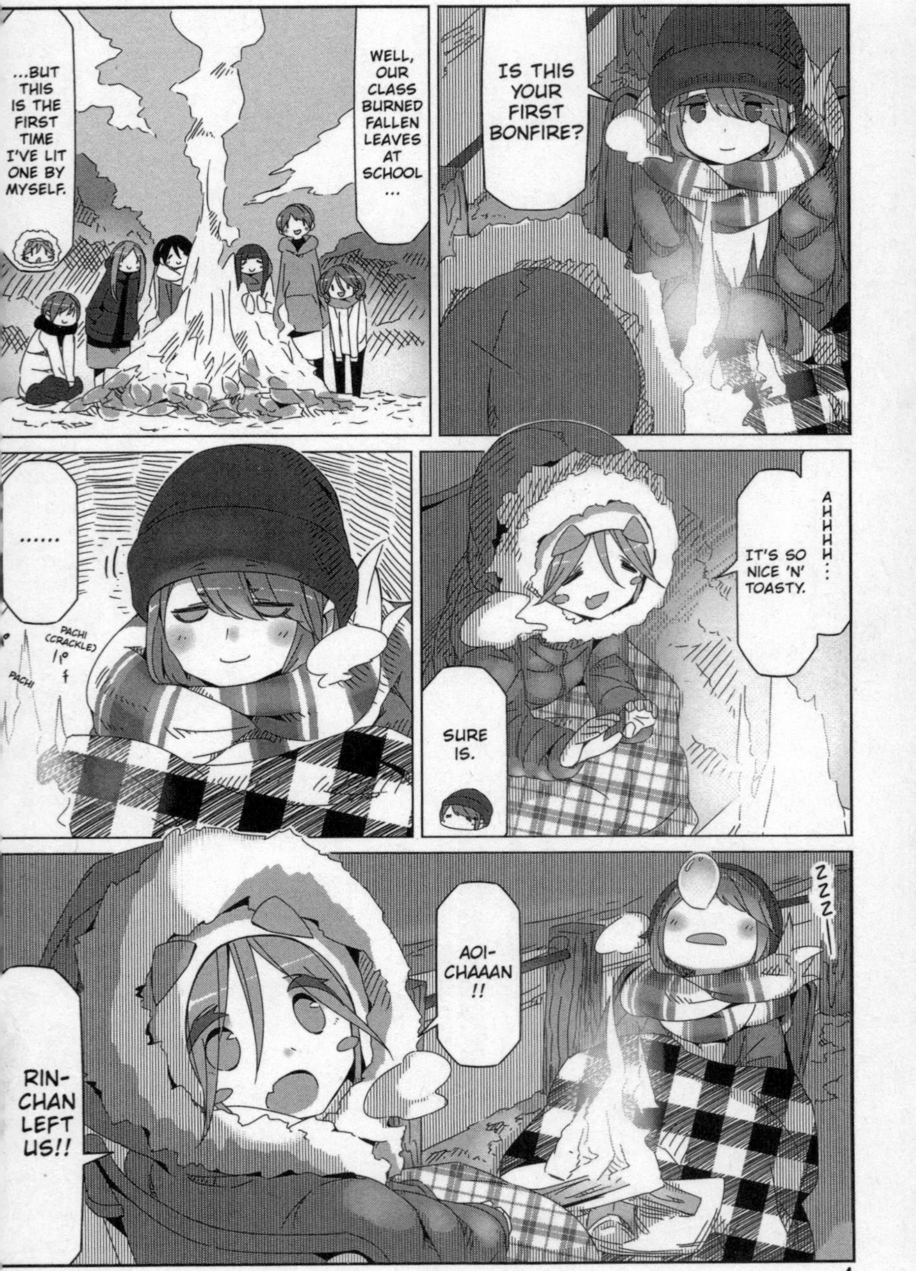
IS THIS YOUR FIRST BONFIRE?
WELL, OUR CLASS BURNED FALLEN LEAVES AT SCHOOL...
...BUT THIS IS THE FIRST TIME I'VE LIT ONE BY MYSELF.
AHHHH...
IT'S SO NICE 'N' TOASTY.
SURE IS.
......
PACHI (CRACKLE)
PACHI
ZZZ
AOI-CHAAAN!!
RIN-CHAN LEFT US!!

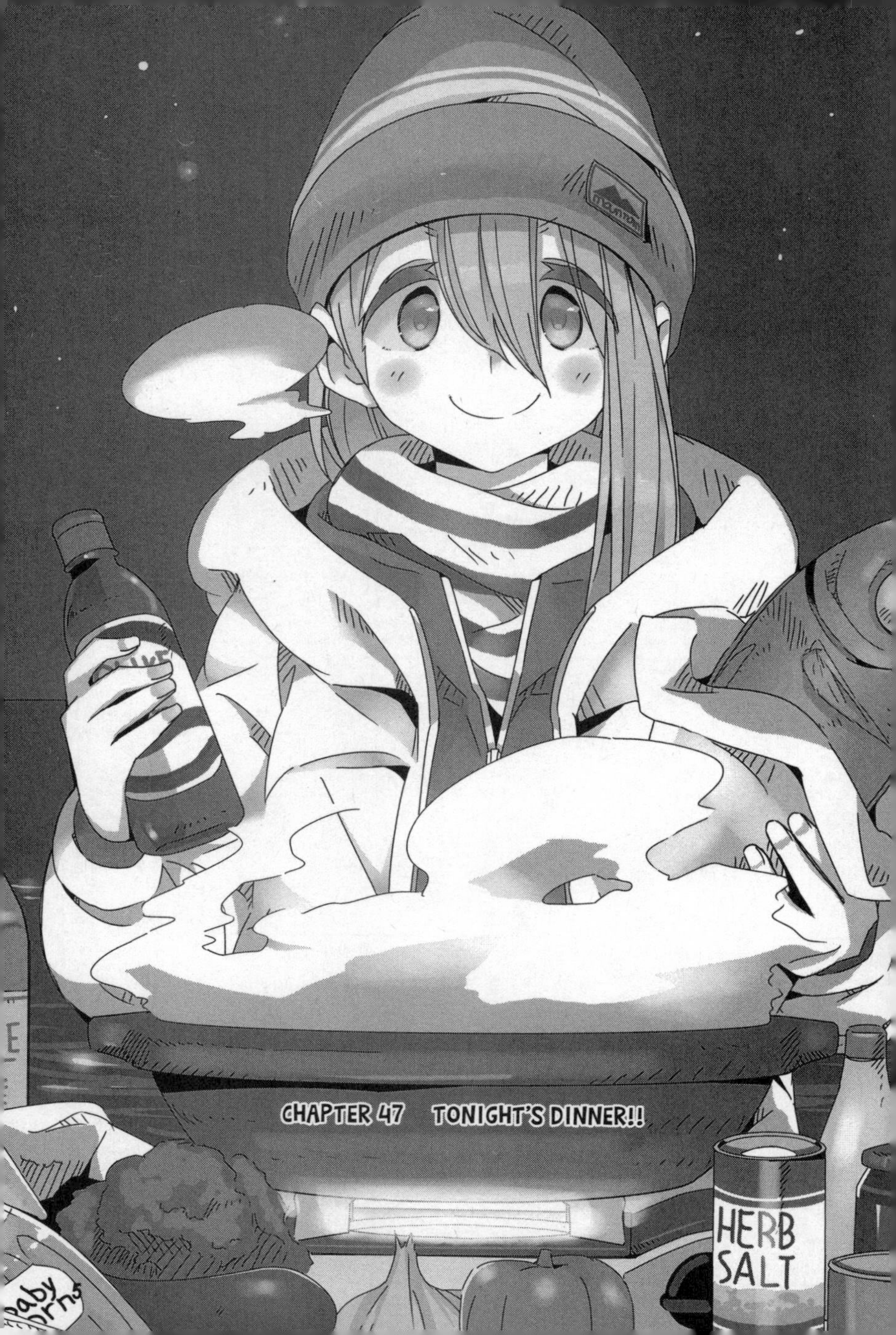
CHAPTER 47 TONIGHT'S DINNER!!
HERB SALT

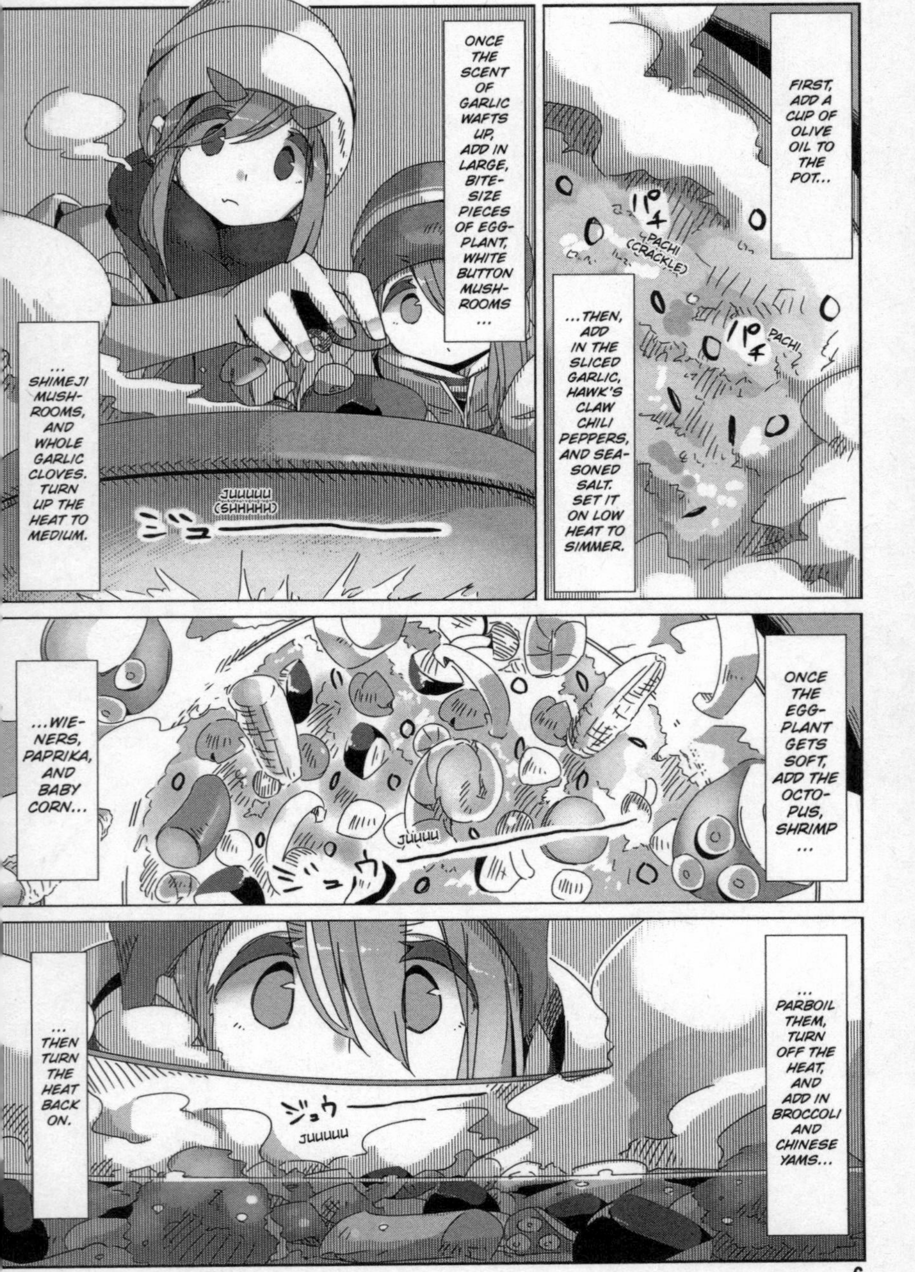
FIRST, ADD A CUP OF OLIVE OIL TO THE POT...
パチ
PACHI (CRACKLE)
パチ
PACHI
...THEN, ADD IN THE SLICED GARLIC, HAWK'S CLAW CHILI PEPPERS, AND SEASONED SALT. SET IT ON LOW HEAT TO SIMMER.
ONCE THE SCENT OF GARLIC WAFTS UP, ADD IN LARGE, BITE-SIZE PIECES OF EGGPLANT, WHITE BUTTON MUSHROOMS...
...SHIMEJI MUSHROOMS, AND WHOLE GARLIC CLOVES. TURN UP THE HEAT TO MEDIUM.
ジュー
JUUUUU (SHHHHH)
ONCE THE EGGPLANT GETS SOFT, ADD THE OCTOPUS, SHRIMP...
ジュウ
JUUUU
...WIENERS, PAPRIKA, AND BABY CORN...
...PARBOIL THEM, TURN OFF THE HEAT, AND ADD IN BROCCOLI AND CHINESE YAMS...
ジュウ
JUUUUU
...THEN TURN THE HEAT BACK ON.

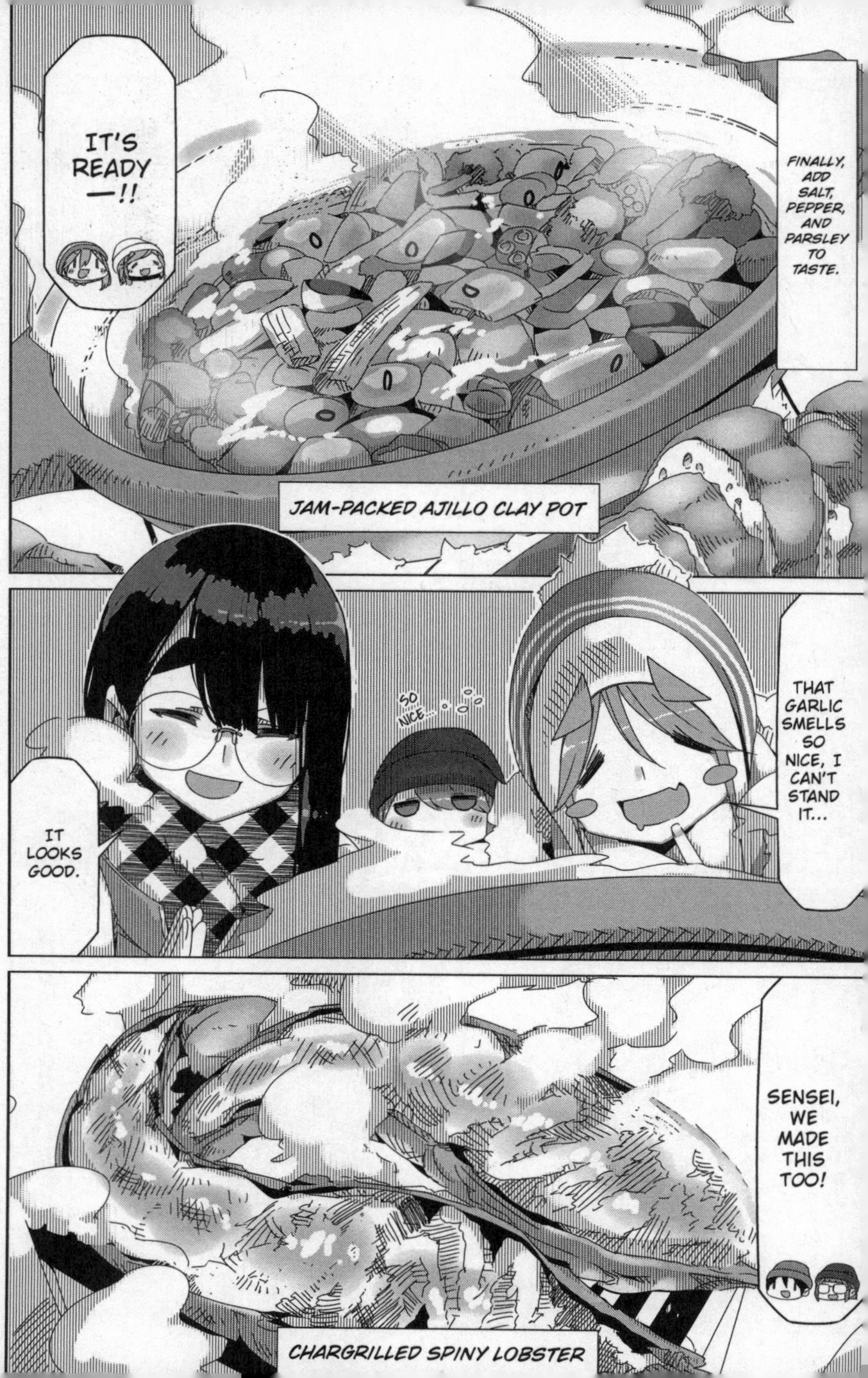
FINALLY, ADD SALT, PEPPER, AND PARSLEY TO TASTE.
IT'S READY—!!
JAM-PACKED AJILLO CLAY POT
THAT GARLIC SMELLS SO NICE, I CAN'T STAND IT...
SO NICE...
IT LOOKS GOOD.
SENSEI, WE MADE THIS TOO!
CHARGRILLED SPINY LOBSTER

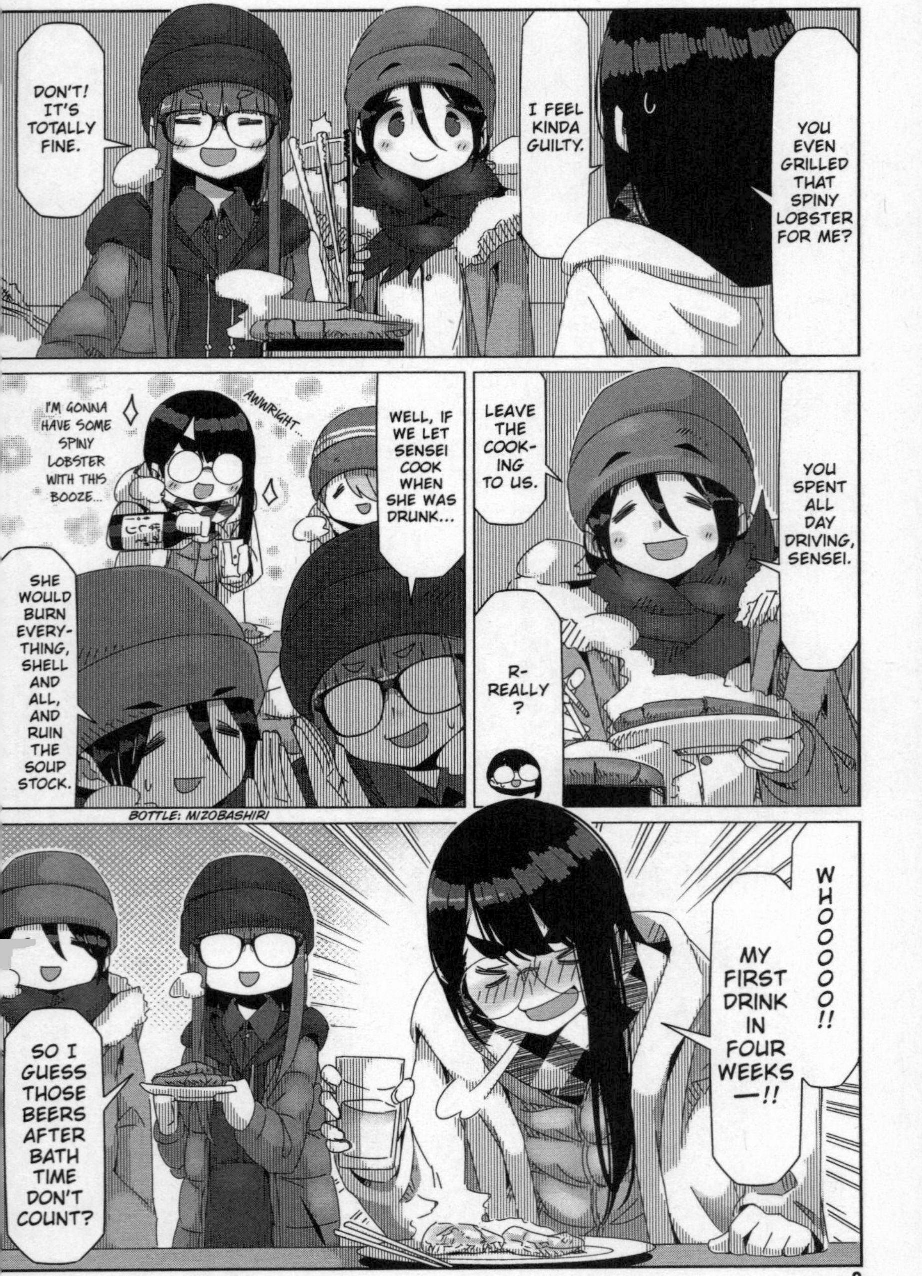
YOU EVEN GRILLED THAT SPINY LOBSTER FOR ME?
I FEEL KINDA GUILTY.
DON'T! IT'S TOTALLY FINE.
YOU SPENT ALL DAY DRIVING, SENSEI.
LEAVE THE COOK-ING TO US.
R-REALLY?
WELL, IF WE LET SENSEI COOK WHEN SHE WAS DRUNK...
AWWRIGHT...
I'M GONNA HAVE SOME SPINY LOBSTER WITH THIS BOOZE...
SHE WOULD BURN EVERY-THING, SHELL AND ALL, AND RUIN THE SOUP STOCK.
BOTTLE: MIZOBASHIRI
WHOOOOOO!!
MY FIRST DRINK IN FOUR WEEKS—!!
SO I GUESS THOSE BEERS AFTER BATH TIME DON'T COUNT?

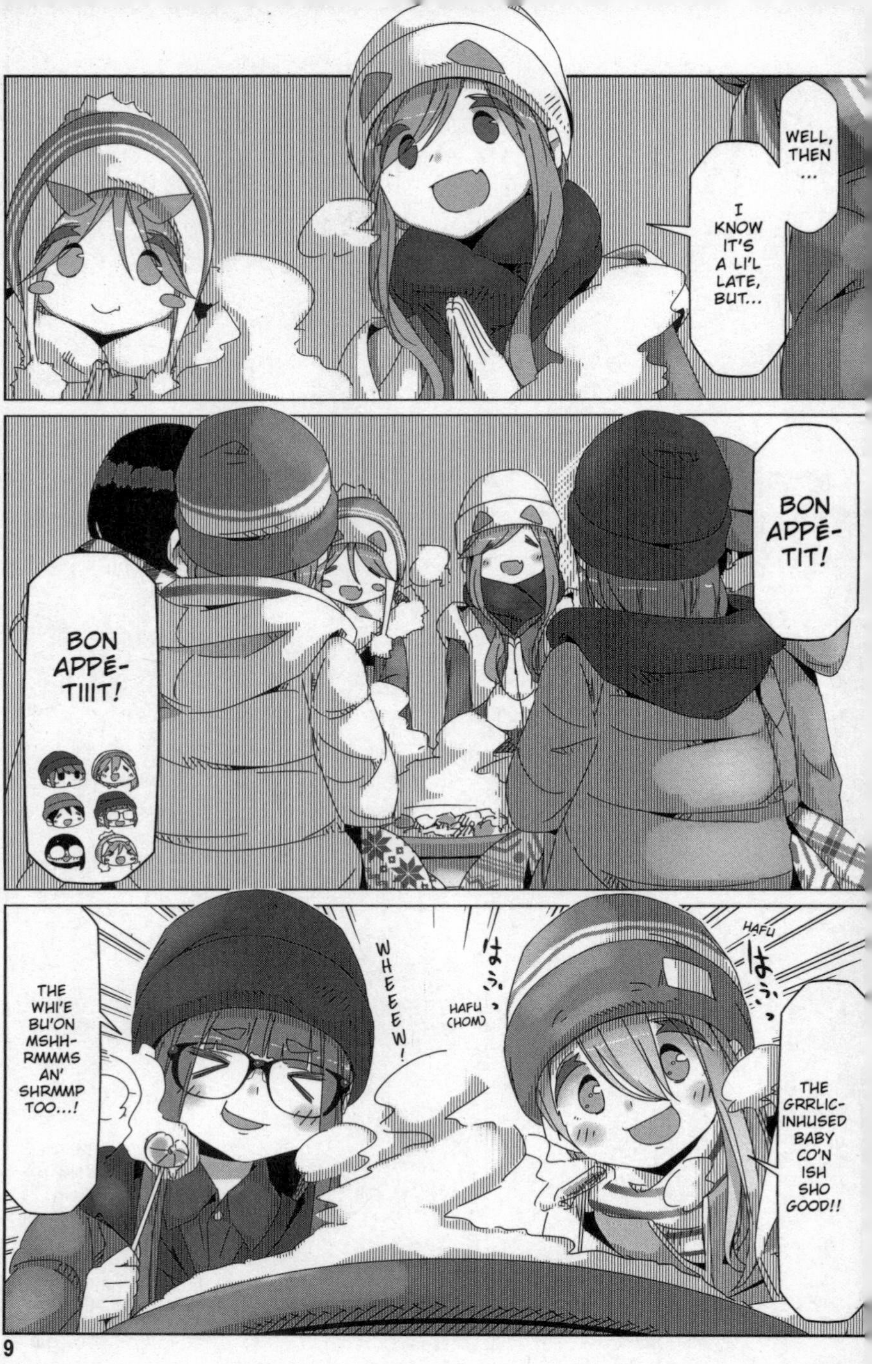

WELL, THEN ...
I KNOW IT'S A LI'L LATE, BUT...
BON APPÉ-TIT!
BON APPÉ-TIIIT!
HAFU
はふっ
THE GRRLIC-INHUSED BABY CO'N ISH SHO GOOD!!
HAFU (HOM)
はふっ
WHEEEEW!
THE WHI'E BU'ON MSHH-RMMMS AN' SHRMMP TOO...!

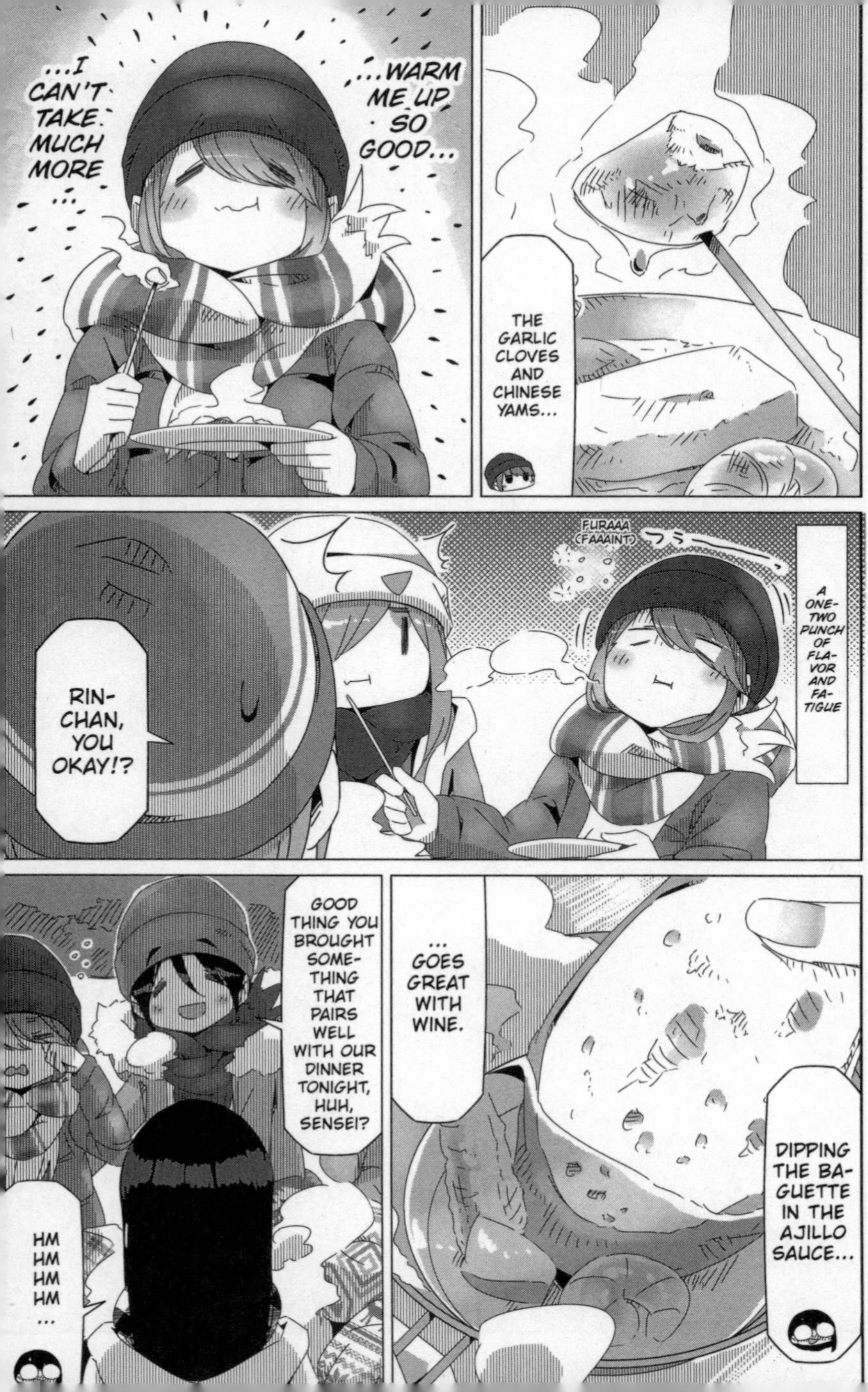

THE GARLIC CLOVES AND CHINESE YAMS...
...WARM ME UP SO GOOD...
...I CAN'T TAKE MUCH MORE...
A ONE-TWO PUNCH OF FLAVOR AND FATIGUE
FURAAA (FAAAINT)
RIN-CHAN, YOU OKAY!?
DIPPING THE BAGUETTE IN THE AJILLO SAUCE...
...GOES GREAT WITH WINE.
GOOD THING YOU BROUGHT SOMETHING THAT PAIRS WELL WITH OUR DINNER TONIGHT, HUH, SENSEI?
HM HM HM HM...

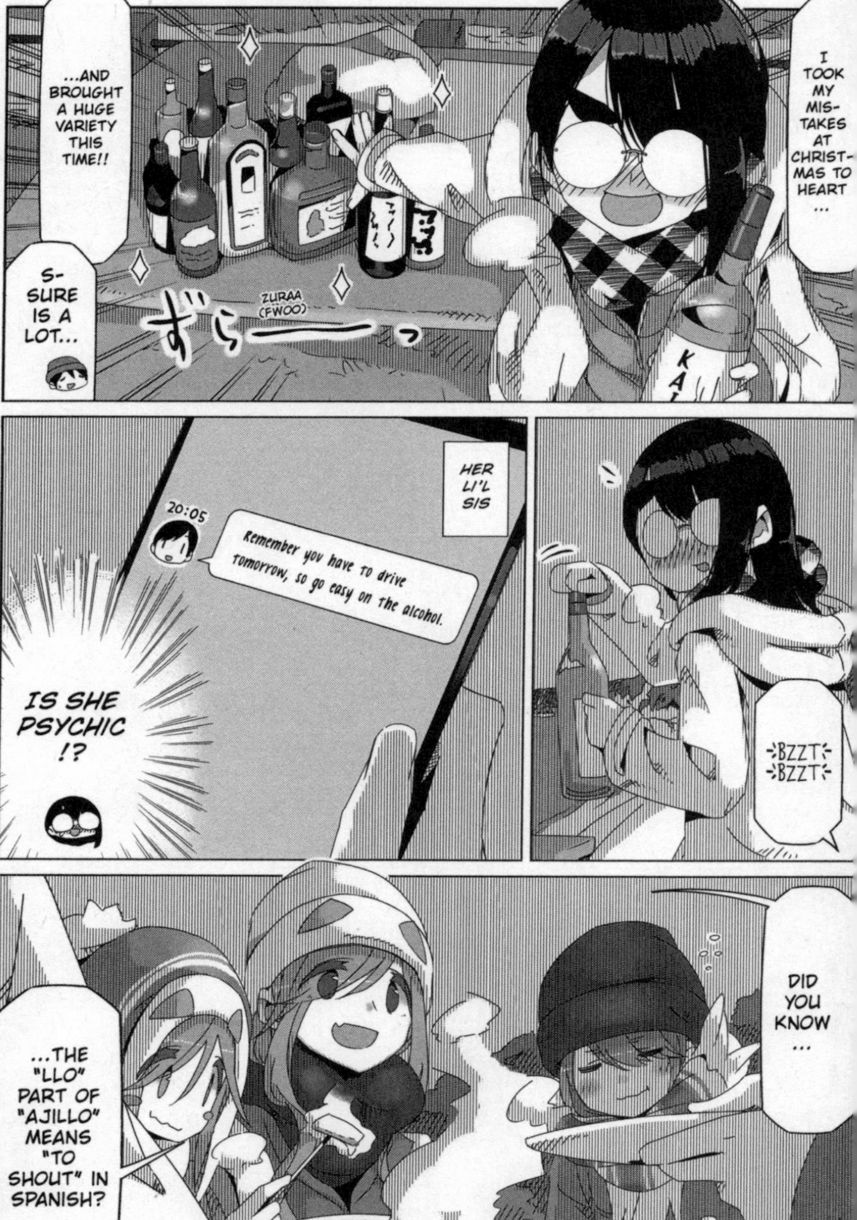
I TOOK MY MIS-TAKES AT CHRIST-MAS TO HEART ...
...AND BROUGHT A HUGE VARIETY THIS TIME!!
ずらーーっ
ZURAA (FWOO)
S-SURE IS A LOT...
BZZT BZZT
HER LI'L SIS
20:05
Remember you have to drive tomorrow, so go easy on the alcohol.
IS SHE PSYCHIC !?
DID YOU KNOW ...
...THE "LLO" PART OF "AJILLO" MEANS "TO SHOUT" IN SPANISH?

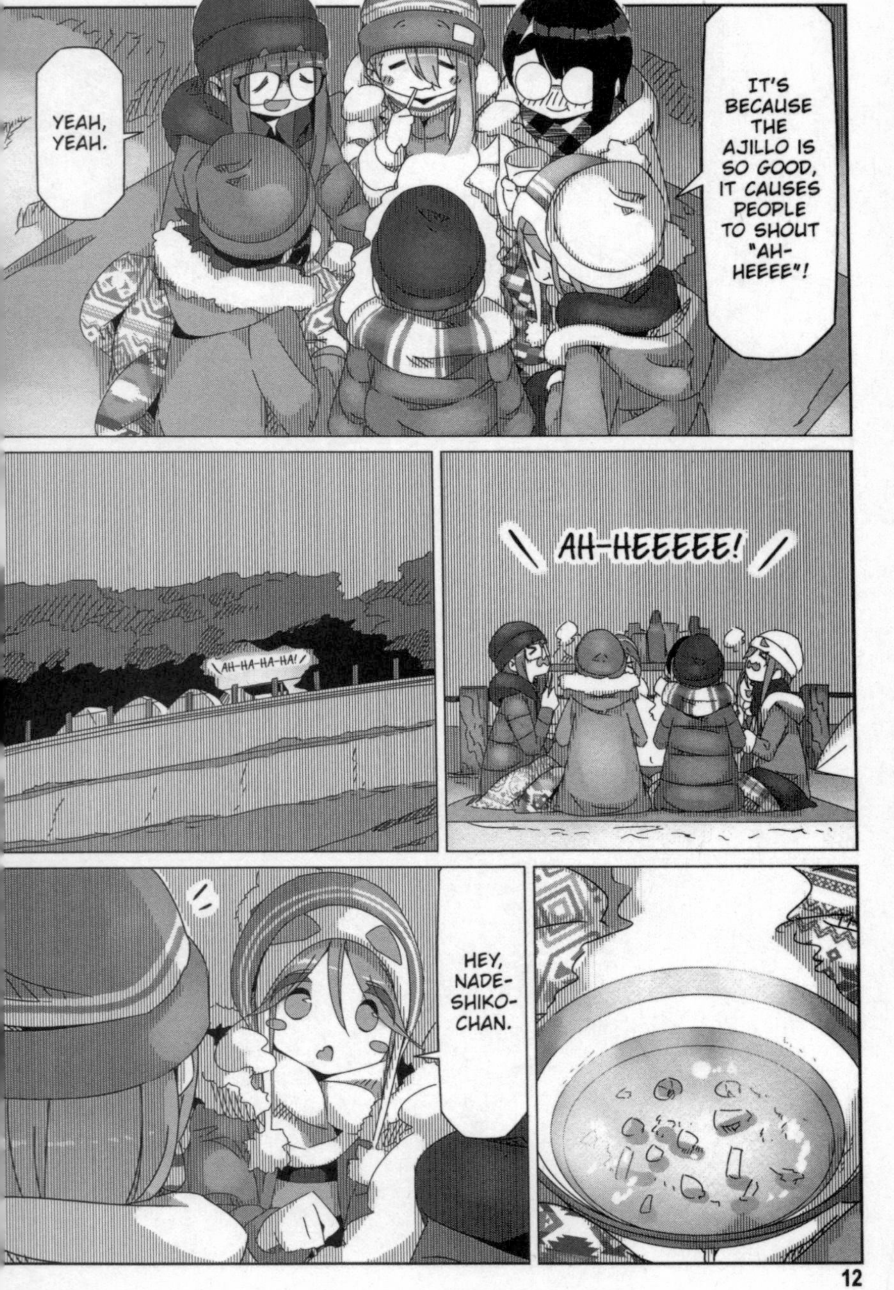
IT'S BECAUSE THE AJILLO IS SO GOOD, IT CAUSES PEOPLE TO SHOUT "AH-HEEEE"!
YEAH, YEAH.
AH-HEEEEE!
AH-HA-HA-HA!
HEY, NADE-SHIKO-CHAN.

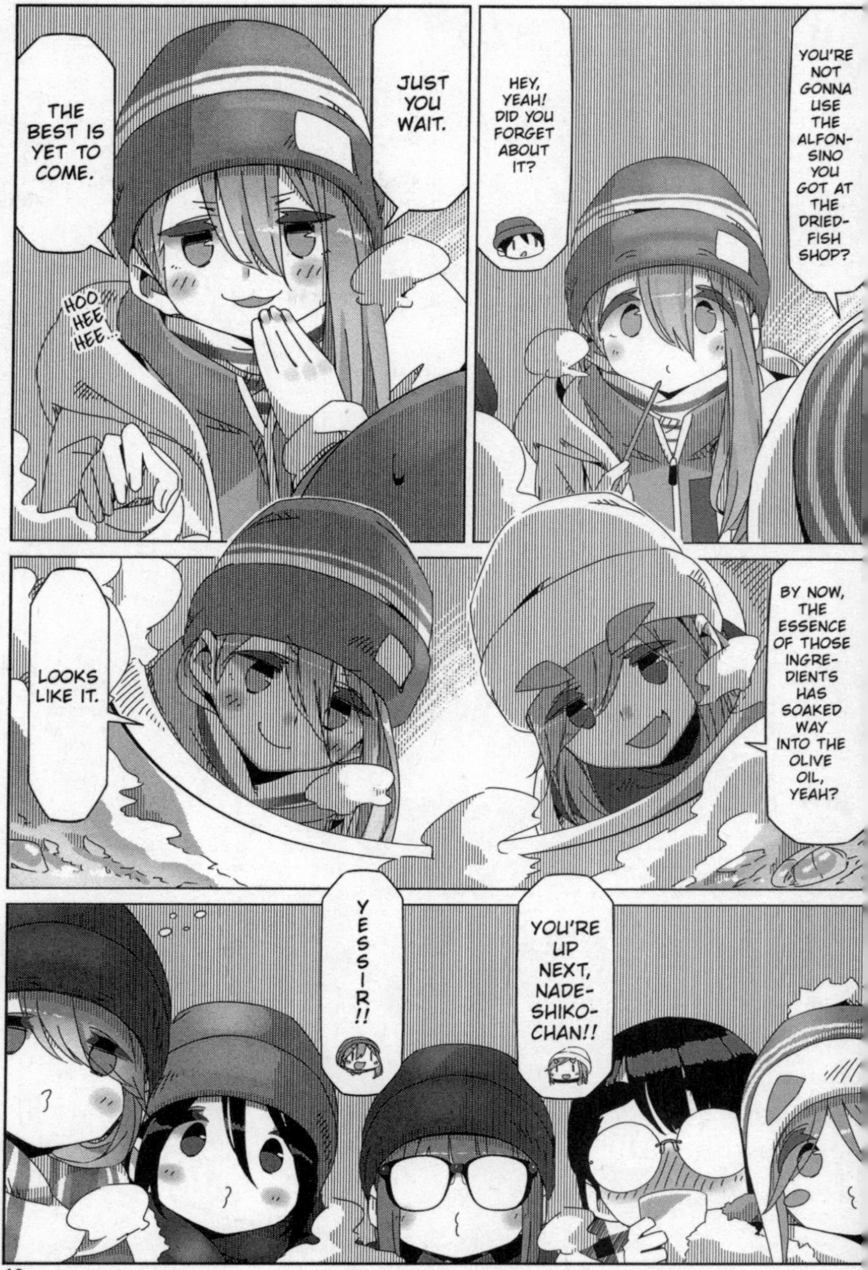
YOU'RE NOT GONNA USE THE ALFONSINO YOU GOT AT THE DRIED-FISH SHOP?
HEY, YEAH! DID YOU FORGET ABOUT IT?
JUST YOU WAIT.
THE BEST IS YET TO COME.
HOO HEE HEE...
BY NOW, THE ESSENCE OF THOSE INGREDIENTS HAS SOAKED WAY INTO THE OLIVE OIL, YEAH?
LOOKS LIKE IT.
YOU'RE UP NEXT, NADESHIKO-CHAN!!
YESSIR!!

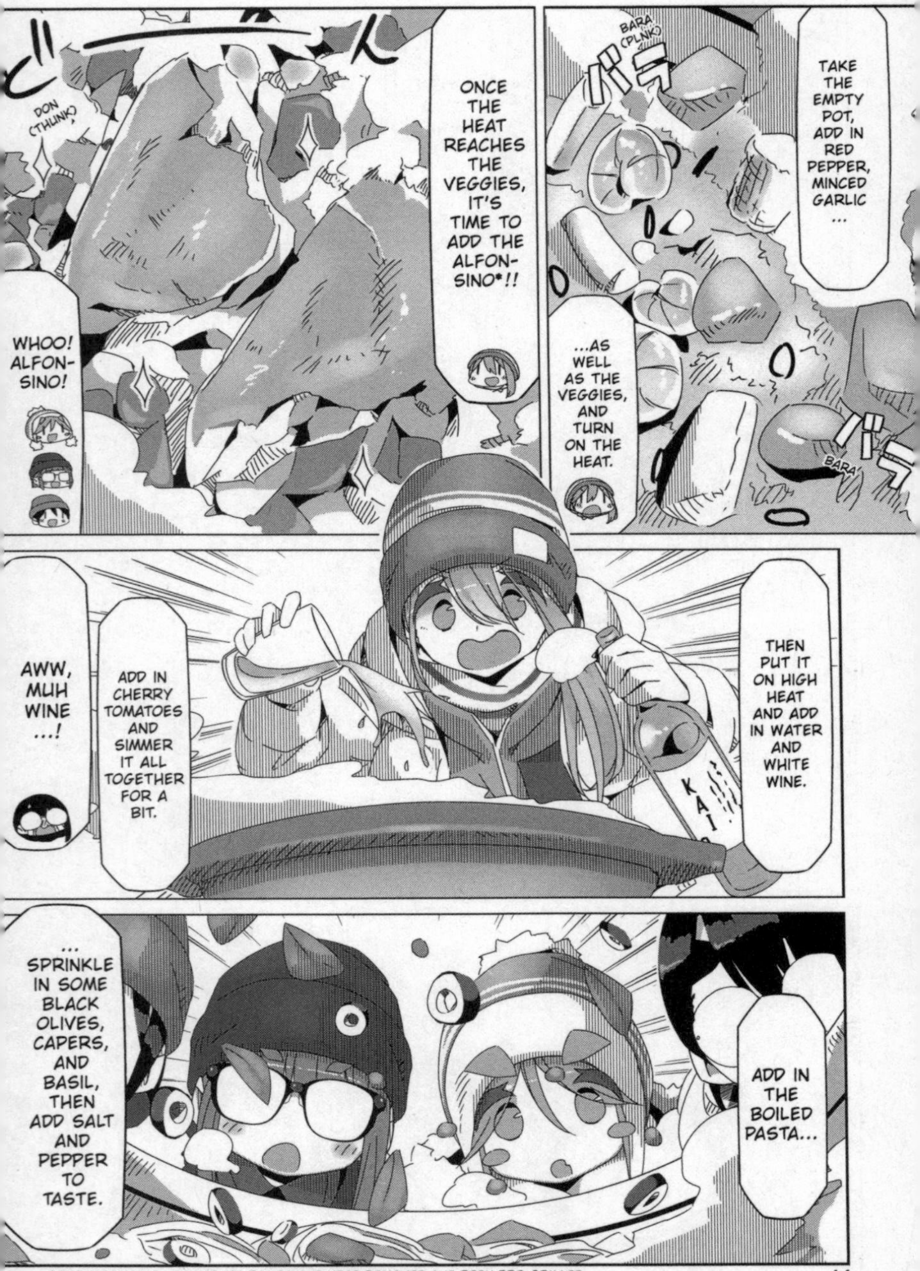
TAKE THE EMPTY POT, ADD IN RED PEPPER, MINCED GARLIC ...
BARA (PLNK)
...AS WELL AS THE VEGGIES, AND TURN ON THE HEAT.
BARA
ONCE THE HEAT REACHES THE VEGGIES, IT'S TIME TO ADD THE ALFONSINO*!!
DON (THUNK)
WHOO! ALFONSINO!
THEN PUT IT ON HIGH HEAT AND ADD IN WATER AND WHITE WINE.
KAI
ADD IN CHERRY TOMATOES AND SIMMER IT ALL TOGETHER FOR A BIT.
AWW, MUH WINE ...!
ADD IN THE BOILED PASTA...
... SPRINKLE IN SOME BLACK OLIVES, CAPERS, AND BASIL, THEN ADD SALT AND PEPPER TO TASTE.

*THE ALFONSINO HAS HAD ITS BONES AND HEAD REMOVED AND BEEN PRE-GRILLED.

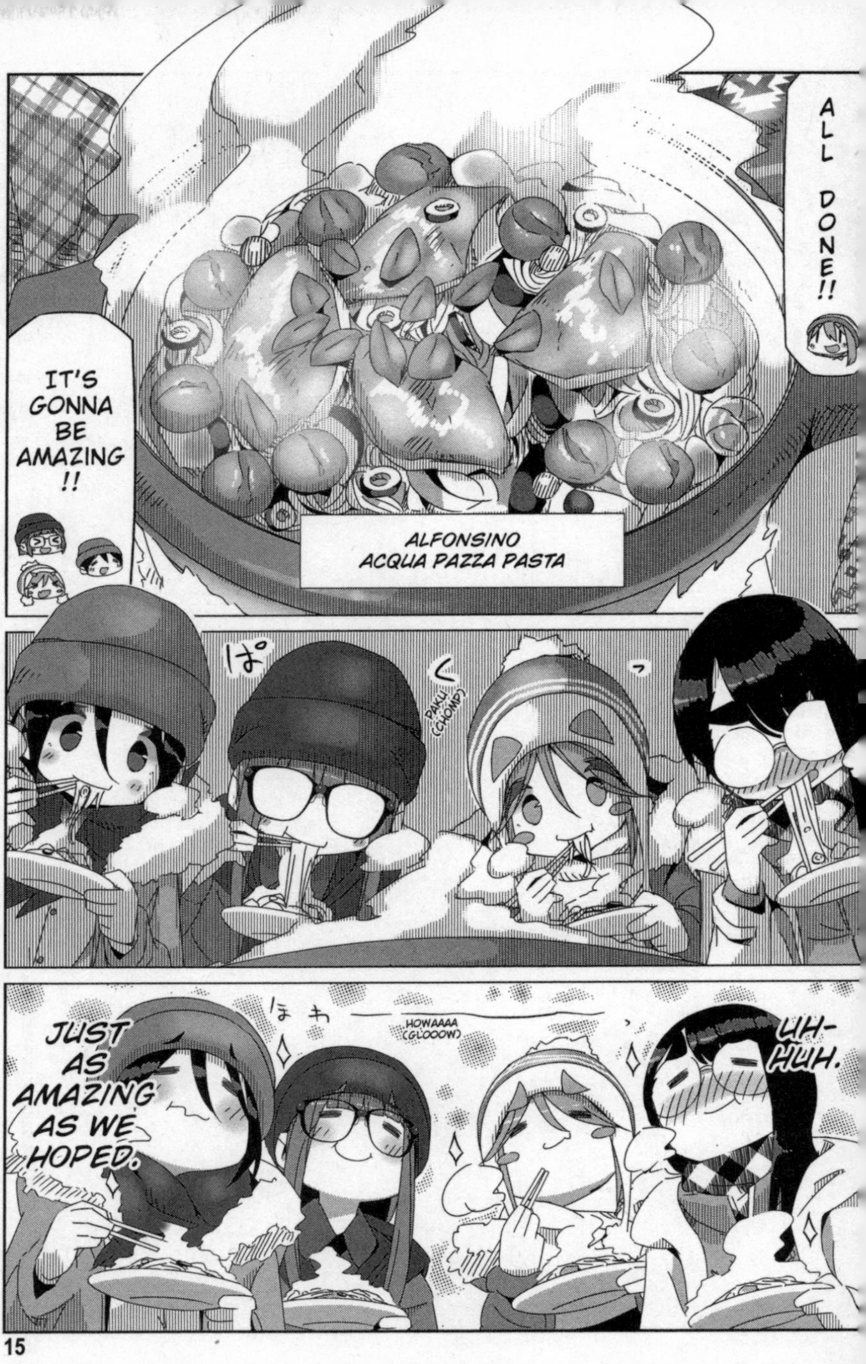
ALL DONE!!
ALFONSINO ACQUA PAZZA PASTA
IT'S GONNA BE AMAZING!!
ぱくっ
PAKU (CHOMP)
ほわ——
HOWAAAA (GLOOOW)
UH-HUH.
JUST AS AMAZING AS WE HOPED.

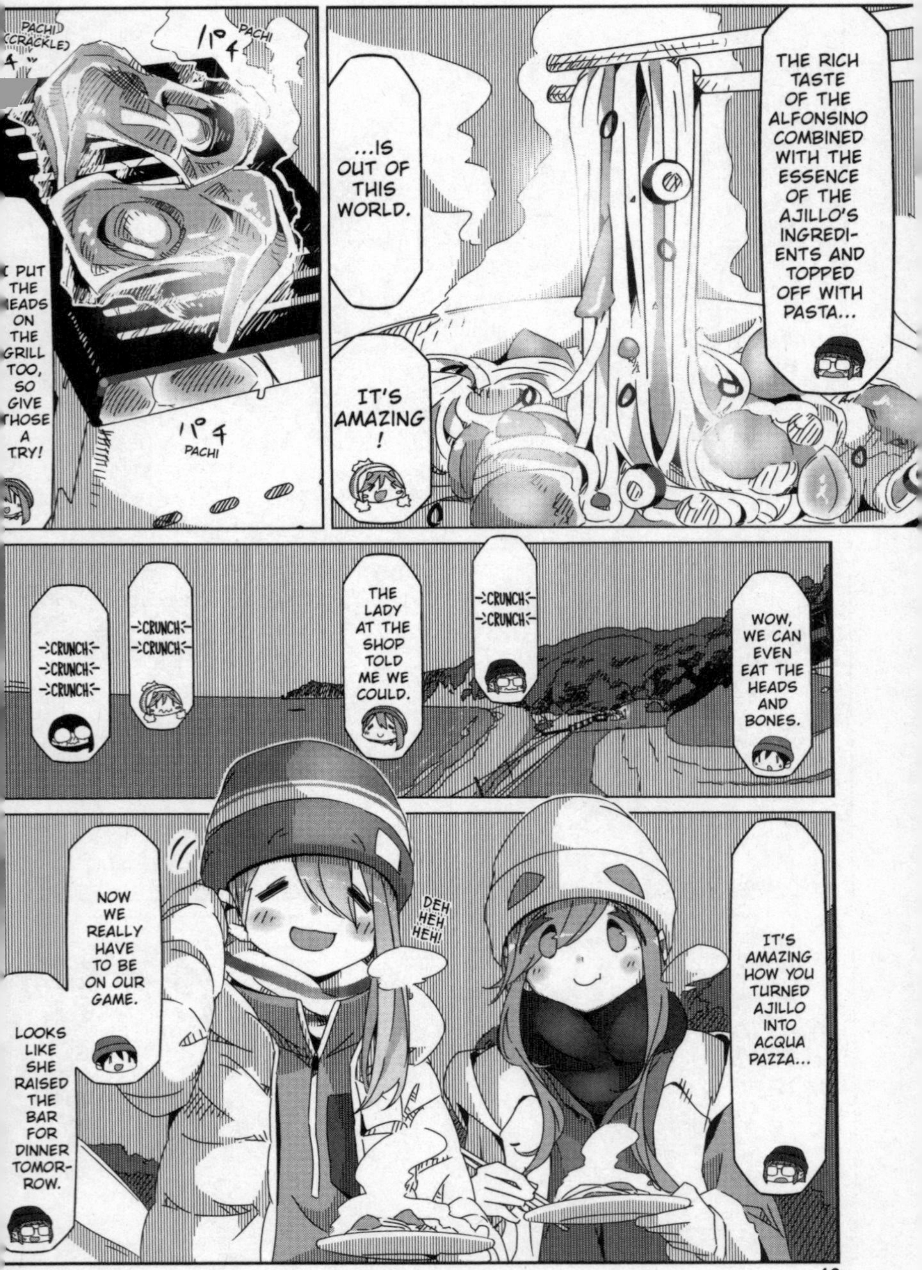
THE RICH TASTE OF THE ALFONSINO COMBINED WITH THE ESSENCE OF THE AJILLO'S INGREDIENTS AND TOPPED OFF WITH PASTA...
...IS OUT OF THIS WORLD.
IT'S AMAZING!
PACHI (CRACKLE)
PACHI
I PUT THE HEADS ON THE GRILL TOO, SO GIVE THOSE A TRY!
PACHI
WOW, WE CAN EVEN EAT THE HEADS AND BONES.
CRUNCH CRUNCH
THE LADY AT THE SHOP TOLD ME WE COULD.
CRUNCH CRUNCH
CRUNCH CRUNCH CRUNCH
IT'S AMAZING HOW YOU TURNED AJILLO INTO ACQUA PAZZA...
DEH HEH HEH!
NOW WE REALLY HAVE TO BE ON OUR GAME.
LOOKS LIKE SHE RAISED THE BAR FOR DINNER TOMORROW.

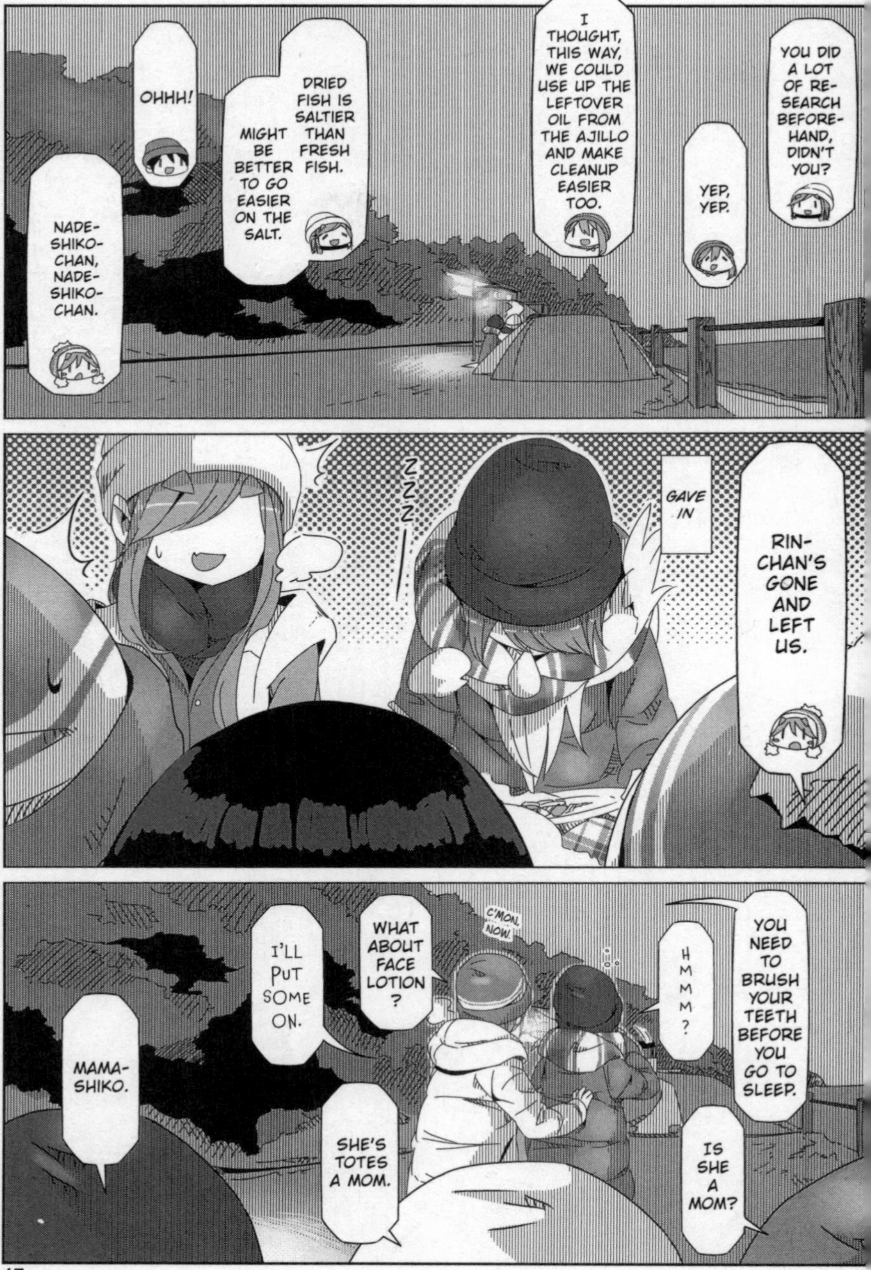
YOU DID A LOT OF RE-SEARCH BEFORE-HAND, DIDN'T YOU?
YEP, YEP.
I THOUGHT, THIS WAY, WE COULD USE UP THE LEFTOVER OIL FROM THE AJILLO AND MAKE CLEANUP EASIER TOO.
DRIED FISH IS SALTIER THAN FRESH FISH.
MIGHT BE BETTER TO GO EASIER ON THE SALT.
OHHH!
NADE-SHIKO-CHAN, NADE-SHIKO-CHAN.
RIN-CHAN'S GONE AND LEFT US.
GAVE IN
ZZZ
YOU NEED TO BRUSH YOUR TEETH BEFORE YOU GO TO SLEEP.
HMMM?
C'MON, NOW.
WHAT ABOUT FACE LOTION?
I'LL PUT SOME ON.
IS SHE A MOM?
SHE'S TOTES A MOM.
MAMA-SHIKO.

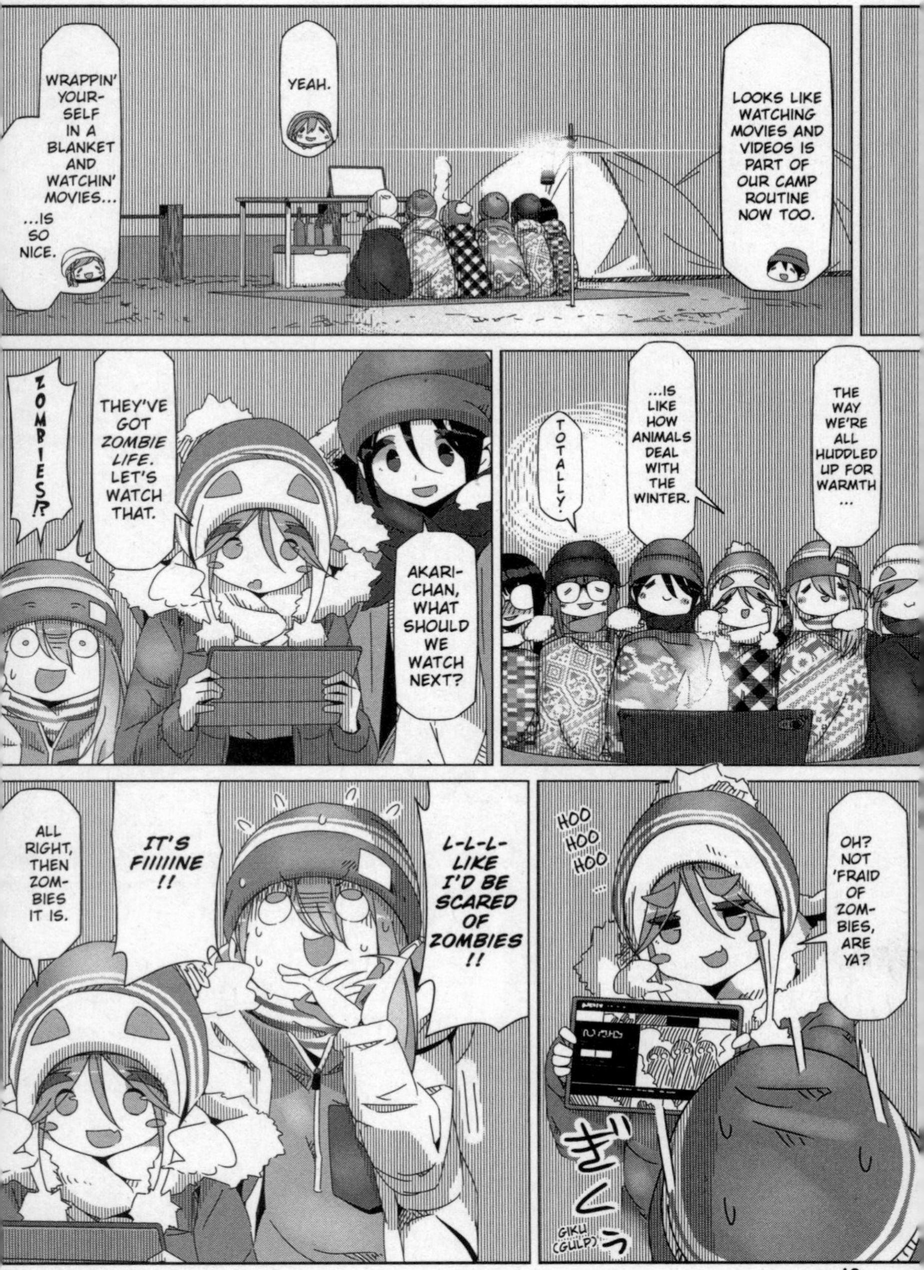
LOOKS LIKE WATCHING MOVIES AND VIDEOS IS PART OF OUR CAMP ROUTINE NOW TOO.
YEAH.
WRAPPIN' YOURSELF IN A BLANKET AND WATCHIN' MOVIES...
...IS SO NICE.
THE WAY WE'RE ALL HUDDLED UP FOR WARMTH...
...IS LIKE HOW ANIMALS DEAL WITH THE WINTER.
TOTALLY!
AKARI-CHAN, WHAT SHOULD WE WATCH NEXT?
THEY'VE GOT ZOMBIE LIFE. LET'S WATCH THAT.
ZOMBIES!?
OH? NOT 'FRAID OF ZOMBIES, ARE YA?
HOO HOO HOO...
GIKU (GULP)
L-L-L-LIKE I'D BE SCARED OF ZOMBIES!!
IT'S FIIIIINE!!
ALL RIGHT, THEN ZOMBIES IT IS.

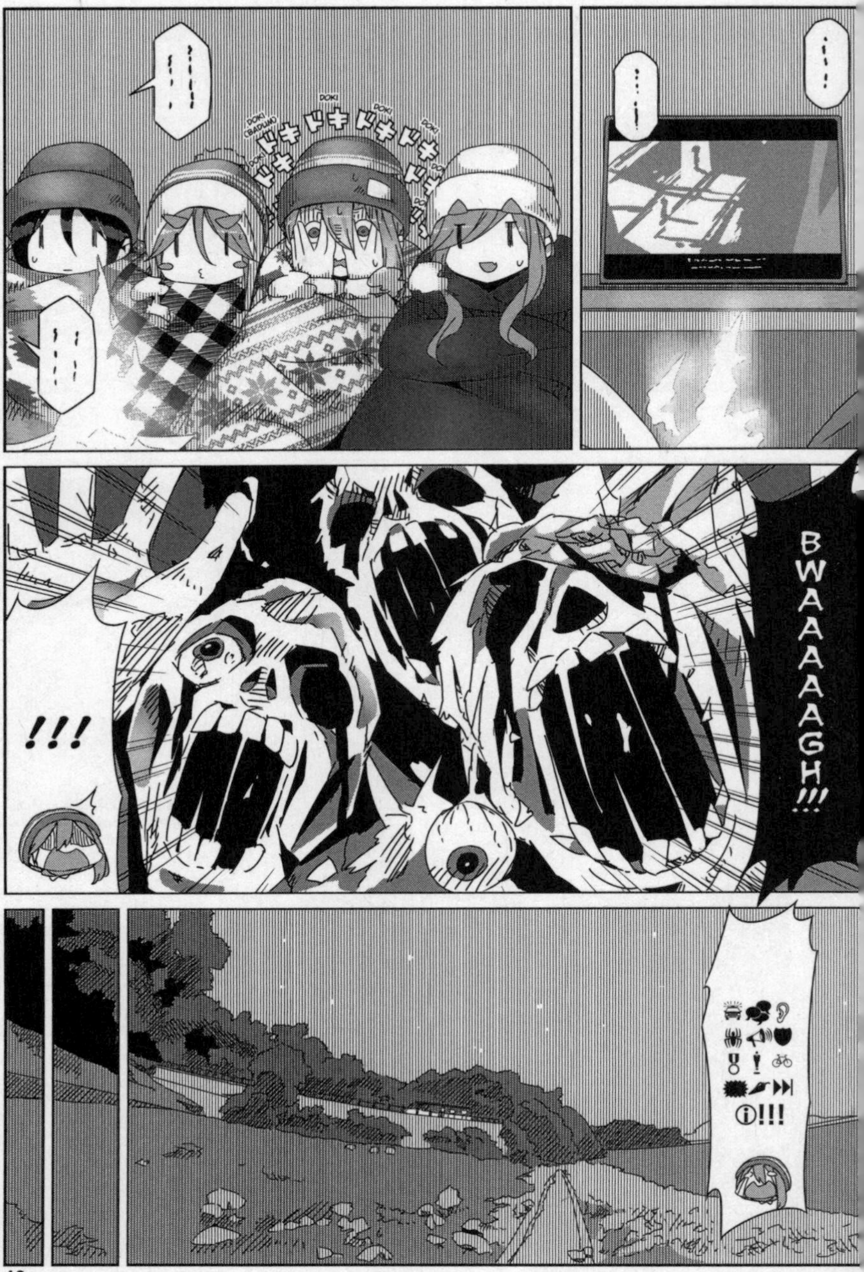
......!
......!
......!!
ドキドキドキドキドキドキ
DOKI (BADUM)
DOKI
DOKI
DOKI
DOKI
DOKI
......!
BWAAAAAAGH!!!
!!!
!!!

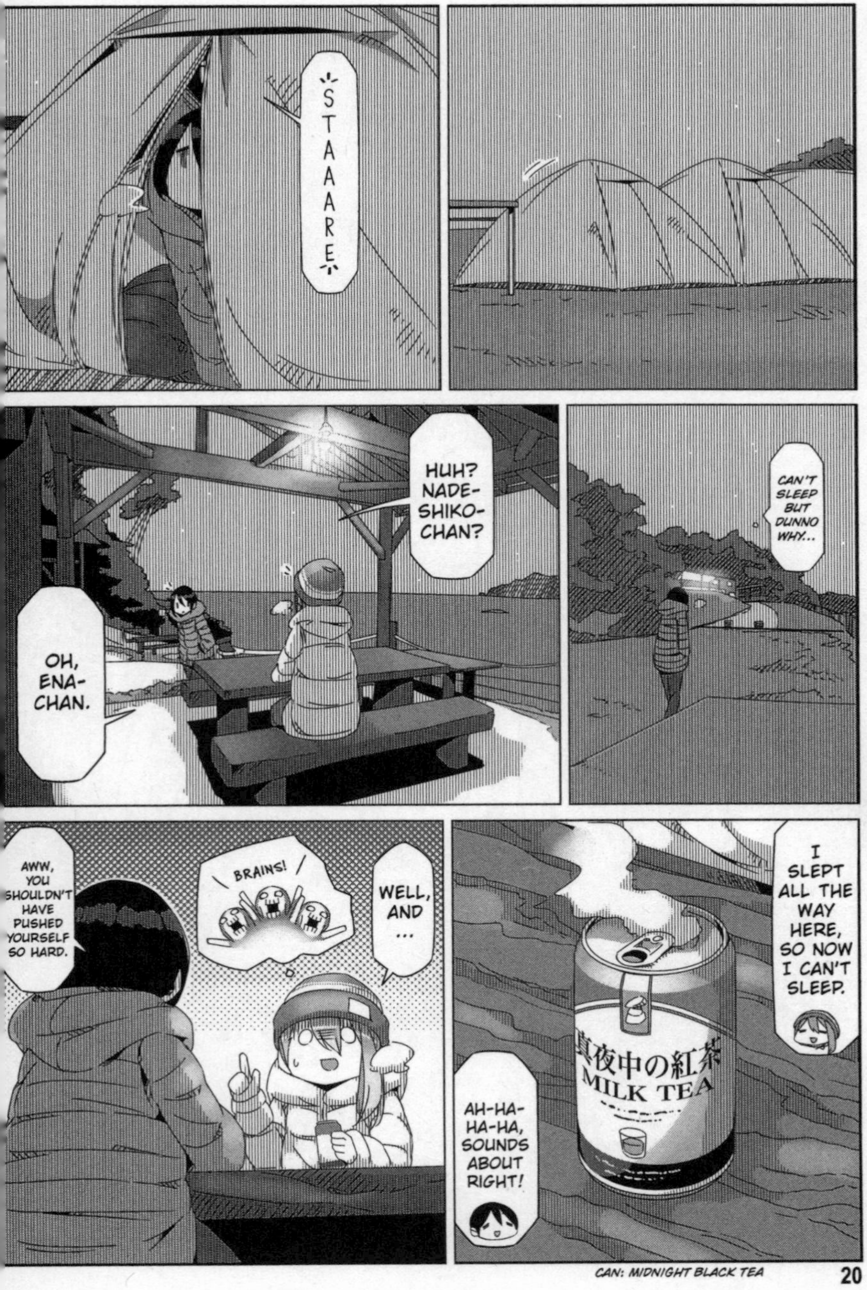
STAAAARE
CAN'T SLEEP BUT DUNNO WHY...
HUH? NADE-SHIKO-CHAN?
OH, ENA-CHAN.
I SLEPT ALL THE WAY HERE, SO NOW I CAN'T SLEEP.
真夜中の紅茶
MILK TEA
AH-HA-HA-HA, SOUNDS ABOUT RIGHT!
WELL, AND ...
BRAINS!
AWW, YOU SHOULDN'T HAVE PUSHED YOURSELF SO HARD.

CAN: MIDNIGHT BLACK TEA

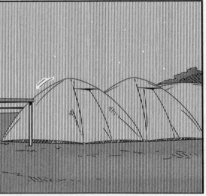

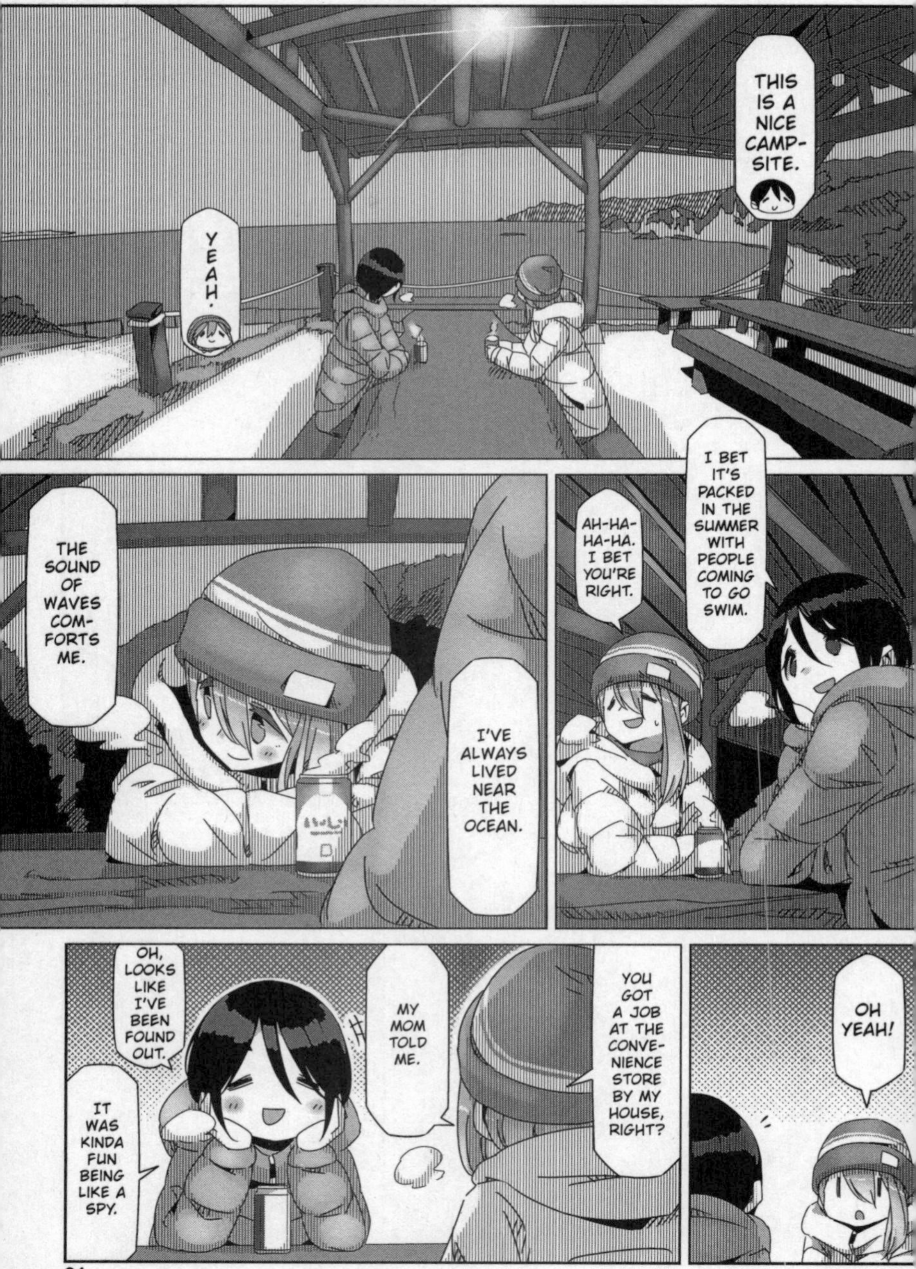
THIS IS A NICE CAMP-SITE.
YEAH.
I BET IT'S PACKED IN THE SUMMER WITH PEOPLE COMING TO GO SWIM.
AH-HA-HA-HA. I BET YOU'RE RIGHT.
I'VE ALWAYS LIVED NEAR THE OCEAN.
THE SOUND OF WAVES COMFORTS ME.
OH YEAH!
YOU GOT A JOB AT THE CONVENIENCE STORE BY MY HOUSE, RIGHT?
MY MOM TOLD ME.
OH, LOOKS LIKE I'VE BEEN FOUND OUT.
IT WAS KINDA FUN BEING LIKE A SPY.

CAN: MAJIUMA COCOA

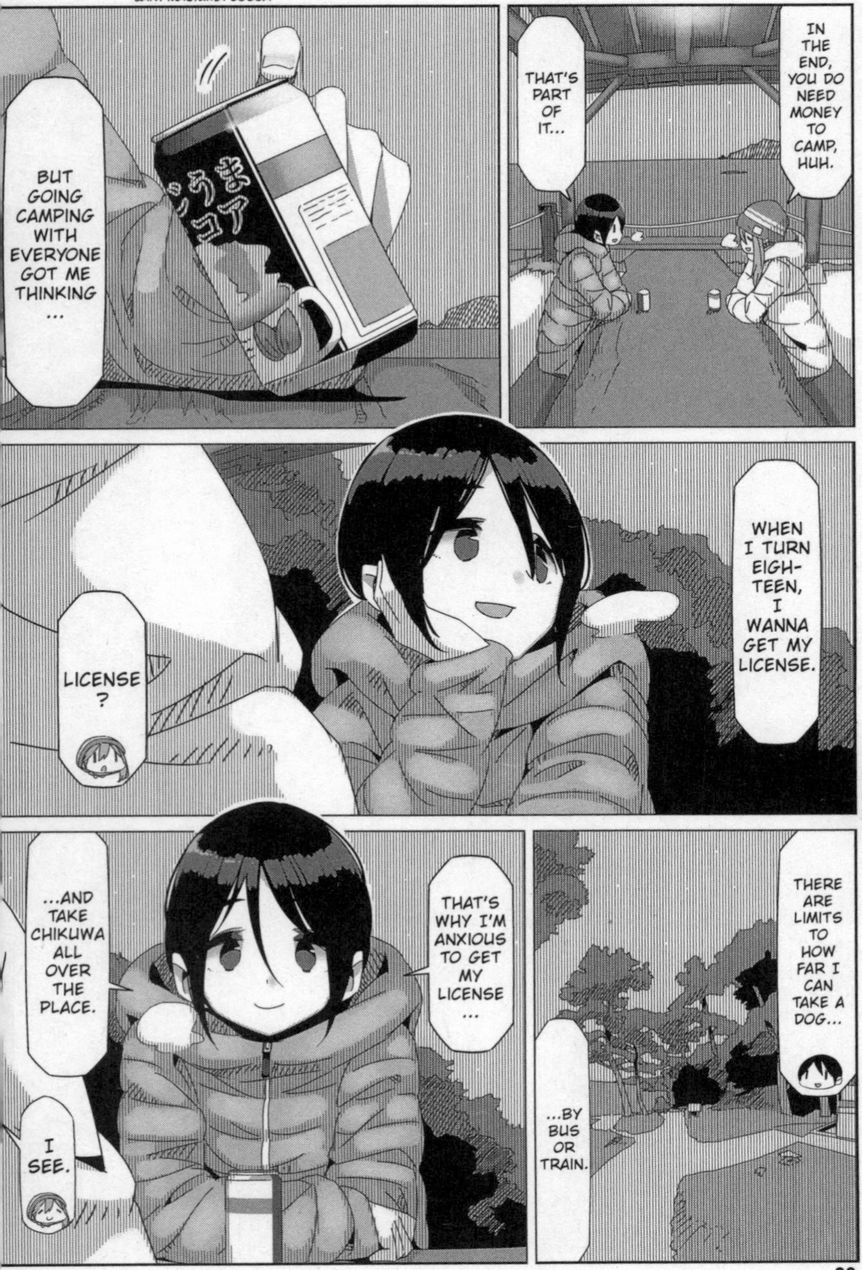
IN THE END, YOU DO NEED MONEY TO CAMP, HUH.
THAT'S PART OF IT...
BUT GOING CAMPING WITH EVERYONE GOT ME THINKING...
WHEN I TURN EIGHTEEN, I WANNA GET MY LICENSE.
LICENSE?
THERE ARE LIMITS TO HOW FAR I CAN TAKE A DOG...
...BY BUS OR TRAIN.
THAT'S WHY I'M ANXIOUS TO GET MY LICENSE...
...AND TAKE CHIKUWA ALL OVER THE PLACE.
I SEE.

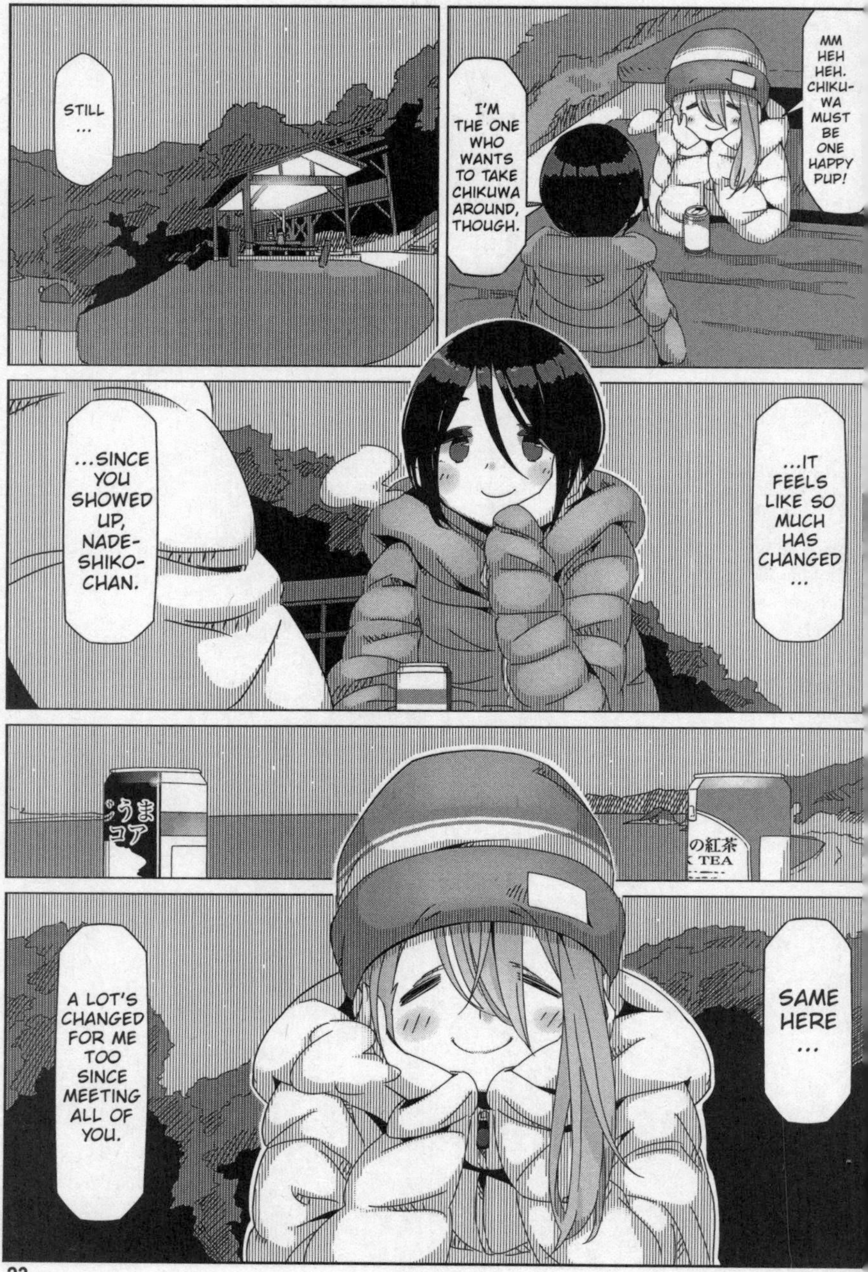
MM HEH HEH. CHIKUWA MUST BE ONE HAPPY PUP!
I'M THE ONE WHO WANTS TO TAKE CHIKUWA AROUND, THOUGH.
STILL ...
...IT FEELS LIKE SO MUCH HAS CHANGED ...
...SINCE YOU SHOWED UP, NADE-SHIKO-CHAN.
の紅茶
K TEA
うま
コア
SAME HERE ...
A LOT'S CHANGED FOR ME TOO SINCE MEETING ALL OF YOU.

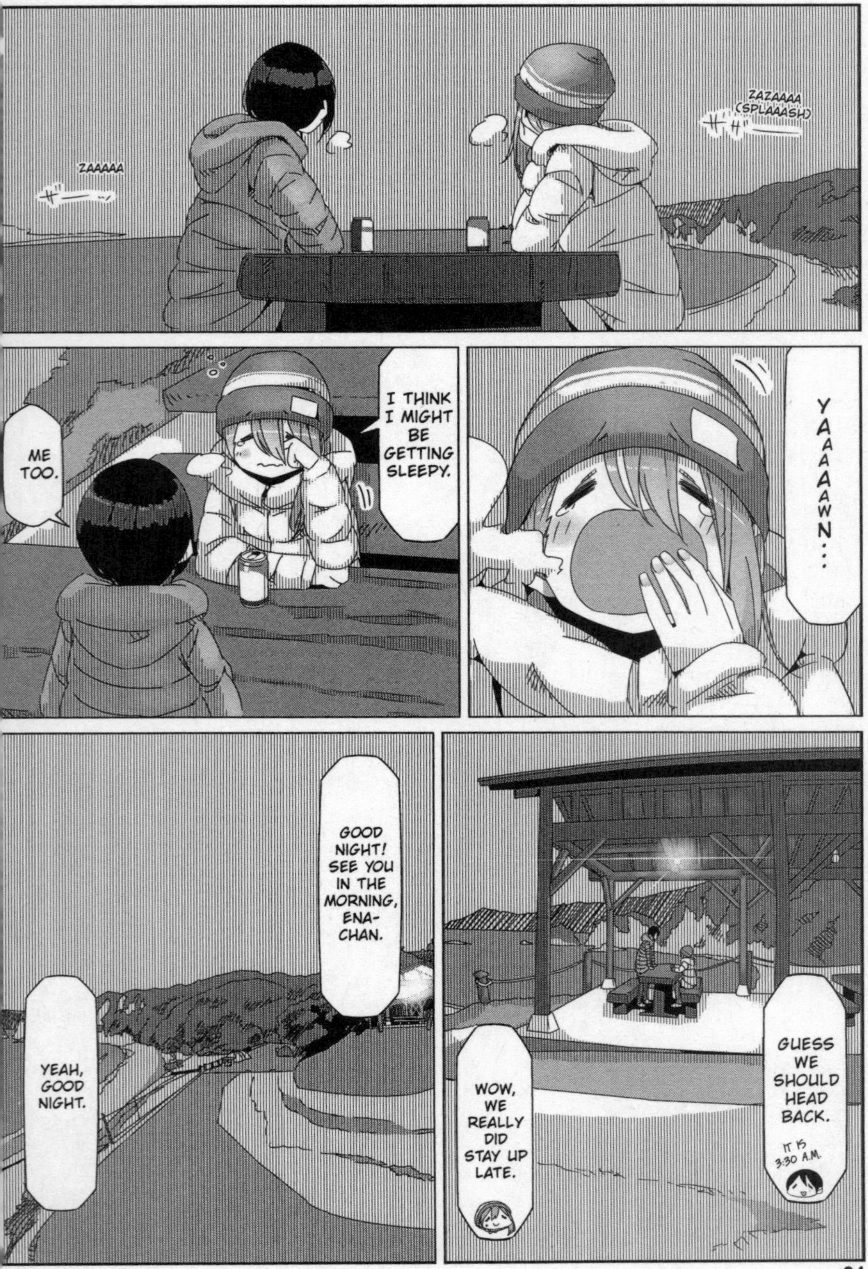
ZAZAAAA (SPLAAASH)
ZAAAAA
YAAAAAAWN...
I THINK I MIGHT BE GETTING SLEEPY.
ME TOO.
GUESS WE SHOULD HEAD BACK.
IT IS 3:30 A.M.
WOW, WE REALLY DID STAY UP LATE.
GOOD NIGHT! SEE YOU IN THE MORNING, ENA-CHAN.
YEAH, GOOD NIGHT.

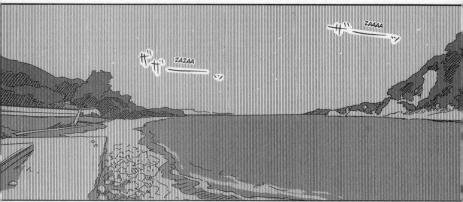

ザザ゛ー゛ー゛ ZAZAA ↝

ザ゛ザ゛ー ZAAAA ↝

ぱ
ち。
PACHI
(BLINK)

BOY,
DID I
SLEEP
...

MMM ━━━━━ ооо

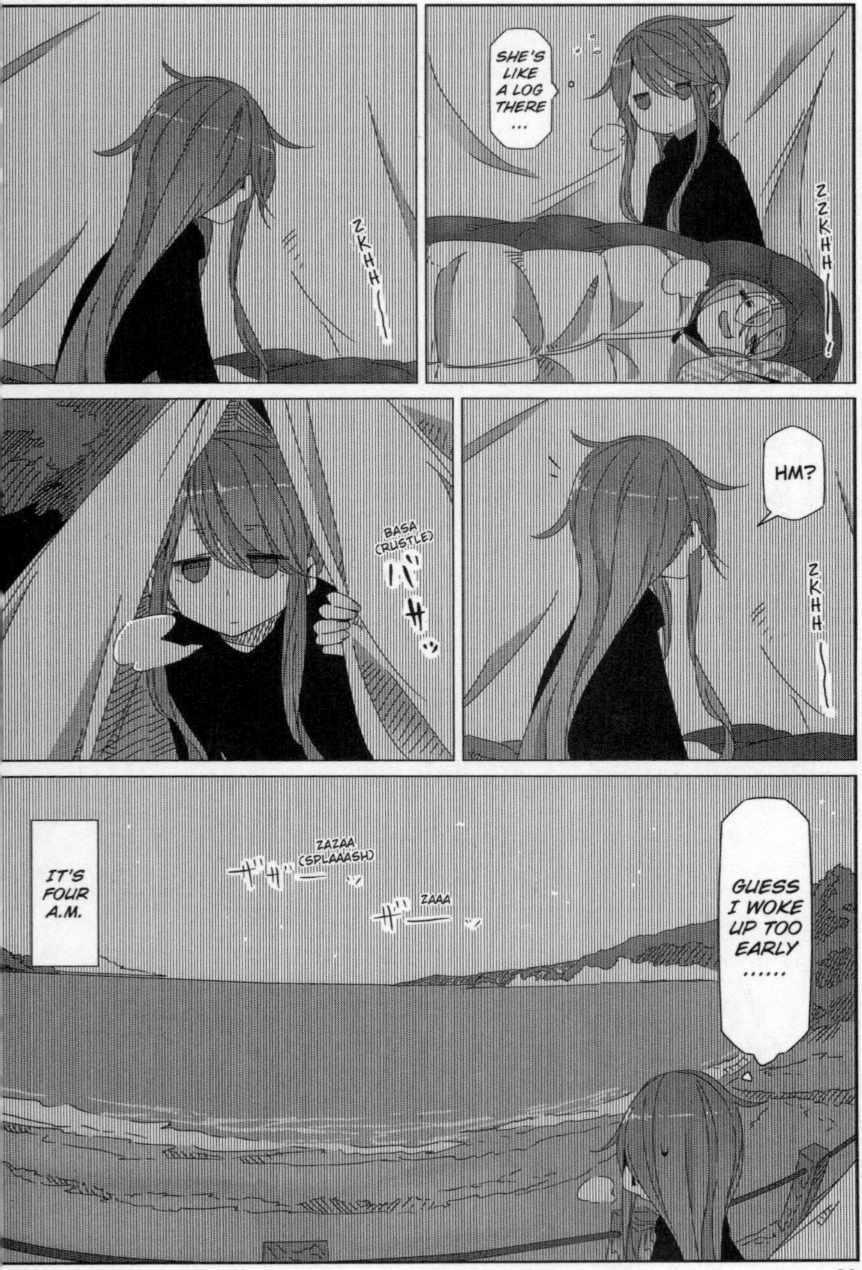
SHE'S LIKE A LOG THERE ...
ZKHH
ZKHH
HM?
ZKHH
BASA (RUSTLE)
バサッ
GUESS I WOKE UP TOO EARLY ......
ZAZAA (SPLAAASH)
ZAAA
IT'S FOUR A.M.

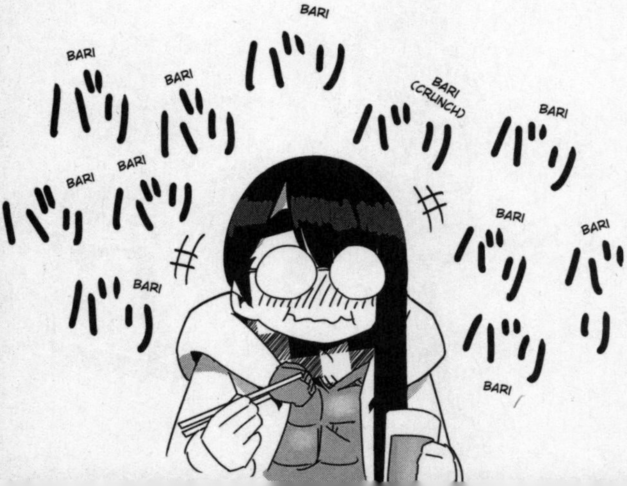
BARI
バリ
BARI
バリ
BARI (CRUNCH)
バリ
BARI
バリ
BARI
バリ
BARI
バリ
BARI
バリ
BARI
バリ
BARI
バリ
BARI
バリ
BARI
バリ

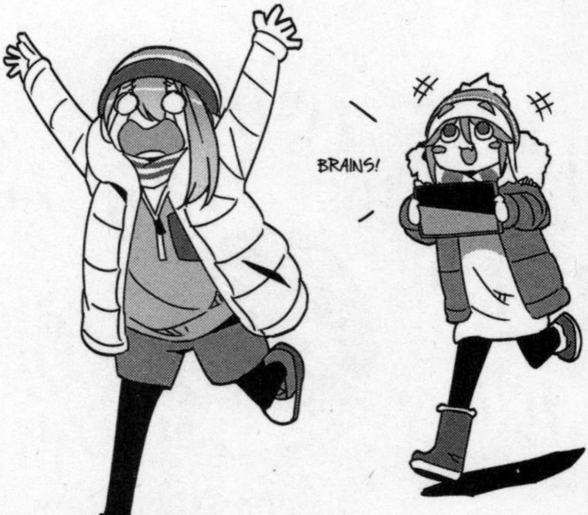
BRAINS!

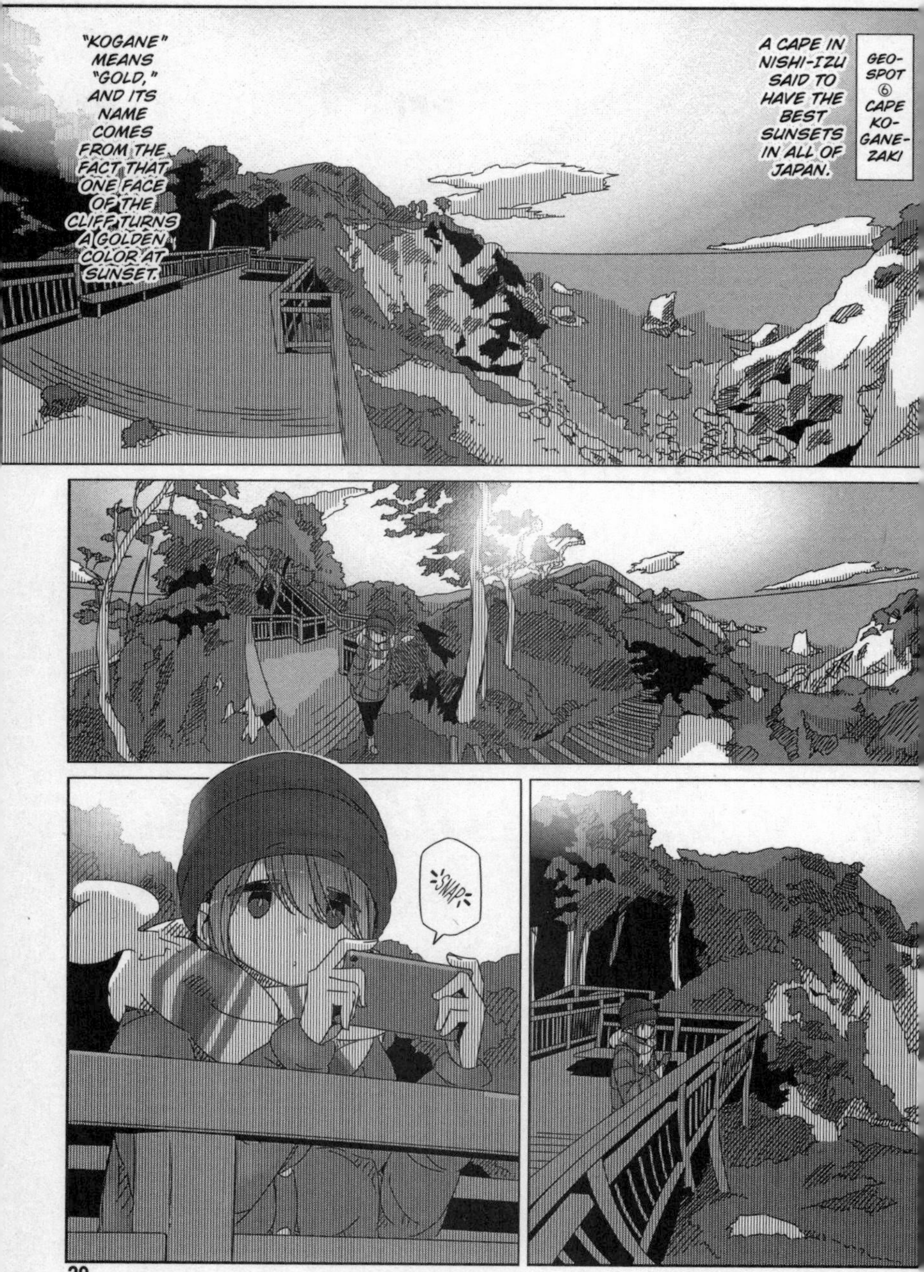
GEO-SPOT ⑥ CAPE KO-GANE-ZAKI
A CAPE IN NISHI-IZU SAID TO HAVE THE BEST SUNSETS IN ALL OF JAPAN.
"KOGANE" MEANS "GOLD," AND ITS NAME COMES FROM THE FACT THAT ONE FACE OF THE CLIFF TURNS A GOLDEN COLOR AT SUNSET.
SNAP

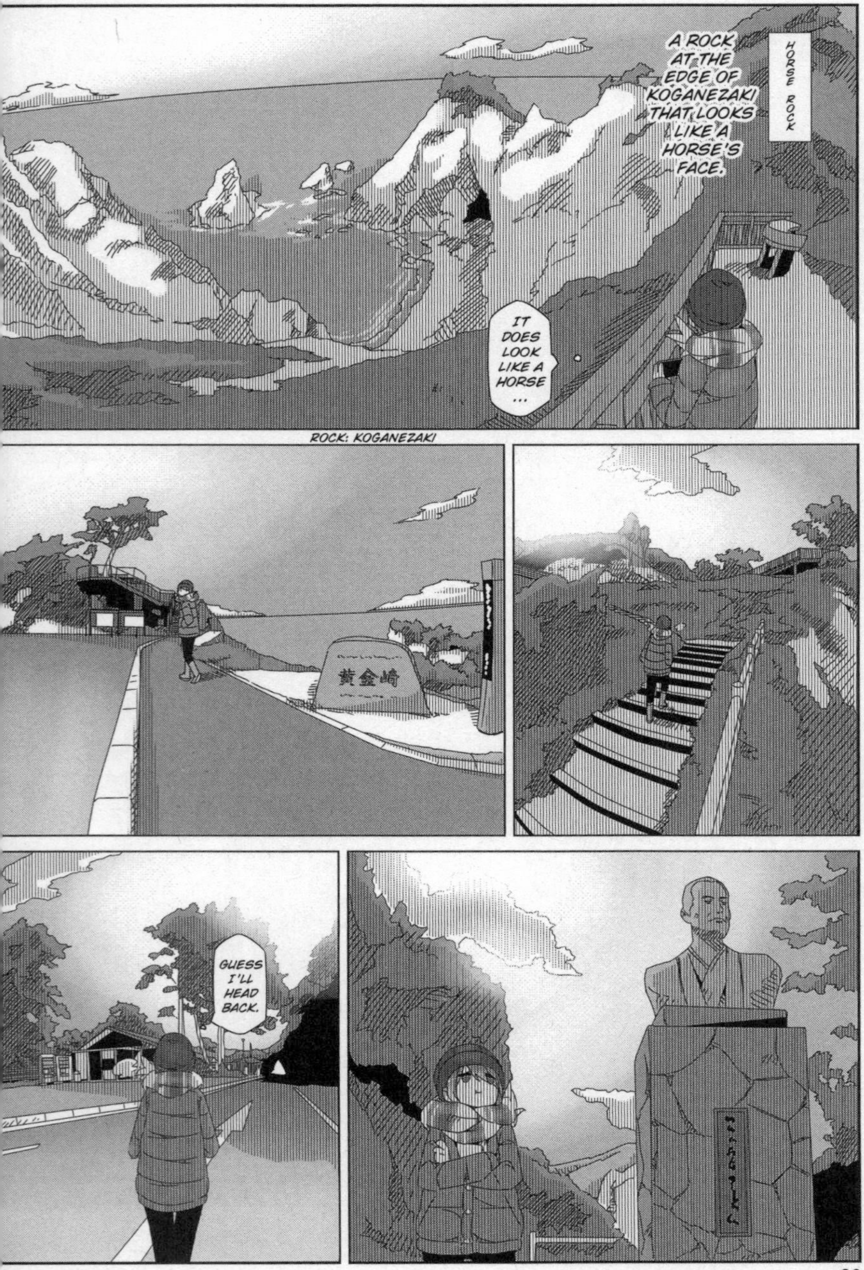
HORSE ROCK
A ROCK AT THE EDGE OF KOGANEZAKI THAT LOOKS LIKE A HORSE'S FACE.
IT DOES LOOK LIKE A HORSE...
ROCK: KOGANEZAKI
黄金崎
GUESS I'LL HEAD BACK.

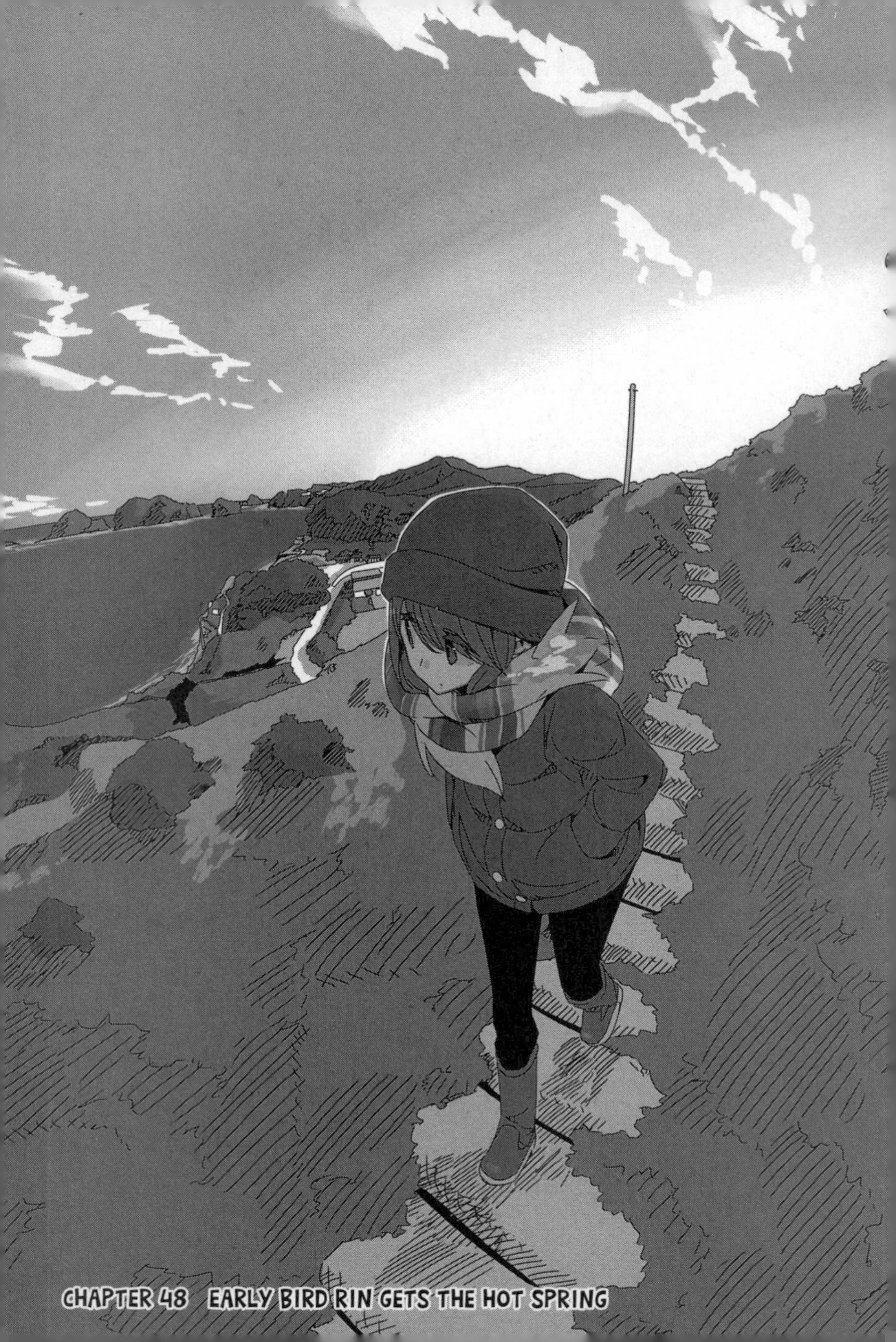

CHAPTER 48 EARLY BIRD RIN GETS THE HOT SPRING

PAN
(PAT)
ぽん

PAN
(PAT)
ぽん

ALL MY STUFF IS PACKED.

ド

ドサ
(PLOP)

BUT IT'S STILL ONLY EIGHT A.M...

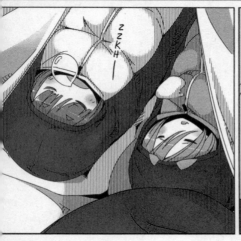

ZZKH—

ジ—
(STAAARE)

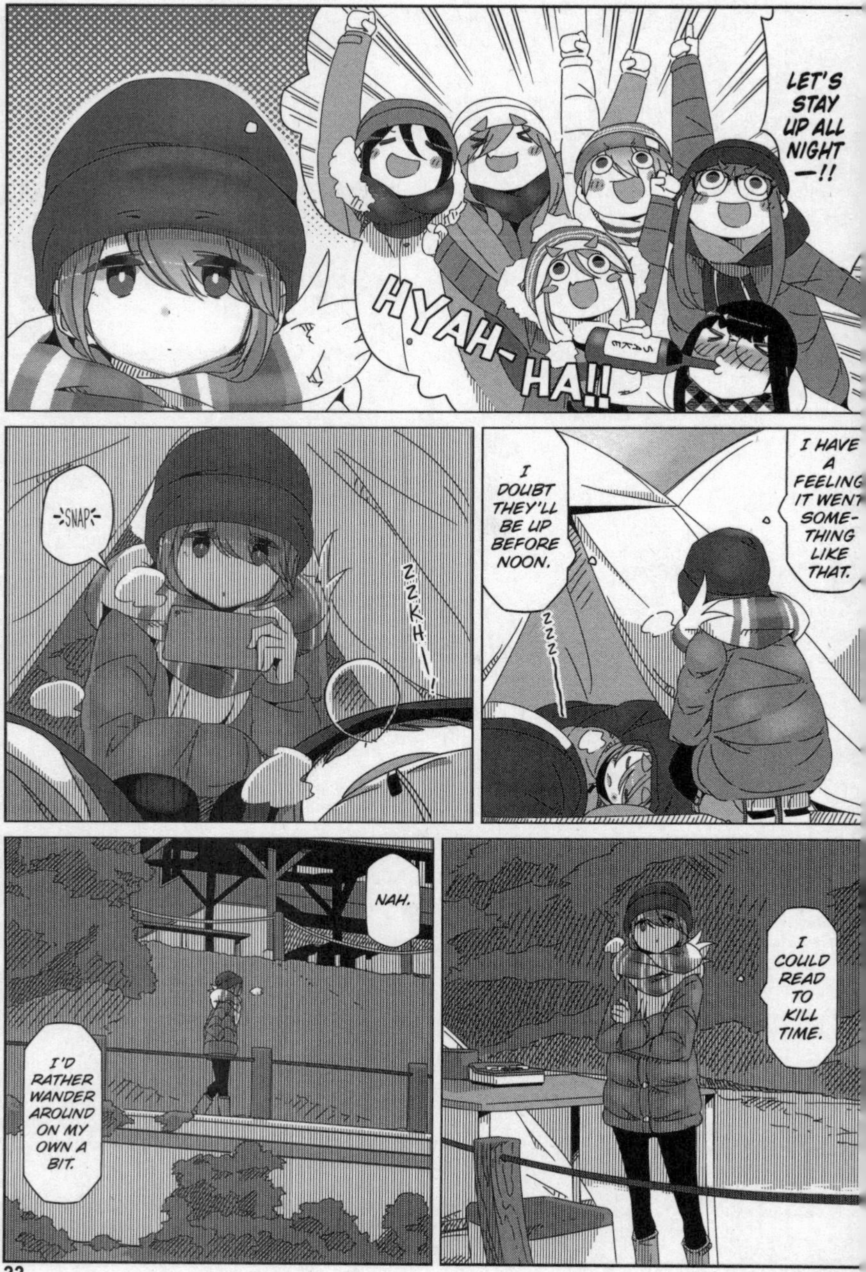

LET'S STAY UP ALL NIGHT—!!
HYAH-HA!!
I HAVE A FEELING IT WENT SOMETHING LIKE THAT.
I DOUBT THEY'LL BE UP BEFORE NOON.
ZZZ—
ZZKH—!
-SNAP-
I COULD READ TO KILL TIME.
NAH.
I'D RATHER WANDER AROUND ON MY OWN A BIT.

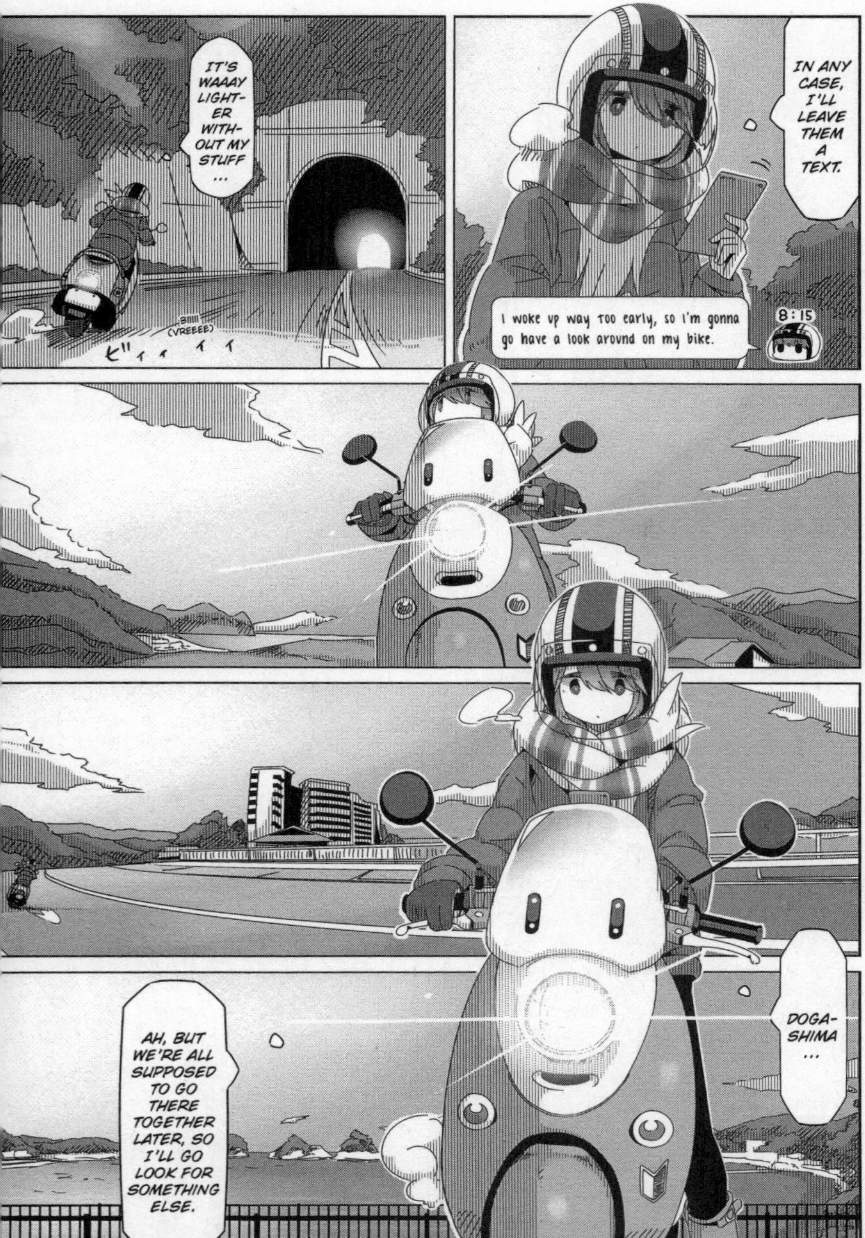
IN ANY CASE, I'LL LEAVE THEM A TEXT.
I woke up way too early, so I'm gonna go have a look around on my bike.
8:15
IT'S WAAAY LIGHTER WITHOUT MY STUFF ...
BIIII (VREEEE)
ビィィイイ
DOGASHIMA ...
AH, BUT WE'RE ALL SUPPOSED TO GO THERE TOGETHER LATER, SO I'LL GO LOOK FOR SOMETHING ELSE.

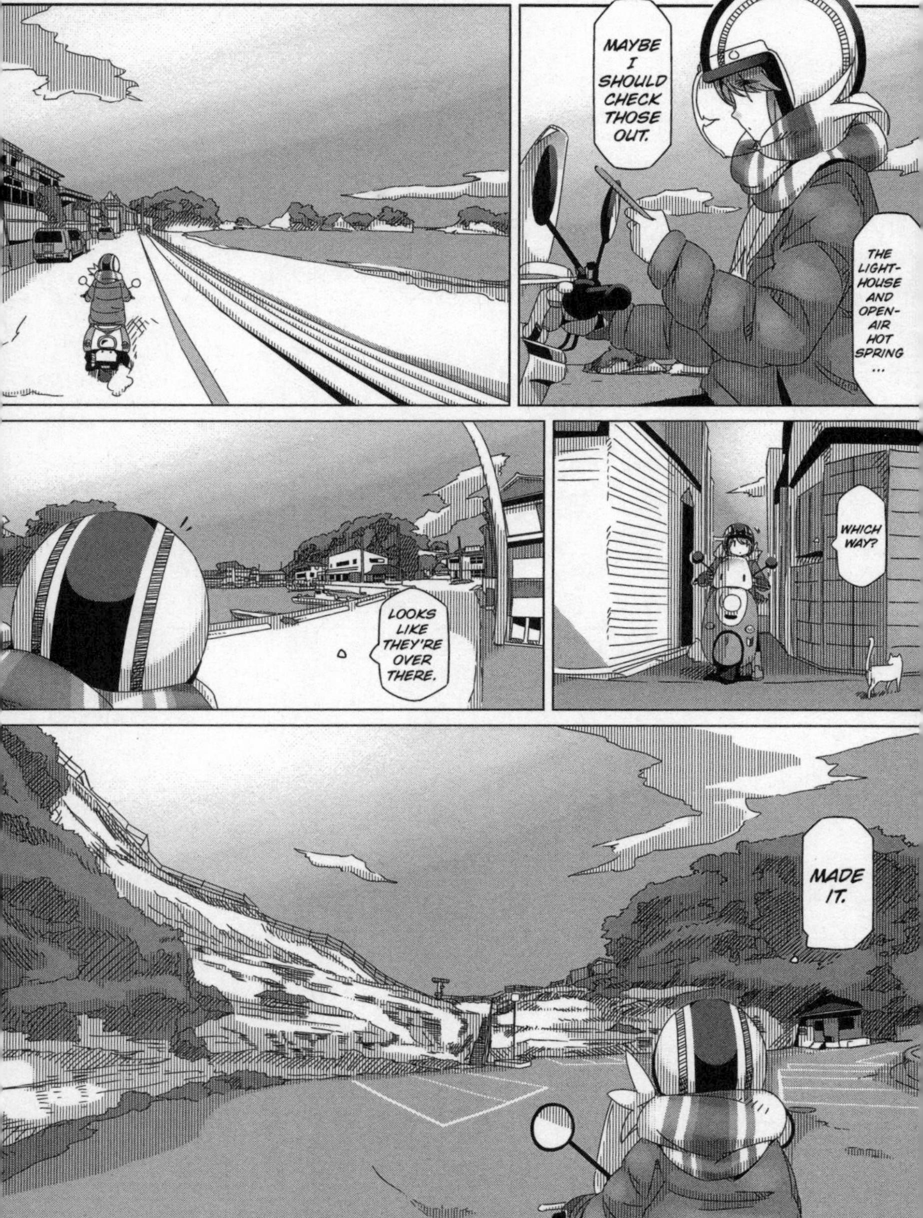
THE LIGHTHOUSE AND OPEN-AIR HOT SPRING...
MAYBE I SHOULD CHECK THOSE OUT.
WHICH WAY?
LOOKS LIKE THEY'RE OVER THERE.
MADE IT.

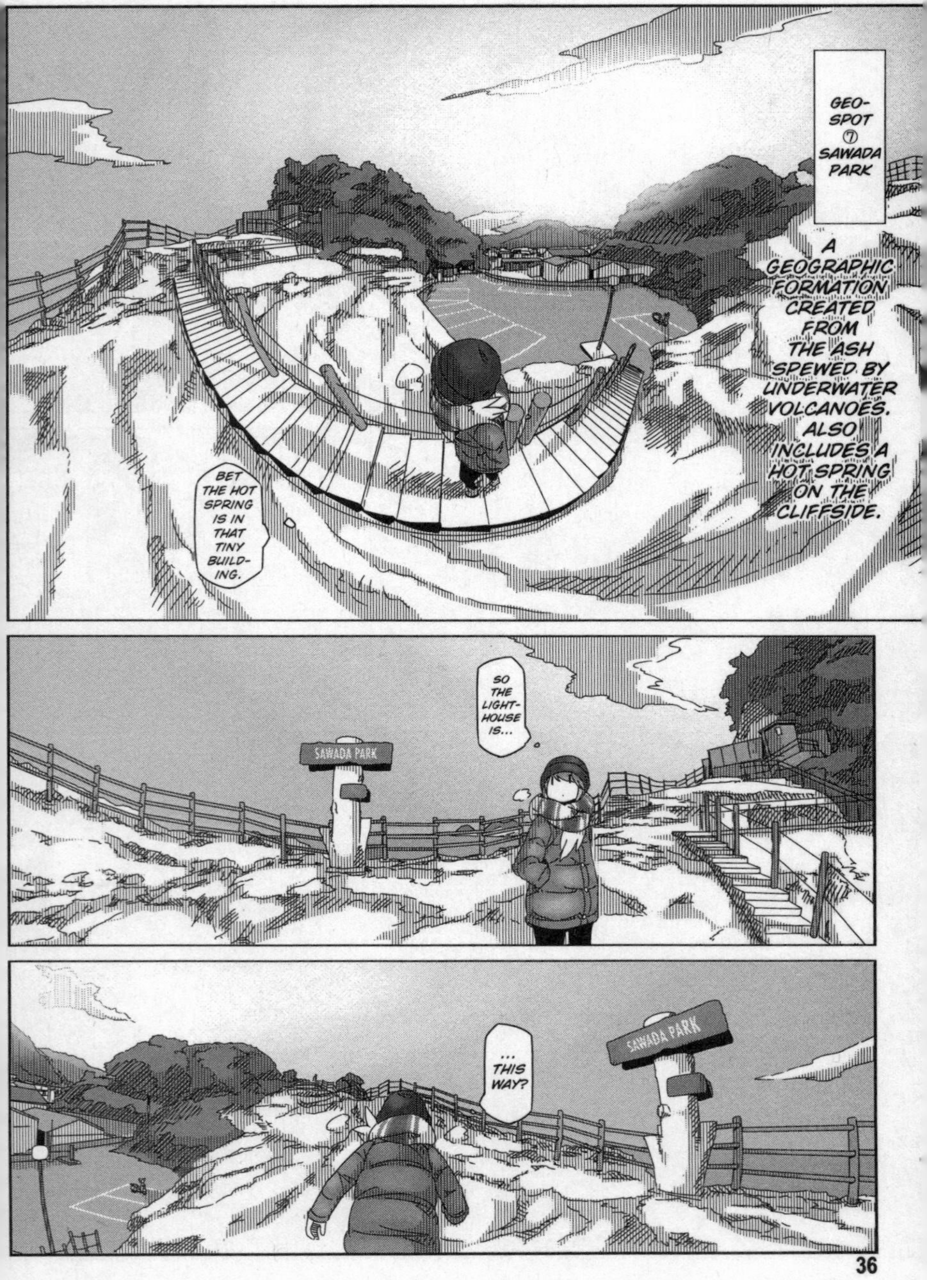
GEO-SPOT ⑦ SAWADA PARK
A GEOGRAPHIC FORMATION CREATED FROM THE ASH SPEWED BY UNDERWATER VOLCANOES. ALSO INCLUDES A HOT SPRING ON THE CLIFFSIDE.
BET THE HOT SPRING IS IN THAT TINY BUILDING.
SO THE LIGHTHOUSE IS...
SAWADA PARK
...THIS WAY?
SAWADA PARK

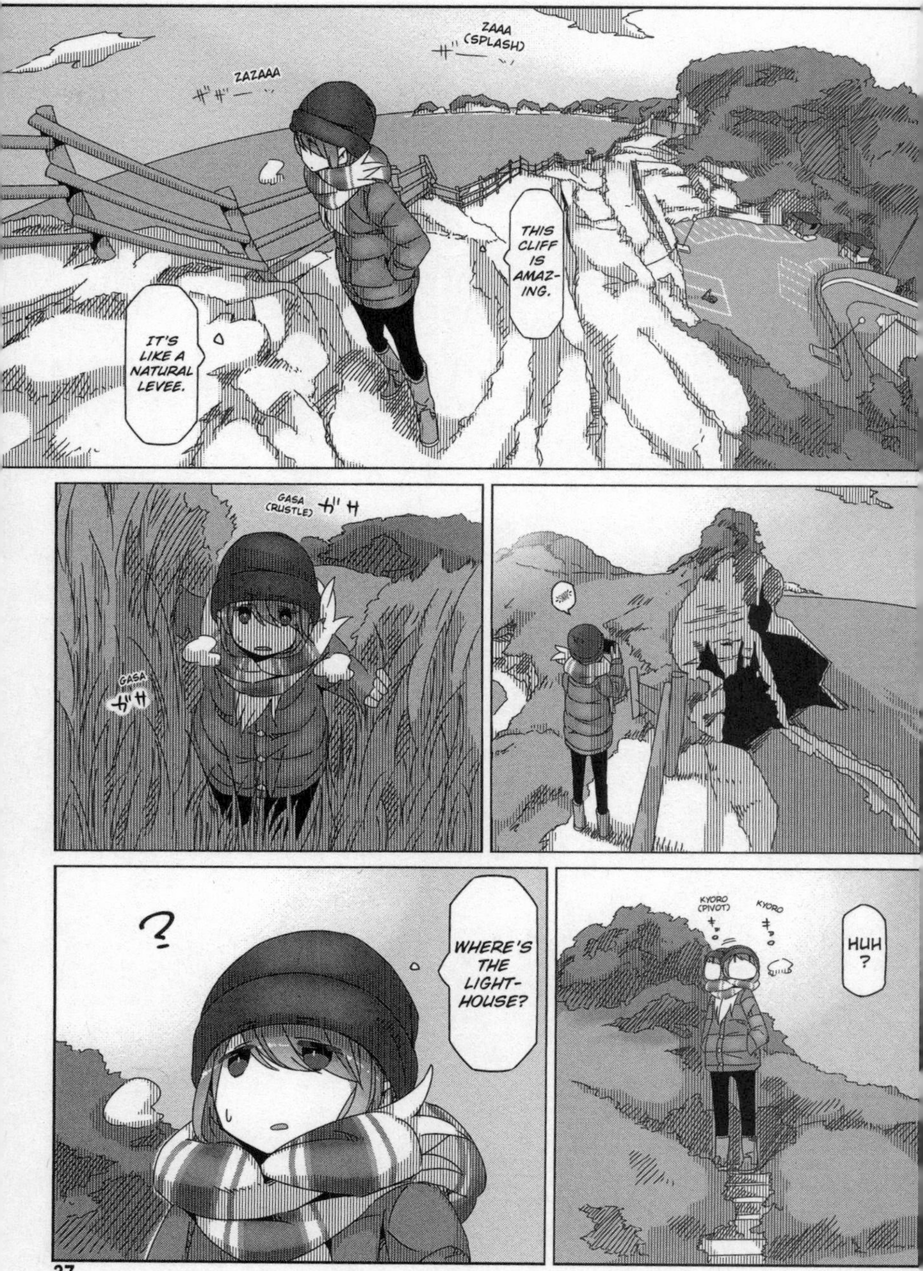
ZAAA (SPLASH)
ZAZAAA
THIS CLIFF IS AMAZING.
IT'S LIKE A NATURAL LEVEE.
GASA (RUSTLE)
GASA
HUH?
KYORO (PIVOT)
KYORO
WHERE'S THE LIGHTHOUSE?
?

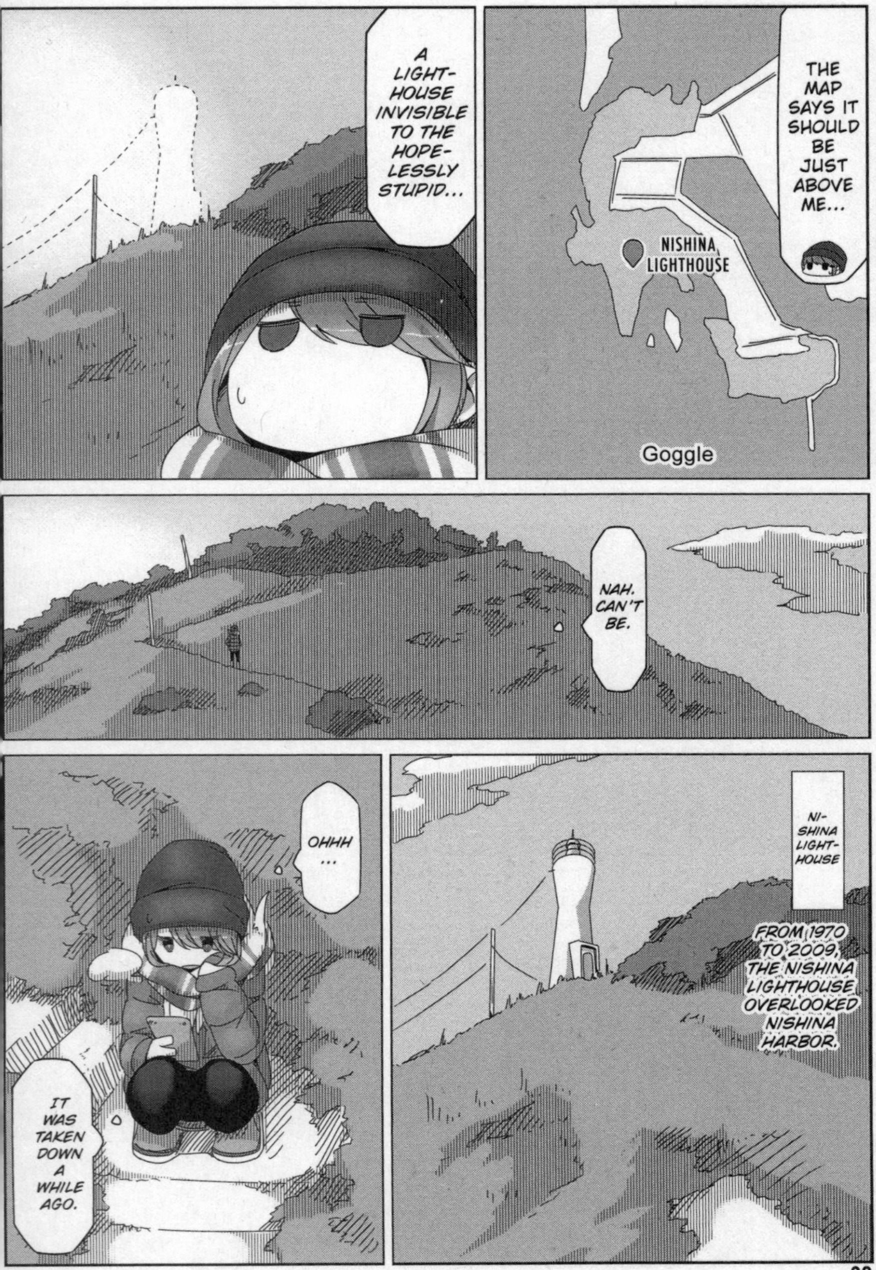
THE MAP SAYS IT SHOULD BE JUST ABOVE ME...
NISHINA LIGHTHOUSE
Goggle
A LIGHT-HOUSE INVISIBLE TO THE HOPE-LESSLY STUPID...
NAH. CAN'T BE.
NI-SHINA LIGHT-HOUSE
FROM 1970 TO 2009, THE NISHINA LIGHTHOUSE OVERLOOKED NISHINA HARBOR.
OHHH ...
IT WAS TAKEN DOWN A WHILE AGO.

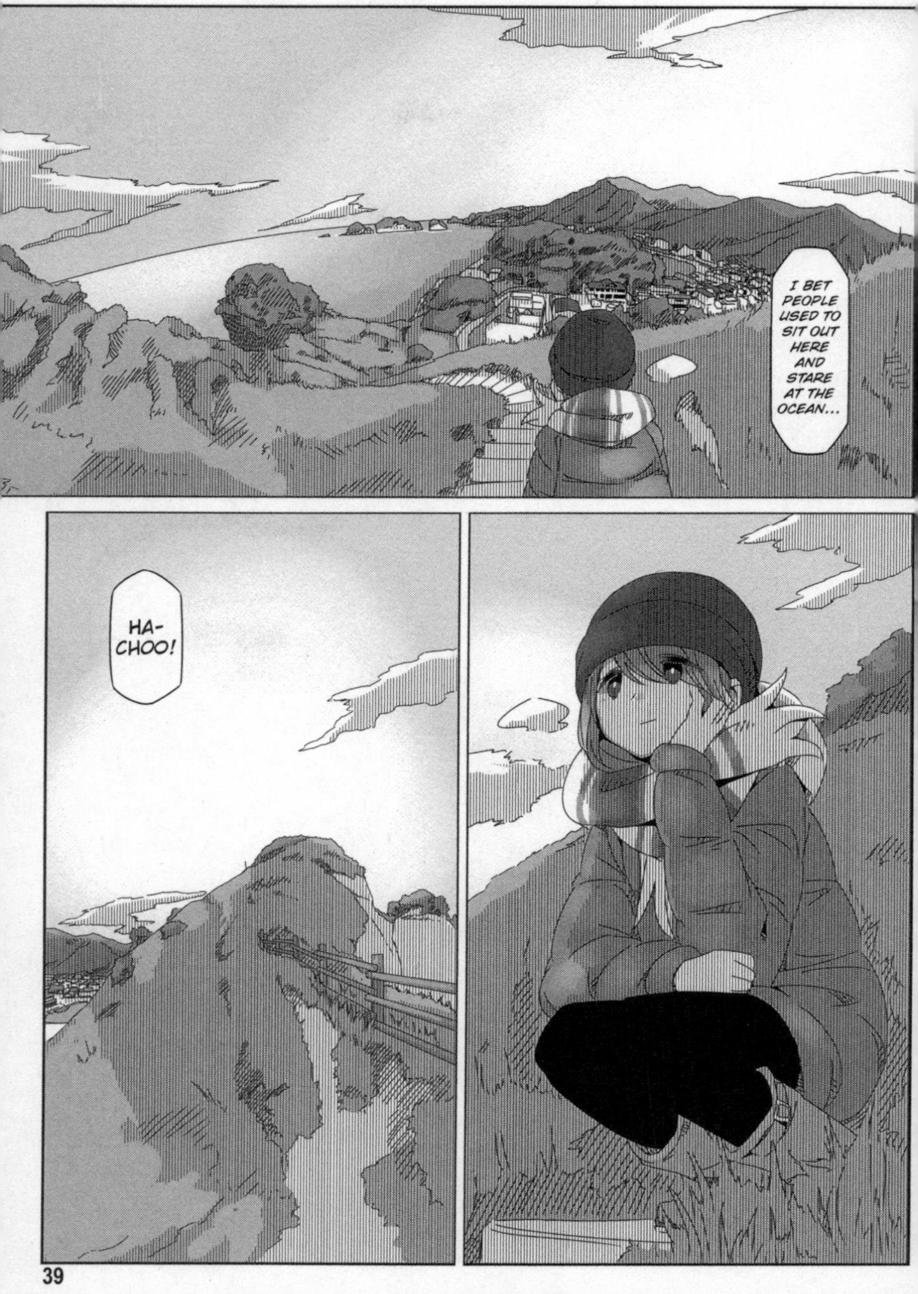
I BET PEOPLE USED TO SIT OUT HERE AND STARE AT THE OCEAN...
HA-CHOO!

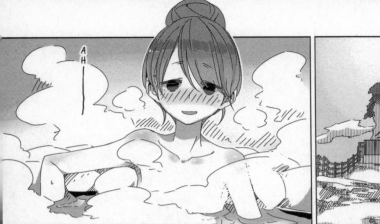

AH—
GETTING IN THE HOT SPRING RIGHT AS THE DAY BEGINS...
ZAAA (SPLASH)
ZAZAAA
...IS SO NICE AND RELAXING—
AND BEATING EVERY-ONE TO IT...
...FEELS THE BEST.

SIGN: SAWADA PARK

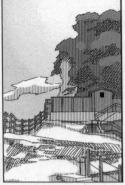

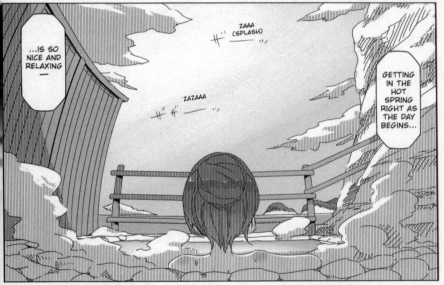

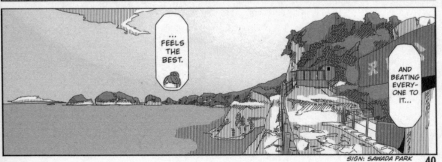

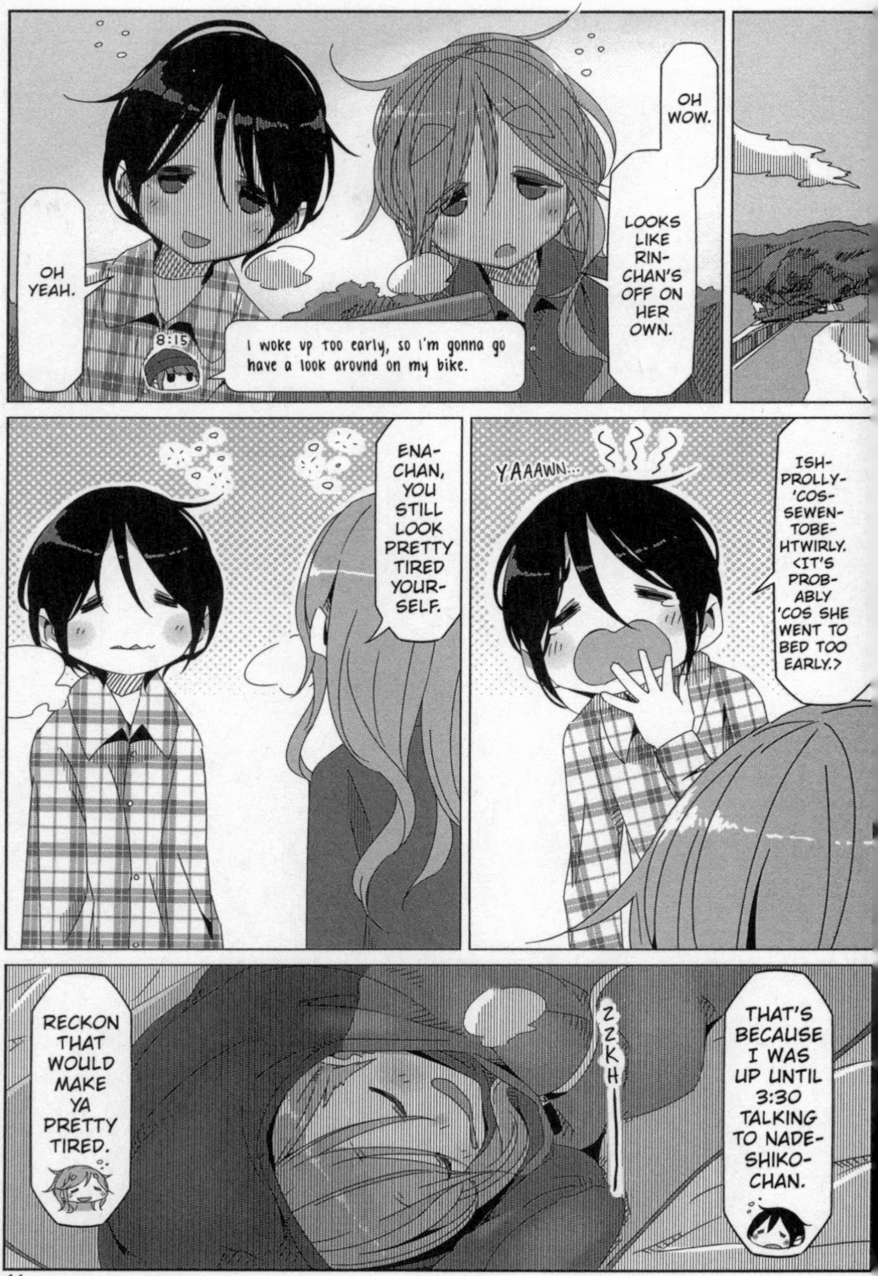
OH WOW.
LOOKS LIKE RIN-CHAN'S OFF ON HER OWN.
8:15
I woke up too early, so I'm gonna go have a look around on my bike.
OH YEAH.
ISH-PROLLY-'COS-SEWEN-TOBE-HTWIRLY. <IT'S PROBABLY 'COS SHE WENT TO BED TOO EARLY.>
YAAAWN...
ENA-CHAN, YOU STILL LOOK PRETTY TIRED YOURSELF.
THAT'S BECAUSE I WAS UP UNTIL 3:30 TALKING TO NADESHIKO-CHAN.
ZZKH
RECKON THAT WOULD MAKE YA PRETTY TIRED.

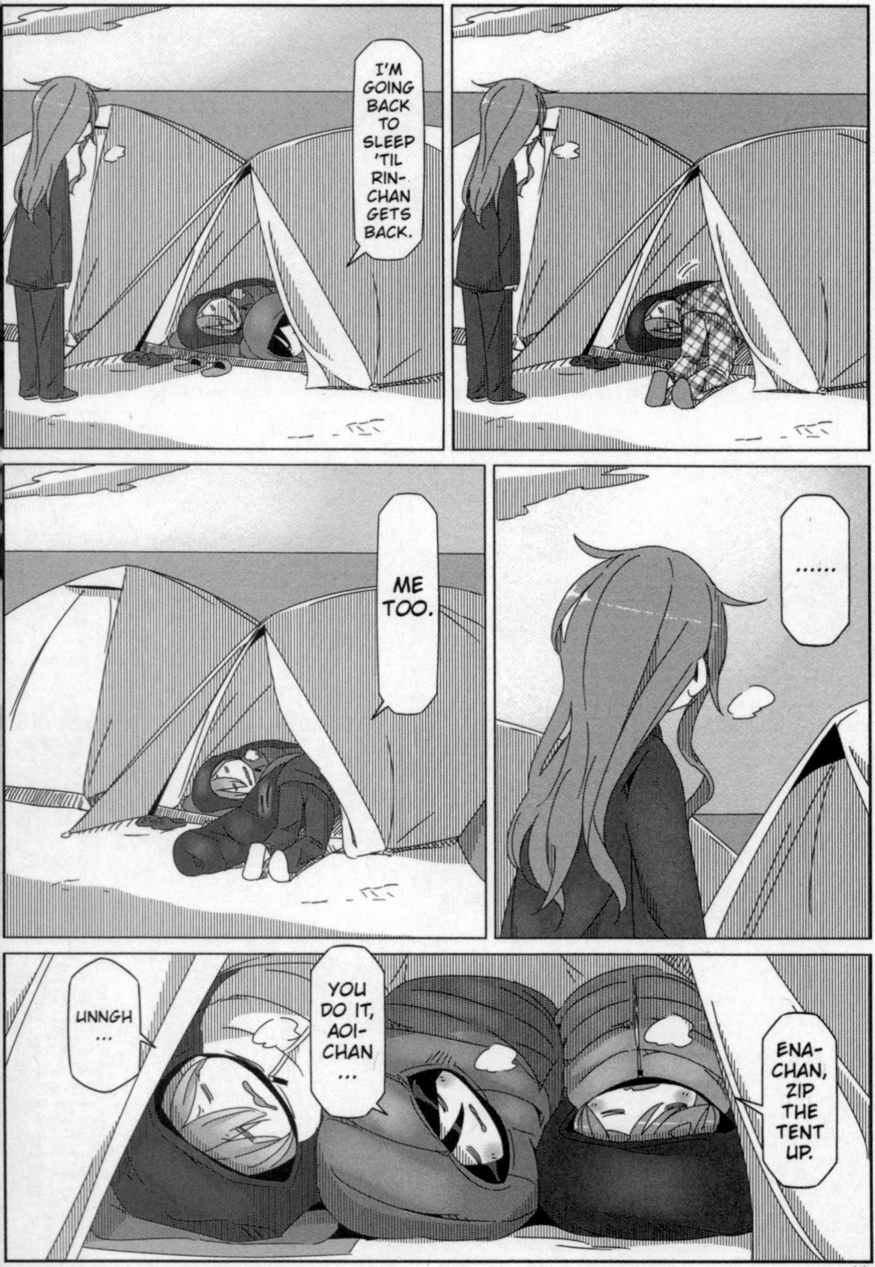
I'M GOING BACK TO SLEEP 'TIL RIN-CHAN GETS BACK.
......
ME TOO.
ENA-CHAN, ZIP THE TENT UP.
YOU DO IT, AOI-CHAN...
UNNGH...

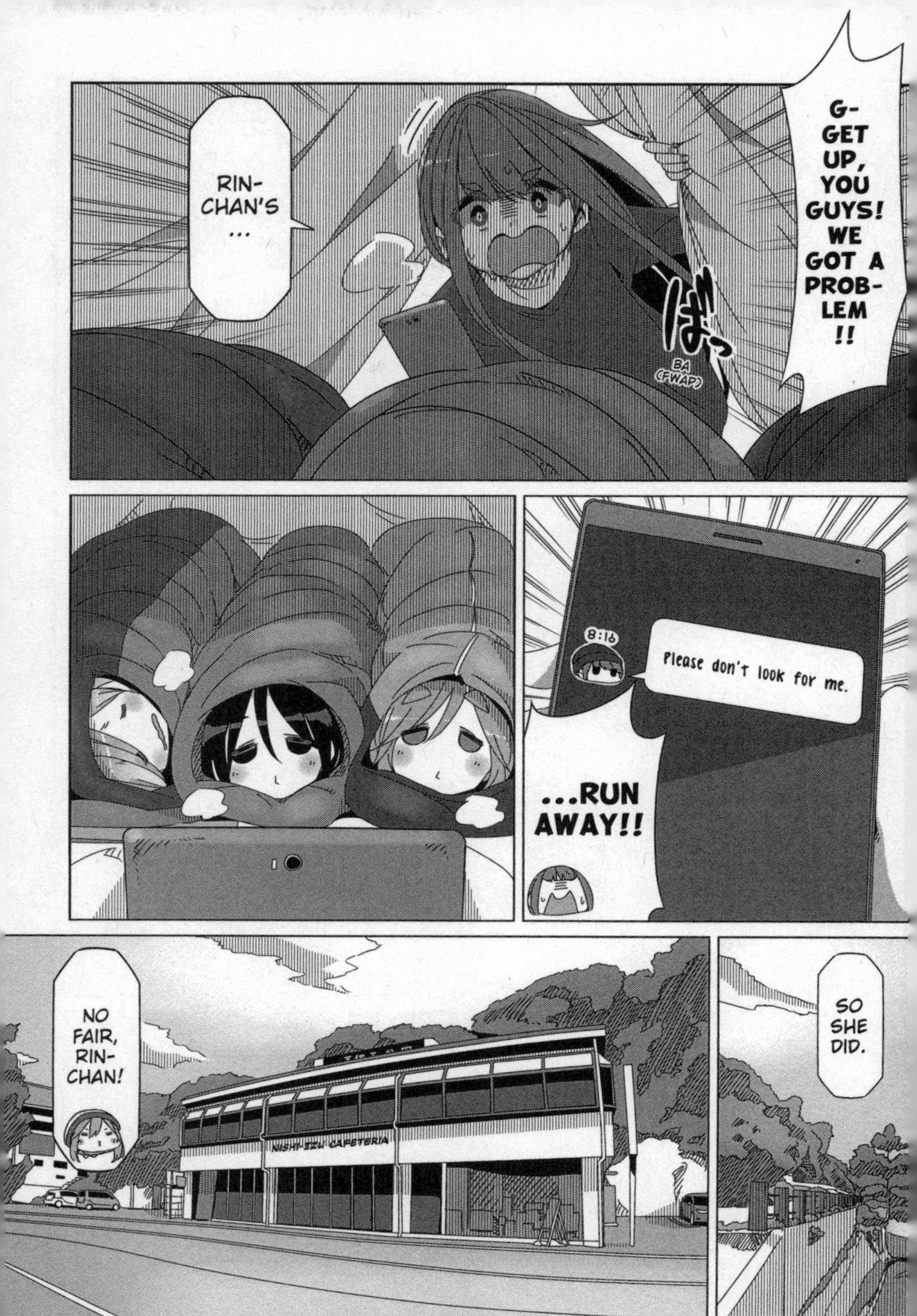
G-GET UP, YOU GUYS! WE GOT A PROBLEM!!
ぱっ
BA (FWAP)
RIN-CHAN'S...
8:16
Please don't look for me.
...RUN AWAY!!
SO SHE DID.
NO FAIR, RIN-CHAN!
NISHI-IZU CAFETERIA

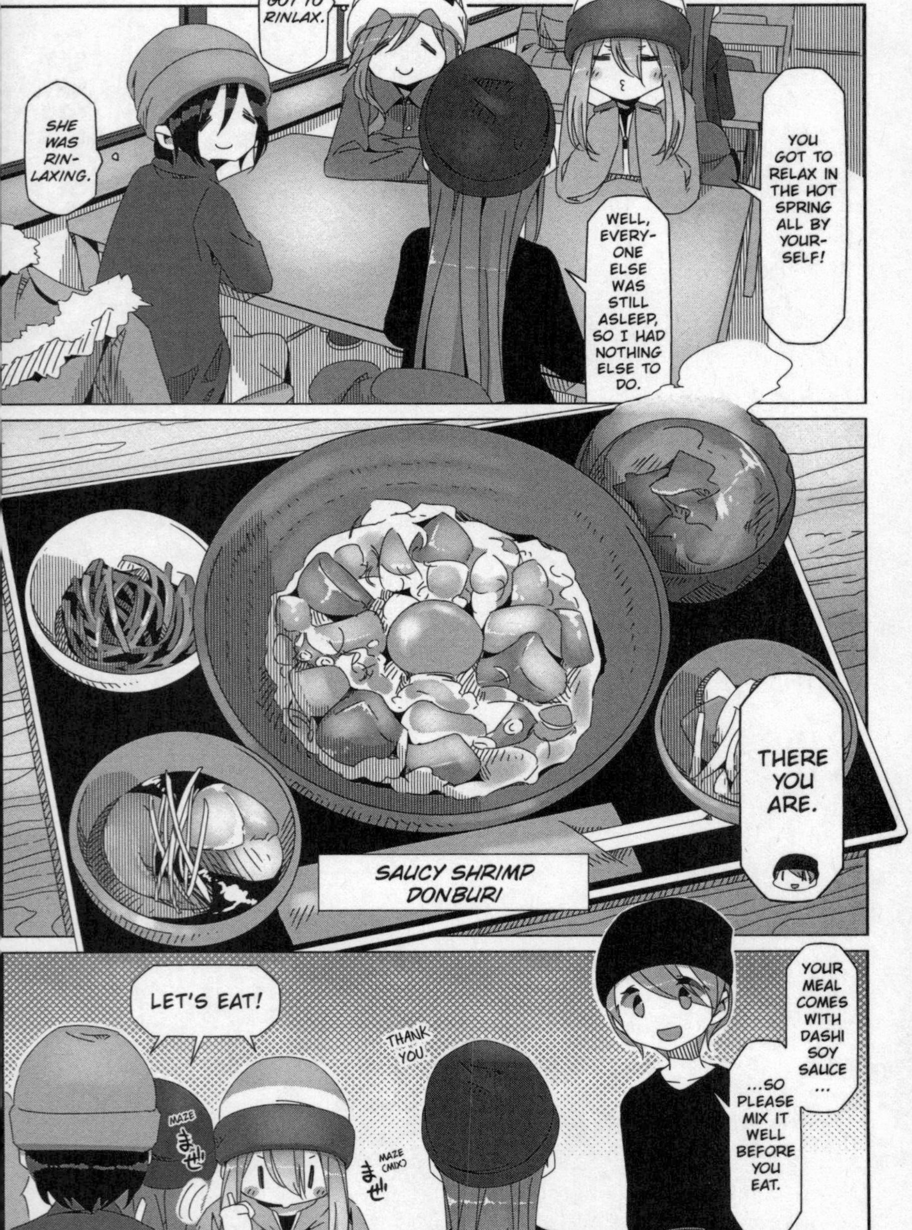
YOU GOT TO RELAX IN THE HOT SPRING ALL BY YOURSELF!
WELL, EVERYONE ELSE WAS STILL ASLEEP, SO I HAD NOTHING ELSE TO DO.
GOT TO RINLAX.
SHE WAS RINLAXING.
THERE YOU ARE.
SAUCY SHRIMP DONBURI
YOUR MEAL COMES WITH DASHI SOY SAUCE ...
...SO PLEASE MIX IT WELL BEFORE YOU EAT.
THANK YOU.
LET'S EAT!
MAZE (MIX) まぜ
MAZE まぜ

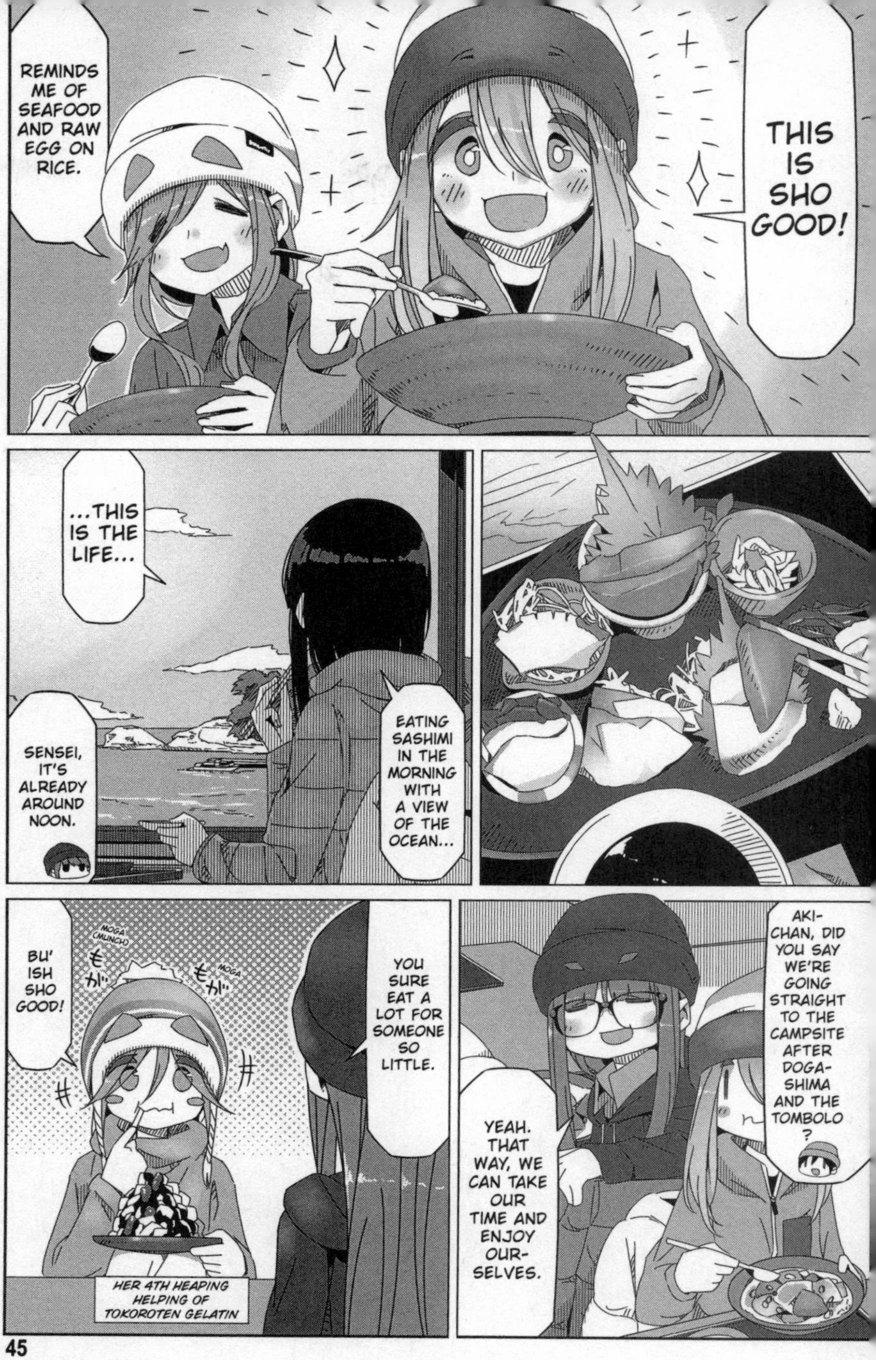
THIS IS SHO GOOD!
REMINDS ME OF SEAFOOD AND RAW EGG ON RICE.
...THIS IS THE LIFE...
EATING SASHIMI IN THE MORNING WITH A VIEW OF THE OCEAN...
SENSEI, IT'S ALREADY AROUND NOON.
AKI-CHAN, DID YOU SAY WE'RE GOING STRAIGHT TO THE CAMPSITE AFTER DOGA-SHIMA AND THE TOMBOLO?
YEAH. THAT WAY, WE CAN TAKE OUR TIME AND ENJOY OUR-SELVES.
YOU SURE EAT A LOT FOR SOMEONE SO LITTLE.
MOGA (MUNCH)
MOGA
BU' ISH SHO GOOD!
HER 4TH HEAPING HELPING OF TOKOROTEN GELATIN

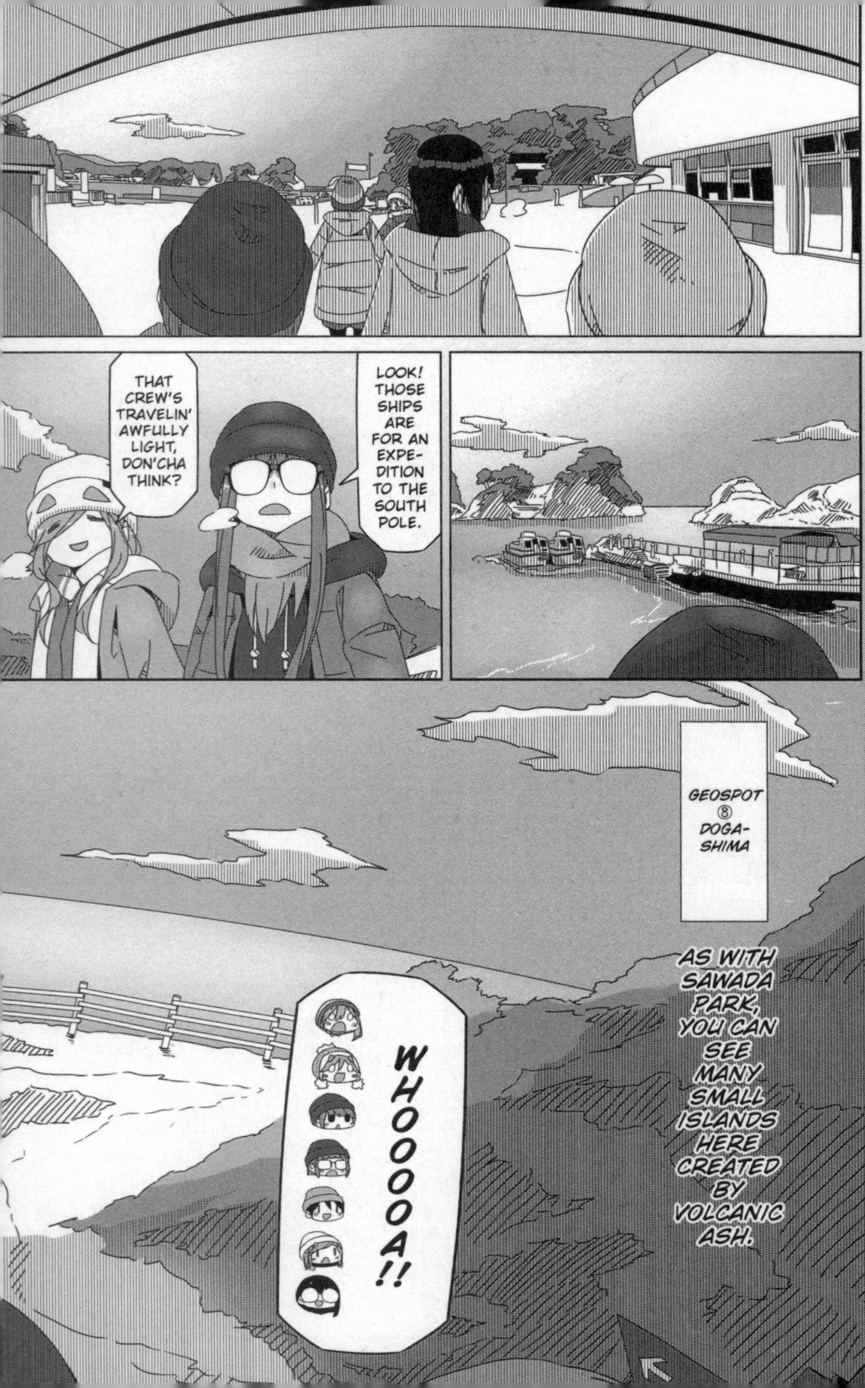
LOOK! THOSE SHIPS ARE FOR AN EXPEDITION TO THE SOUTH POLE.
THAT CREW'S TRAVELIN' AWFULLY LIGHT, DON'CHA THINK?
GEOSPOT ⑧ DOGA-SHIMA
AS WITH SAWADA PARK, YOU CAN SEE MANY SMALL ISLANDS HERE CREATED BY VOLCANIC ASH.
WHOOOOA!!

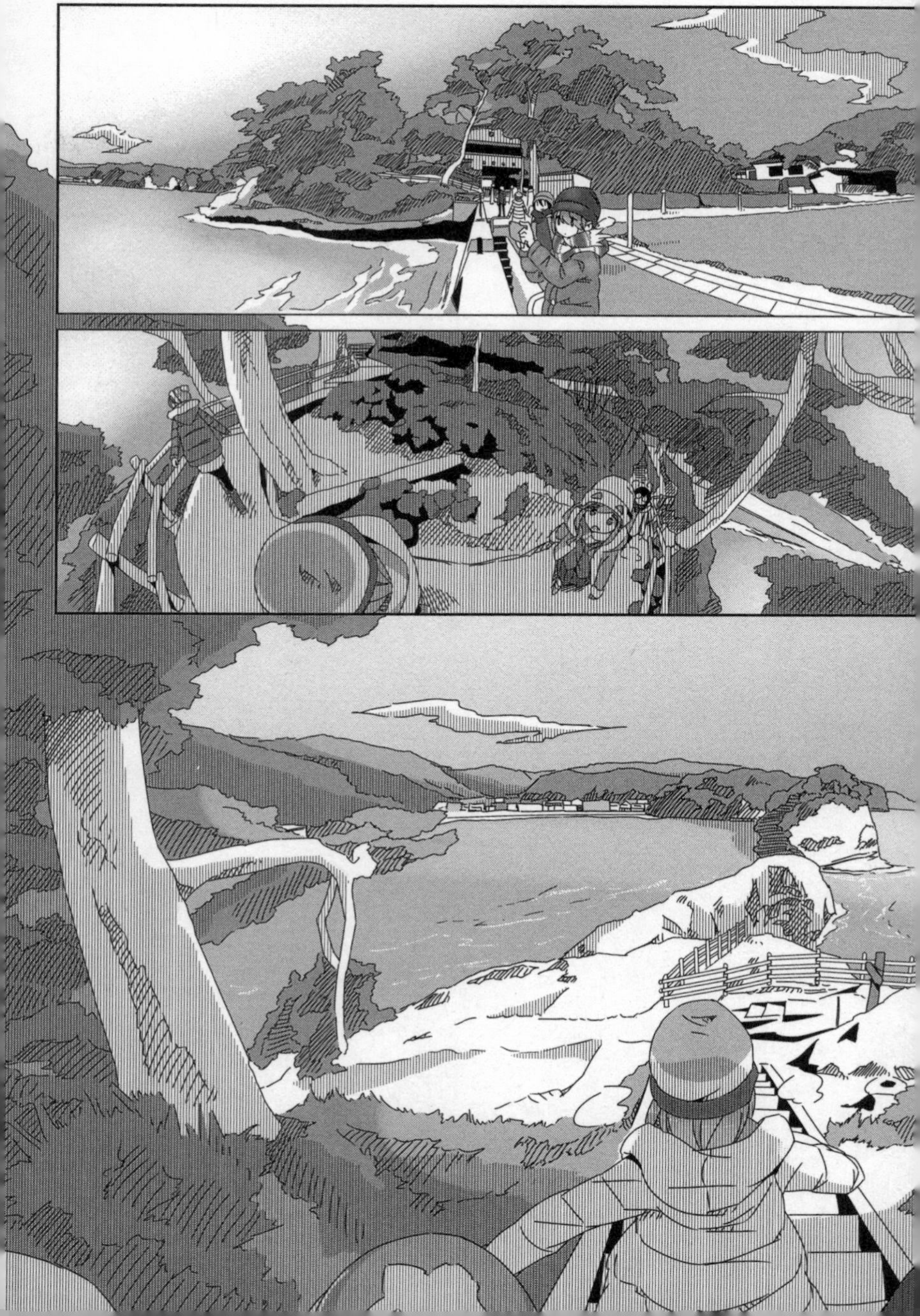

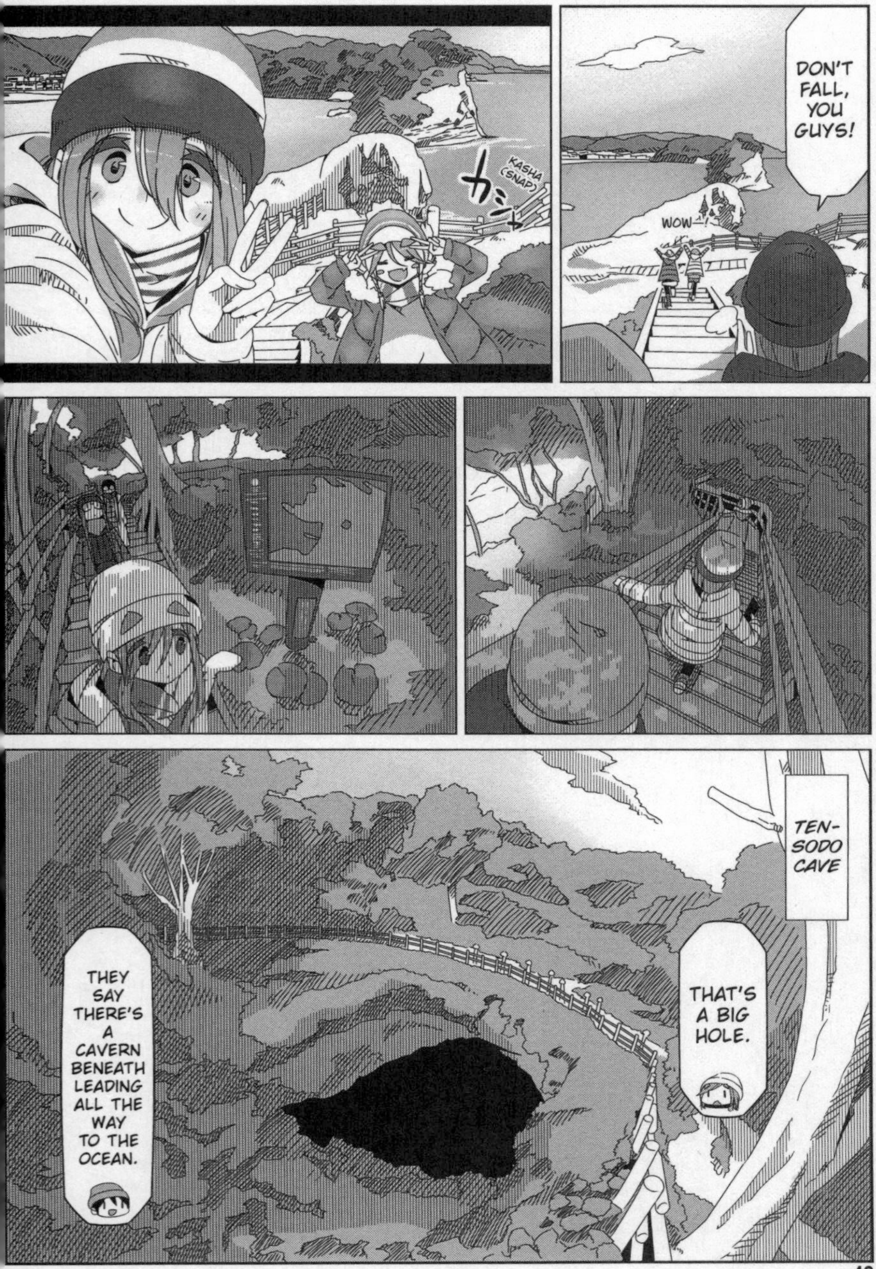
DON'T FALL, YOU GUYS!
WOW—!
カシャ
KASHA (SNAP)
TEN-SODO CAVE
THAT'S A BIG HOLE.
THEY SAY THERE'S A CAVERN BENEATH LEADING ALL THE WAY TO THE OCEAN.

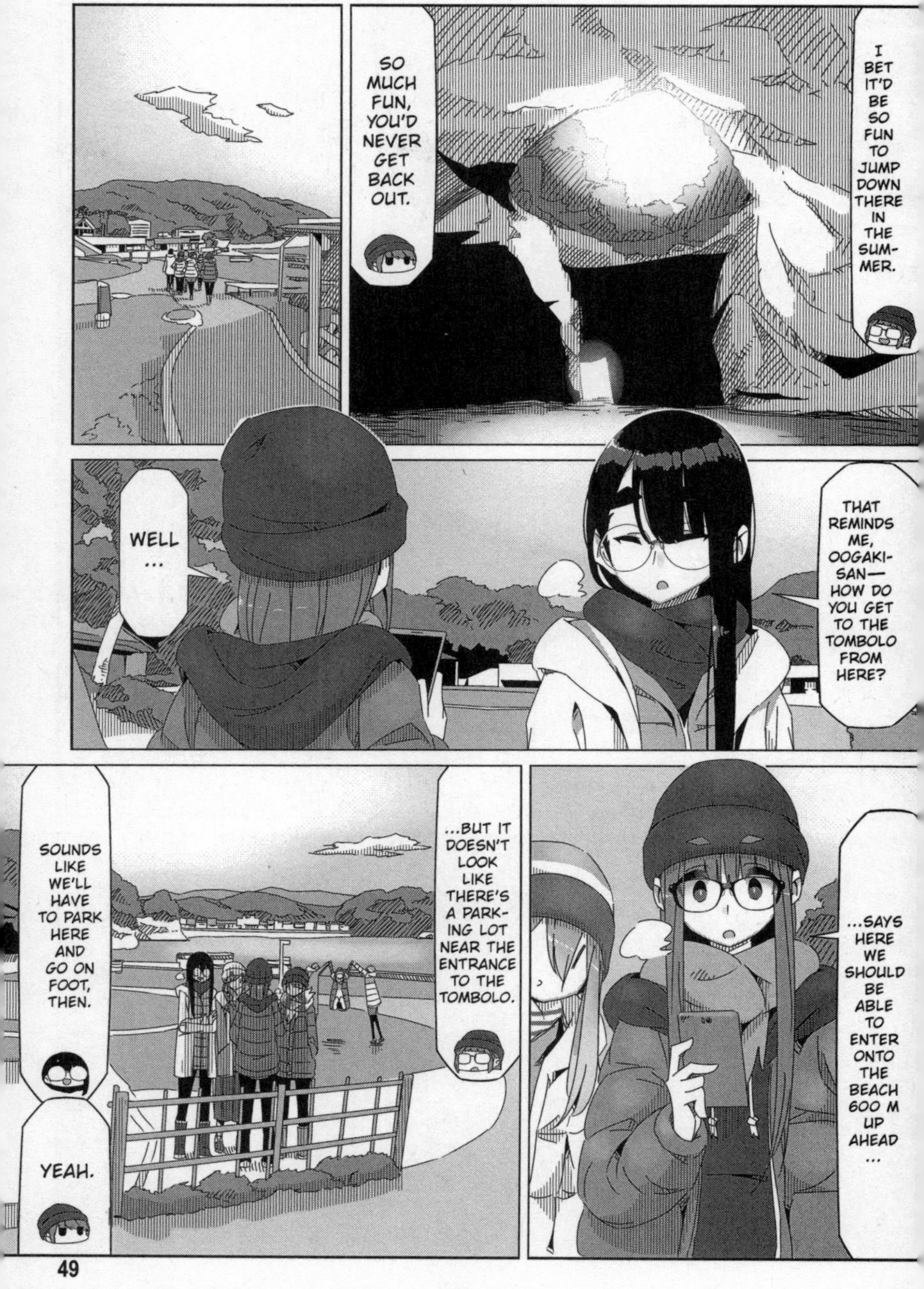
I BET IT'D BE SO FUN TO JUMP DOWN THERE IN THE SUMMER.
SO MUCH FUN, YOU'D NEVER GET BACK OUT.
THAT REMINDS ME, OOGAKI-SAN—HOW DO YOU GET TO THE TOMBOLO FROM HERE?
WELL...
...SAYS HERE WE SHOULD BE ABLE TO ENTER ONTO THE BEACH 600 M UP AHEAD...
...BUT IT DOESN'T LOOK LIKE THERE'S A PARKING LOT NEAR THE ENTRANCE TO THE TOMBOLO.
SOUNDS LIKE WE'LL HAVE TO PARK HERE AND GO ON FOOT, THEN.
YEAH.

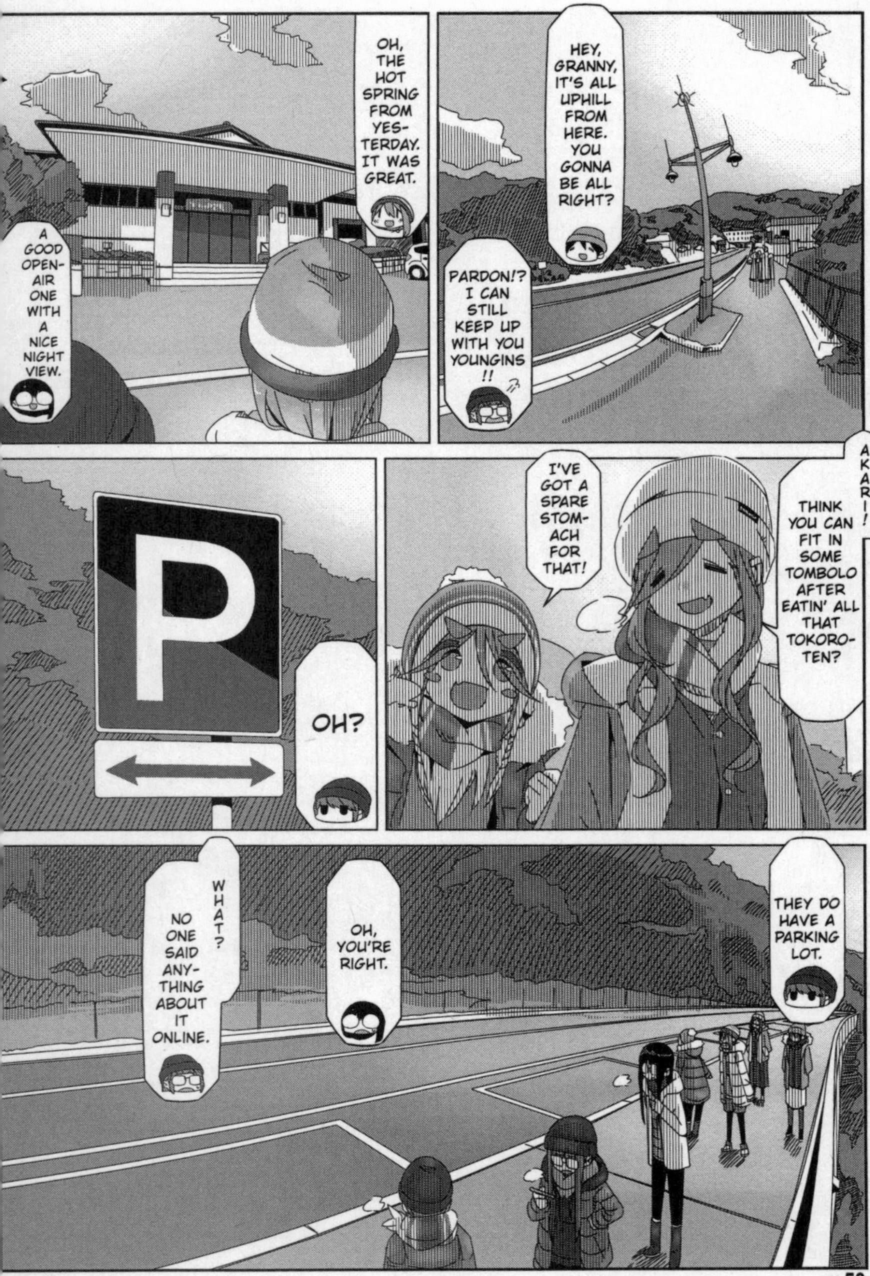
HEY, GRANNY, IT'S ALL UPHILL FROM HERE. YOU GONNA BE ALL RIGHT?
PARDON!? I CAN STILL KEEP UP WITH YOU YOUNGINS!!
OH, THE HOT SPRING FROM YES-TERDAY. IT WAS GREAT.
A GOOD OPEN-AIR ONE WITH A NICE NIGHT VIEW.
AKARI!
THINK YOU CAN FIT IN SOME TOMBOLO AFTER EATIN' ALL THAT TOKORO-TEN?
I'VE GOT A SPARE STOM-ACH FOR THAT!
OH?
THEY DO HAVE A PARKING LOT.
OH, YOU'RE RIGHT.
WHAT?
NO ONE SAID ANY-THING ABOUT IT ONLINE.

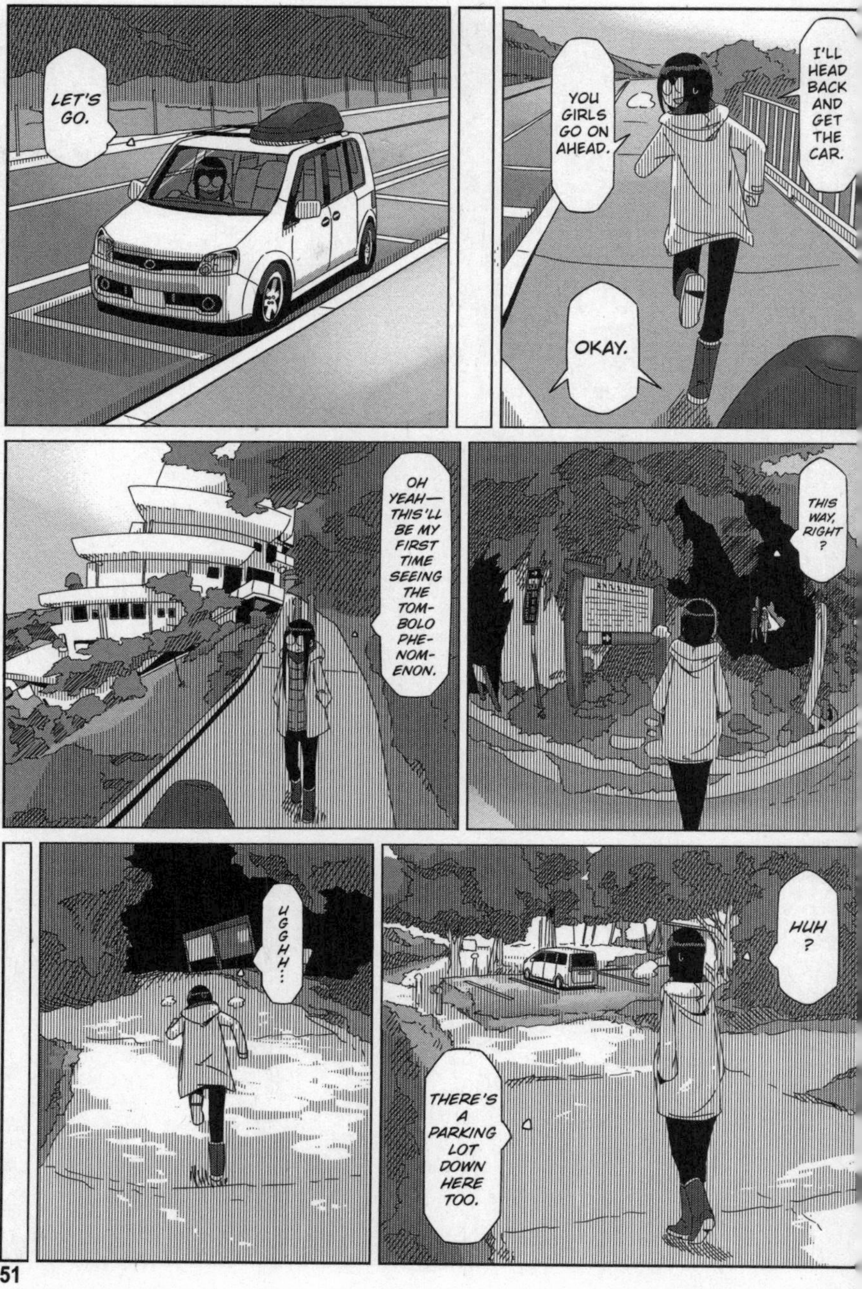
I'LL HEAD BACK AND GET THE CAR.
YOU GIRLS GO ON AHEAD.
OKAY.
LET'S GO.
THIS WAY, RIGHT?
OH YEAH— THIS'LL BE MY FIRST TIME SEEING THE TOMBOLO PHENOMENON.
HUH?
THERE'S A PARKING LOT DOWN HERE TOO.
UGGHH...

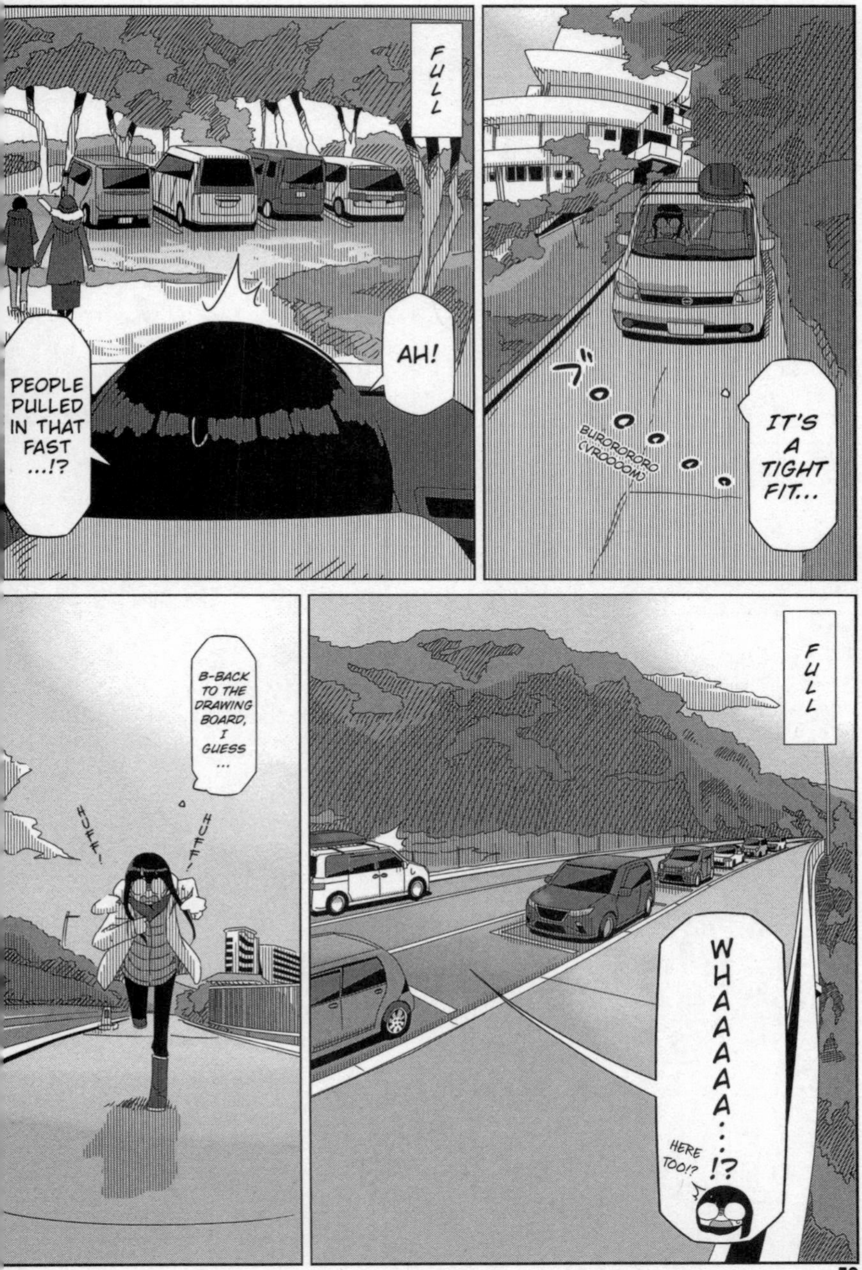
IT'S A TIGHT FIT...
BURORORORO (VROOOOM)
FULL
AH!
PEOPLE PULLED IN THAT FAST ...!?
FULL
WHAAAAAA...!?
HERE TOO!?
B-BACK TO THE DRAWING BOARD, I GUESS ...
HUFF! HUFF!

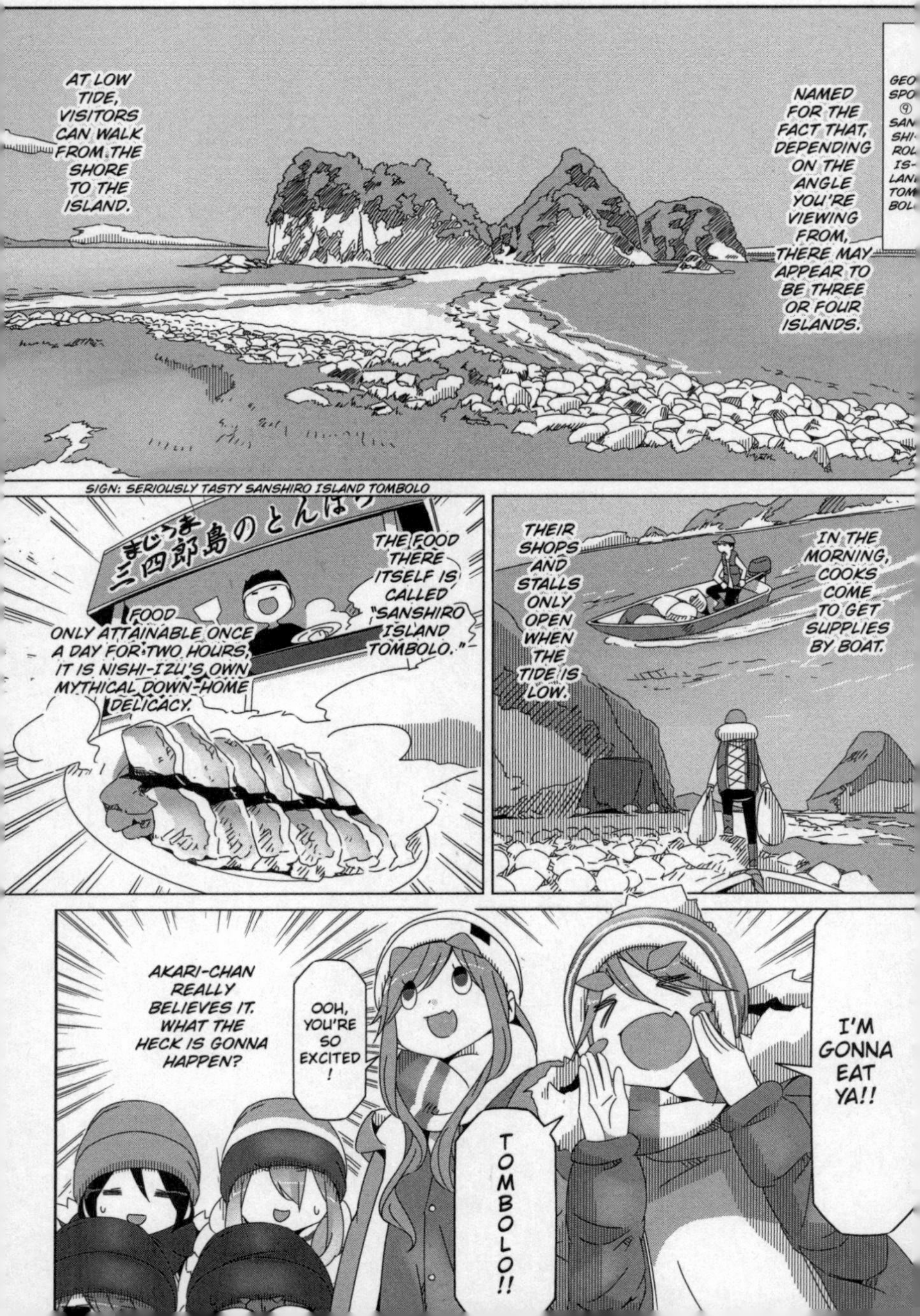
GEO SPO ⑨ SAN SHI ROL IS- LAN TOM BOL
NAMED FOR THE FACT THAT, DEPENDING ON THE ANGLE YOU'RE VIEWING FROM, THERE MAY APPEAR TO BE THREE OR FOUR ISLANDS.
AT LOW TIDE, VISITORS CAN WALK FROM THE SHORE TO THE ISLAND.
IN THE MORNING, COOKS COME TO GET SUPPLIES BY BOAT.
THEIR SHOPS AND STALLS ONLY OPEN WHEN THE TIDE IS LOW.
SIGN: SERIOUSLY TASTY SANSHIRO ISLAND TOMBOLO
まじうま
三四郎島のとんぼ
THE FOOD THERE ITSELF IS CALLED "SANSHIRO ISLAND TOMBOLO."
FOOD ONLY ATTAINABLE ONCE A DAY FOR TWO HOURS, IT IS NISHI-IZU'S OWN MYTHICAL DOWN-HOME DELICACY.
I'M GONNA EAT YA!!
TOMBOLO!!
OOH, YOU'RE SO EXCITED!
AKARI-CHAN REALLY BELIEVES IT. WHAT THE HECK IS GONNA HAPPEN?

CHAPTER 49
THE PATH OF OCEAN AND THE PATH OF SKY

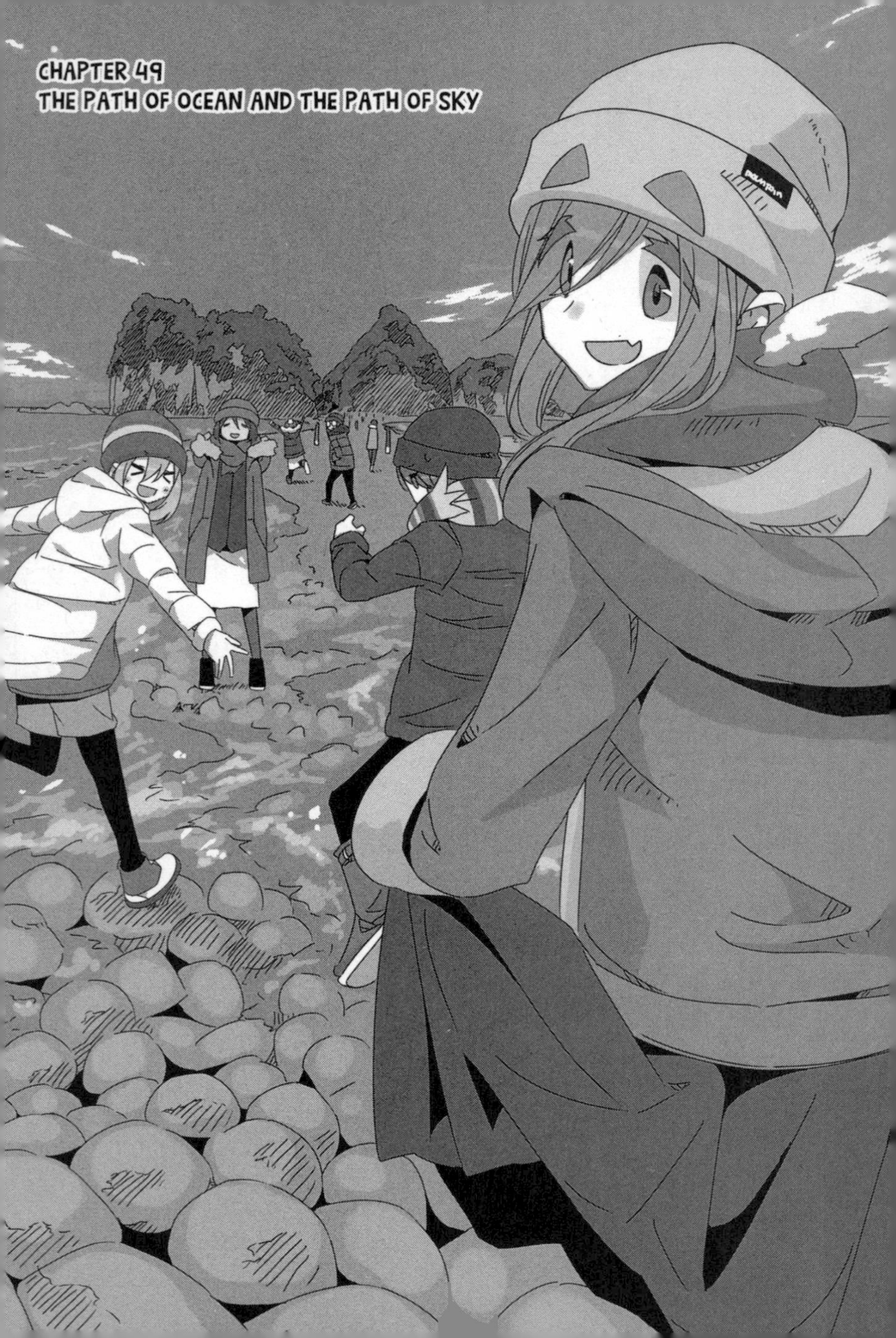

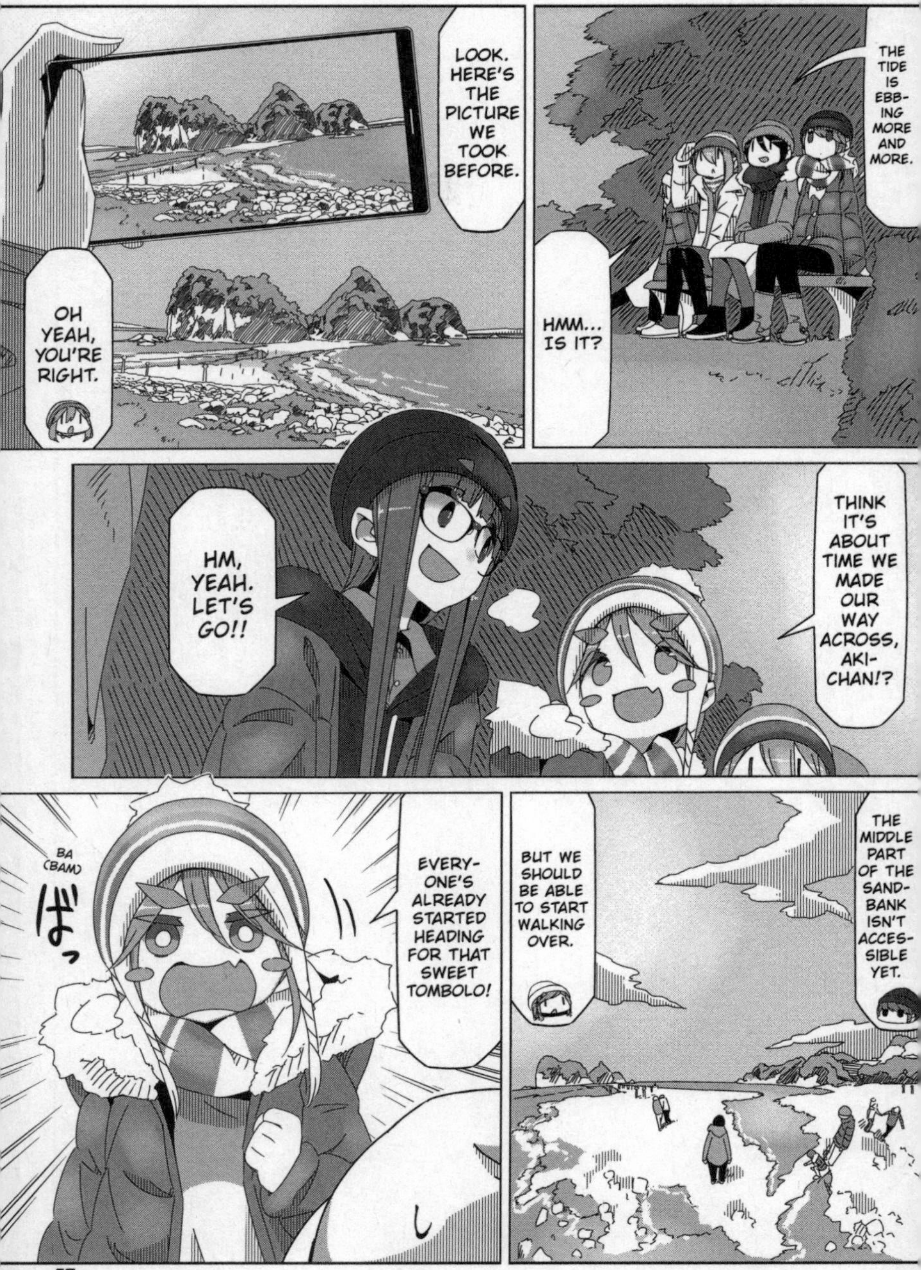
THE TIDE IS EBBING MORE AND MORE.
HMM... IS IT?
LOOK. HERE'S THE PICTURE WE TOOK BEFORE.
OH YEAH, YOU'RE RIGHT.
THINK IT'S ABOUT TIME WE MADE OUR WAY ACROSS, AKI-CHAN!?
HM, YEAH. LET'S GO!!
THE MIDDLE PART OF THE SANDBANK ISN'T ACCESSIBLE YET.
BUT WE SHOULD BE ABLE TO START WALKING OVER.
EVERYONE'S ALREADY STARTED HEADING FOR THAT SWEET TOMBOLO!
ばっ
BA (BAM)

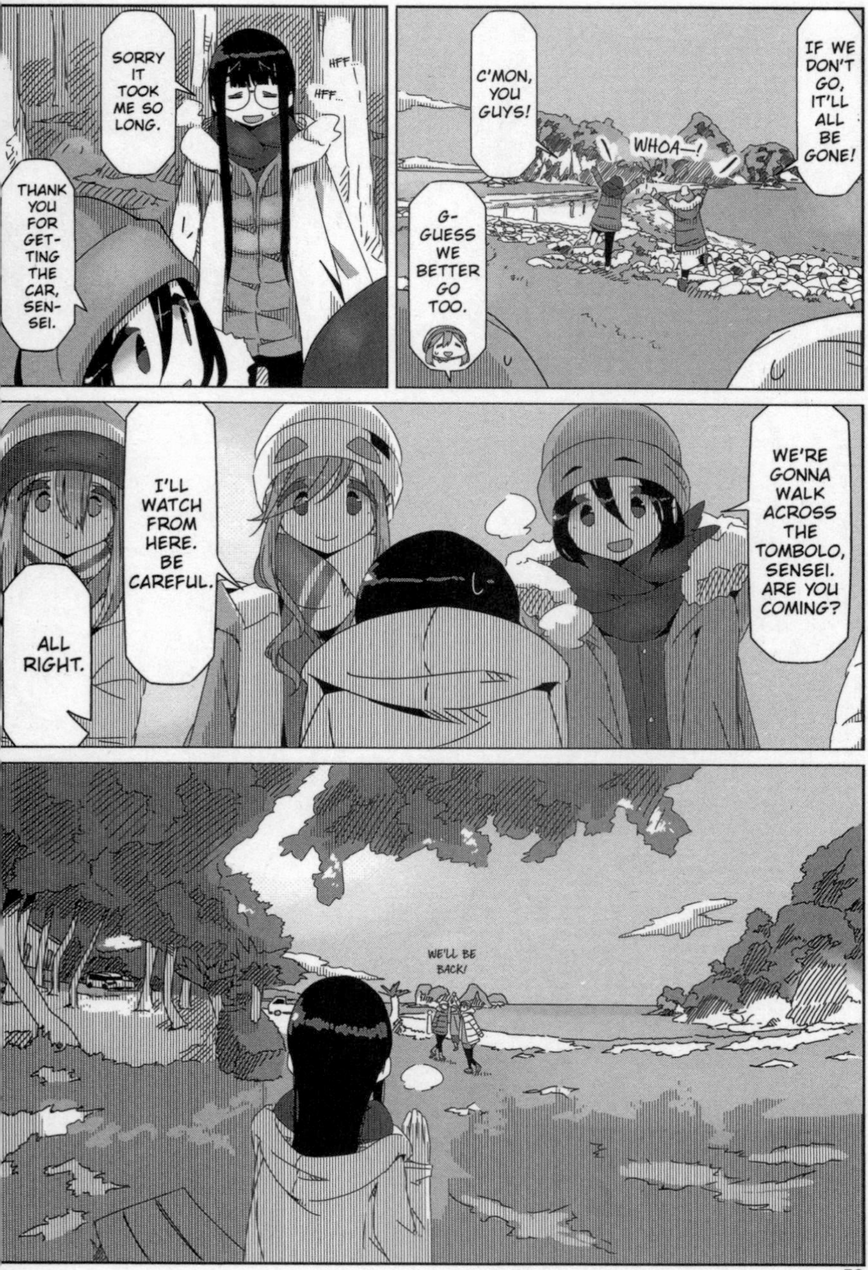
IF WE DON'T GO, IT'LL ALL BE GONE!
WHOA—!
C'MON, YOU GUYS!
G-GUESS WE BETTER GO TOO.
HFF...
HFF...
SORRY IT TOOK ME SO LONG.
THANK YOU FOR GETTING THE CAR, SENSEI.
WE'RE GONNA WALK ACROSS THE TOMBOLO, SENSEI. ARE YOU COMING?
I'LL WATCH FROM HERE. BE CAREFUL.
ALL RIGHT.
WE'LL BE BACK!

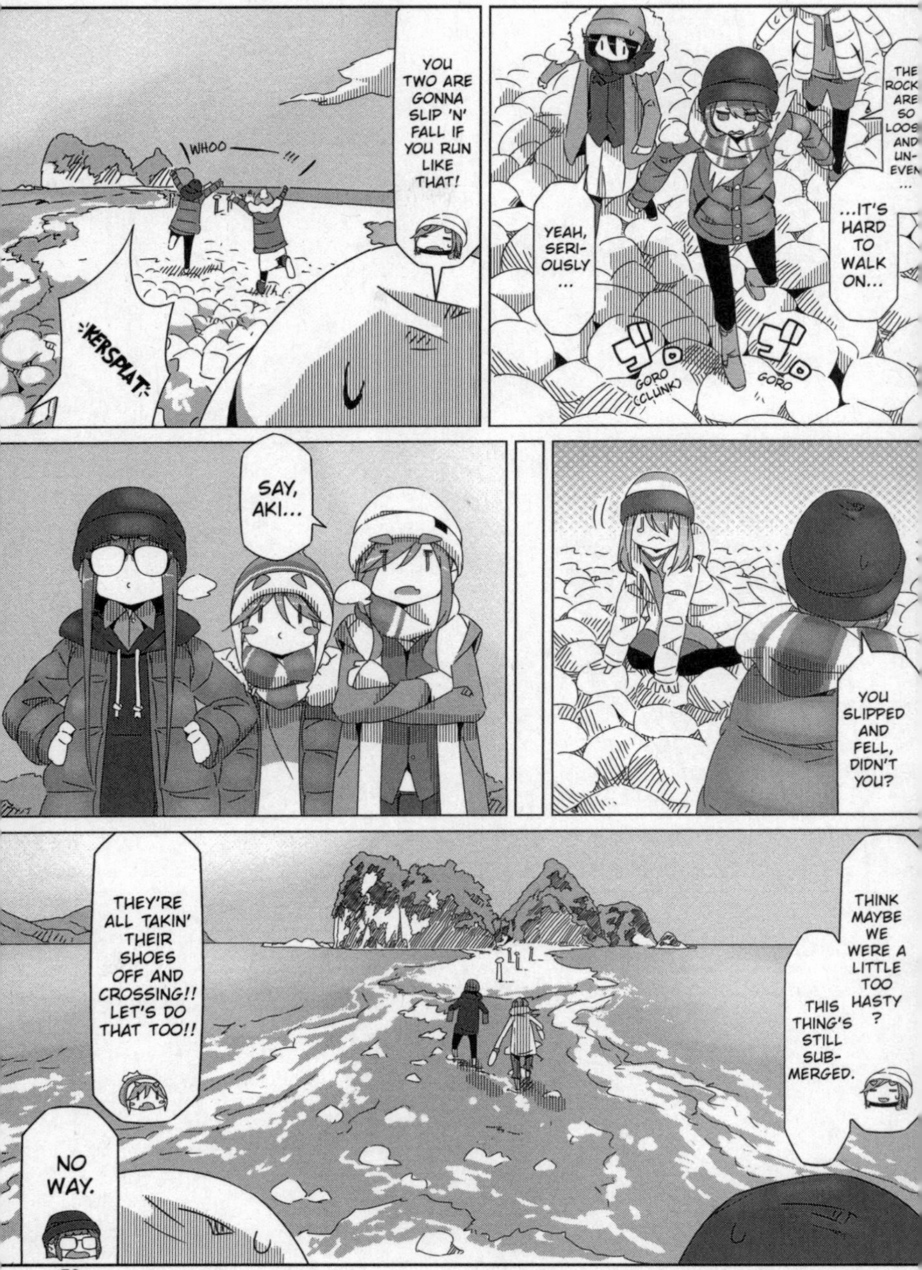
THE ROCK ARE SO LOOS AND UN-EVEN …
…IT'S HARD TO WALK ON…
YEAH, SERIOUSLY …
GORO (CLLINK)
GORO
YOU TWO ARE GONNA SLIP 'N' FALL IF YOU RUN LIKE THAT!
WHOO—!!!
KERSPLAT
YOU SLIPPED AND FELL, DIDN'T YOU?
SAY, AKI…
THINK MAYBE WE WERE A LITTLE TOO HASTY?
THIS THING'S STILL SUBMERGED.
THEY'RE ALL TAKIN' THEIR SHOES OFF AND CROSSING!! LET'S DO THAT TOO!!
NO WAY.

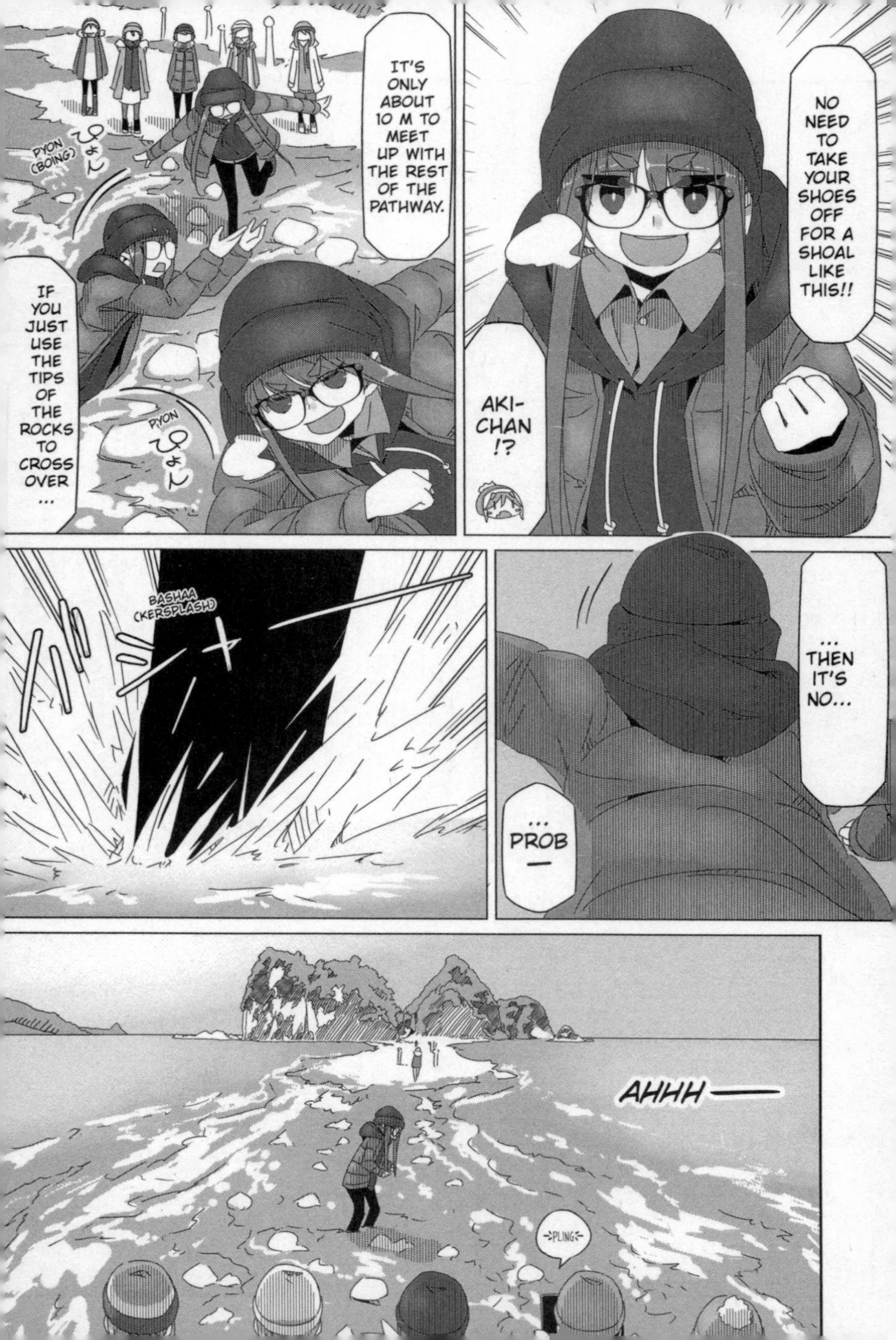
NO NEED TO TAKE YOUR SHOES OFF FOR A SHOAL LIKE THIS!!
AKI-CHAN!?
IT'S ONLY ABOUT 10 M TO MEET UP WITH THE REST OF THE PATHWAY.
PYON (BOING)
ぴょん
IF YOU JUST USE THE TIPS OF THE ROCKS TO CROSS OVER...
PYON
ぴょん
...THEN IT'S NO...
...PROB—
BASHAA (KERSPLASH)
AHHH—
PLING

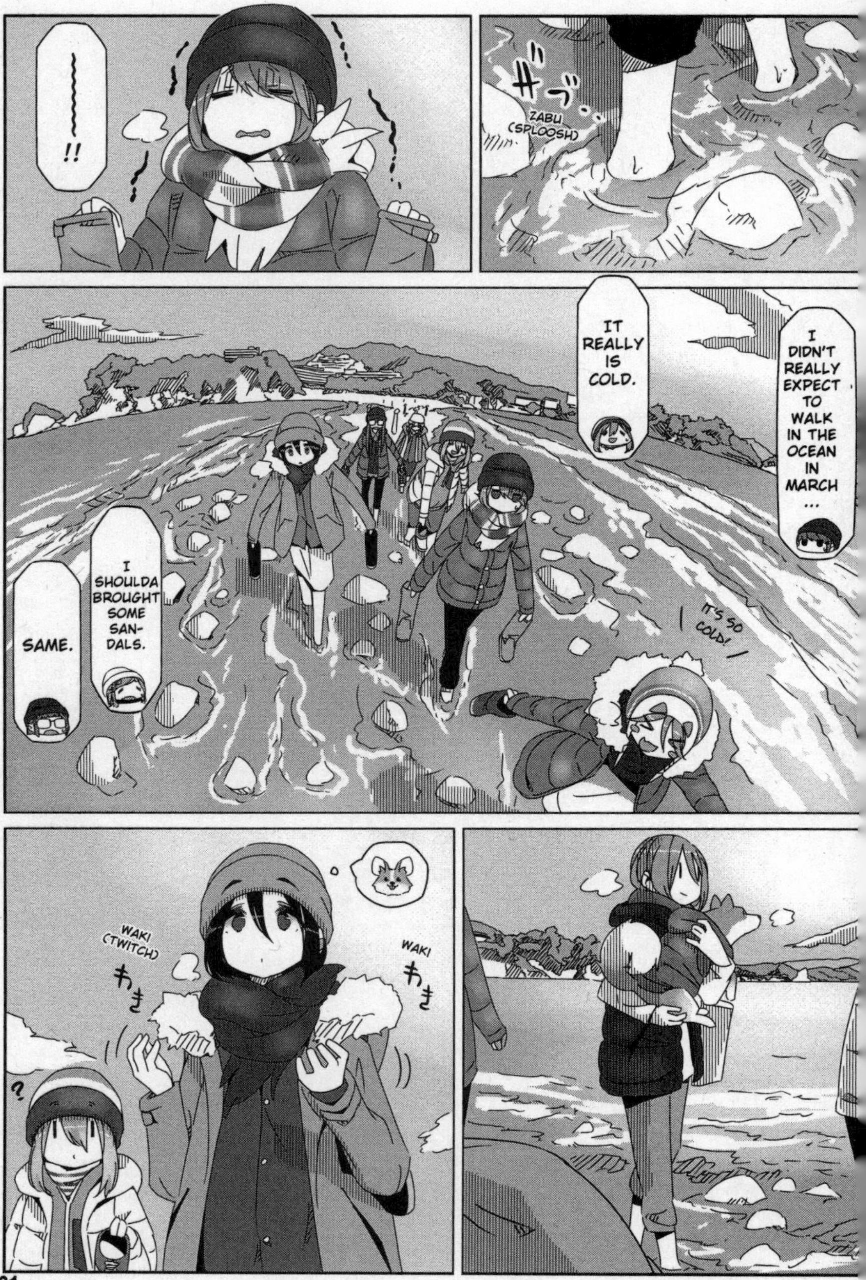

ザブ
ZABU (SPLOOSH)
〜〜〜〜!!
I DIDN'T REALLY EXPECT TO WALK IN THE OCEAN IN MARCH...
IT REALLY IS COLD.
IT'S SO COLD!
I SHOULDA BROUGHT SOME SAN-DALS.
SAME.
WAKI
わき
WAKI (TWITCH)
わき
?

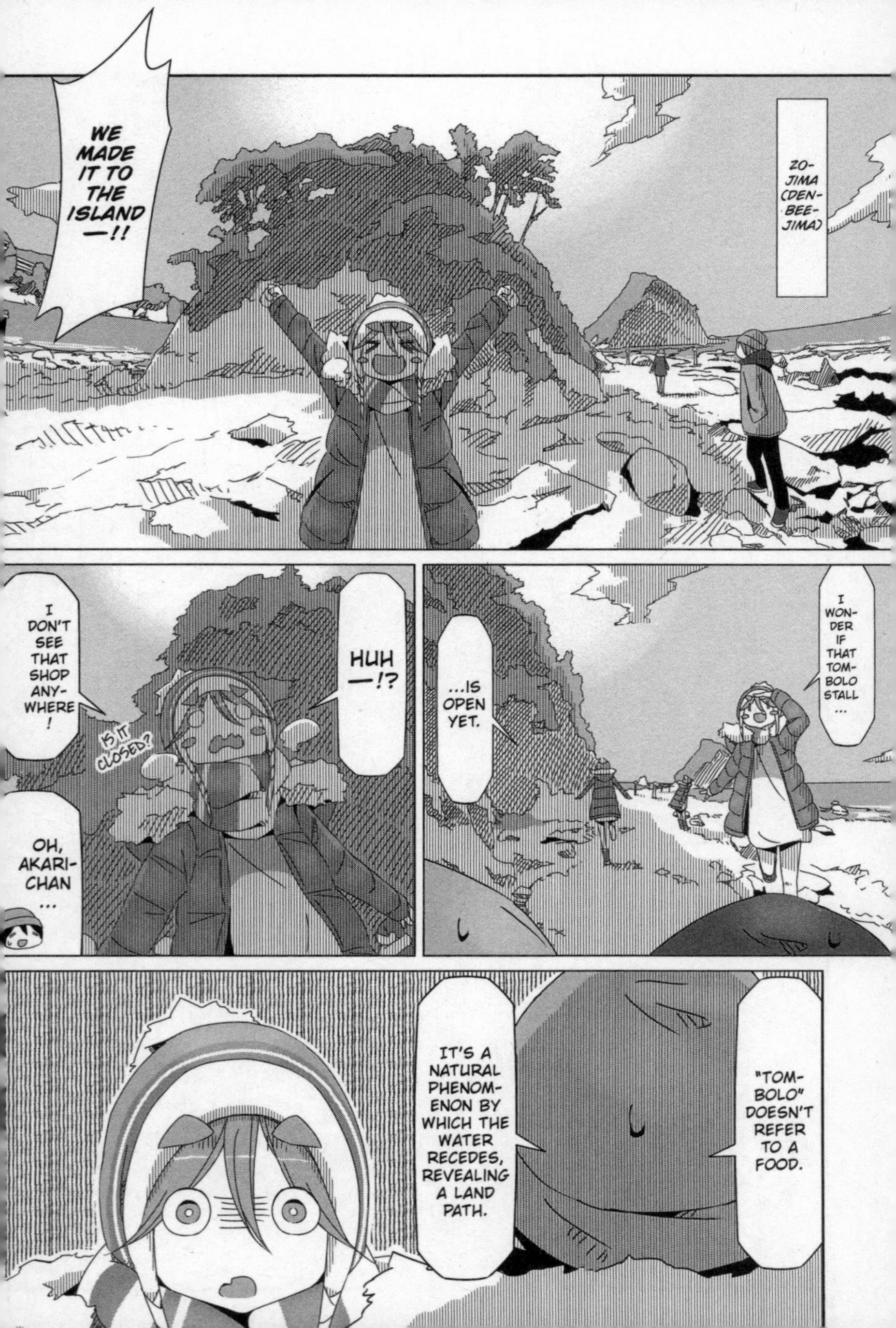
WE MADE IT TO THE ISLAND—!!
ZO-JIMA (DEN-BEE-JIMA)
I WONDER IF THAT TOMBOLO STALL...
...IS OPEN YET.
HUH—!?
I DON'T SEE THAT SHOP ANYWHERE!
IS IT CLOSED?
OH, AKARI-CHAN...
"TOMBOLO" DOESN'T REFER TO A FOOD.
IT'S A NATURAL PHENOMENON BY WHICH THE WATER RECEDES, REVEALING A LAND PATH.

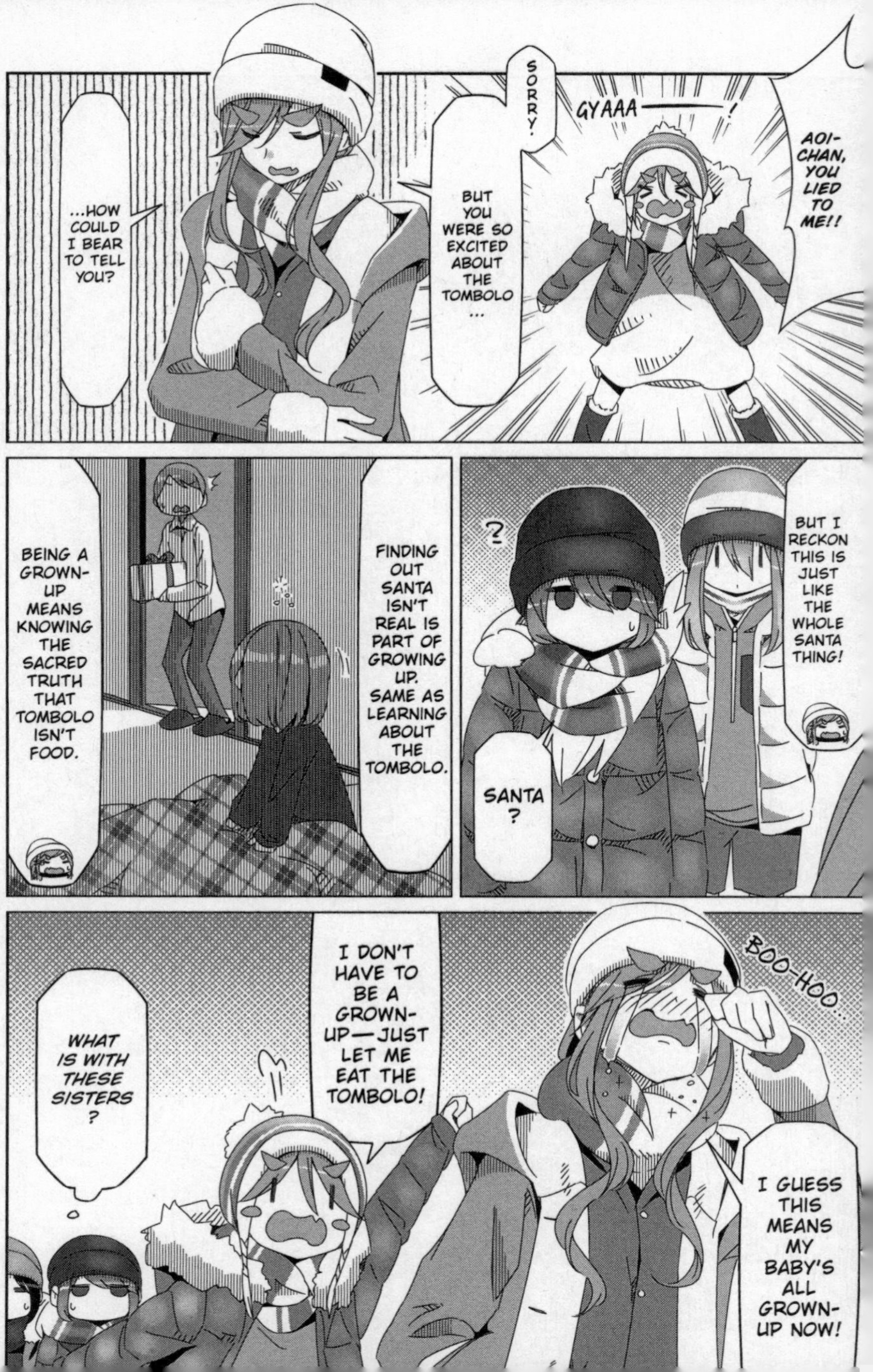
AOI-CHAN, YOU LIED TO ME!!
GYAAA——!
SORRY.
BUT YOU WERE SO EXCITED ABOUT THE TOMBOLO...
...HOW COULD I BEAR TO TELL YOU?
BUT I RECKON THIS IS JUST LIKE THE WHOLE SANTA THING!
SANTA?
FINDING OUT SANTA ISN'T REAL IS PART OF GROWING UP. SAME AS LEARNING ABOUT THE TOMBOLO.
BEING A GROWN-UP MEANS KNOWING THE SACRED TRUTH THAT TOMBOLO ISN'T FOOD.
BOO-HOO...
I GUESS THIS MEANS MY BABY'S ALL GROWN-UP NOW!
I DON'T HAVE TO BE A GROWN-UP—JUST LET ME EAT THE TOMBOLO!
WHAT IS WITH THESE SISTERS?

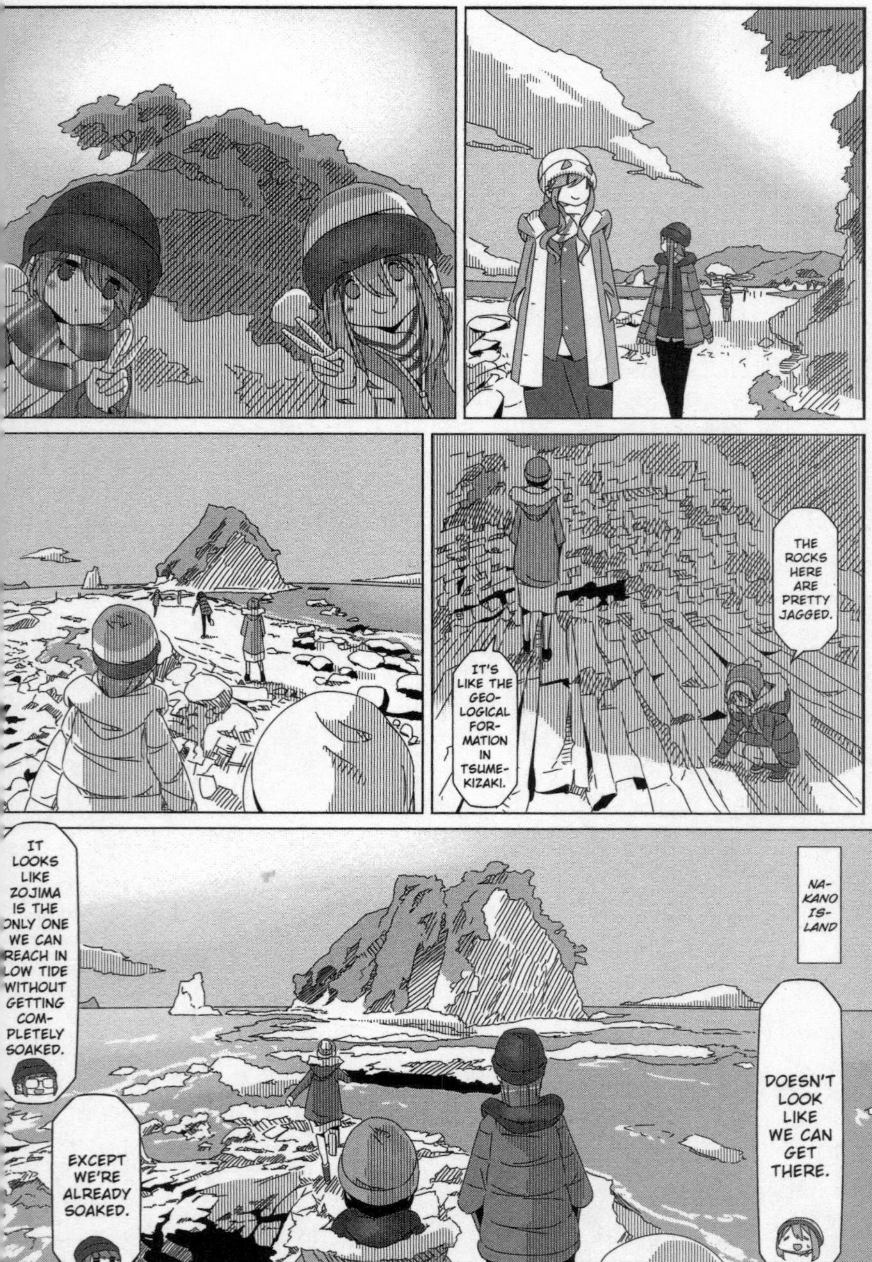
THE ROCKS HERE ARE PRETTY JAGGED.
IT'S LIKE THE GEO-LOGICAL FOR-MATION IN TSUME-KIZAKI.
NA-KANO IS-LAND
DOESN'T LOOK LIKE WE CAN GET THERE.
IT LOOKS LIKE ZOJIMA IS THE ONLY ONE WE CAN REACH IN LOW TIDE WITHOUT GETTING COM-PLETELY SOAKED.
EXCEPT WE'RE ALREADY SOAKED.

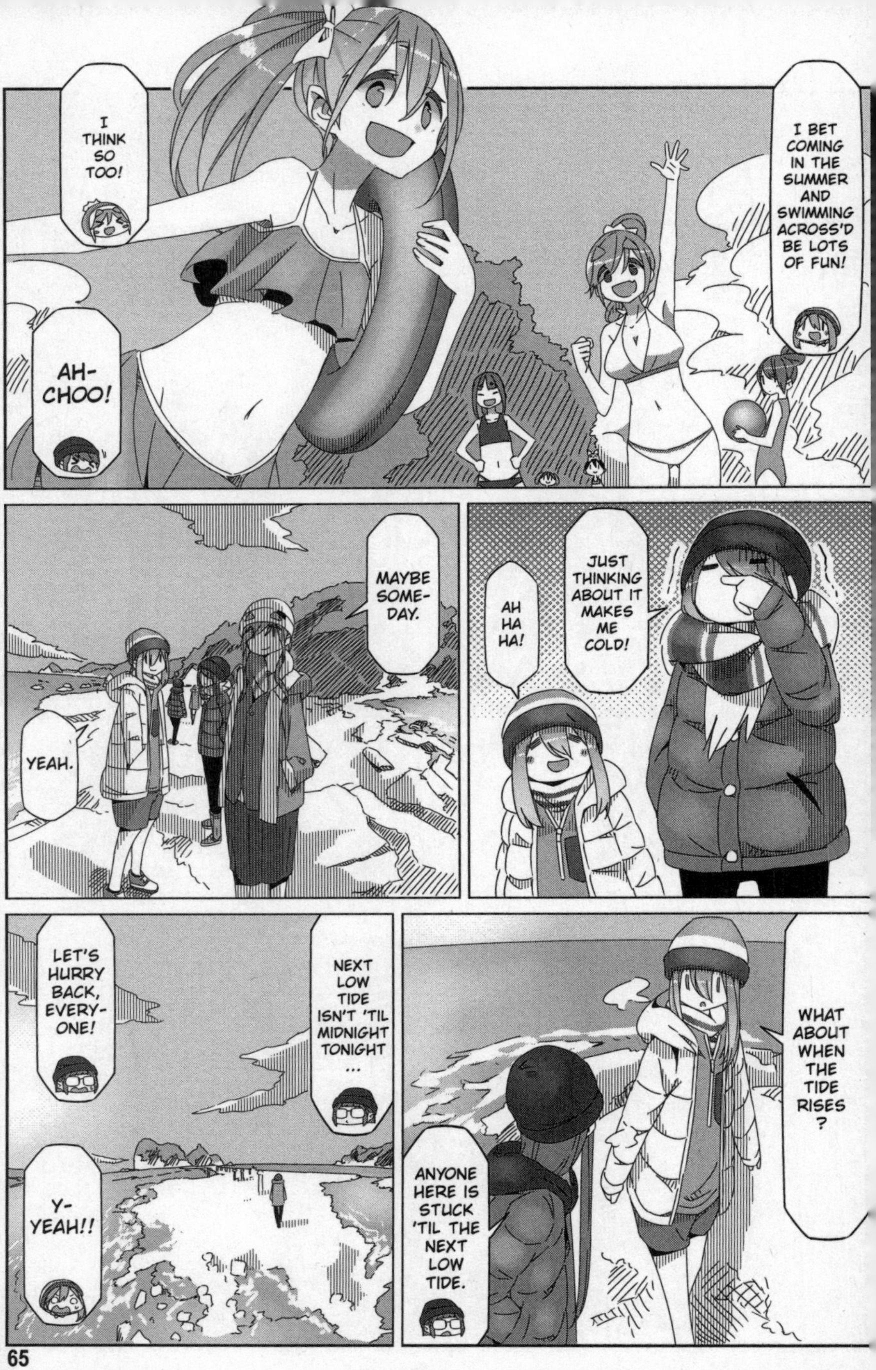
I BET COMING IN THE SUMMER AND SWIMMING ACROSS'D BE LOTS OF FUN!
I THINK SO TOO!
AH-CHOO!
JUST THINKING ABOUT IT MAKES ME COLD!
AH HA HA!
MAYBE SOME-DAY.
YEAH.
WHAT ABOUT WHEN THE TIDE RISES?
ANYONE HERE IS STUCK 'TIL THE NEXT LOW TIDE.
NEXT LOW TIDE ISN'T 'TIL MIDNIGHT TONIGHT...
LET'S HURRY BACK, EVERY-ONE!
Y-YEAH!!

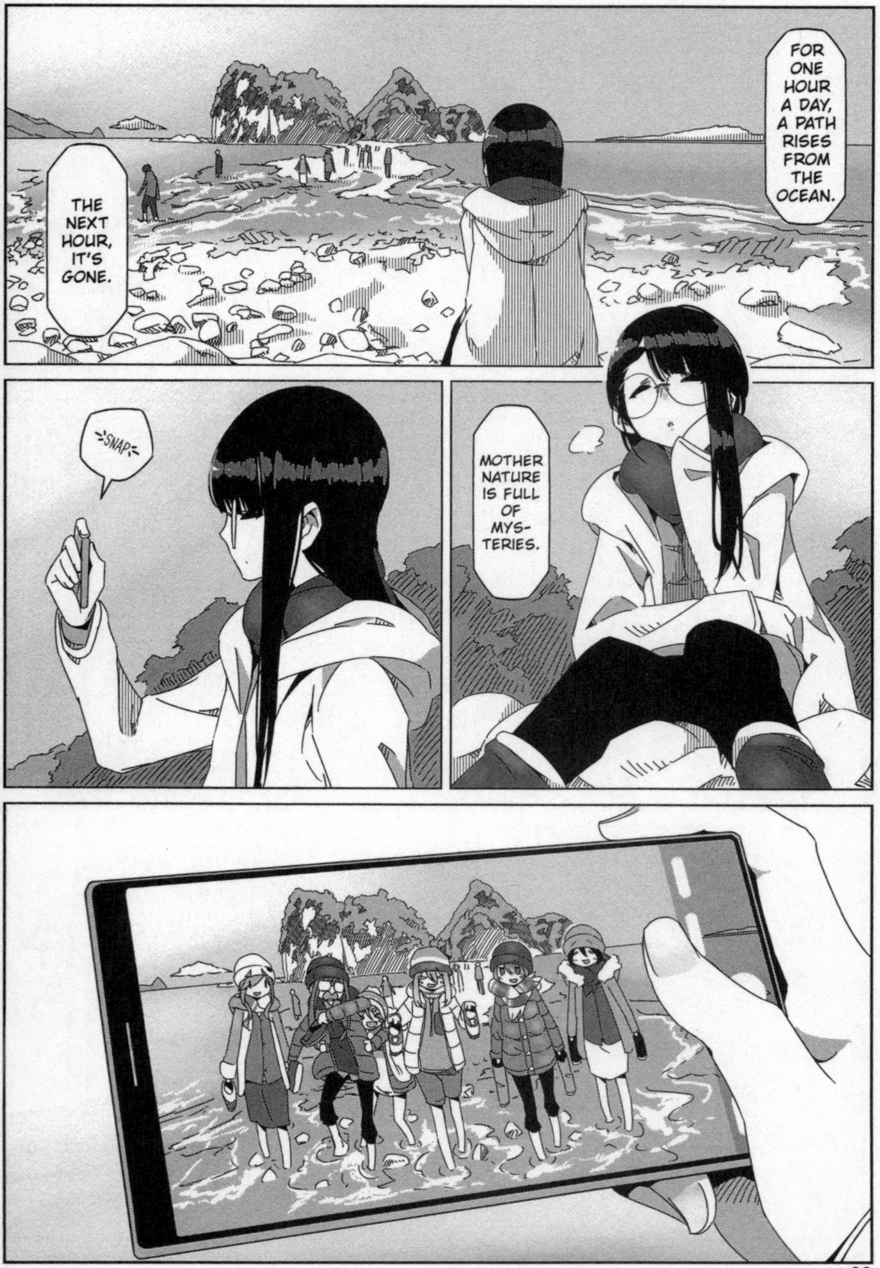
FOR ONE HOUR A DAY, A PATH RISES FROM THE OCEAN.
THE NEXT HOUR, IT'S GONE.
MOTHER NATURE IS FULL OF MYS-TERIES.
SNAP

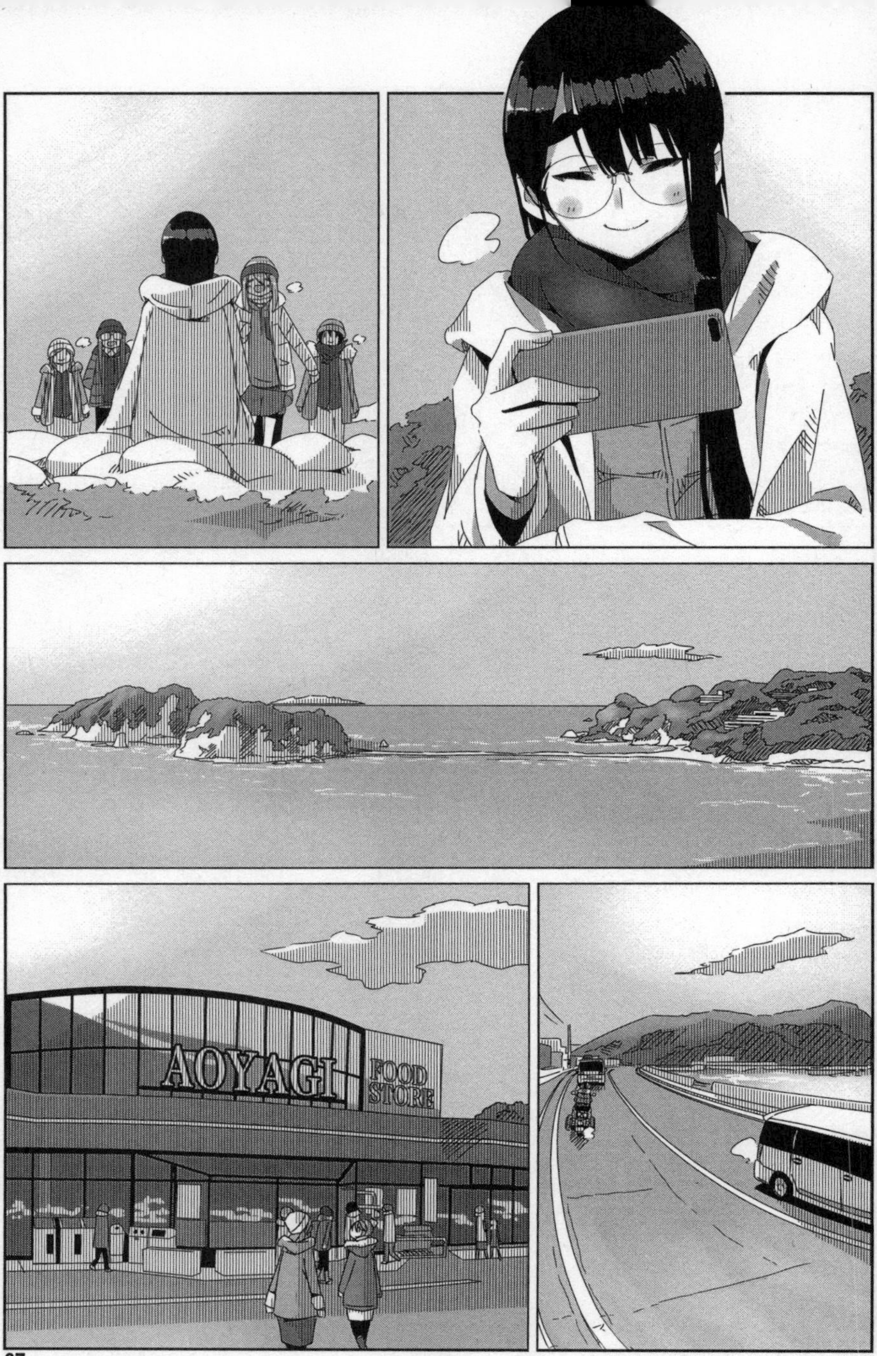
AOYAGI
FOOD STORE

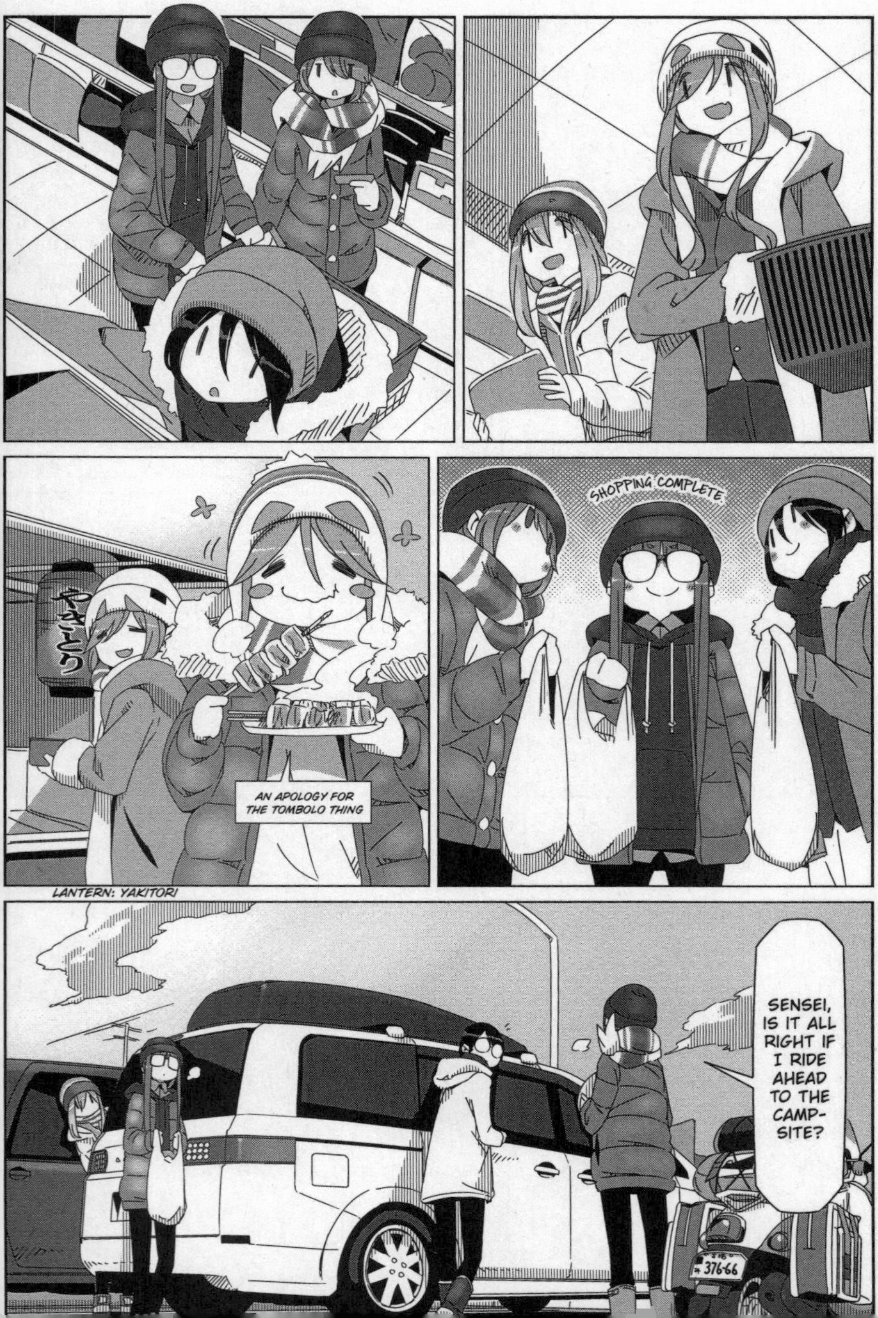
SHOPPING COMPLETE.
AN APOLOGY FOR THE TOMBOLO THING
LANTERN: YAKITORI
SENSEI, IS IT ALL RIGHT IF I RIDE AHEAD TO THE CAMP-SITE?

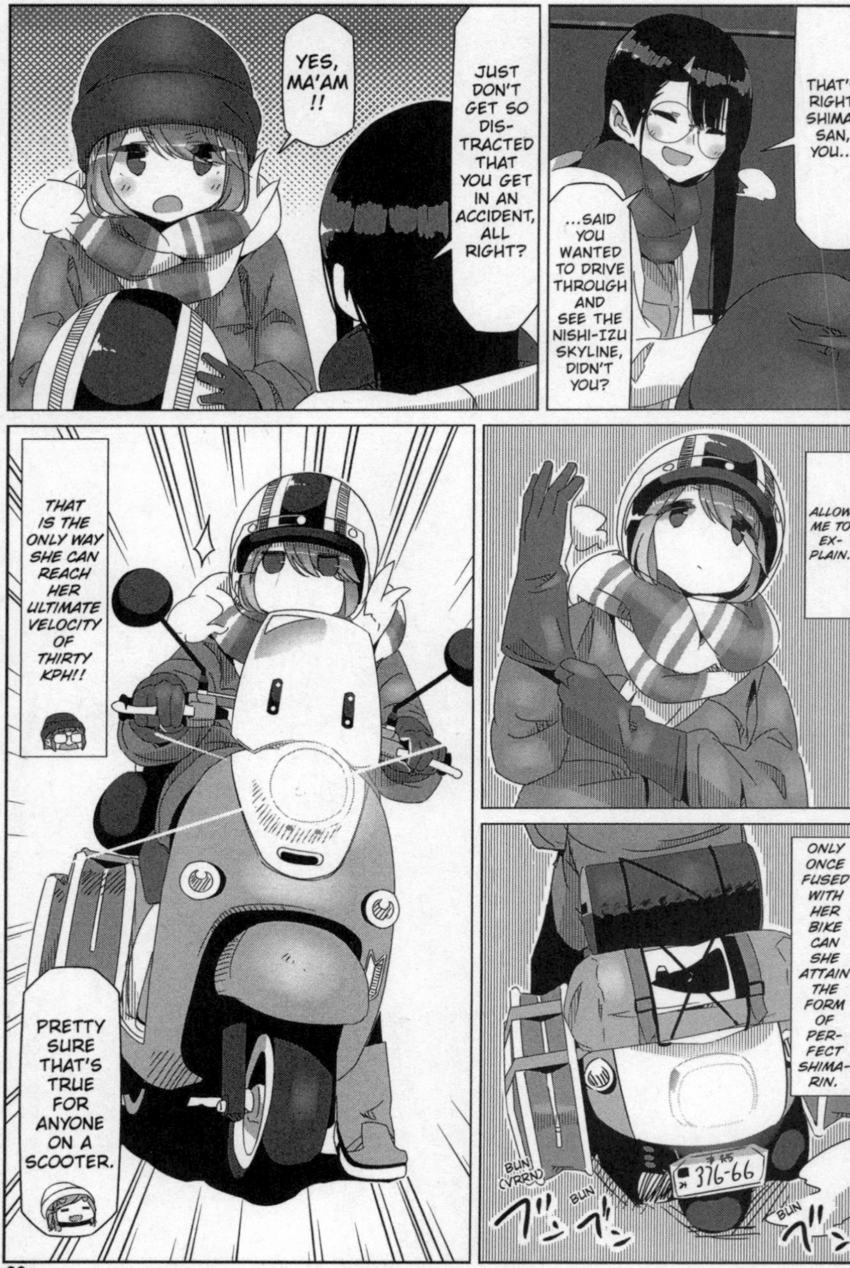
THAT'S RIGHT, SHIMA-SAN, YOU...
...SAID YOU WANTED TO DRIVE THROUGH AND SEE THE NISHI-IZU SKYLINE, DIDN'T YOU?
JUST DON'T GET SO DIS-TRACTED THAT YOU GET IN AN ACCIDENT, ALL RIGHT?
YES, MA'AM!!
ALLOW ME TO EX-PLAIN.
ONLY ONCE FUSED WITH HER BIKE CAN SHE ATTAIN THE FORM OF PER-FECT SHIMA-RIN.
BUN (VRRN)
BUN
BUN
THAT IS THE ONLY WAY SHE CAN REACH HER ULTIMATE VELOCITY OF THIRTY KPH!!
PRETTY SURE THAT'S TRUE FOR ANYONE ON A SCOOTER.

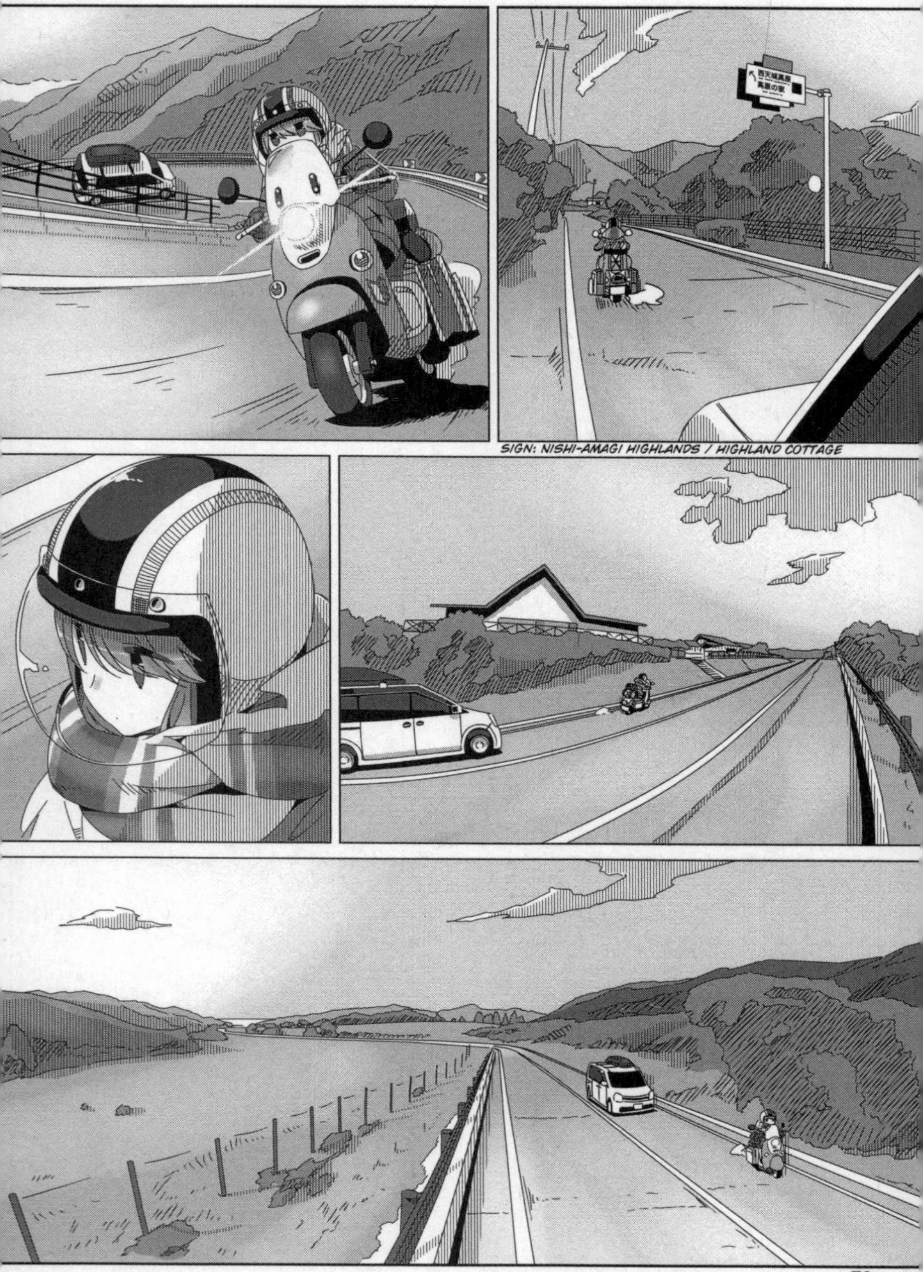
西天城高原
高原の家
SIGN: NISHI-AMAGI HIGHLANDS / HIGHLAND COTTAGE

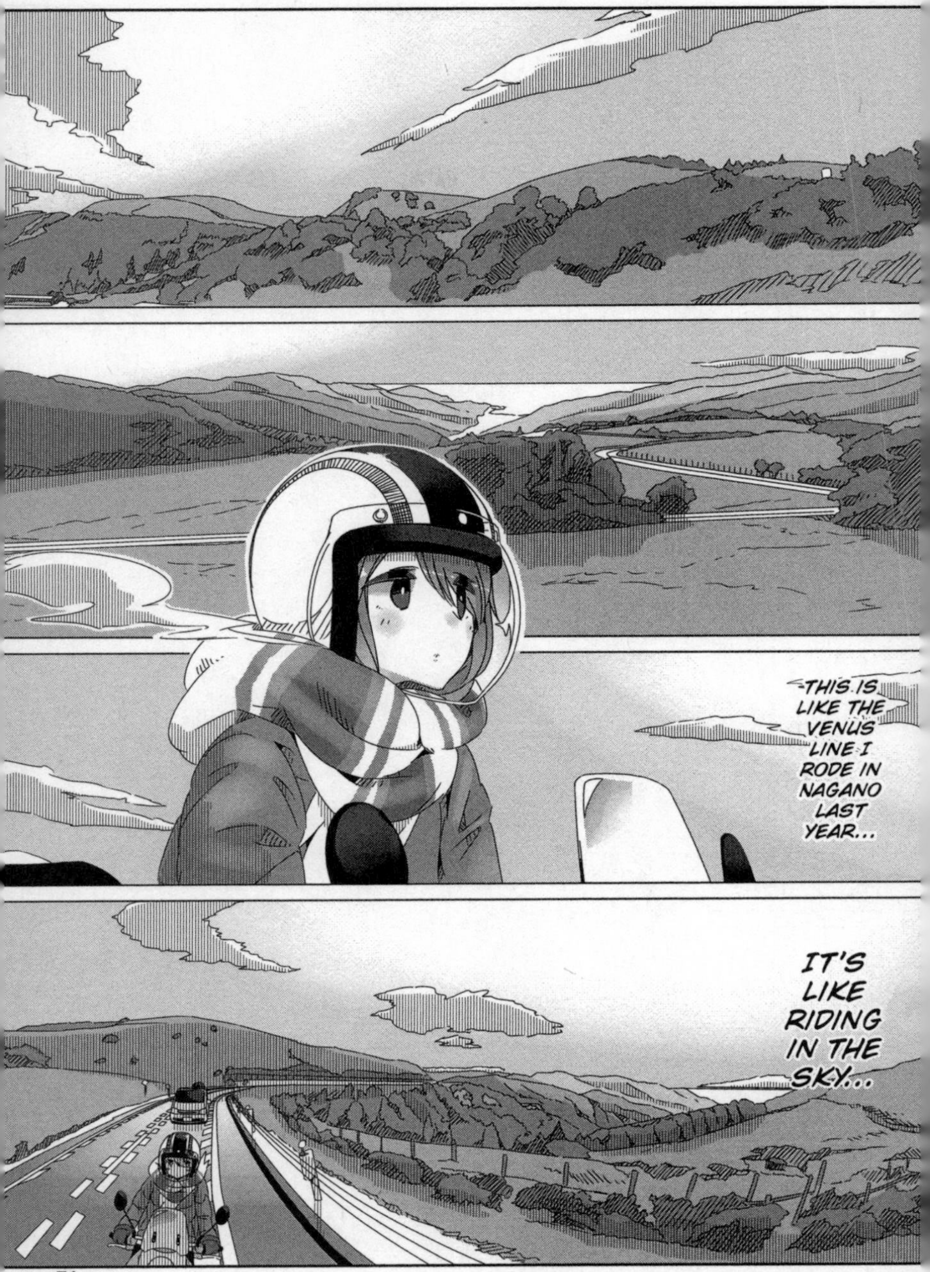
THIS IS LIKE THE VENUS LINE I RODE IN NAGANO LAST YEAR...
IT'S LIKE RIDING IN THE SKY...

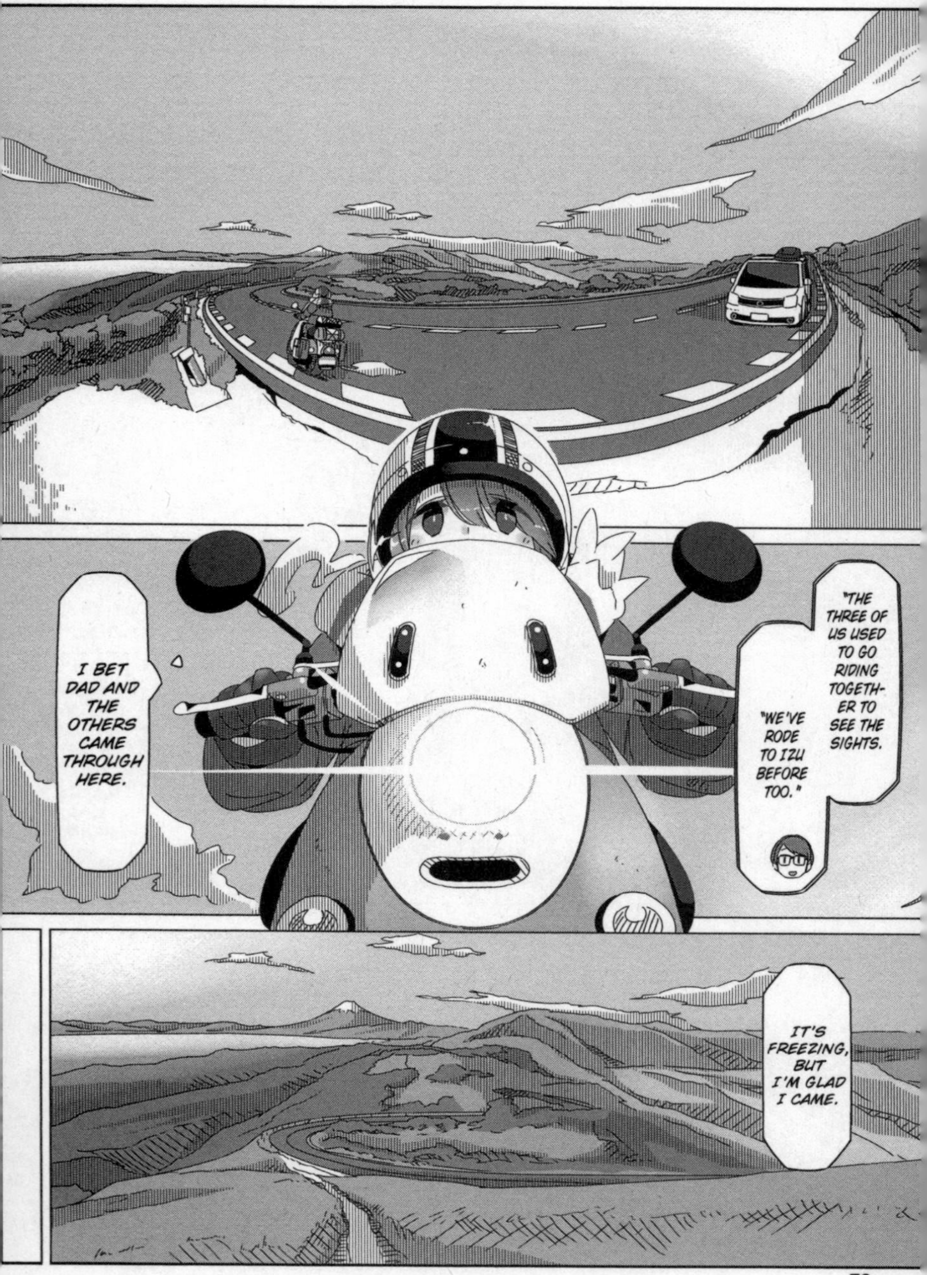
"THE THREE OF US USED TO GO RIDING TOGETHER TO SEE THE SIGHTS.
"WE'VE RODE TO IZU BEFORE TOO."
I BET DAD AND THE OTHERS CAME THROUGH HERE.
IT'S FREEZING, BUT I'M GLAD I CAME.

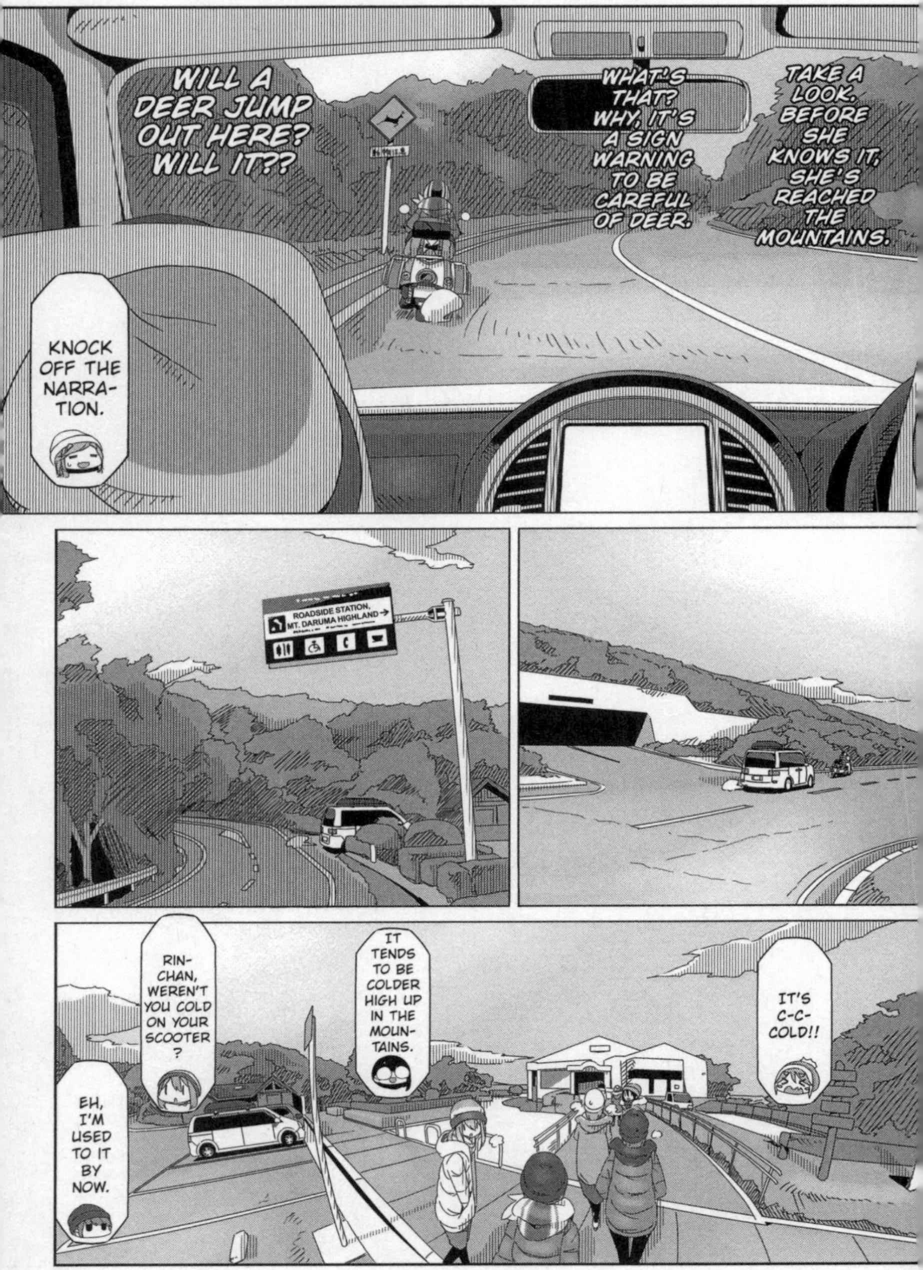
TAKE A LOOK. BEFORE SHE KNOWS IT, SHE'S REACHED THE MOUNTAINS.
WHAT'S THAT? WHY, IT'S A SIGN WARNING TO BE CAREFUL OF DEER.
WILL A DEER JUMP OUT HERE? WILL IT??
KNOCK OFF THE NARRA-TION.
ROADSIDE STATION, MT. DARUMA HIGHLAND →
IT'S C-C-COLD!!
IT TENDS TO BE COLDER HIGH UP IN THE MOUN-TAINS.
RIN-CHAN, WEREN'T YOU COLD ON YOUR SCOOTER?
EH, I'M USED TO IT BY NOW.

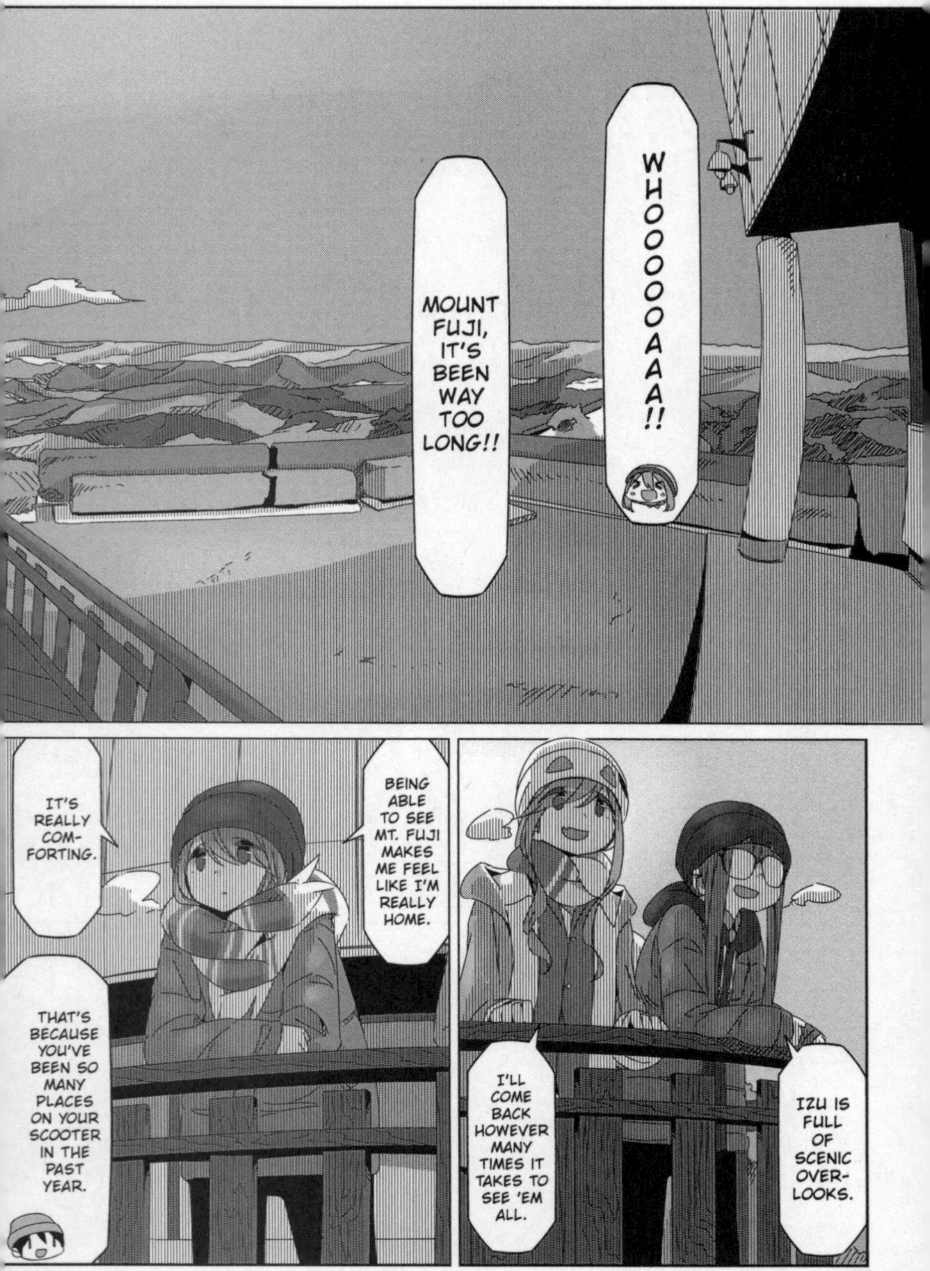
WHOOOOOOAAAA!!
MOUNT FUJI, IT'S BEEN WAY TOO LONG!!
IZU IS FULL OF SCENIC OVER-LOOKS.
I'LL COME BACK HOWEVER MANY TIMES IT TAKES TO SEE 'EM ALL.
BEING ABLE TO SEE MT. FUJI MAKES ME FEEL LIKE I'M REALLY HOME.
IT'S REALLY COM-FORTING.
THAT'S BECAUSE YOU'VE BEEN SO MANY PLACES ON YOUR SCOOTER IN THE PAST YEAR.

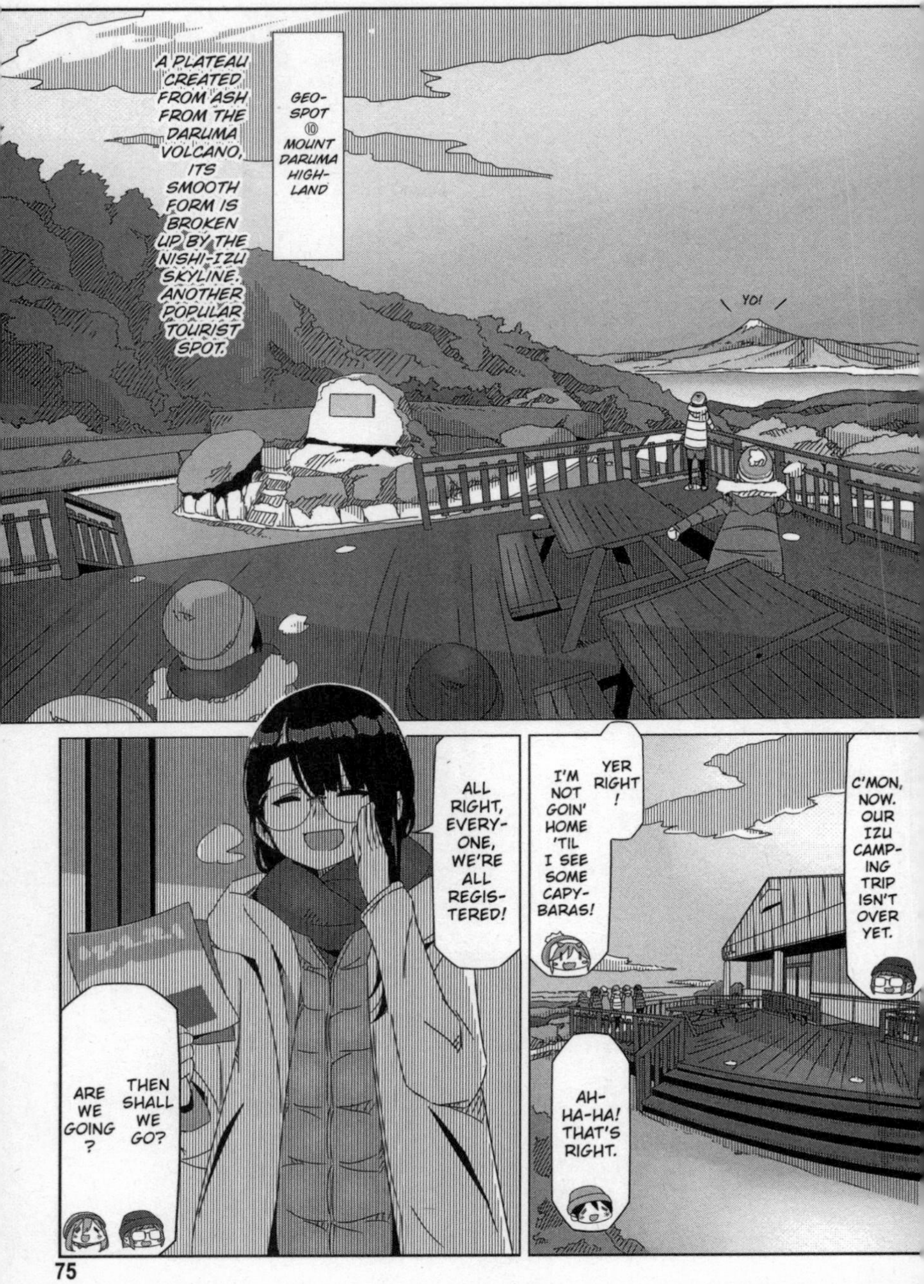
GEO-SPOT ⑩ MOUNT DARUMA HIGHLAND
A PLATEAU CREATED FROM ASH FROM THE DARUMA VOLCANO, ITS SMOOTH FORM IS BROKEN UP BY THE NISHI-IZU SKYLINE. ANOTHER POPULAR TOURIST SPOT.
YO!
C'MON, NOW. OUR IZU CAMPING TRIP ISN'T OVER YET.
YER RIGHT!
I'M NOT GOIN' HOME 'TIL I SEE SOME CAPYBARAS!
AH-HA-HA! THAT'S RIGHT.
ALL RIGHT, EVERYONE, WE'RE ALL REGISTERED!
THEN SHALL WE GO?
ARE WE GOING?

LICENSE PLATE: MOUNT FUJI 502 / SA 10-225

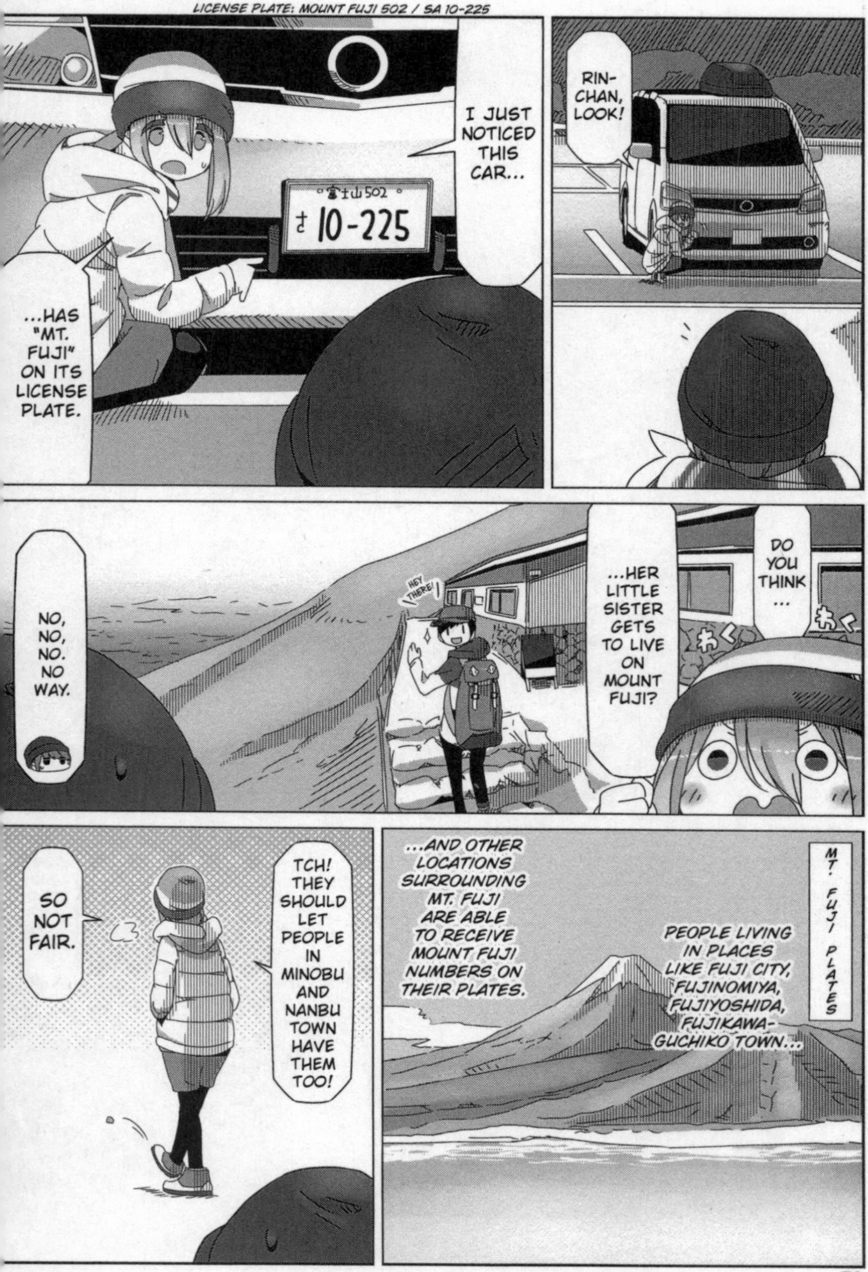
RIN-CHAN, LOOK!
I JUST NOTICED THIS CAR...
富士山502
さ 10-225
...HAS "MT. FUJI" ON ITS LICENSE PLATE.
DO YOU THINK...
わく わく
...HER LITTLE SISTER GETS TO LIVE ON MOUNT FUJI?
HEY THERE!
NO, NO, NO. NO WAY.
MT. FUJI PLATES
PEOPLE LIVING IN PLACES LIKE FUJI CITY, FUJINOMIYA, FUJIYOSHIDA, FUJIKAWA-GUCHIKO TOWN...
...AND OTHER LOCATIONS SURROUNDING MT. FUJI ARE ABLE TO RECEIVE MOUNT FUJI NUMBERS ON THEIR PLATES.
TCH! THEY SHOULD LET PEOPLE IN MINOBU AND NANBU TOWN HAVE THEM TOO!
SO NOT FAIR.

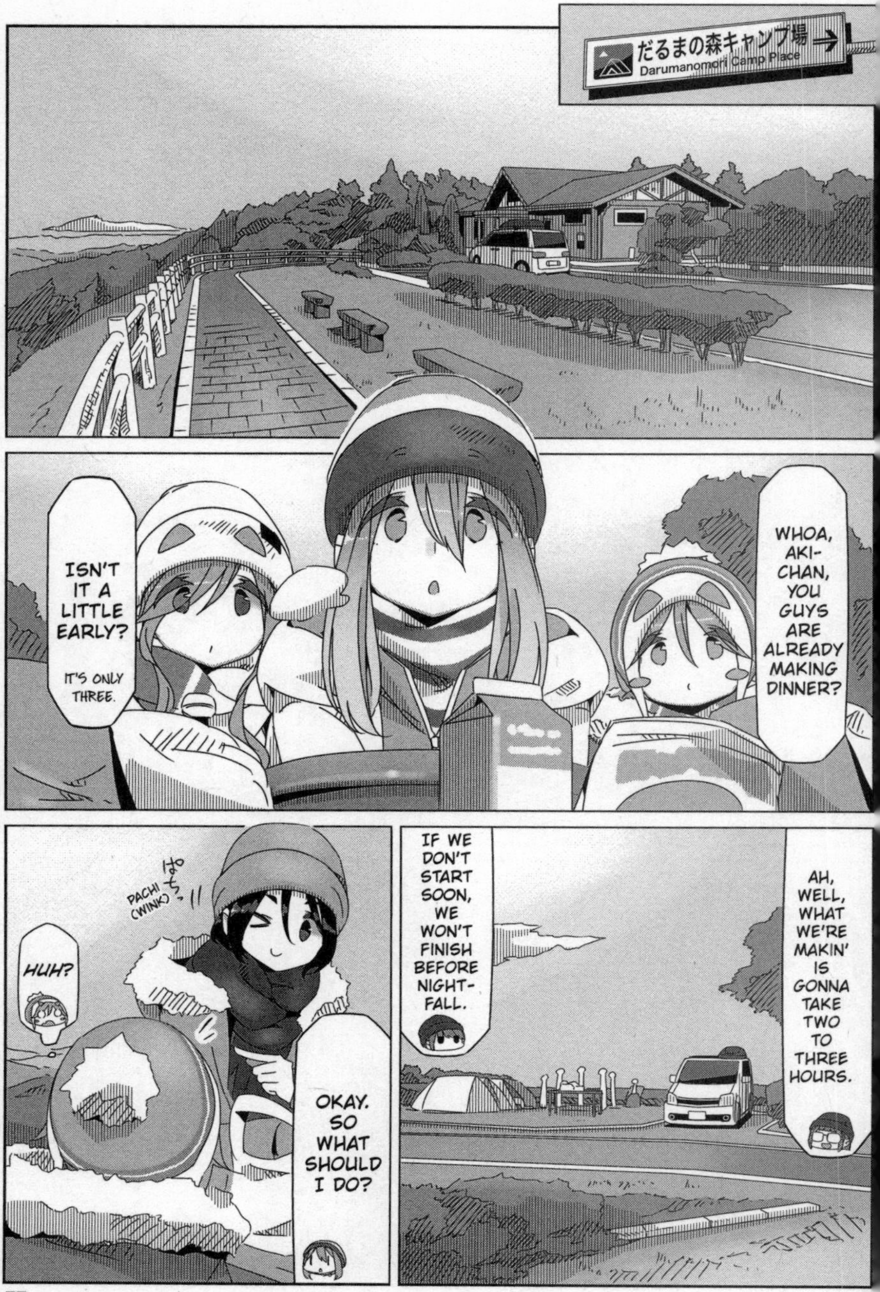
だるまの森キャンプ場
Darumanomori Camp Place
WHOA, AKI-CHAN, YOU GUYS ARE ALREADY MAKING DINNER?
ISN'T IT A LITTLE EARLY?
IT'S ONLY THREE.
AH, WELL, WHAT WE'RE MAKIN' IS GONNA TAKE TWO TO THREE HOURS.
IF WE DON'T START SOON, WE WON'T FINISH BEFORE NIGHT-FALL.
ぱちっ
PACHI (WINK)
HUH?
OKAY. SO WHAT SHOULD I DO?

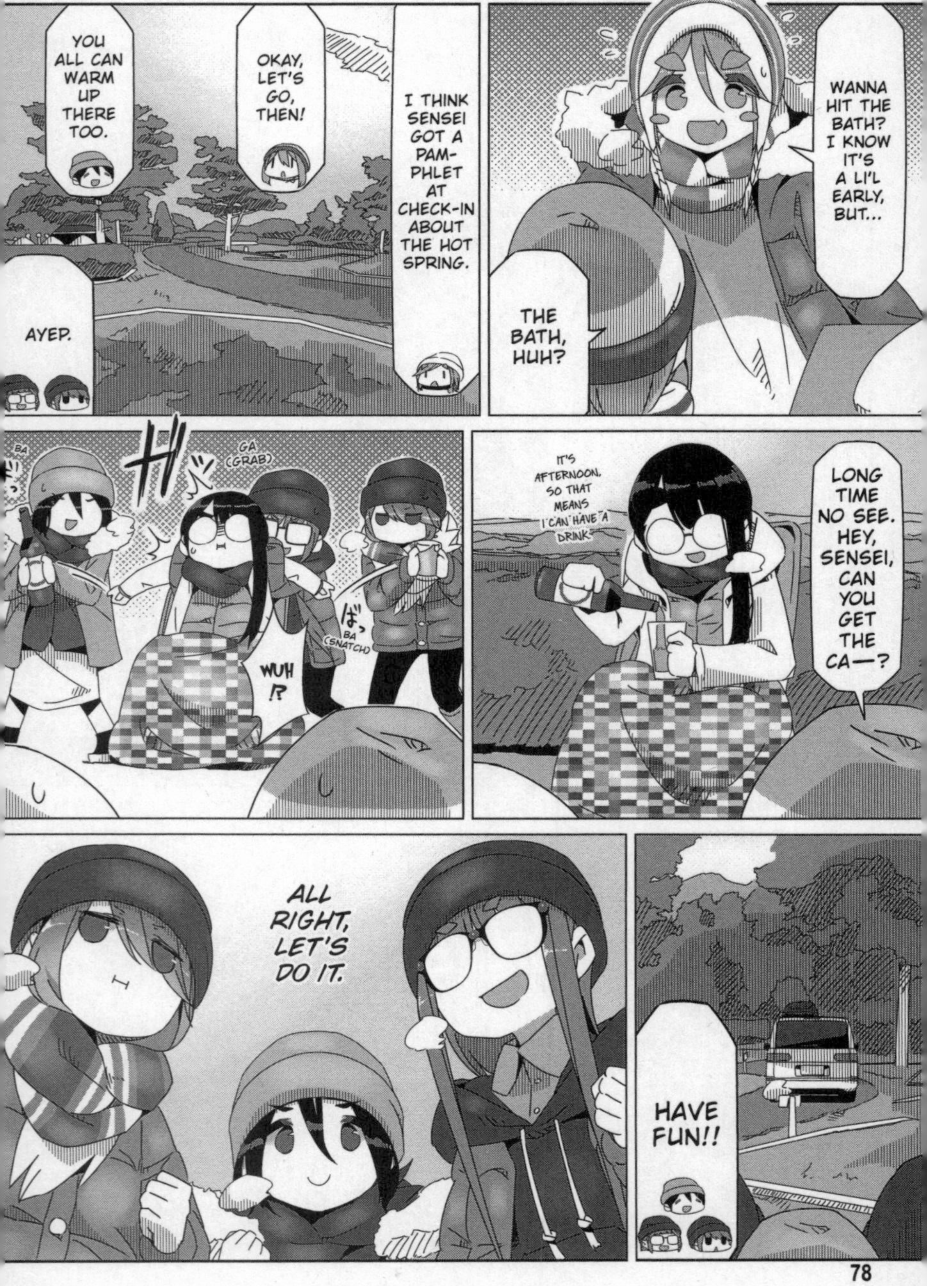

WANNA HIT THE BATH? I KNOW IT'S A LI'L EARLY, BUT...
THE BATH, HUH?
I THINK SENSEI GOT A PAMPHLET AT CHECK-IN ABOUT THE HOT SPRING.
OKAY, LET'S GO, THEN!
YOU ALL CAN WARM UP THERE TOO.
AYEP.
LONG TIME NO SEE. HEY, SENSEI, CAN YOU GET THE CA—?
IT'S AFTERNOON, SO THAT MEANS I CAN HAVE A DRINK
GA (GRAB)
BA
ばっ
BA (SNATCH)
WUH !?
HAVE FUN!!
ALL RIGHT, LET'S DO IT.

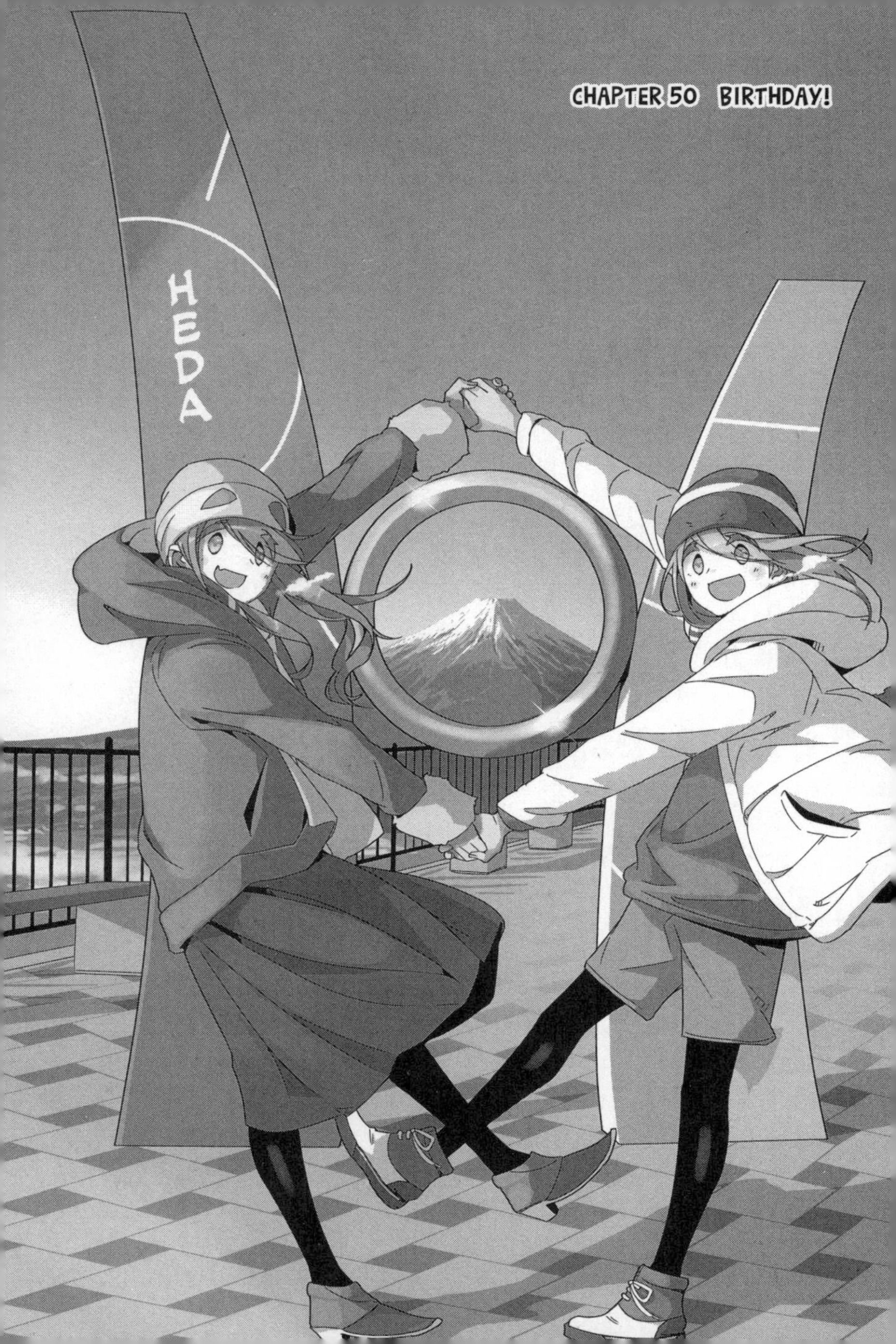
CHAPTER 50 BIRTHDAY!
HEDA

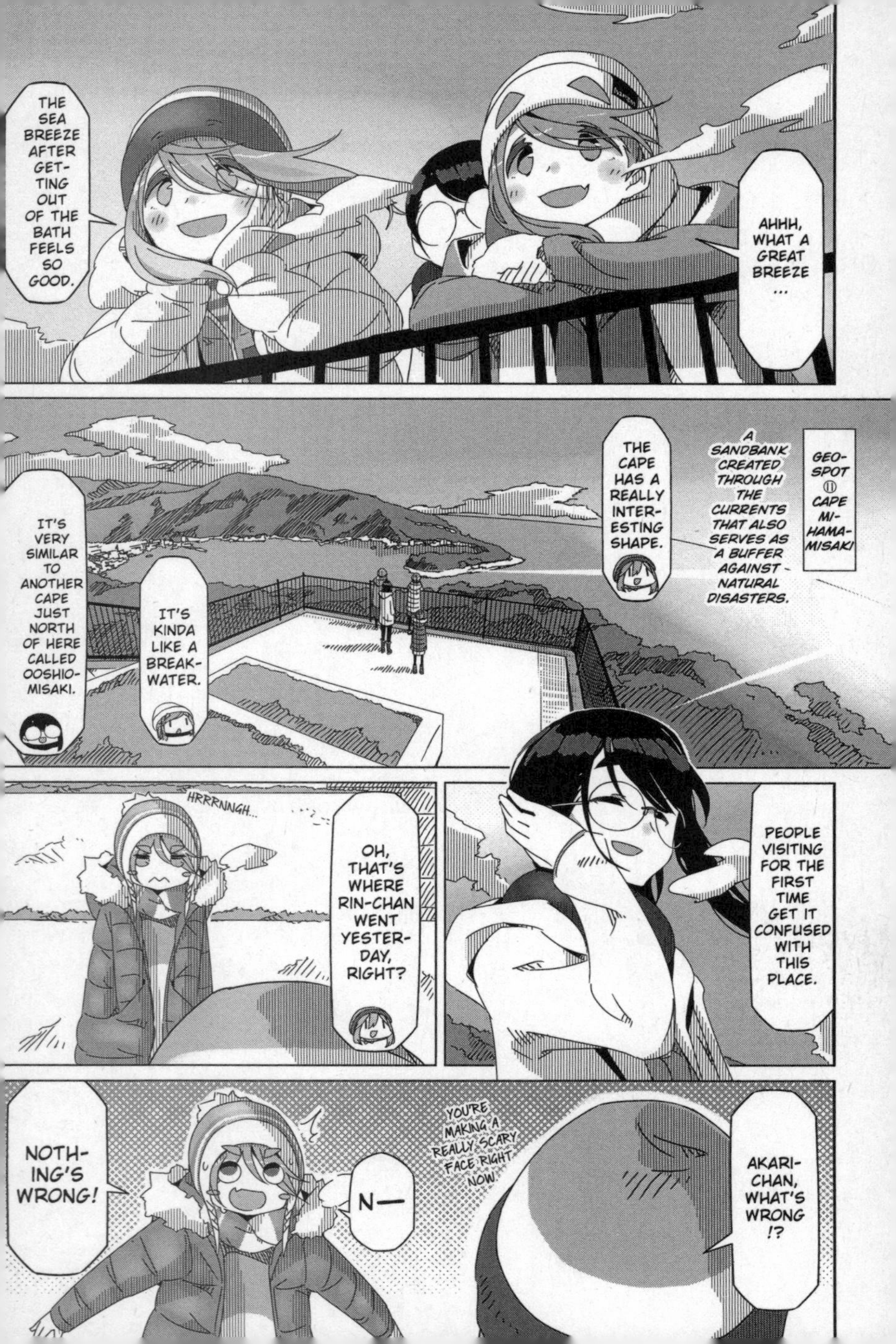
AHHH, WHAT A GREAT BREEZE...
THE SEA BREEZE AFTER GETTING OUT OF THE BATH FEELS SO GOOD.
GEO-SPOT ⑪ CAPE MIHAMA-MISAKI
A SANDBANK CREATED THROUGH THE CURRENTS THAT ALSO SERVES AS A BUFFER AGAINST NATURAL DISASTERS.
THE CAPE HAS A REALLY INTERESTING SHAPE.
IT'S KINDA LIKE A BREAKWATER.
IT'S VERY SIMILAR TO ANOTHER CAPE JUST NORTH OF HERE CALLED OOSHIO-MISAKI.
PEOPLE VISITING FOR THE FIRST TIME GET IT CONFUSED WITH THIS PLACE.
OH, THAT'S WHERE RIN-CHAN WENT YESTERDAY, RIGHT?
HRRRNNGH...
AKARI-CHAN, WHAT'S WRONG!?
YOU'RE MAKING A REALLY SCARY FACE RIGHT NOW.
N—
NOTHING'S WRONG!

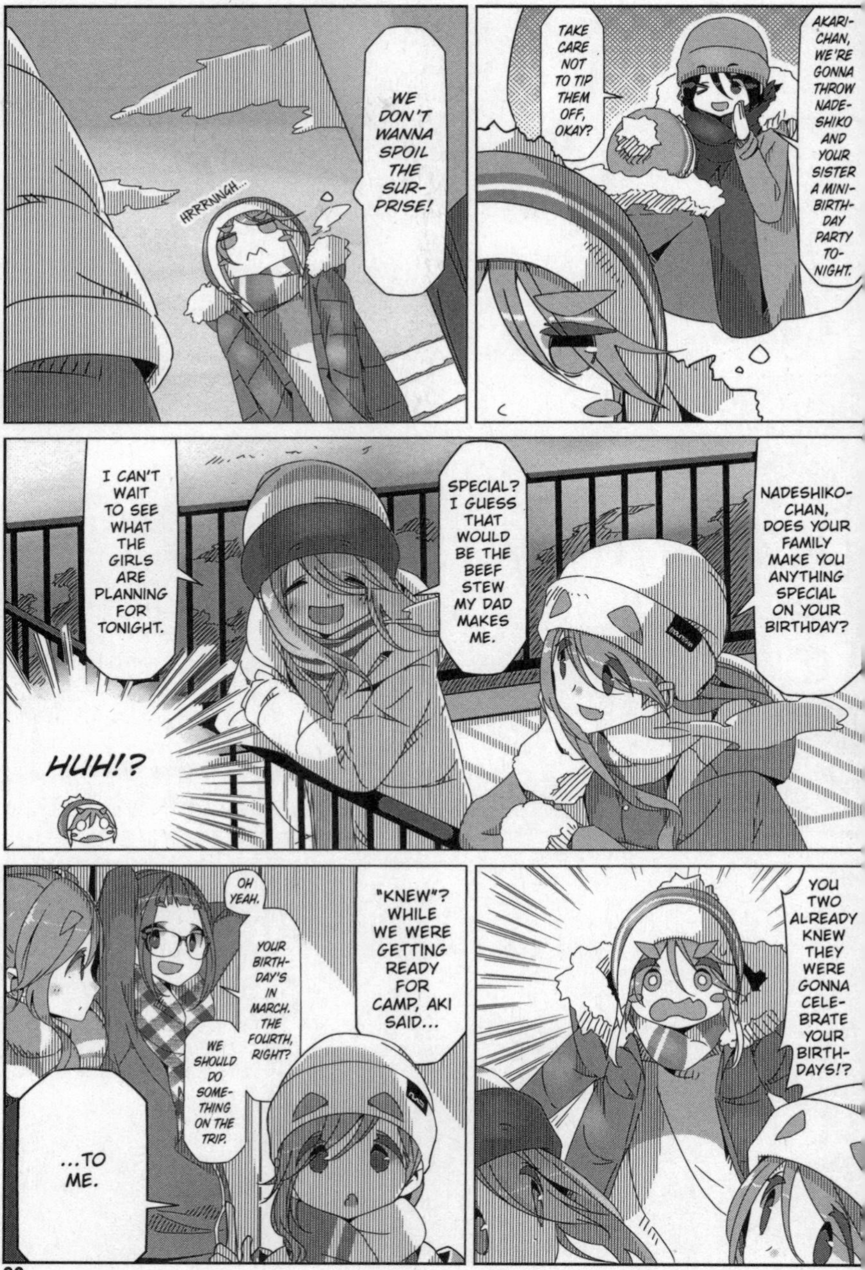
AKARI-CHAN, WE'RE GONNA THROW NADESHIKO AND YOUR SISTER A MINI-BIRTHDAY PARTY TONIGHT.
TAKE CARE NOT TO TIP THEM OFF, OKAY?
WE DON'T WANNA SPOIL THE SURPRISE!
HRRRNNGH...
NADESHIKO-CHAN, DOES YOUR FAMILY MAKE YOU ANYTHING SPECIAL ON YOUR BIRTHDAY?
SPECIAL? I GUESS THAT WOULD BE THE BEEF STEW MY DAD MAKES ME.
I CAN'T WAIT TO SEE WHAT THE GIRLS ARE PLANNING FOR TONIGHT.
HUH!?
YOU TWO ALREADY KNEW THEY WERE GONNA CELEBRATE YOUR BIRTHDAYS!?
"KNEW"? WHILE WE WERE GETTING READY FOR CAMP, AKI SAID...
OH YEAH.
YOUR BIRTHDAY'S IN MARCH. THE FOURTH, RIGHT?
WE SHOULD DO SOMETHING ON THE TRIP.
...TO ME.

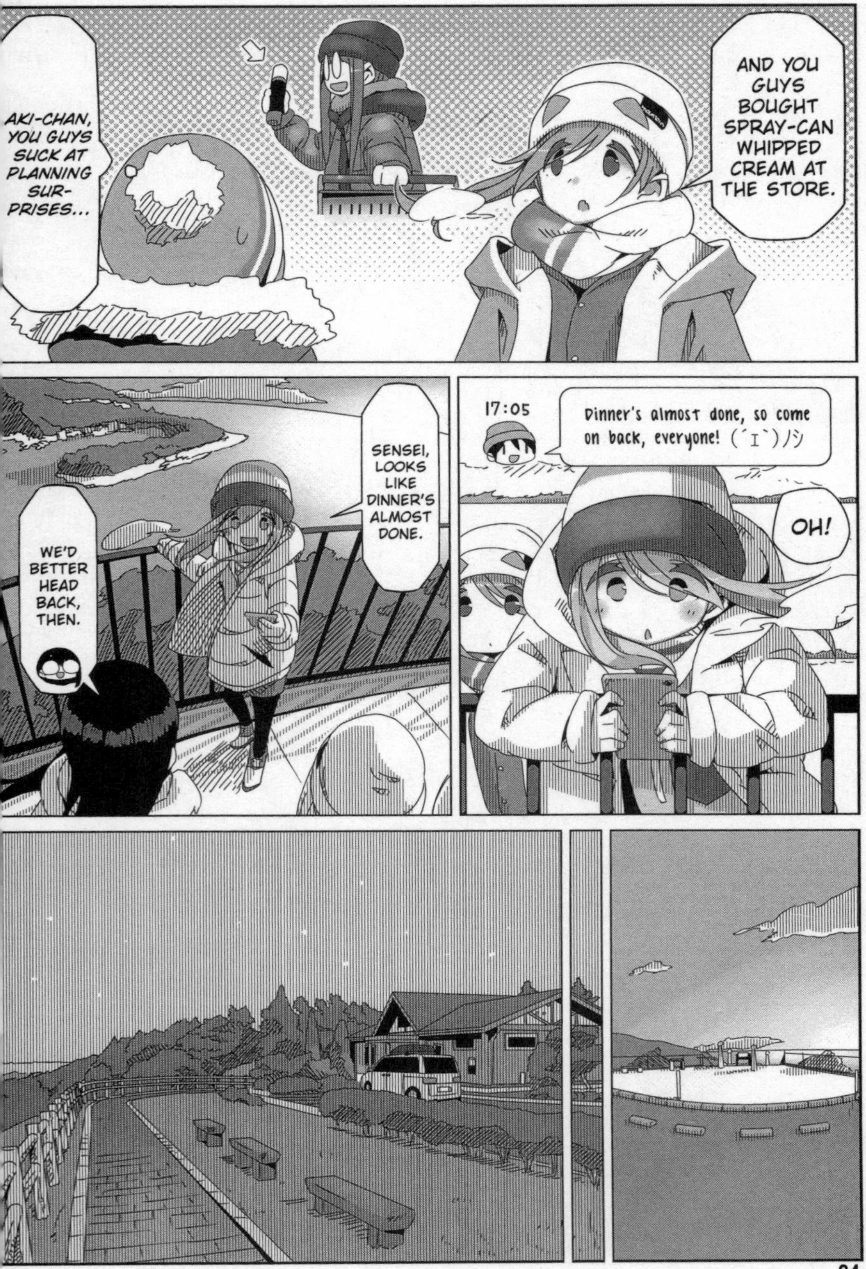
AND YOU GUYS BOUGHT SPRAY-CAN WHIPPED CREAM AT THE STORE.
AKI-CHAN, YOU GUYS SUCK AT PLANNING SUR-PRISES...
17:05
Dinner's almost done, so come on back, everyone! (´ｴ`)ノシ
OH!
SENSEI, LOOKS LIKE DINNER'S ALMOST DONE.
WE'D BETTER HEAD BACK, THEN.

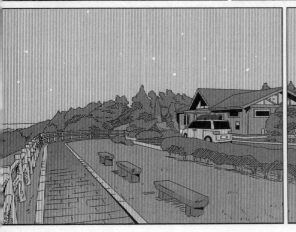

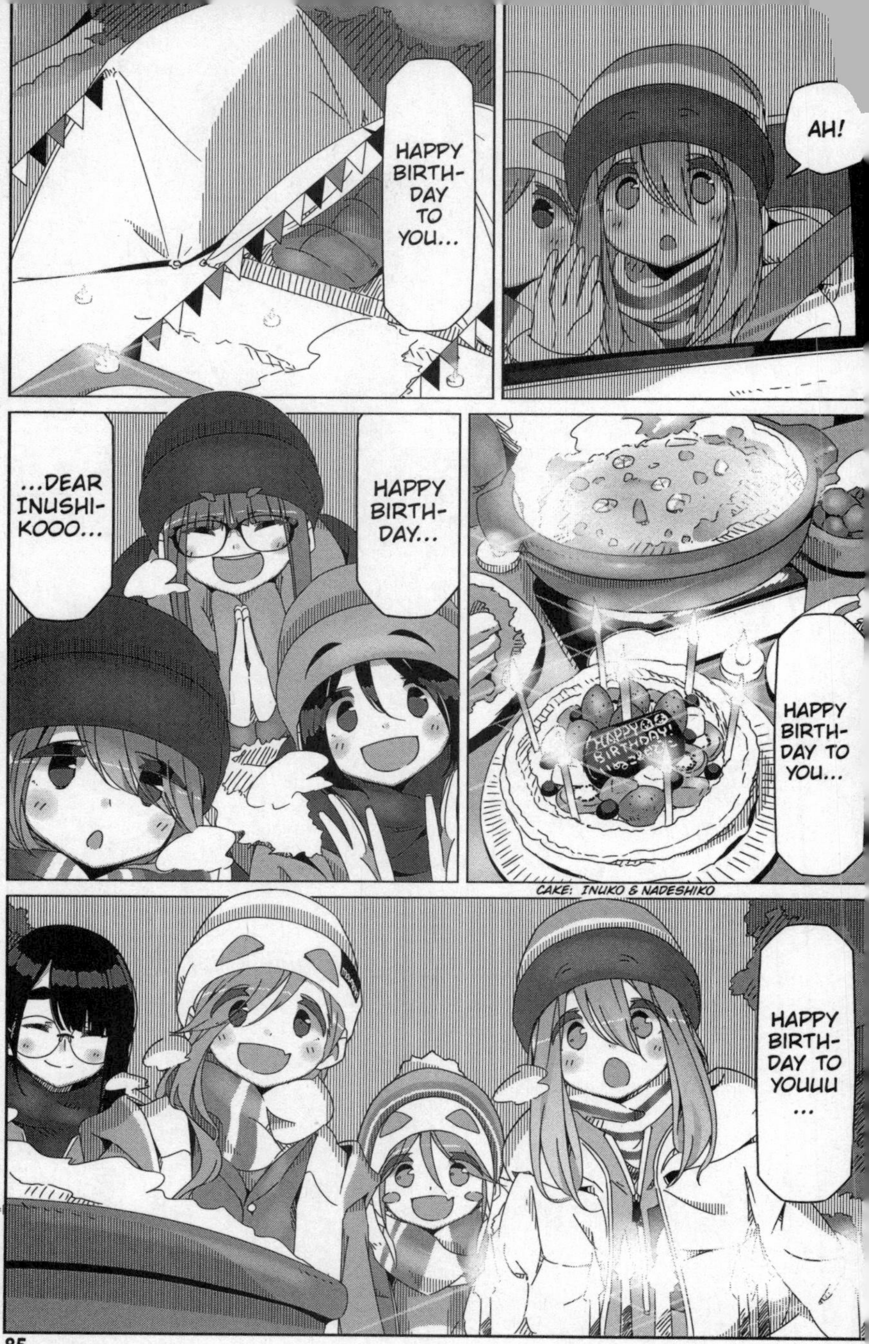
AH!
HAPPY BIRTH-DAY TO YOU...
HAPPY BIRTH-DAY TO YOU...
HAPPY BIRTHDAY
HAPPY BIRTH-DAY...
...DEAR INUSHI-KOOO...
CAKE: INUKO & NADESHIKO
HAPPY BIRTH-DAY TO YOUUU ...

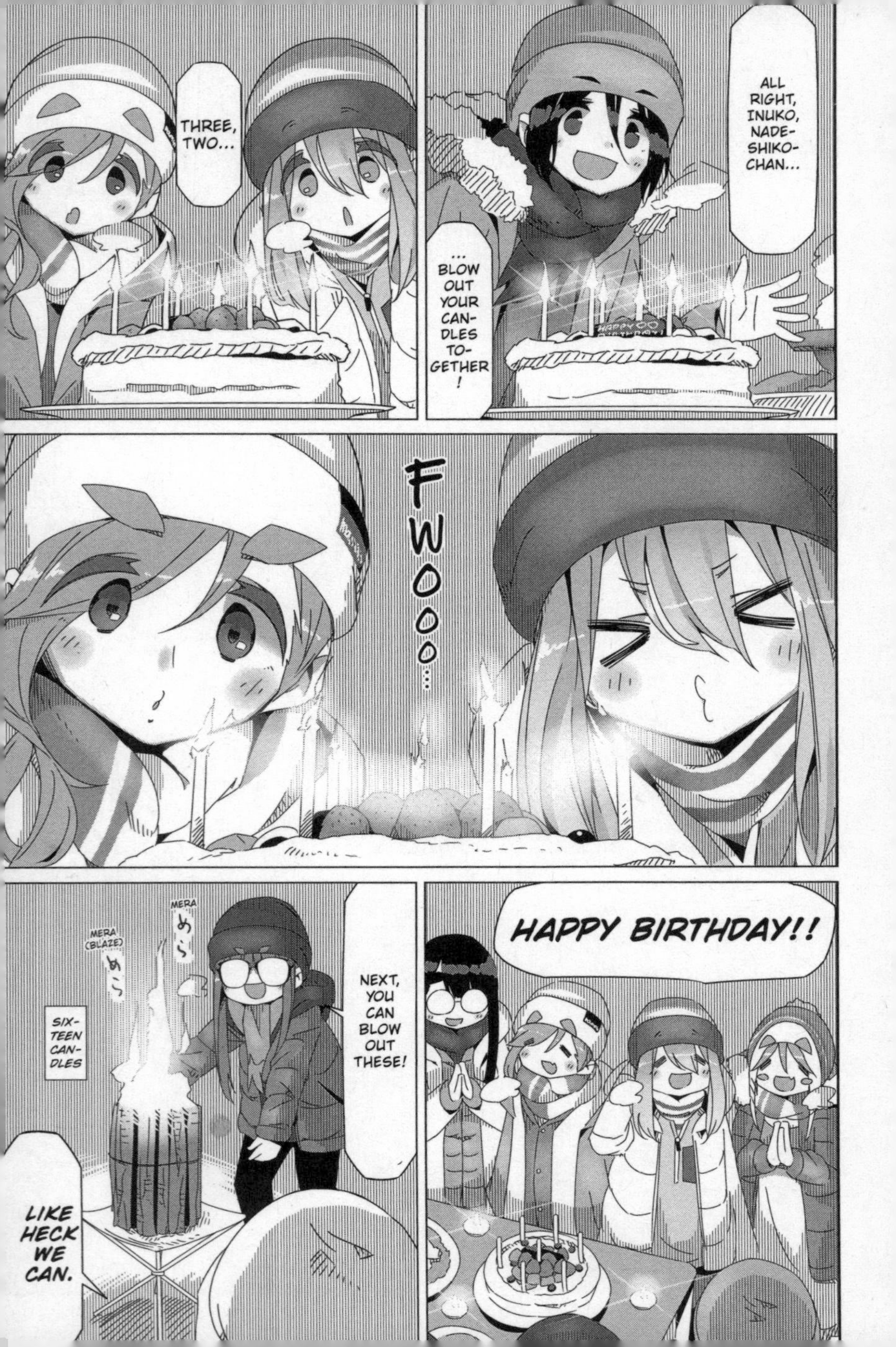
ALL RIGHT, INUKO, NADE-SHIKO-CHAN...
...BLOW OUT YOUR CAN-DLES TO-GETHER!
THREE, TWO...
FWOOO...
HAPPY BIRTHDAY!!
MERA めら
MERA (BLAZE) めら
NEXT, YOU CAN BLOW OUT THESE!
SIX-TEEN CAN-DLES
LIKE HECK WE CAN.

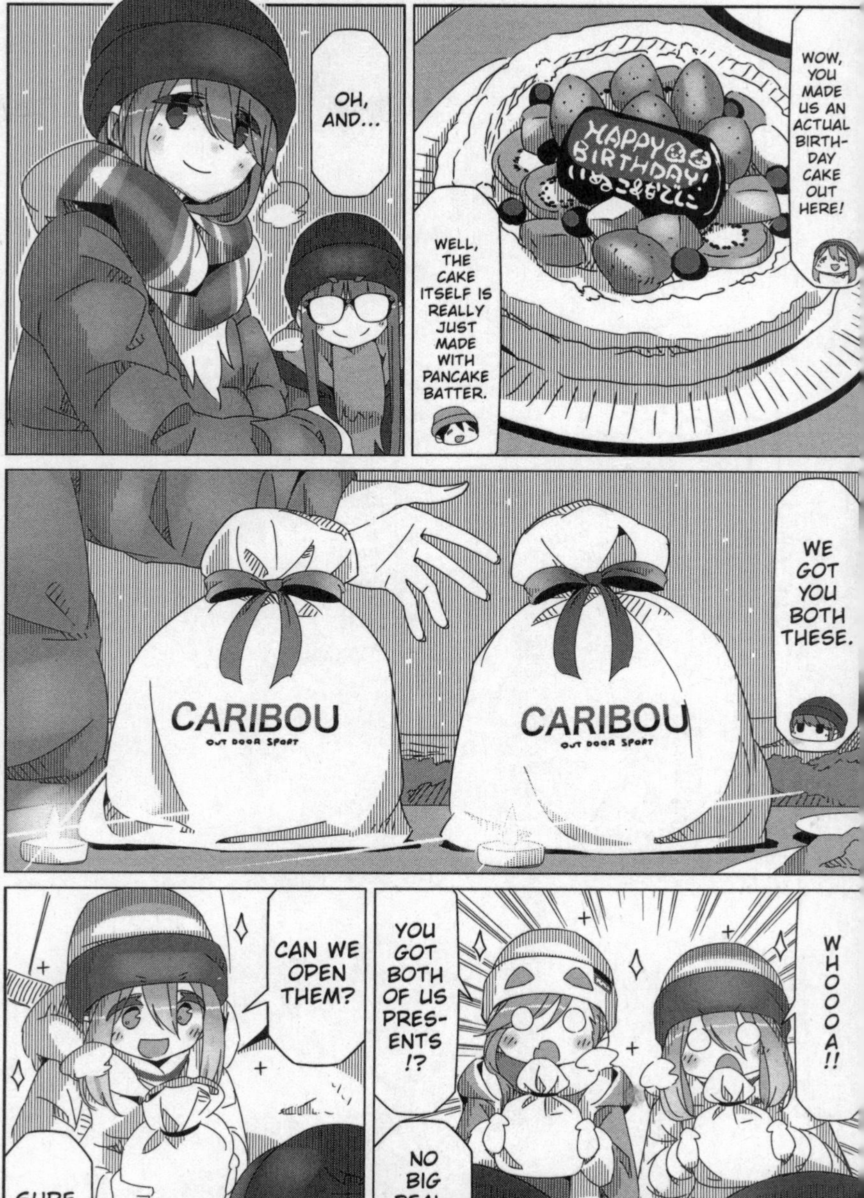
WOW, YOU MADE US AN ACTUAL BIRTHDAY CAKE OUT HERE!
HAPPY BIRTHDAY!
WELL, THE CAKE ITSELF IS REALLY JUST MADE WITH PANCAKE BATTER.
OH, AND...
WE GOT YOU BOTH THESE.
CARIBOU
OUT DOOR SPORT
CARIBOU
OUT DOOR SPORT
WHOOOOA!!
YOU GOT BOTH OF US PRES-ENTS!?
NO BIG DEAL.
CAN WE OPEN THEM?
SURE.

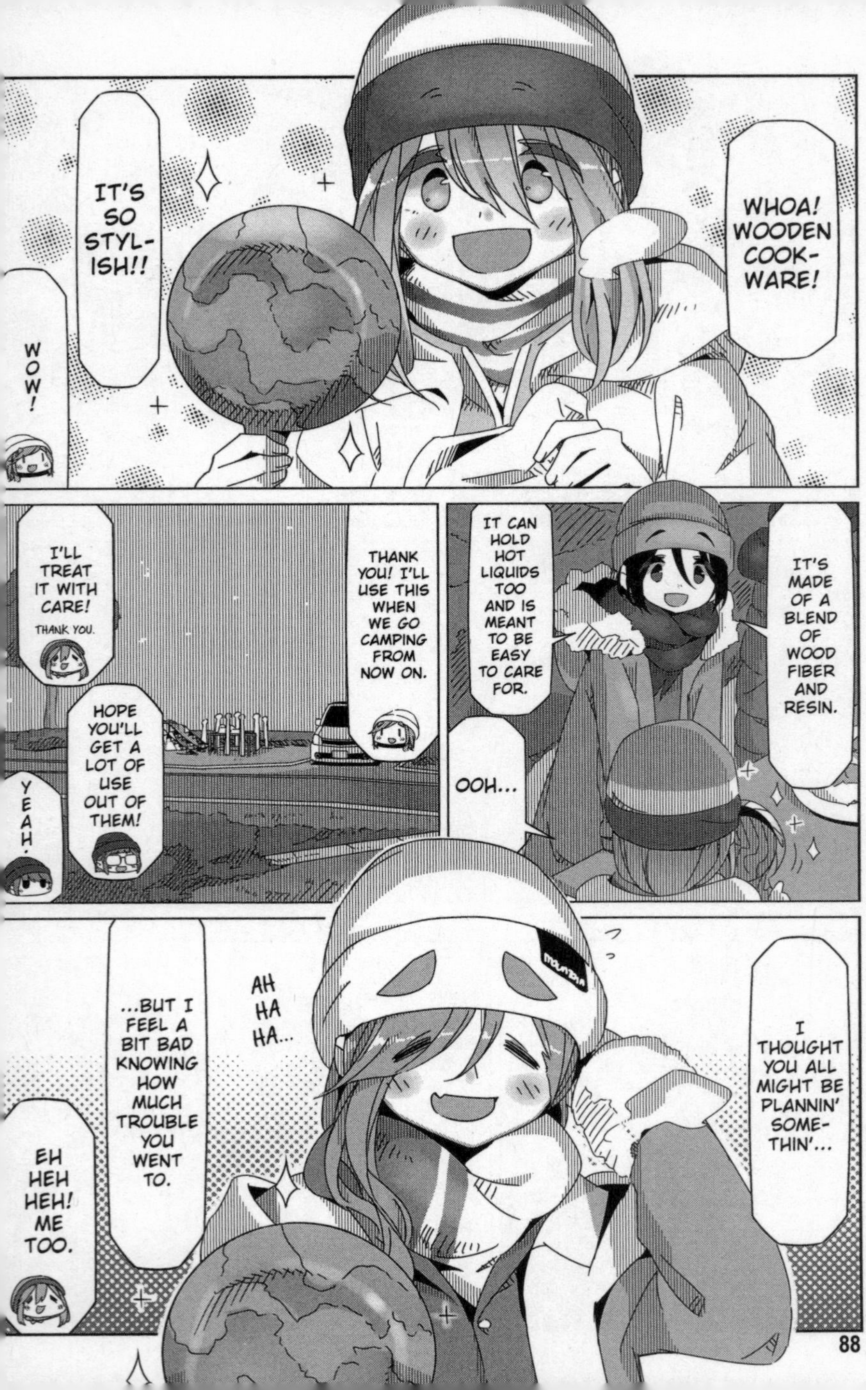

WHOA! WOODEN COOK-WARE!
IT'S SO STYL-ISH!!
WOW!
IT'S MADE OF A BLEND OF WOOD FIBER AND RESIN.
IT CAN HOLD HOT LIQUIDS TOO AND IS MEANT TO BE EASY TO CARE FOR.
OOH...
THANK YOU! I'LL USE THIS WHEN WE GO CAMPING FROM NOW ON.
I'LL TREAT IT WITH CARE!
THANK YOU.
HOPE YOU'LL GET A LOT OF USE OUT OF THEM!
YEAH.
I THOUGHT YOU ALL MIGHT BE PLANNIN' SOME-THIN'...
AH HA HA...
...BUT I FEEL A BIT BAD KNOWING HOW MUCH TROUBLE YOU WENT TO.
EH HEH HEH! ME TOO.

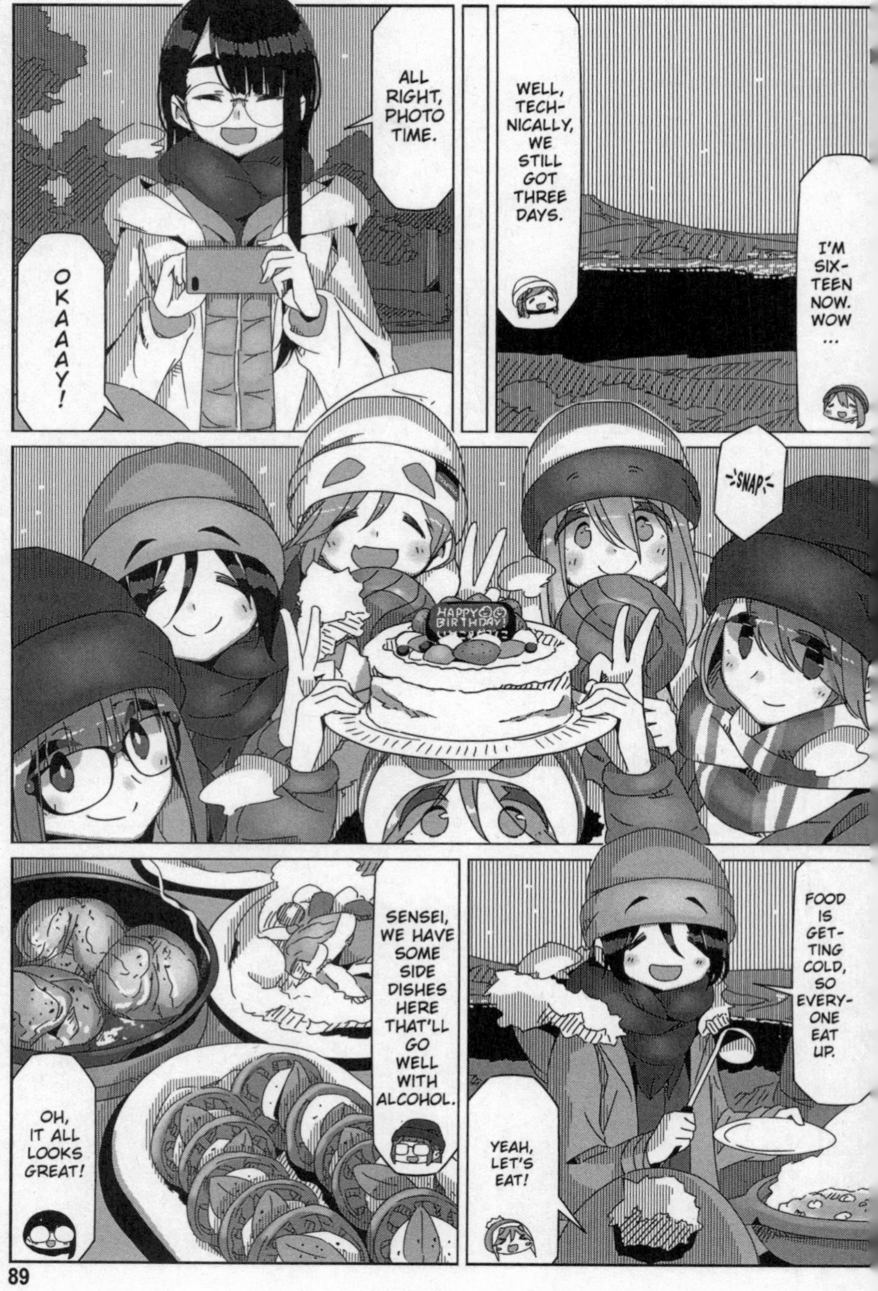
I'M SIXTEEN NOW. WOW...
WELL, TECHNICALLY, WE STILL GOT THREE DAYS.
ALL RIGHT, PHOTO TIME.
OKAAAAY!
SNAP
HAPPY BIRTHDAY!
FOOD IS GETTING COLD, SO EVERYONE EAT UP.
YEAH, LET'S EAT!
SENSEI, WE HAVE SOME SIDE DISHES HERE THAT'LL GO WELL WITH ALCOHOL.
OH, IT ALL LOOKS GREAT!

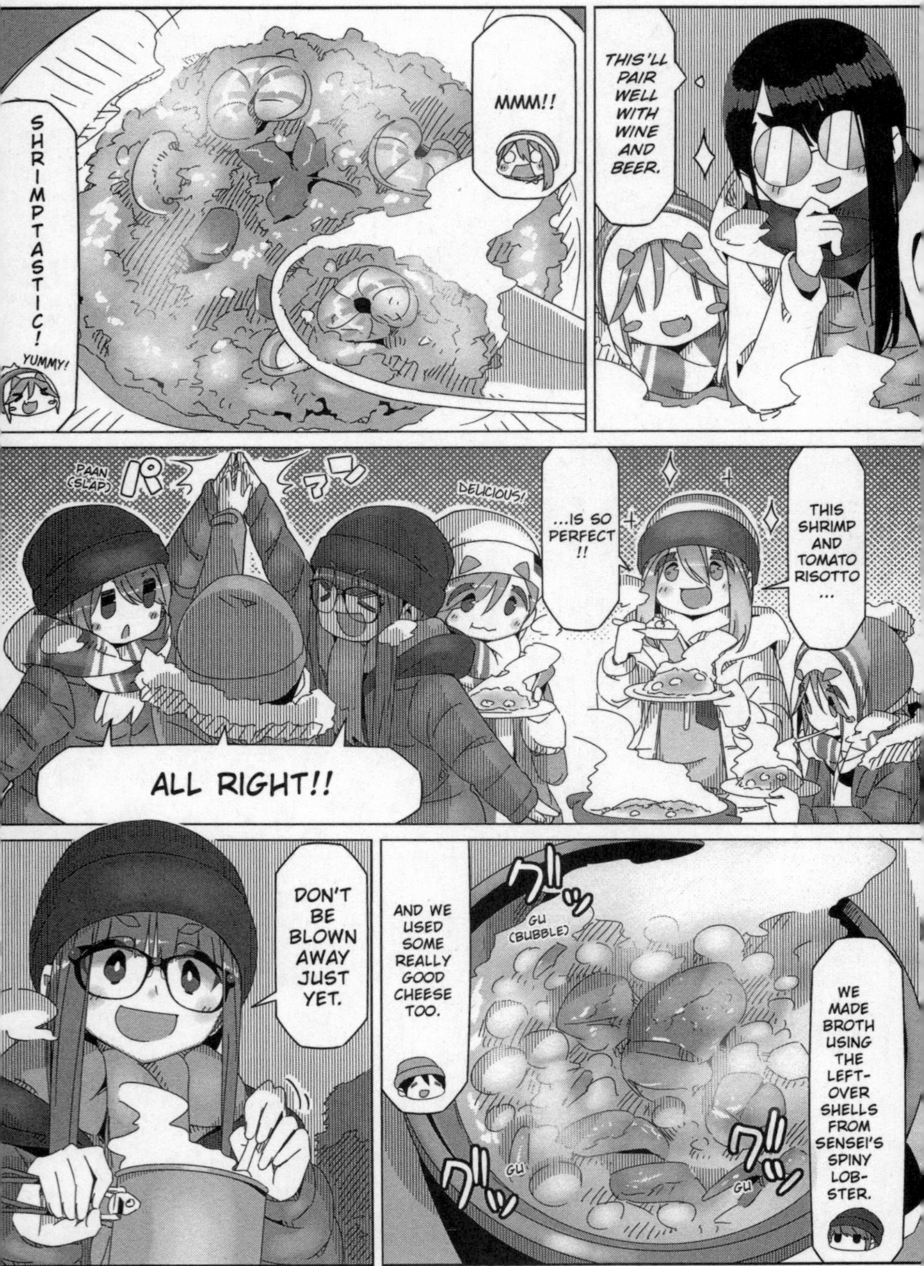
THIS'LL PAIR WELL WITH WINE AND BEER.
MMM!!
SHRIMPTASTIC!
YUMMY!
THIS SHRIMP AND TOMATO RISOTTO...
...IS SO PERFECT!!
DELICIOUS!
PAAN (SLAP)
ALL RIGHT!!
WE MADE BROTH USING THE LEFT-OVER SHELLS FROM SENSEI'S SPINY LOBSTER.
GU (BUBBLE)
AND WE USED SOME REALLY GOOD CHEESE TOO.
GU
GU
DON'T BE BLOWN AWAY JUST YET.

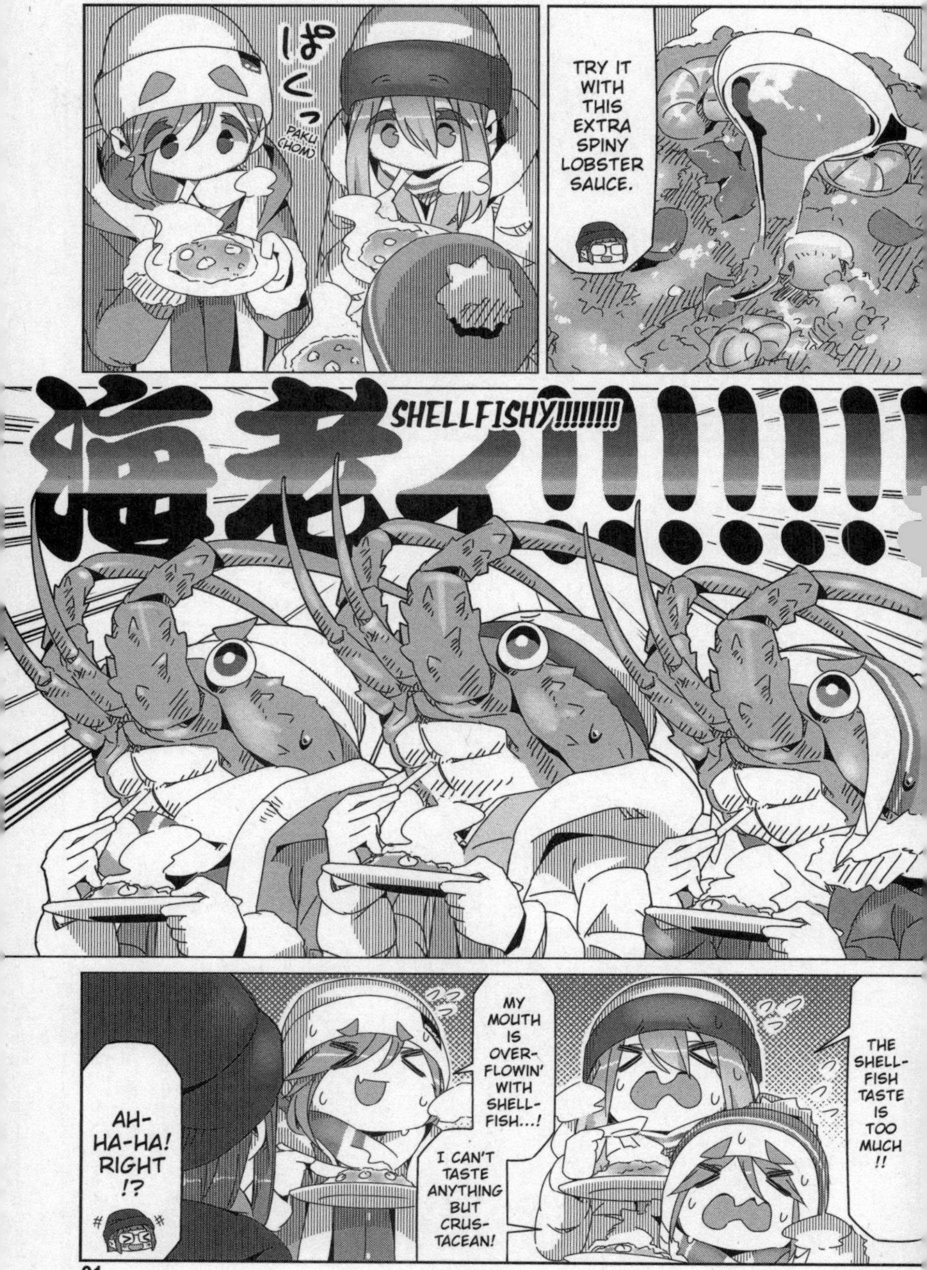
ぱくっ
PAKU (HOM)
TRY IT WITH THIS EXTRA SPINY LOBSTER SAUCE.
海老イ!!!!!!
SHELLFISHY!!!!!!!!!
THE SHELL-FISH TASTE IS TOO MUCH !!
MY MOUTH IS OVER-FLOWIN' WITH SHELL-FISH...!
I CAN'T TASTE ANYTHING BUT CRUS-TACEAN!
AH-HA-HA! RIGHT !?

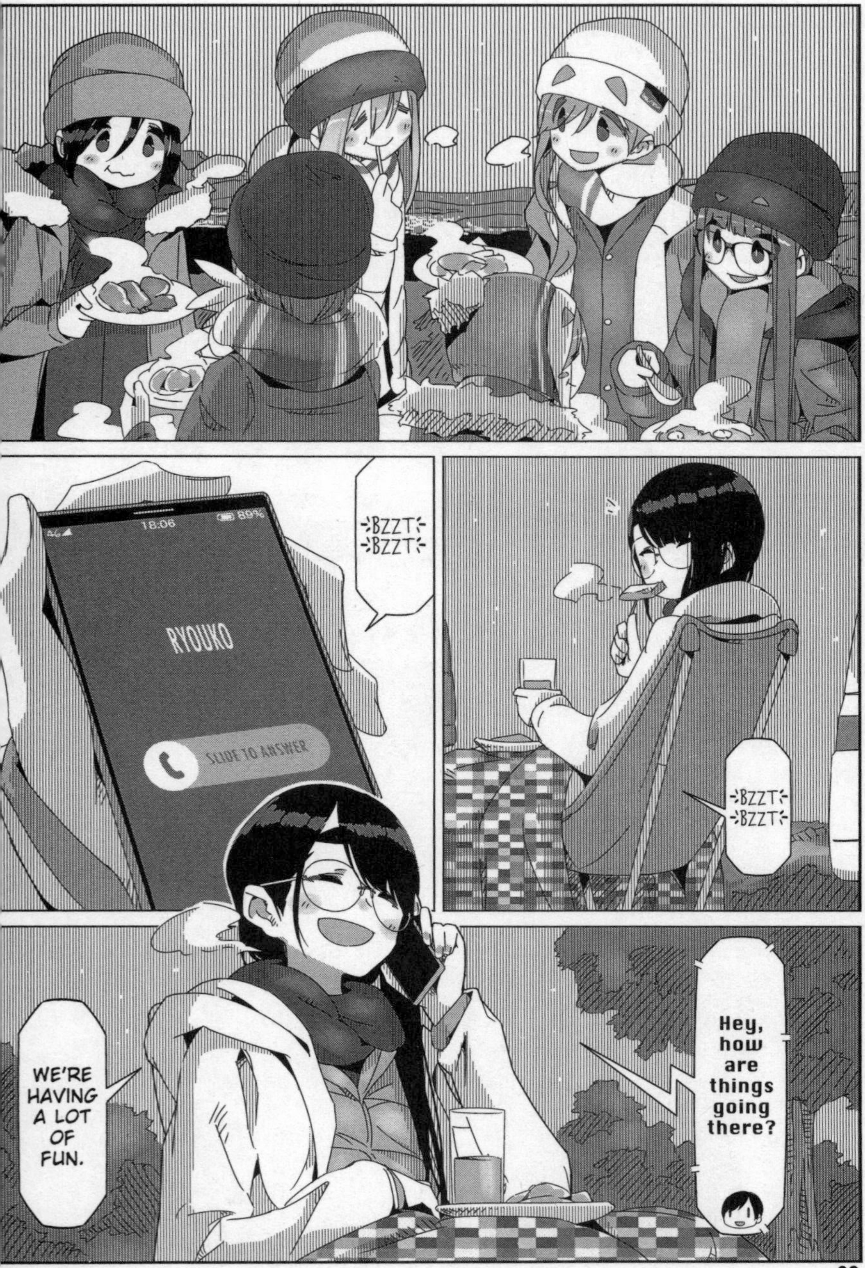
BZZT BZZT
BZZT BZZT
18:06
89%
RYOUKO
SLIDE TO ANSWER
Hey, how are things going there?
WE'RE HAVING A LOT OF FUN.

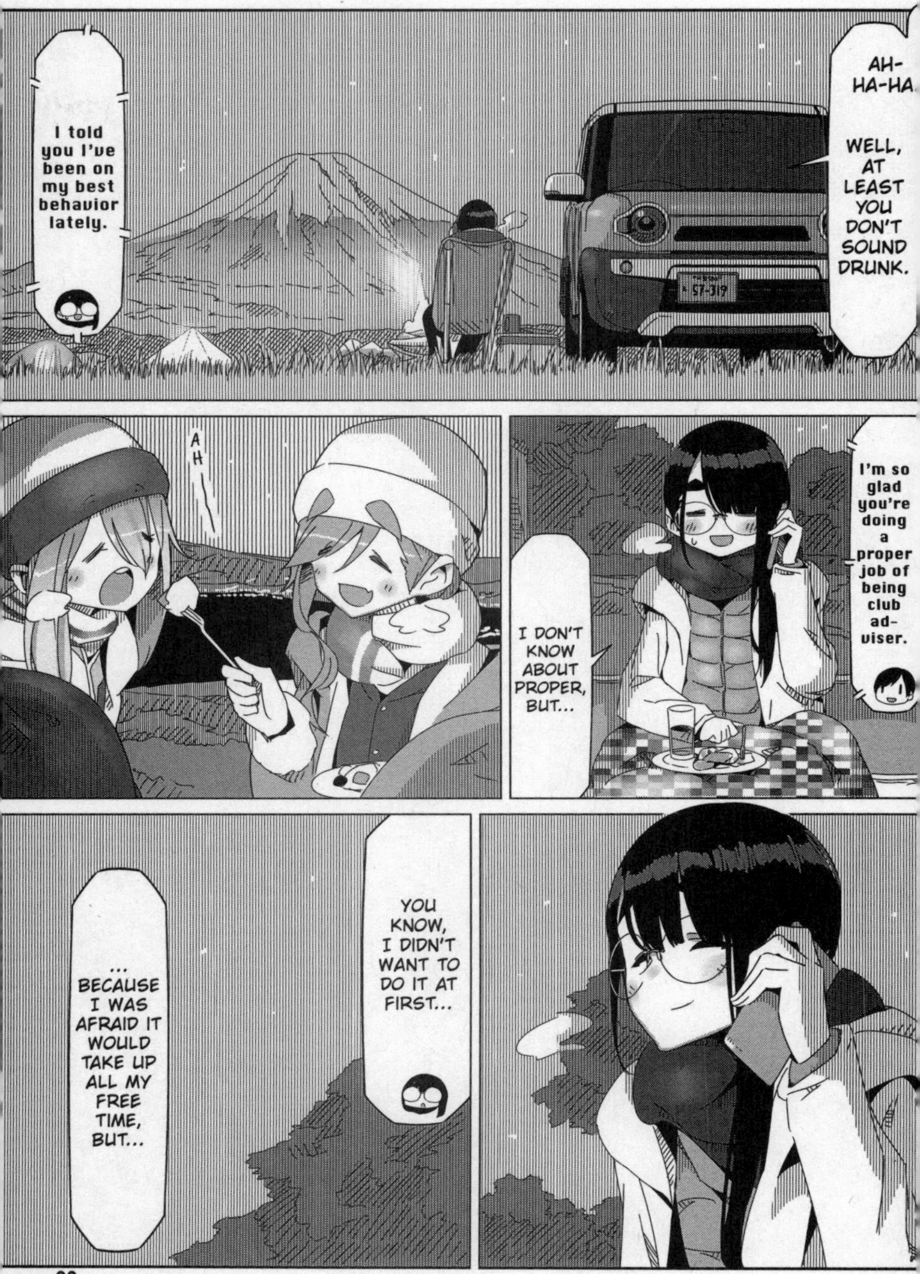
AH-HA-HA.
WELL, AT LEAST YOU DON'T SOUND DRUNK.
I told you I've been on my best behavior lately.
I'm so glad you're doing a proper job of being club ad-viser.
I DON'T KNOW ABOUT PROPER, BUT...
AH
YOU KNOW, I DIDN'T WANT TO DO IT AT FIRST...
...BECAUSE I WAS AFRAID IT WOULD TAKE UP ALL MY FREE TIME, BUT...

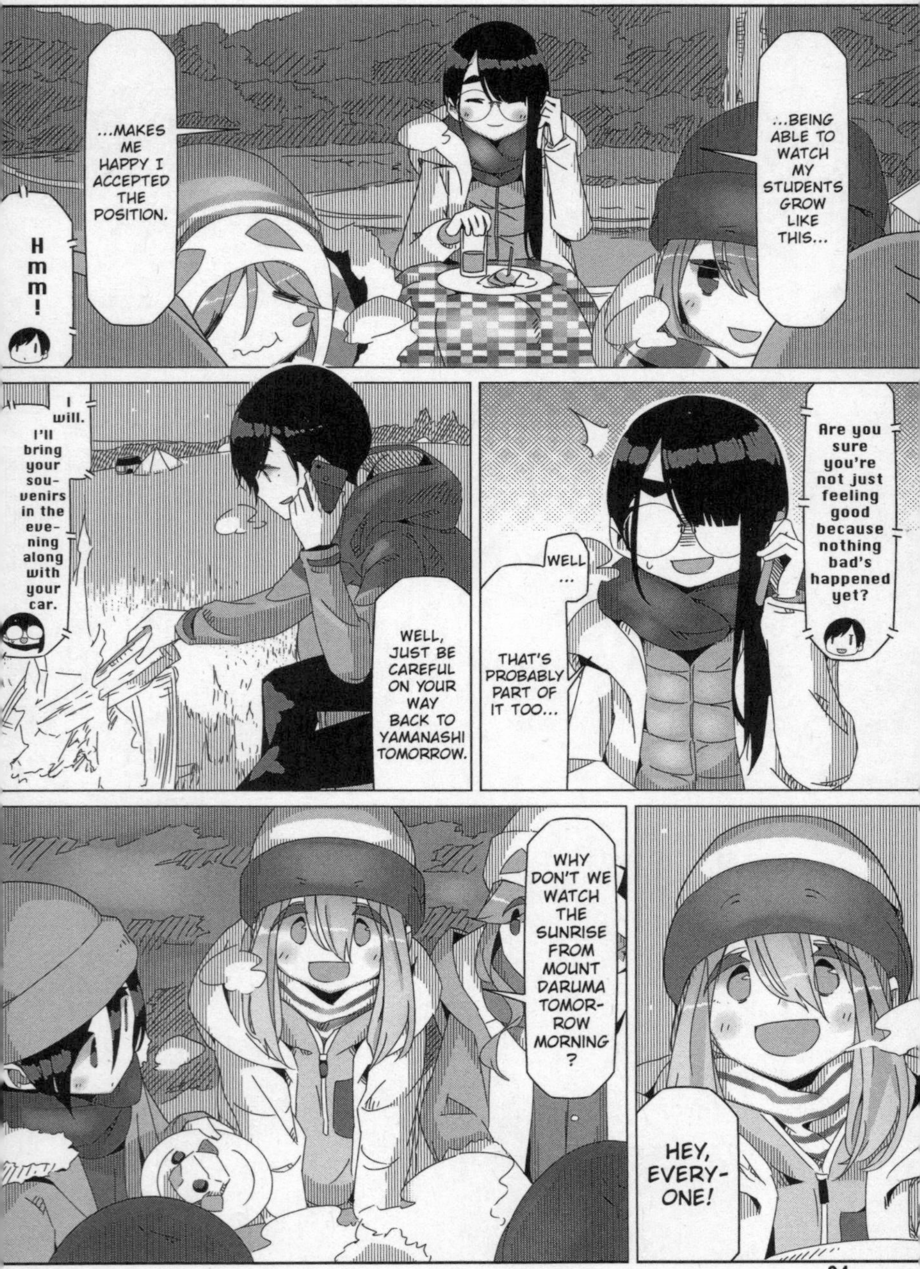
...BEING ABLE TO WATCH MY STUDENTS GROW LIKE THIS...
...MAKES ME HAPPY I ACCEPTED THE POSITION.
Hmm!
Are you sure you're not just feeling good because nothing bad's happened yet?
WELL...
THAT'S PROBABLY PART OF IT TOO...
WELL, JUST BE CAREFUL ON YOUR WAY BACK TO YAMANASHI TOMORROW.
I will. I'll bring your souvenirs in the evening along with your car.
HEY, EVERYONE!
WHY DON'T WE WATCH THE SUNRISE FROM MOUNT DARUMA TOMORROW MORNING?

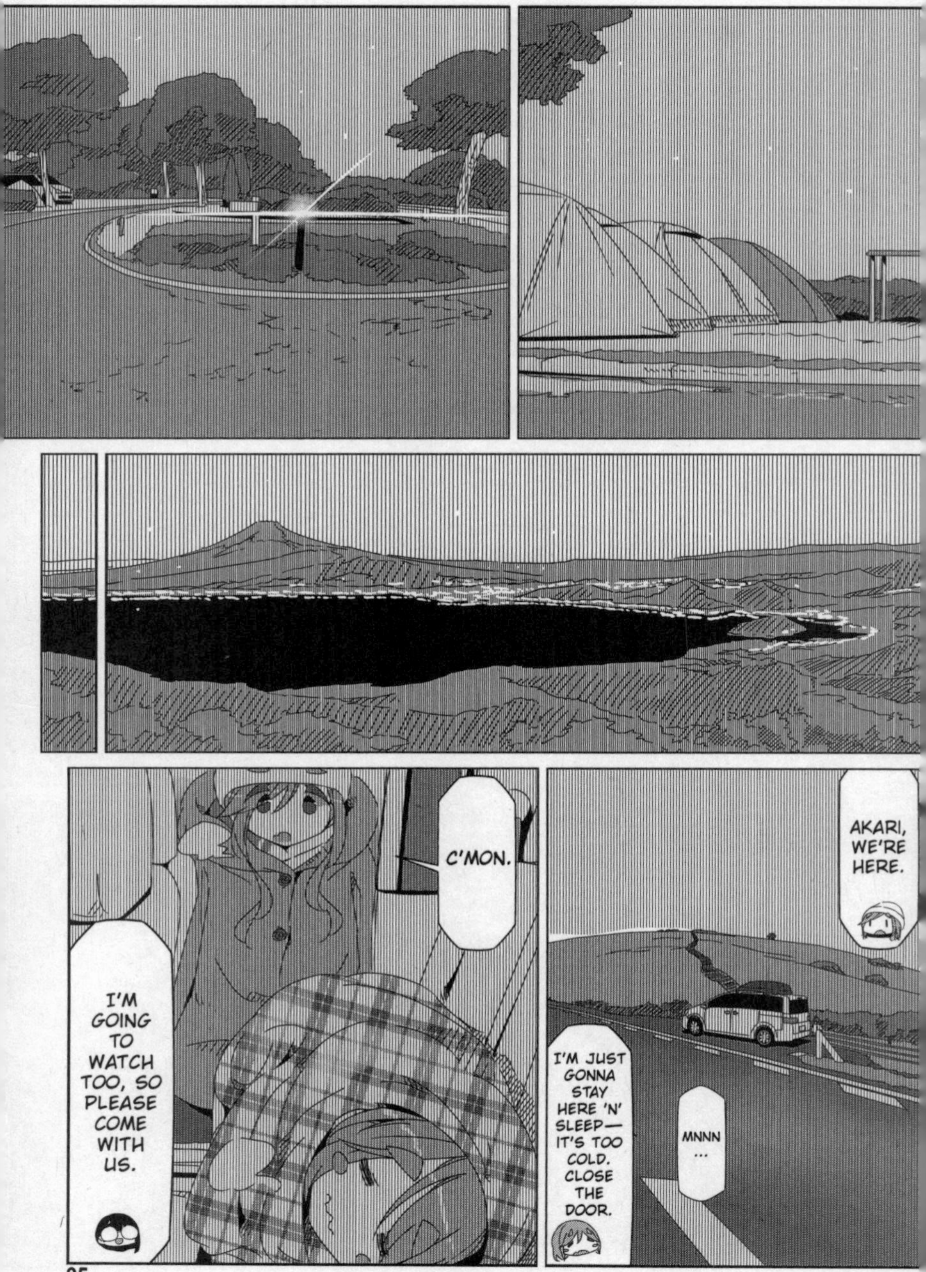
AKARI, WE'RE HERE.
MNNN...
I'M JUST GONNA STAY HERE 'N' SLEEP— IT'S TOO COLD. CLOSE THE DOOR.
C'MON.
I'M GOING TO WATCH TOO, SO PLEASE COME WITH US.

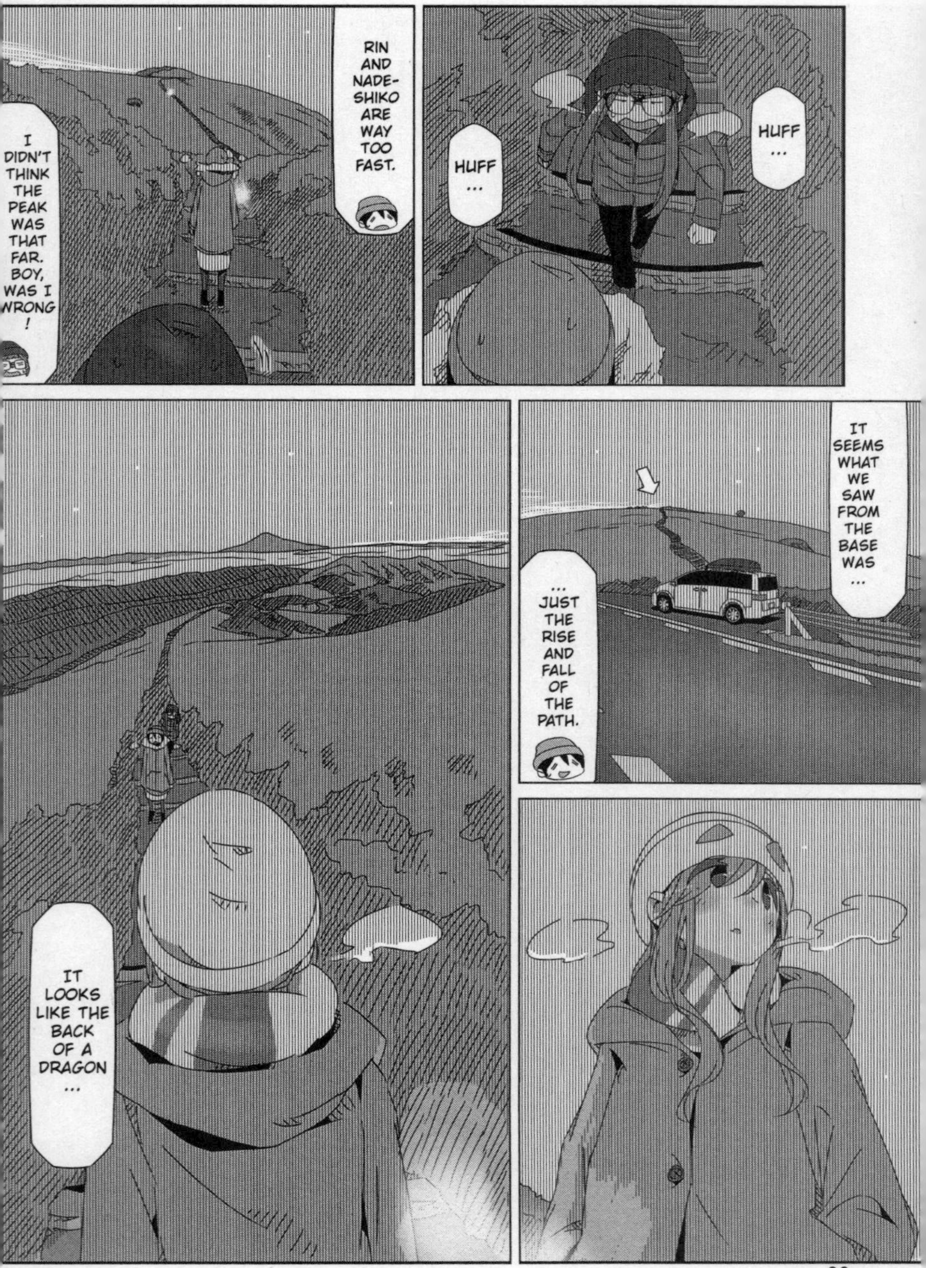
HUFF...
HUFF...
RIN AND NADE-SHIKO ARE WAY TOO FAST.
I DIDN'T THINK THE PEAK WAS THAT FAR. BOY, WAS I WRONG!
IT SEEMS WHAT WE SAW FROM THE BASE WAS...
...JUST THE RISE AND FALL OF THE PATH.
IT LOOKS LIKE THE BACK OF A DRAGON...

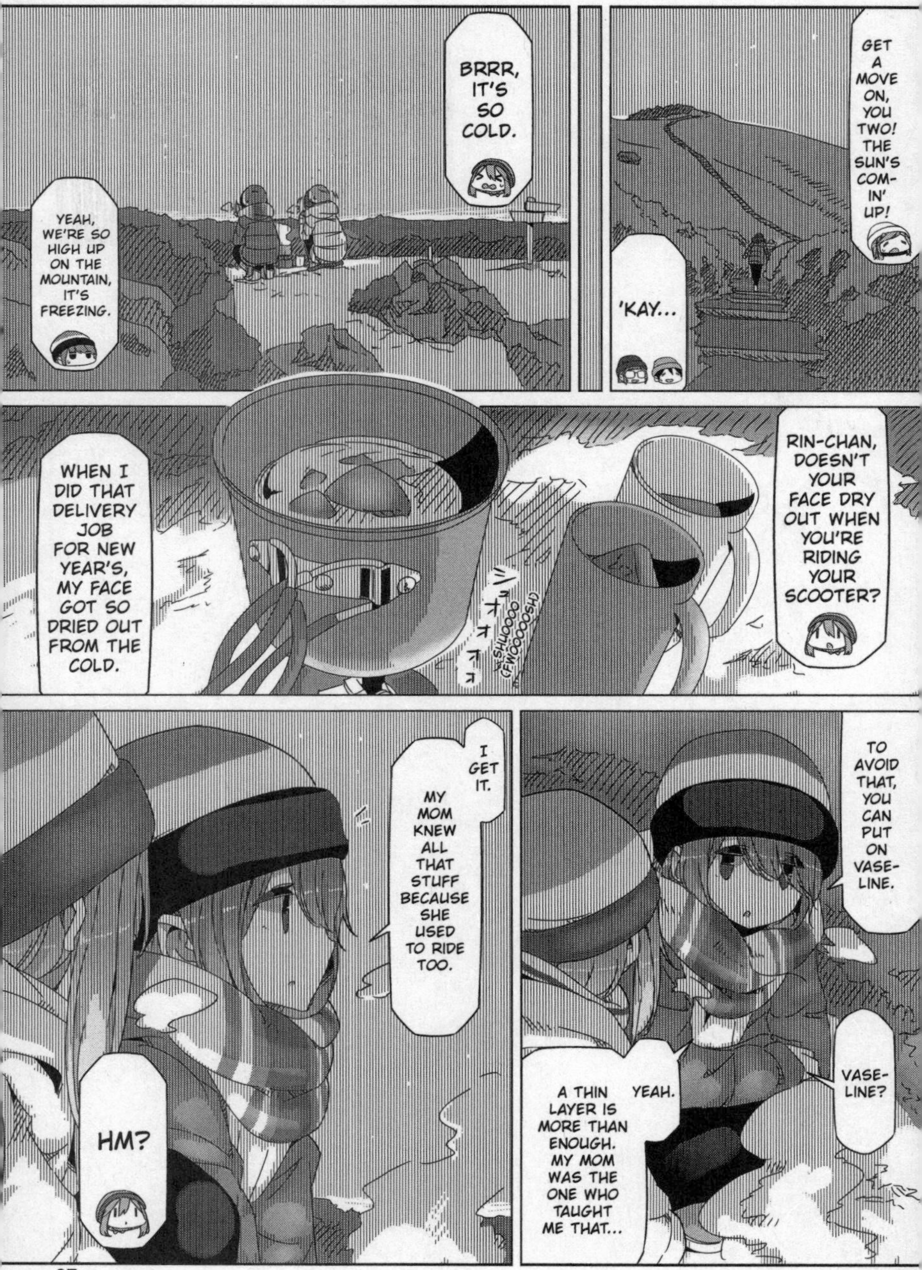
GET A MOVE ON, YOU TWO! THE SUN'S COM-IN' UP!
'KAY...
BRRR, IT'S SO COLD.
YEAH, WE'RE SO HIGH UP ON THE MOUNTAIN, IT'S FREEZING.
RIN-CHAN, DOESN'T YOUR FACE DRY OUT WHEN YOU'RE RIDING YOUR SCOOTER?
(FWOOOOOSH)
WHEN I DID THAT DELIVERY JOB FOR NEW YEAR'S, MY FACE GOT SO DRIED OUT FROM THE COLD.
TO AVOID THAT, YOU CAN PUT ON VASE-LINE.
VASE-LINE?
YEAH.
A THIN LAYER IS MORE THAN ENOUGH. MY MOM WAS THE ONE WHO TAUGHT ME THAT...
I GET IT.
MY MOM KNEW ALL THAT STUFF BECAUSE SHE USED TO RIDE TOO.
HM?

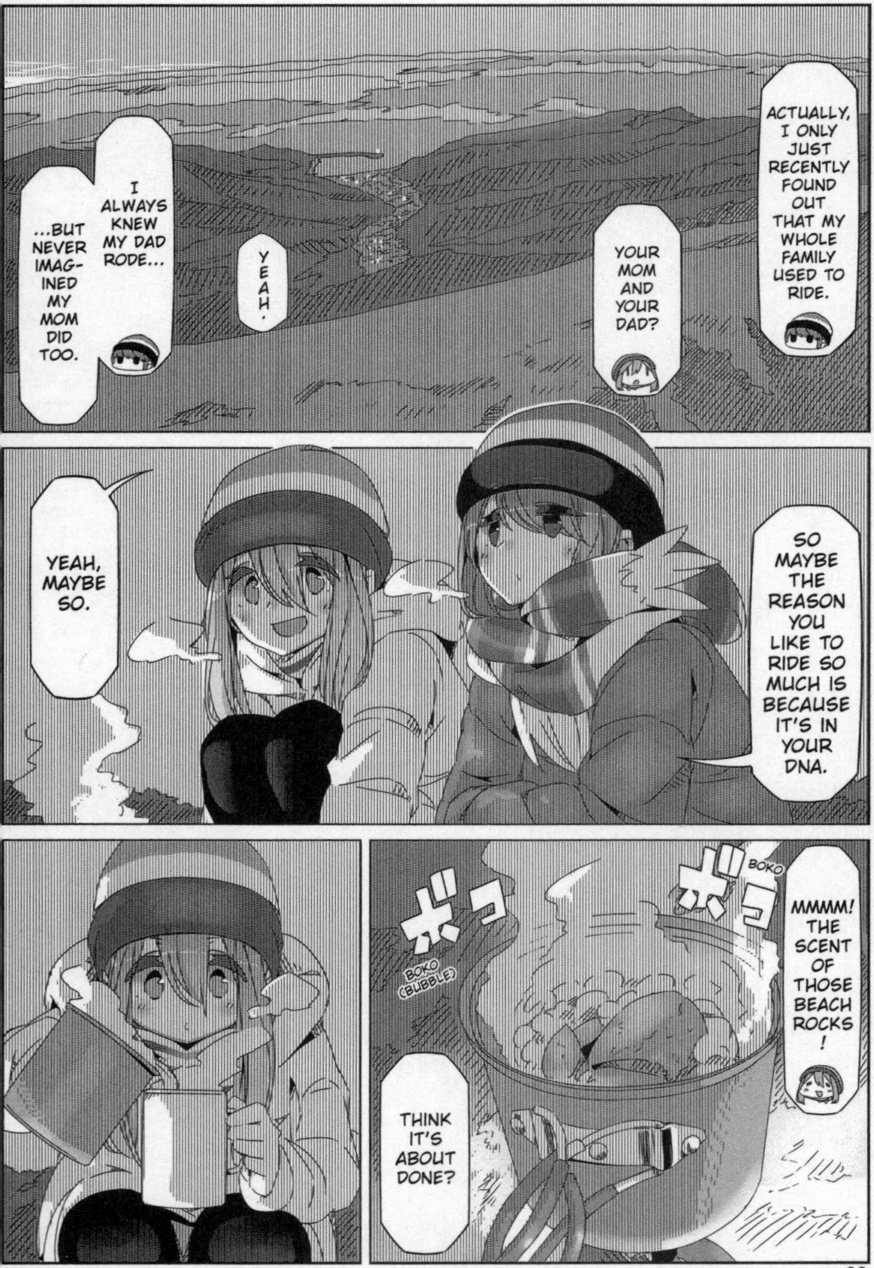
ACTUALLY, I ONLY JUST RECENTLY FOUND OUT THAT MY WHOLE FAMILY USED TO RIDE.
YOUR MOM AND YOUR DAD?
YEAH.
I ALWAYS KNEW MY DAD RODE...
...BUT NEVER IMAG-INED MY MOM DID TOO.
SO MAYBE THE REASON YOU LIKE TO RIDE SO MUCH IS BECAUSE IT'S IN YOUR DNA.
YEAH, MAYBE SO.
BOKO
MMMM! THE SCENT OF THOSE BEACH ROCKS!
BOKO (BUBBLE)
THINK IT'S ABOUT DONE?

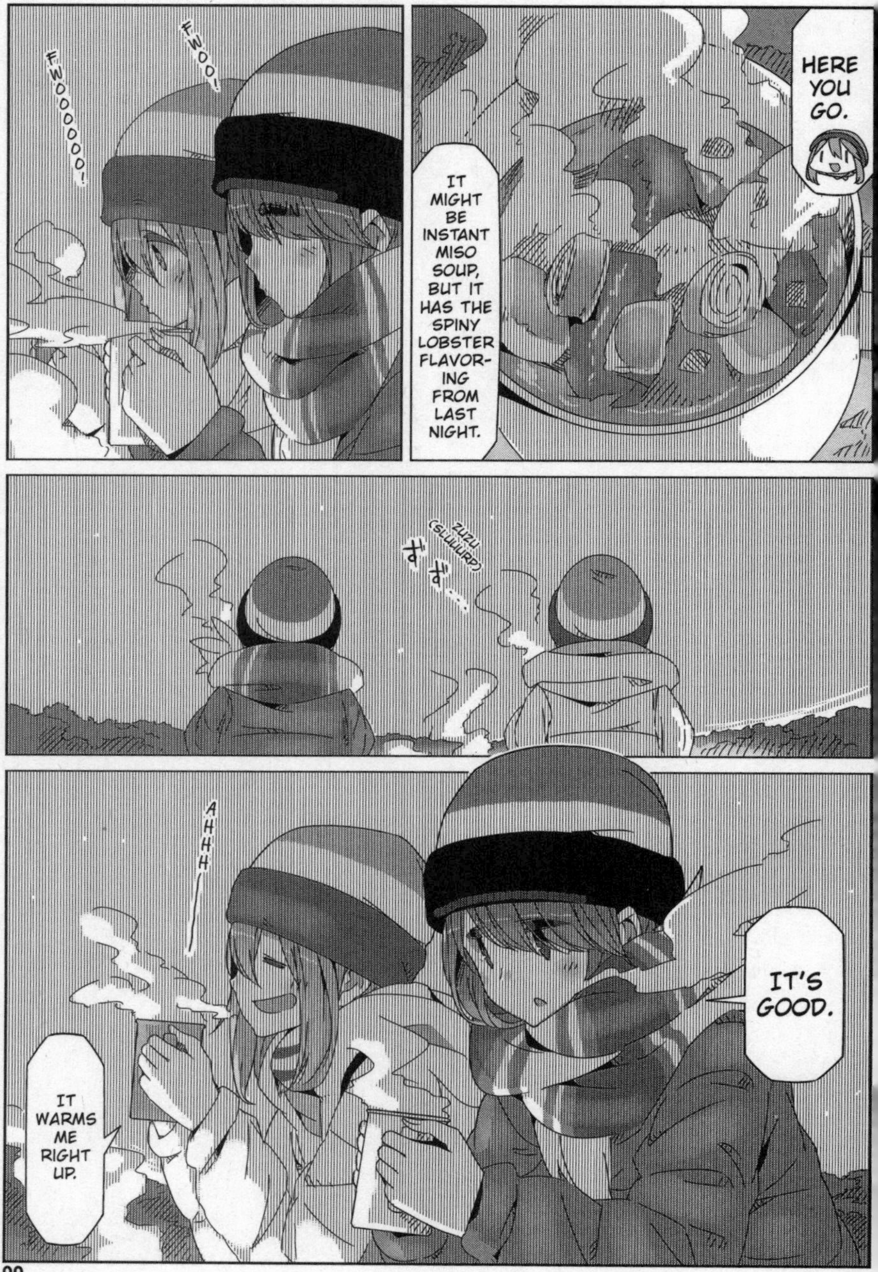
HERE YOU GO.
IT MIGHT BE INSTANT MISO SOUP, BUT IT HAS THE SPINY LOBSTER FLAVORING FROM LAST NIGHT.
FWOO!
FWOOOOOOO!
ずず…
zuzu (sluuurp)
IT'S GOOD.
AHHH
IT WARMS ME RIGHT UP.

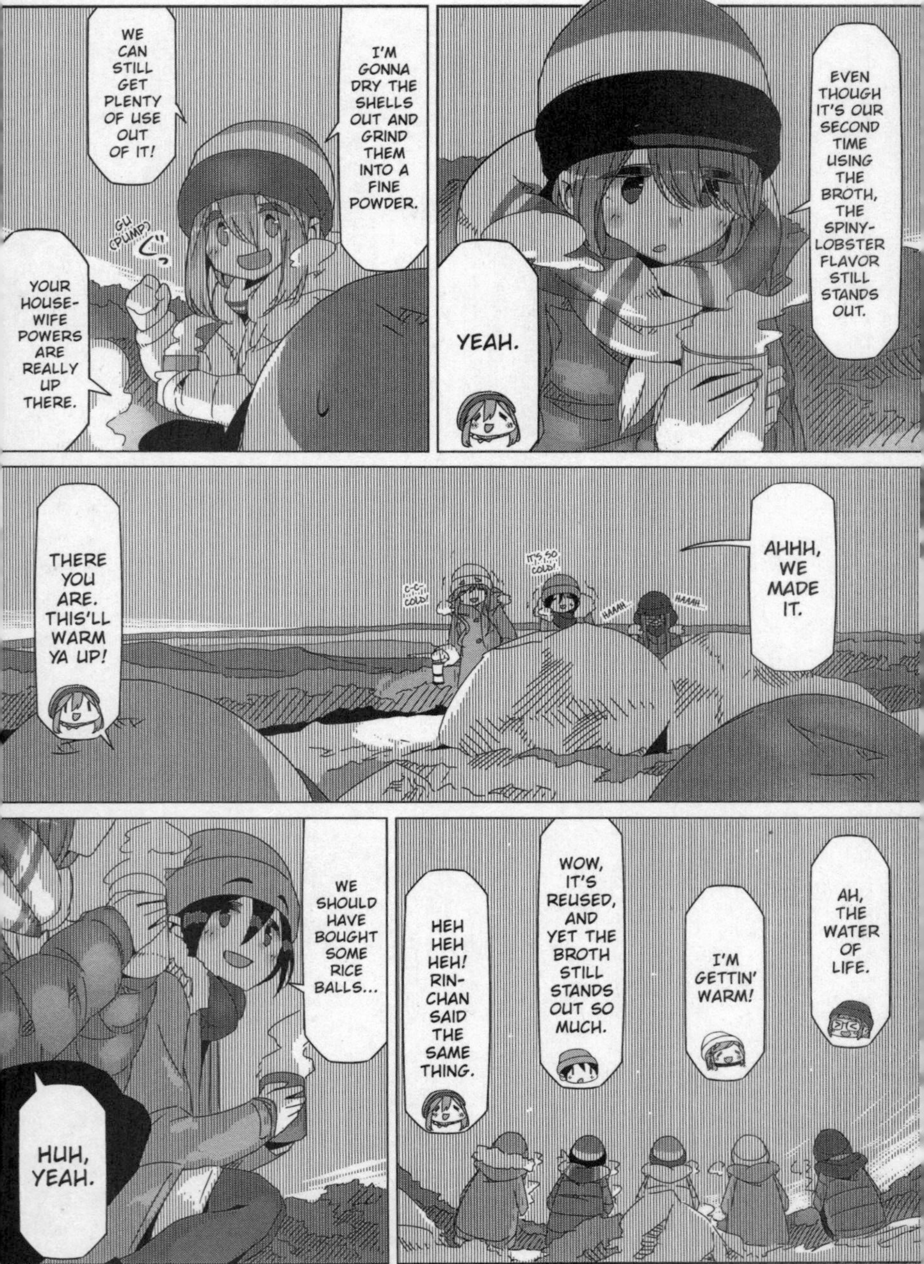
EVEN THOUGH IT'S OUR SECOND TIME USING THE BROTH, THE SPINY-LOBSTER FLAVOR STILL STANDS OUT.
YEAH.
I'M GONNA DRY THE SHELLS OUT AND GRIND THEM INTO A FINE POWDER.
WE CAN STILL GET PLENTY OF USE OUT OF IT!
GU (PUMP)
YOUR HOUSE-WIFE POWERS ARE REALLY UP THERE.
AHHH, WE MADE IT.
HAAAH...
HAAAH
IT'S SO COLD!
C-C-COLD!
THERE YOU ARE. THIS'LL WARM YA UP!
AH, THE WATER OF LIFE.
I'M GETTIN' WARM!
WOW, IT'S REUSED, AND YET THE BROTH STILL STANDS OUT SO MUCH.
HEH HEH HEH! RIN-CHAN SAID THE SAME THING.
WE SHOULD HAVE BOUGHT SOME RICE BALLS...
HUH, YEAH.

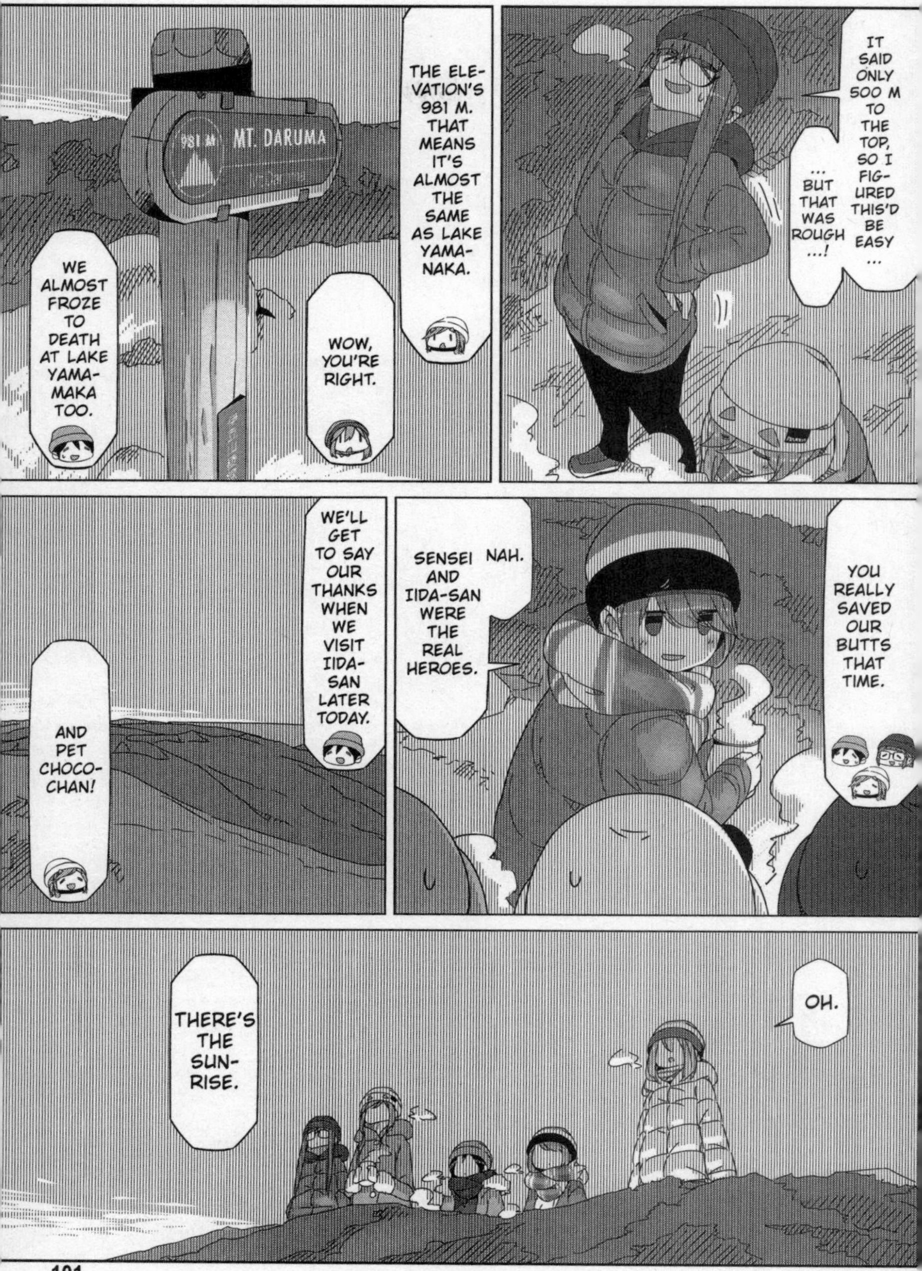
IT SAID ONLY 500 M TO THE TOP, SO I FIGURED THIS'D BE EASY...
...BUT THAT WAS ROUGH...!
981 M MT. DARUMA
THE ELEVATION'S 981 M. THAT MEANS IT'S ALMOST THE SAME AS LAKE YAMANAKA.
WOW, YOU'RE RIGHT.
WE ALMOST FROZE TO DEATH AT LAKE YAMAMAKA TOO.
YOU REALLY SAVED OUR BUTTS THAT TIME.
NAH.
SENSEI AND IIDA-SAN WERE THE REAL HEROES.
WE'LL GET TO SAY OUR THANKS WHEN WE VISIT IIDA-SAN LATER TODAY.
AND PET CHOCO-CHAN!
OH.
THERE'S THE SUNRISE.

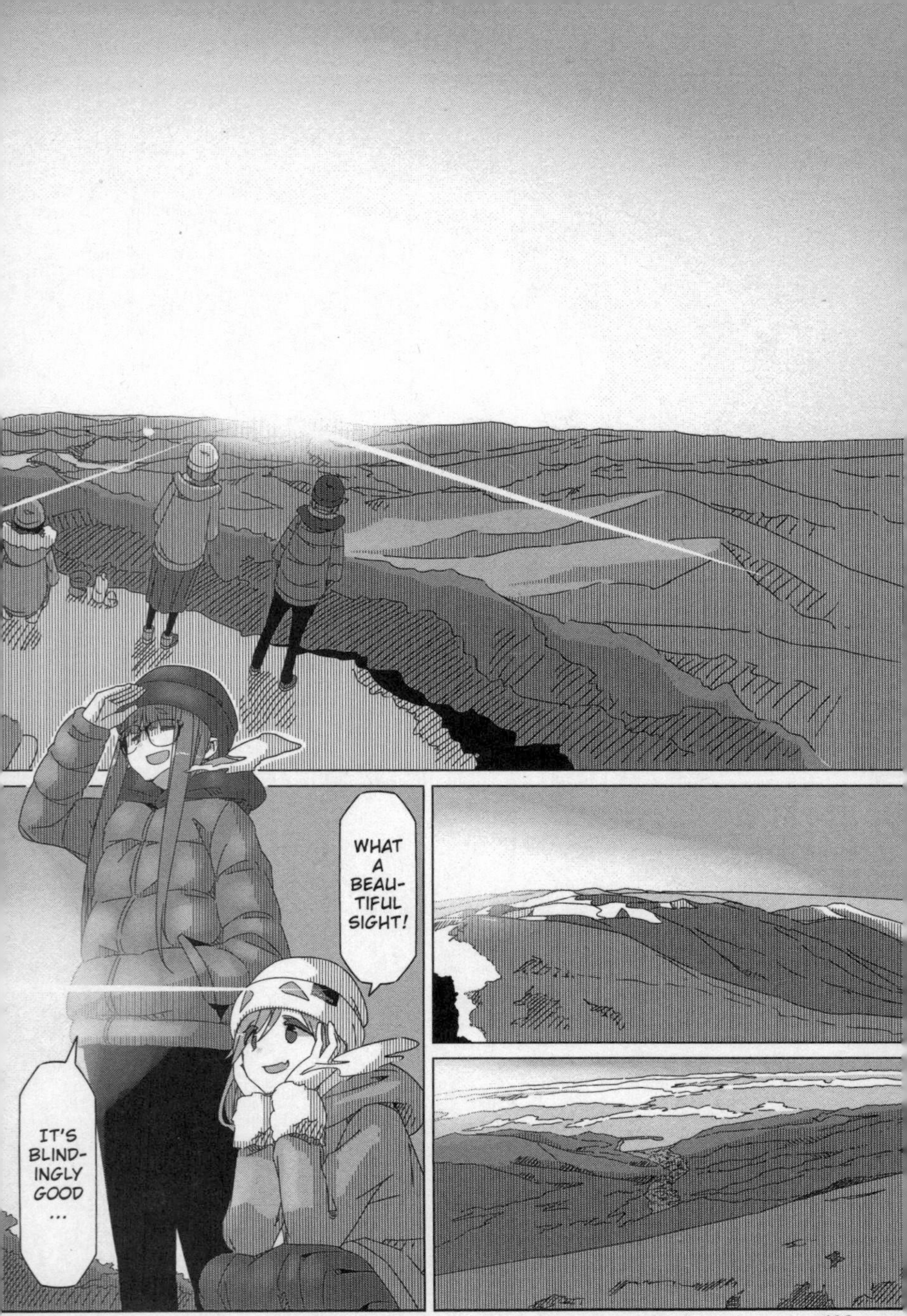
WHAT A BEAUTIFUL SIGHT!
IT'S BLINDINGLY GOOD...

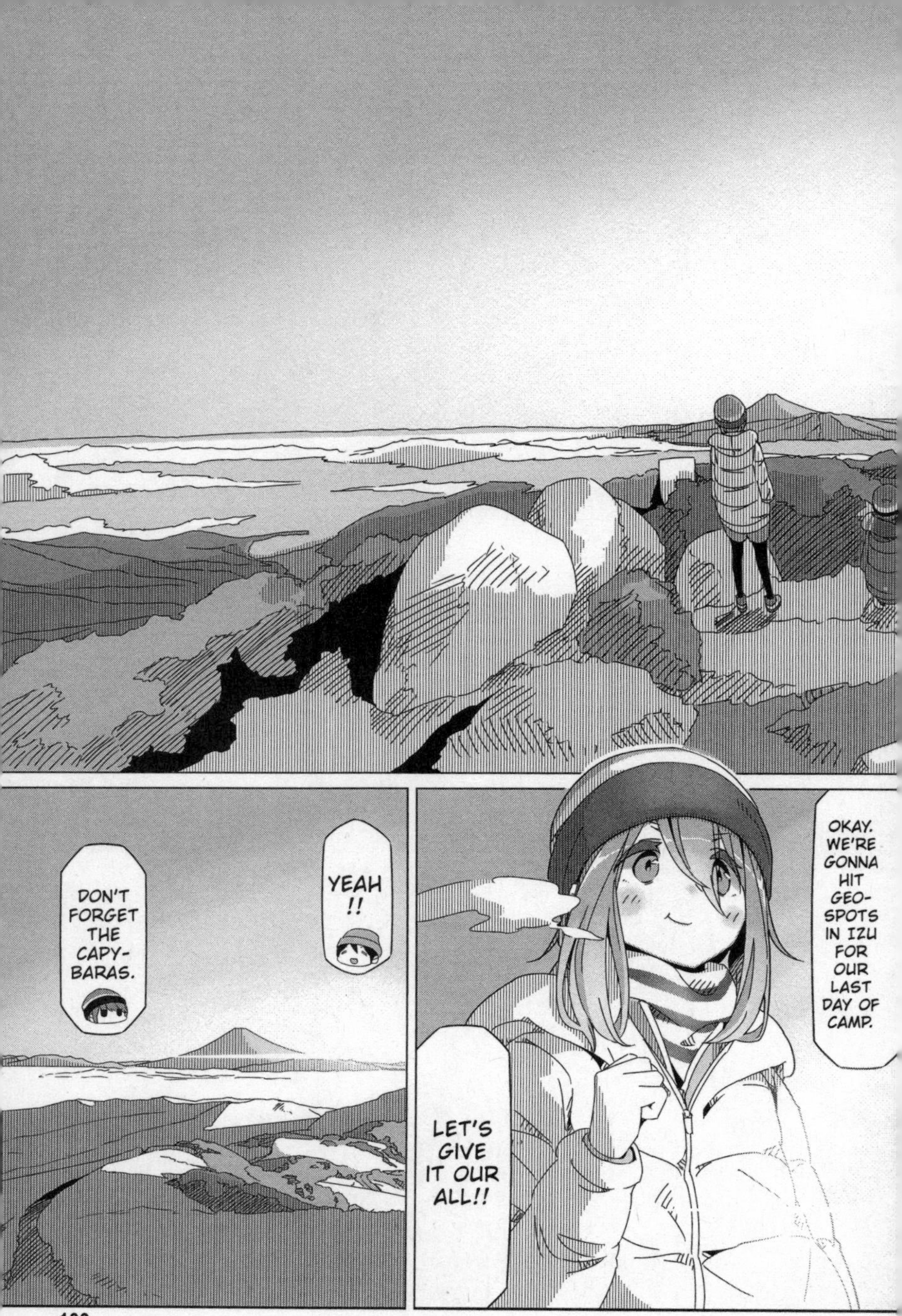
OKAY. WE'RE GONNA HIT GEO-SPOTS IN IZU FOR OUR LAST DAY OF CAMP.
LET'S GIVE IT OUR ALL!!
YEAH !!
DON'T FORGET THE CAPY-BARAS.

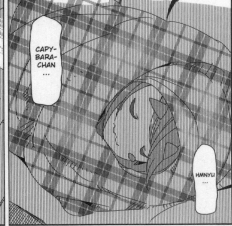

CAPY-
BARA-
CHAN
...

HMNYU
...

104

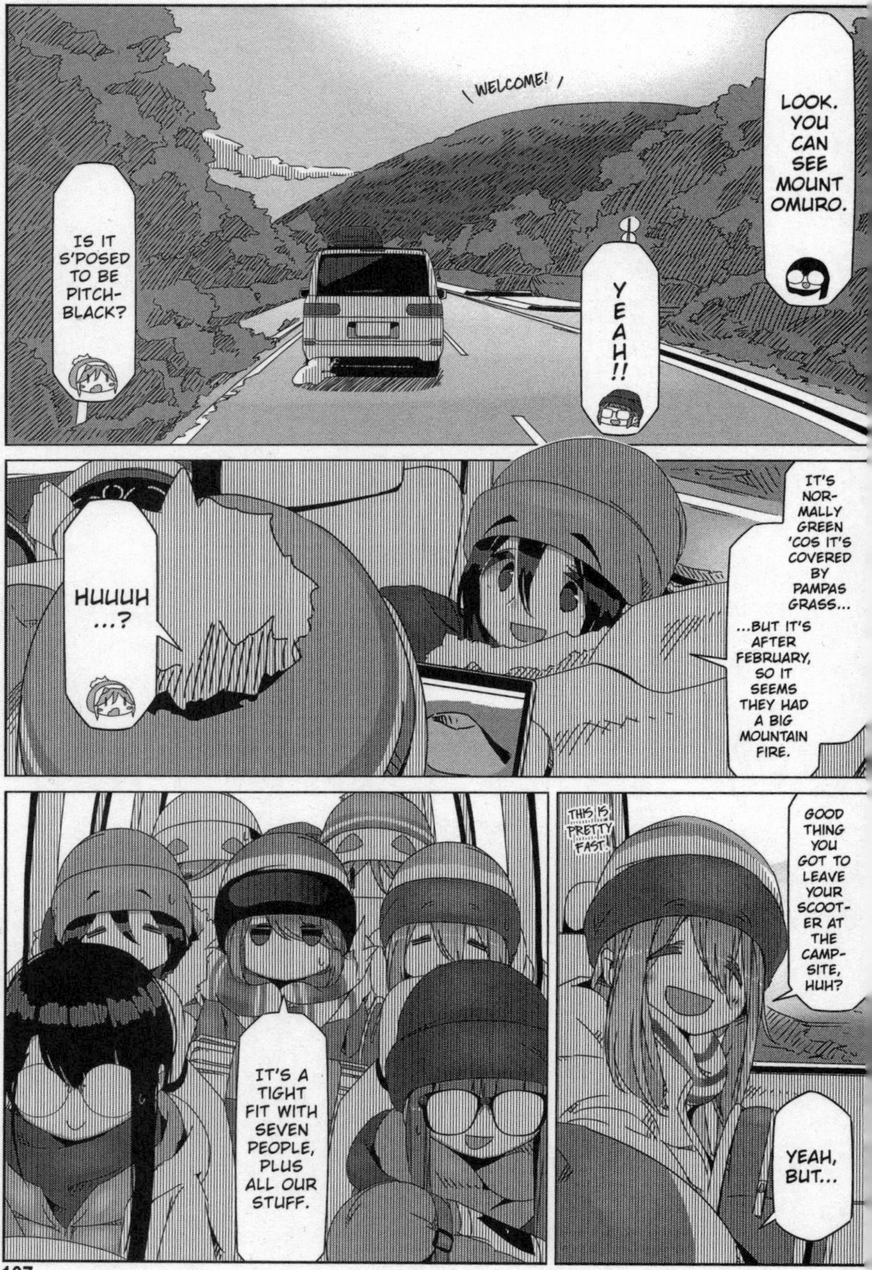
LOOK. YOU CAN SEE MOUNT OMURO.
WELCOME!
YEAH!!
IS IT S'POSED TO BE PITCH-BLACK?
IT'S NORMALLY GREEN 'COS IT'S COVERED BY PAMPAS GRASS...
...BUT IT'S AFTER FEBRUARY, SO IT SEEMS THEY HAD A BIG MOUNTAIN FIRE.
HUUUH ...?
GOOD THING YOU GOT TO LEAVE YOUR SCOOTER AT THE CAMPSITE, HUH?
THIS IS PRETTY FAST.
YEAH, BUT...
IT'S A TIGHT FIT WITH SEVEN PEOPLE, PLUS ALL OUR STUFF.

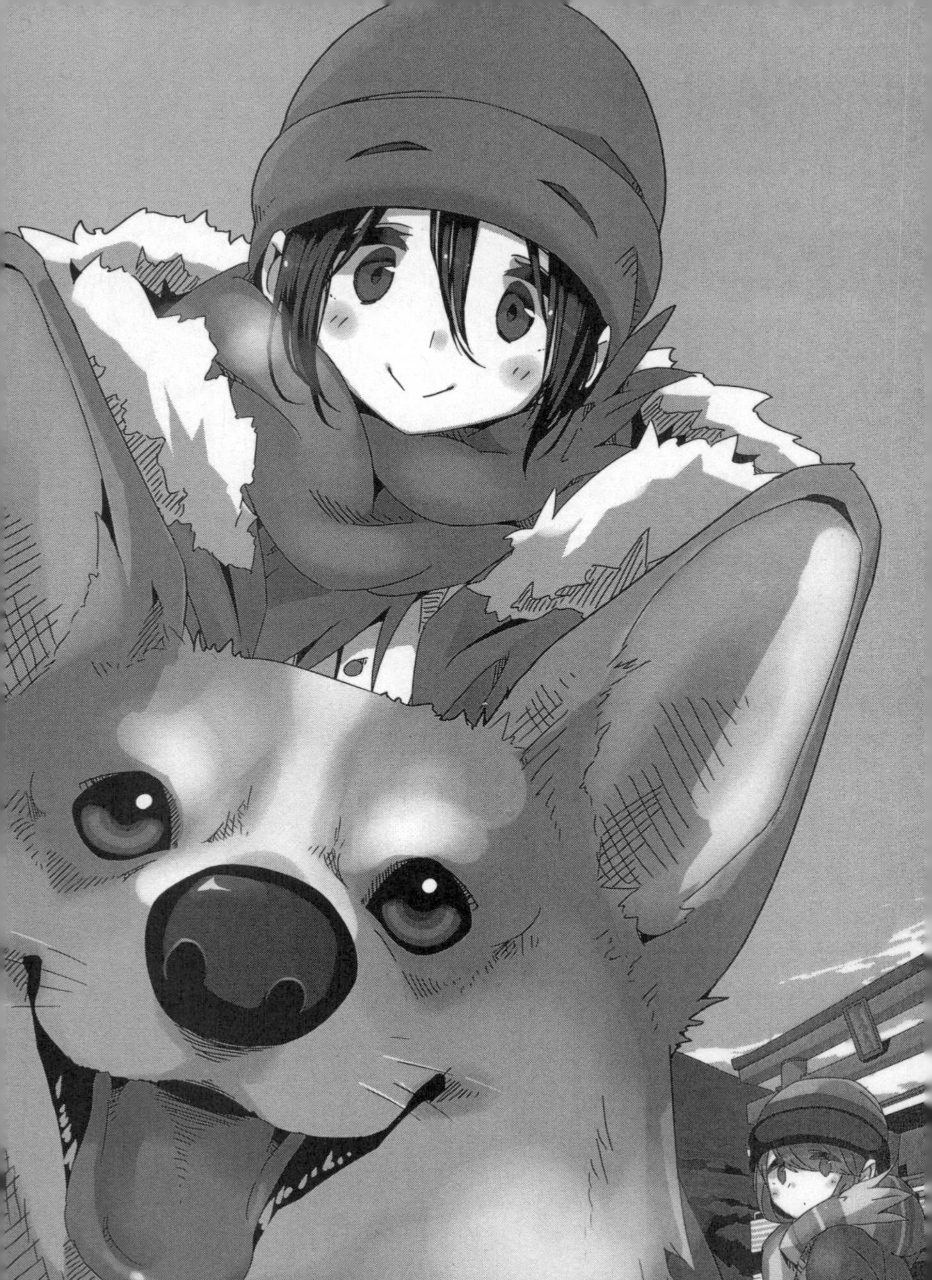

CHAPTER 51 WHAT COLOR IS MOUNT OMURO?

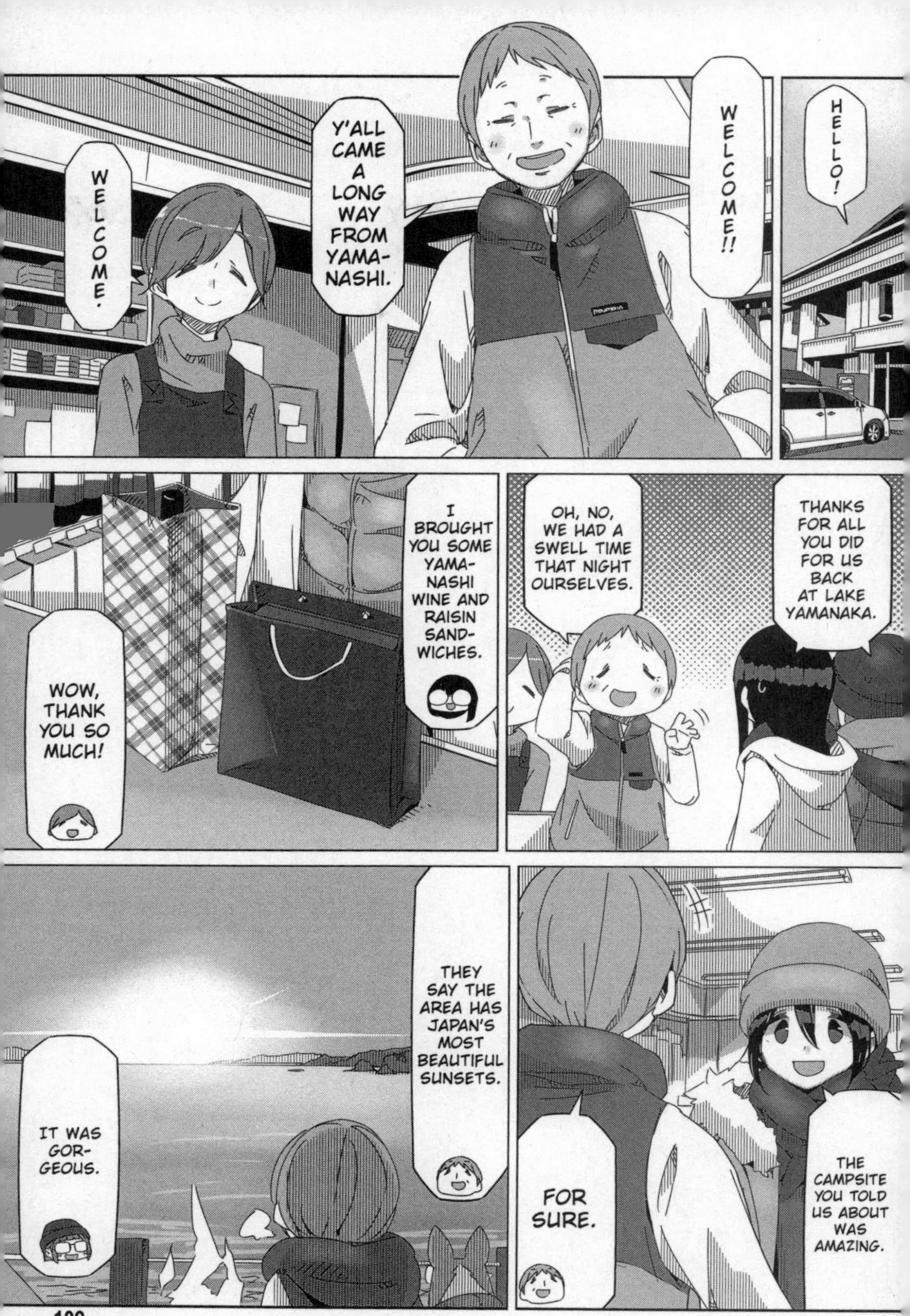
HELLO!
WELCOME!!
Y'ALL CAME A LONG WAY FROM YAMA-NASHI.
WELCOME.
THANKS FOR ALL YOU DID FOR US BACK AT LAKE YAMANAKA.
OH, NO, WE HAD A SWELL TIME THAT NIGHT OURSELVES.
I BROUGHT YOU SOME YAMA-NASHI WINE AND RAISIN SAND-WICHES.
WOW, THANK YOU SO MUCH!
THE CAMPSITE YOU TOLD US ABOUT WAS AMAZING.
FOR SURE.
THEY SAY THE AREA HAS JAPAN'S MOST BEAUTIFUL SUNSETS.
IT WAS GOR-GEOUS.

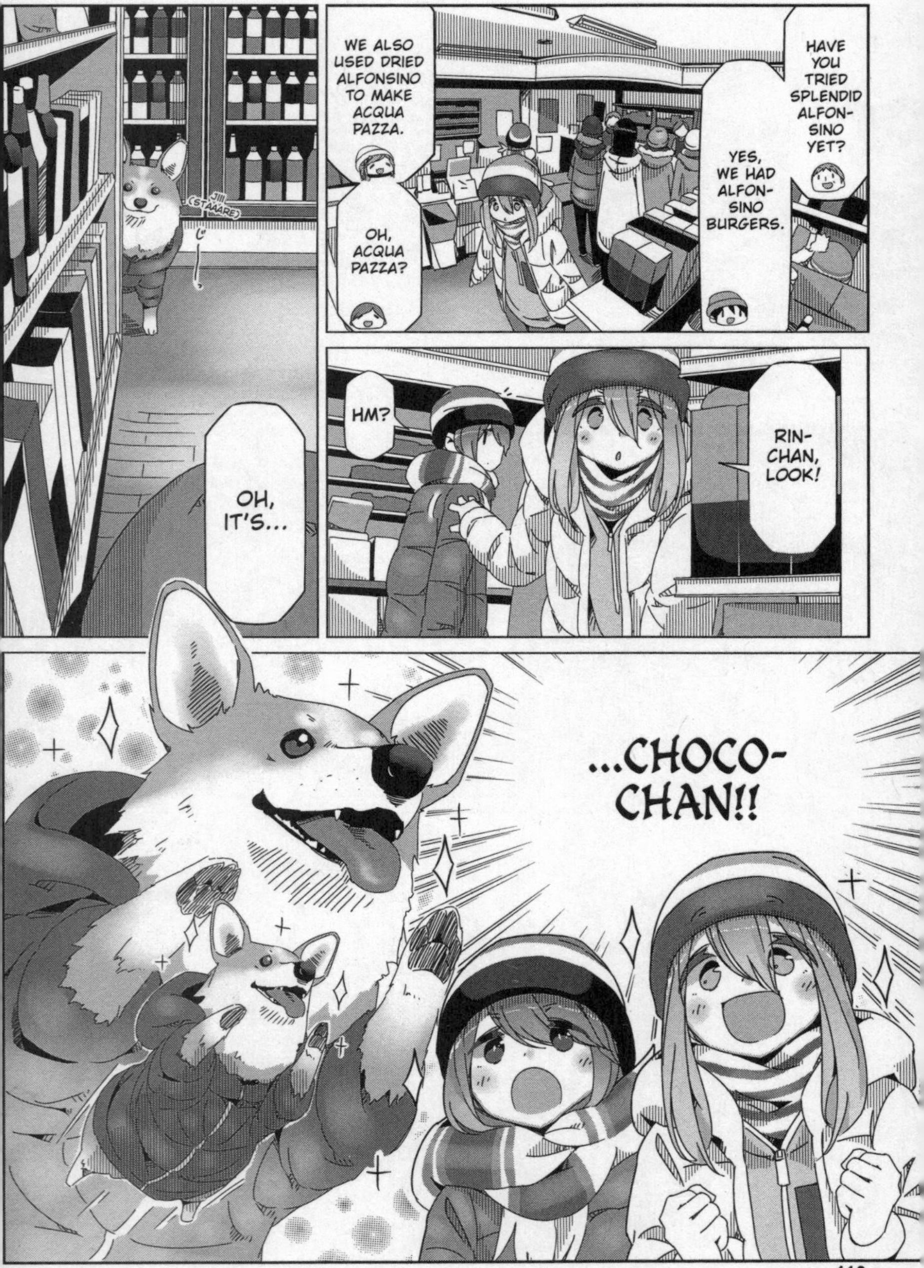
HAVE YOU TRIED SPLENDID ALFONSINO YET?
YES, WE HAD ALFONSINO BURGERS.
WE ALSO USED DRIED ALFONSINO TO MAKE ACQUA PAZZA.
OH, ACQUA PAZZA?
RIN-CHAN, LOOK!
HM?
JIII (STAAARE)
OH, IT'S...
...CHOCO-CHAN!!

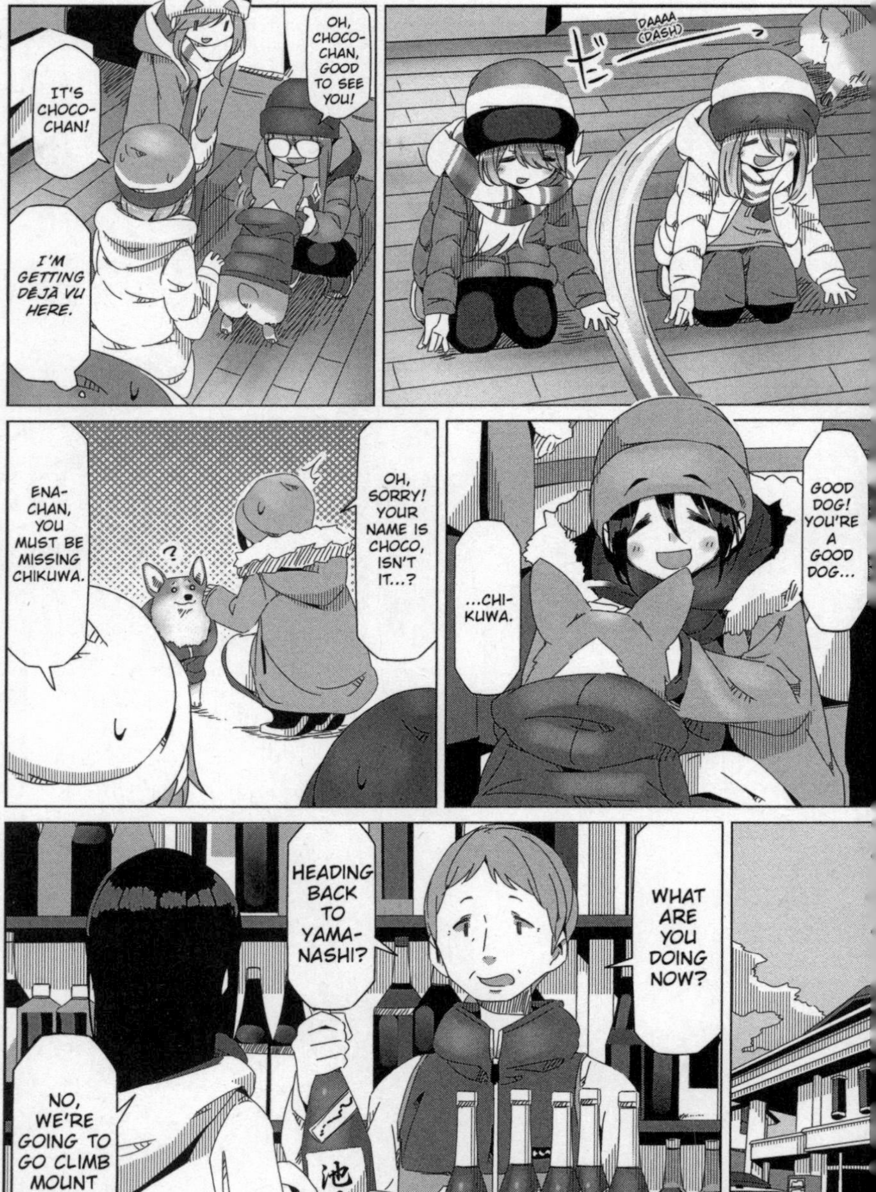
DAAAA (DASH)
OH, CHOCO-CHAN, GOOD TO SEE YOU!
IT'S CHOCO-CHAN!
I'M GETTING DÉJÀ VU HERE.
GOOD DOG! YOU'RE A GOOD DOG...
...CHI-KUWA.
OH, SORRY! YOUR NAME IS CHOCO, ISN'T IT...?
ENA-CHAN, YOU MUST BE MISSING CHIKUWA.
WHAT ARE YOU DOING NOW?
HEADING BACK TO YAMA-NASHI?
NO, WE'RE GOING TO GO CLIMB MOUNT OMURO.
BOTTLES: IKE-IKE

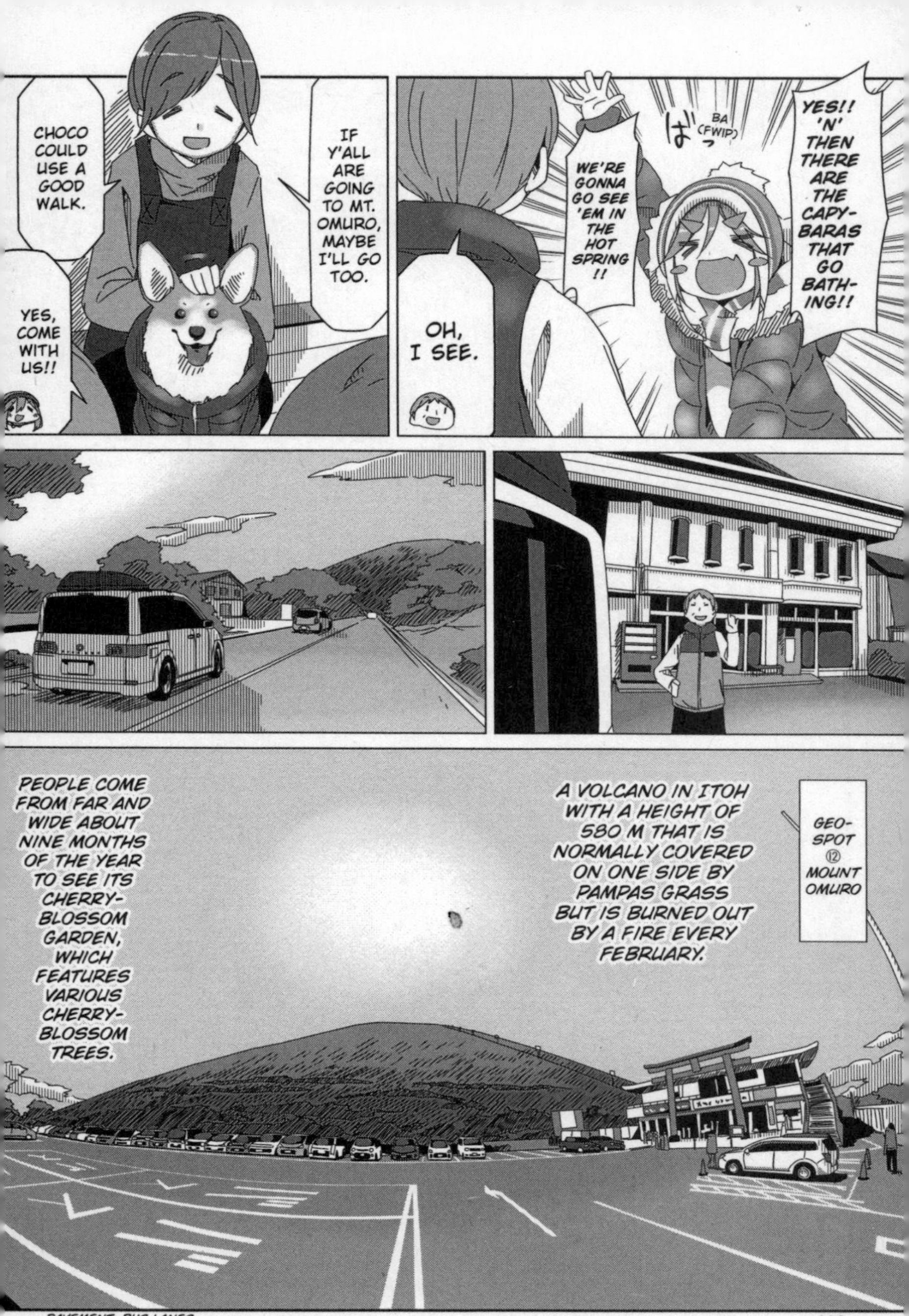
YES!! 'N' THEN THERE ARE THE CAPYBARAS THAT GO BATHING!!
ばっ
BA (FWIP)
WE'RE GONNA GO SEE 'EM IN THE HOT SPRING!!
OH, I SEE.
IF Y'ALL ARE GOING TO MT. OMURO, MAYBE I'LL GO TOO.
CHOCO COULD USE A GOOD WALK.
YES, COME WITH US!!
GEO-SPOT ⑫ MOUNT OMURO
A VOLCANO IN ITOH WITH A HEIGHT OF 580 M THAT IS NORMALLY COVERED ON ONE SIDE BY PAMPAS GRASS BUT IS BURNED OUT BY A FIRE EVERY FEBRUARY.
PEOPLE COME FROM FAR AND WIDE ABOUT NINE MONTHS OF THE YEAR TO SEE ITS CHERRY-BLOSSOM GARDEN, WHICH FEATURES VARIOUS CHERRY-BLOSSOM TREES.

PAVEMENT: BUS LANES

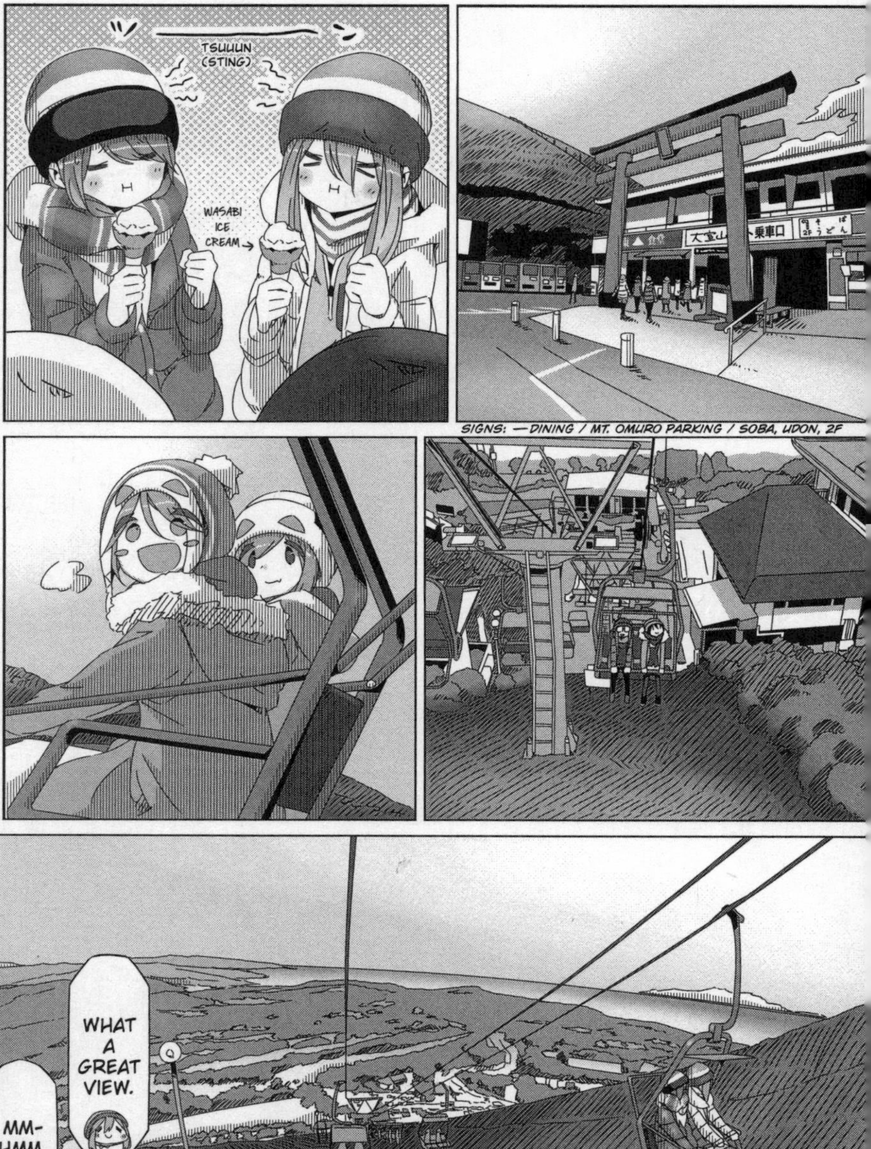
SIGNS: —DINING / MT. OMURO PARKING / SOBA, UDON, 2F
TSUUUN (STING)
WASABI ICE CREAM
WHAT A GREAT VIEW.
MM-HMM.

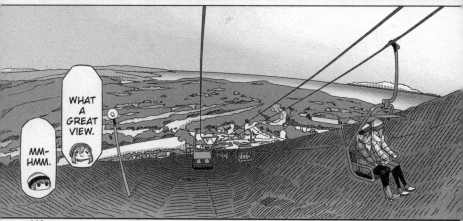

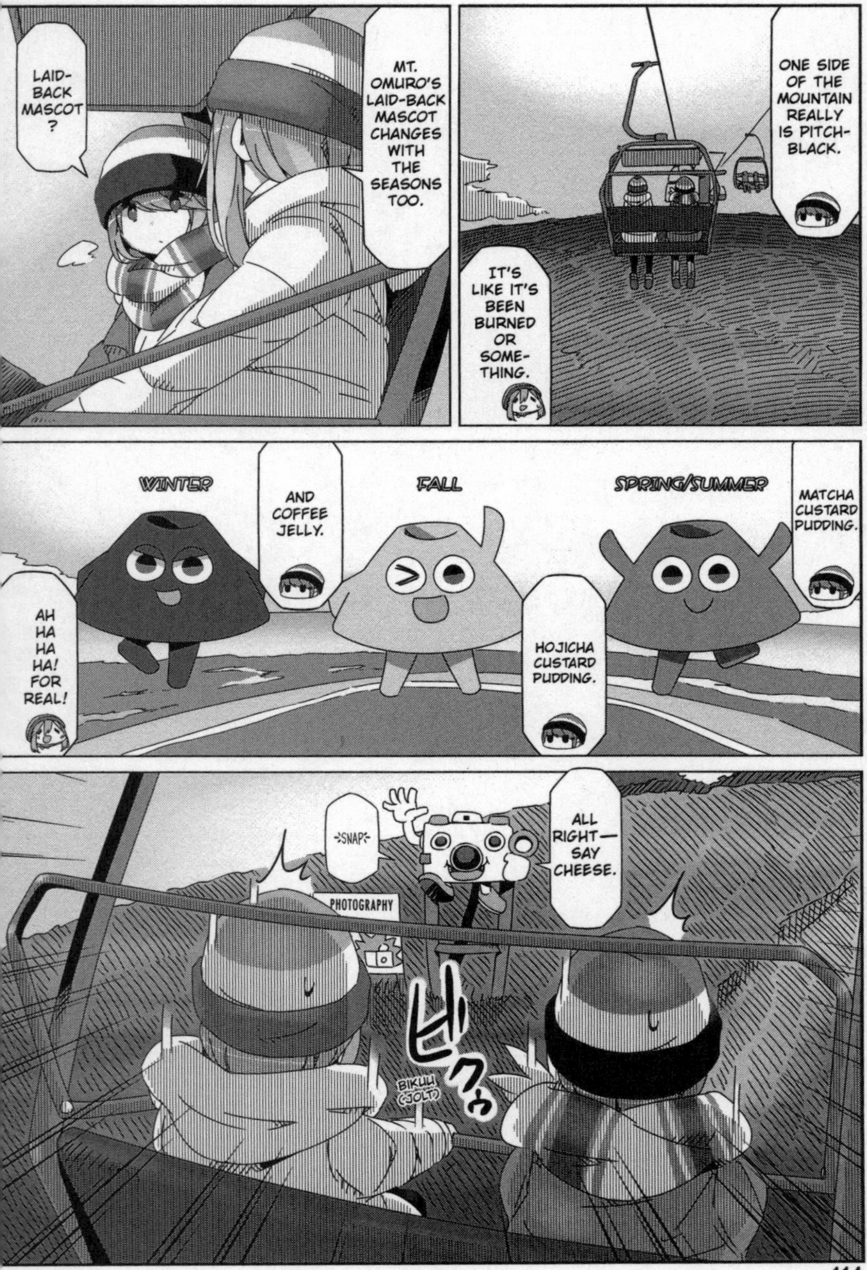
ONE SIDE OF THE MOUNTAIN REALLY IS PITCH-BLACK.
IT'S LIKE IT'S BEEN BURNED OR SOMETHING.
MT. OMURO'S LAID-BACK MASCOT CHANGES WITH THE SEASONS TOO.
LAID-BACK MASCOT?
MATCHA CUSTARD PUDDING.
SPRING/SUMMER
HOJICHA CUSTARD PUDDING.
FALL
AND COFFEE JELLY.
WINTER
AH HA HA HA! FOR REAL!
ALL RIGHT—SAY CHEESE.
-SNAP-
PHOTOGRAPHY
BIKUU (JOLT)

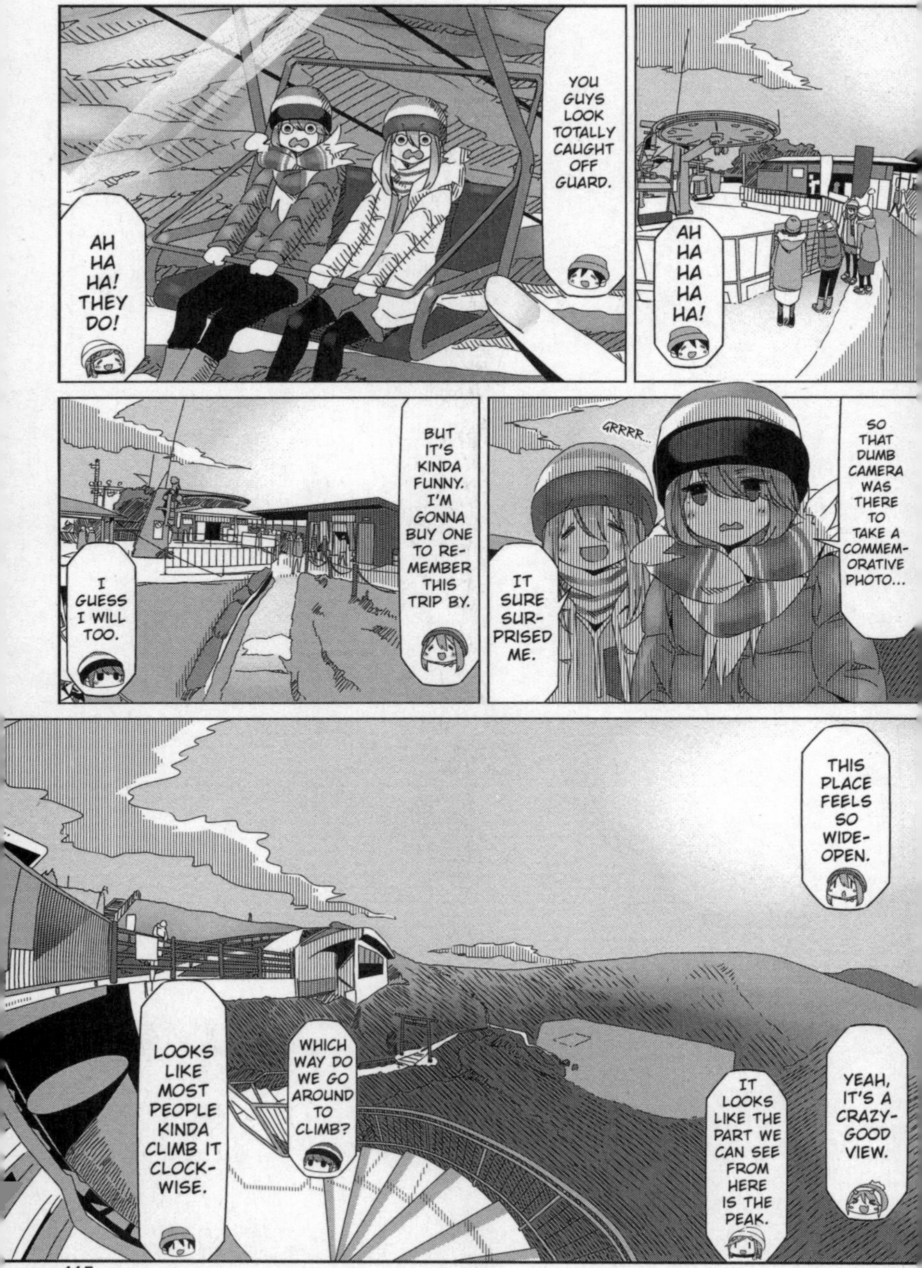
AH HA HA HA HA!
YOU GUYS LOOK TOTALLY CAUGHT OFF GUARD.
AH HA HA! THEY DO!
SO THAT DUMB CAMERA WAS THERE TO TAKE A COMMEMORATIVE PHOTO...
GRRRR...
IT SURE SURPRISED ME.
BUT IT'S KINDA FUNNY. I'M GONNA BUY ONE TO REMEMBER THIS TRIP BY.
I GUESS I WILL TOO.
THIS PLACE FEELS SO WIDE-OPEN.
YEAH, IT'S A CRAZY-GOOD VIEW.
IT LOOKS LIKE THE PART WE CAN SEE FROM HERE IS THE PEAK.
WHICH WAY DO WE GO AROUND TO CLIMB?
LOOKS LIKE MOST PEOPLE KINDA CLIMB IT CLOCKWISE.

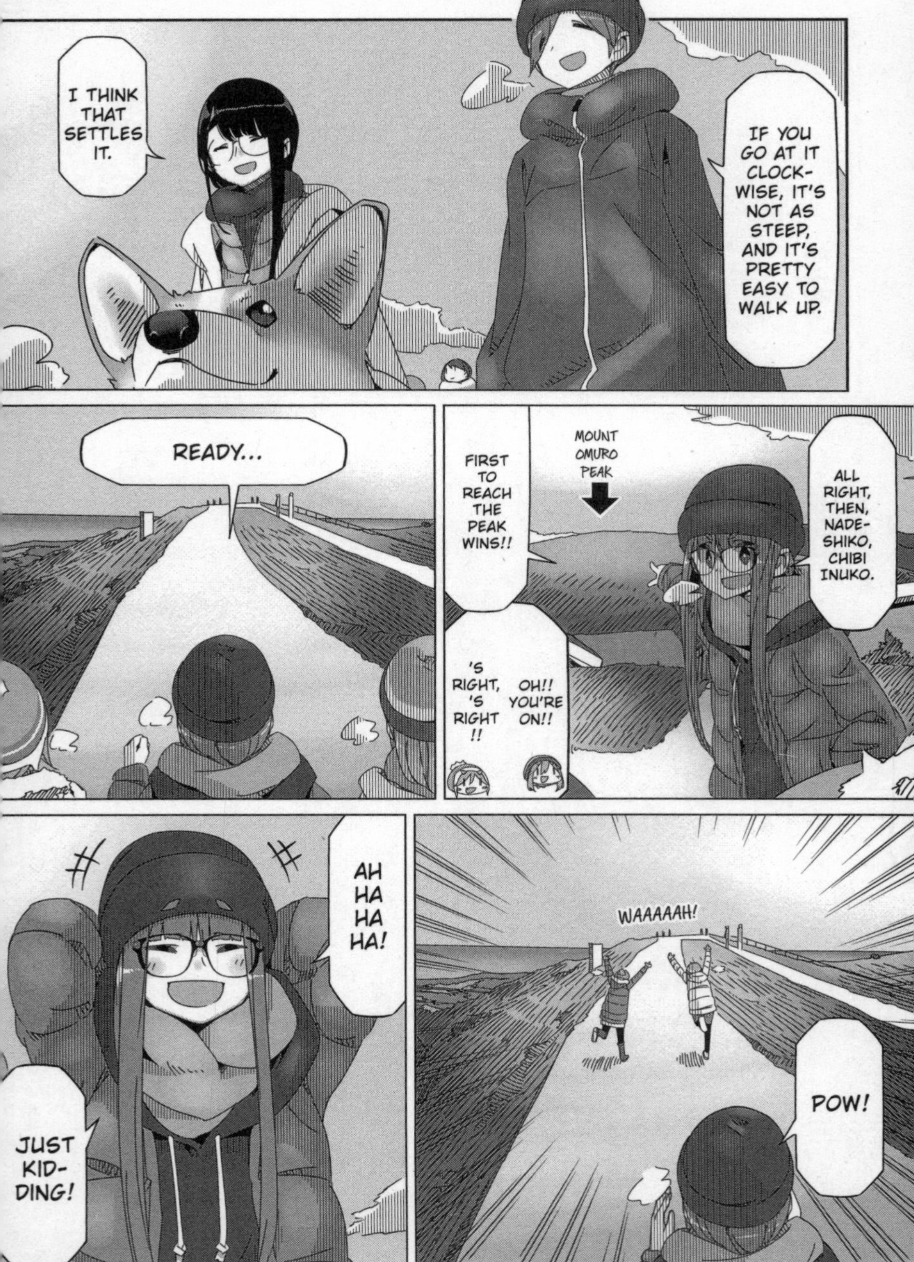

IF YOU GO AT IT CLOCKWISE, IT'S NOT AS STEEP, AND IT'S PRETTY EASY TO WALK UP.
I THINK THAT SETTLES IT.
ALL RIGHT, THEN, NADESHIKO, CHIBI INUKO.
MOUNT OMURO PEAK
FIRST TO REACH THE PEAK WINS!!
OH!! YOU'RE ON!!
'S RIGHT, 'S RIGHT!!
READY...
WAAAAAH!
POW!
AH HA HA HA!
JUST KIDDING!

※ PLEASE DON'T RACE ONE ANOTHER UP MT. OMURO!

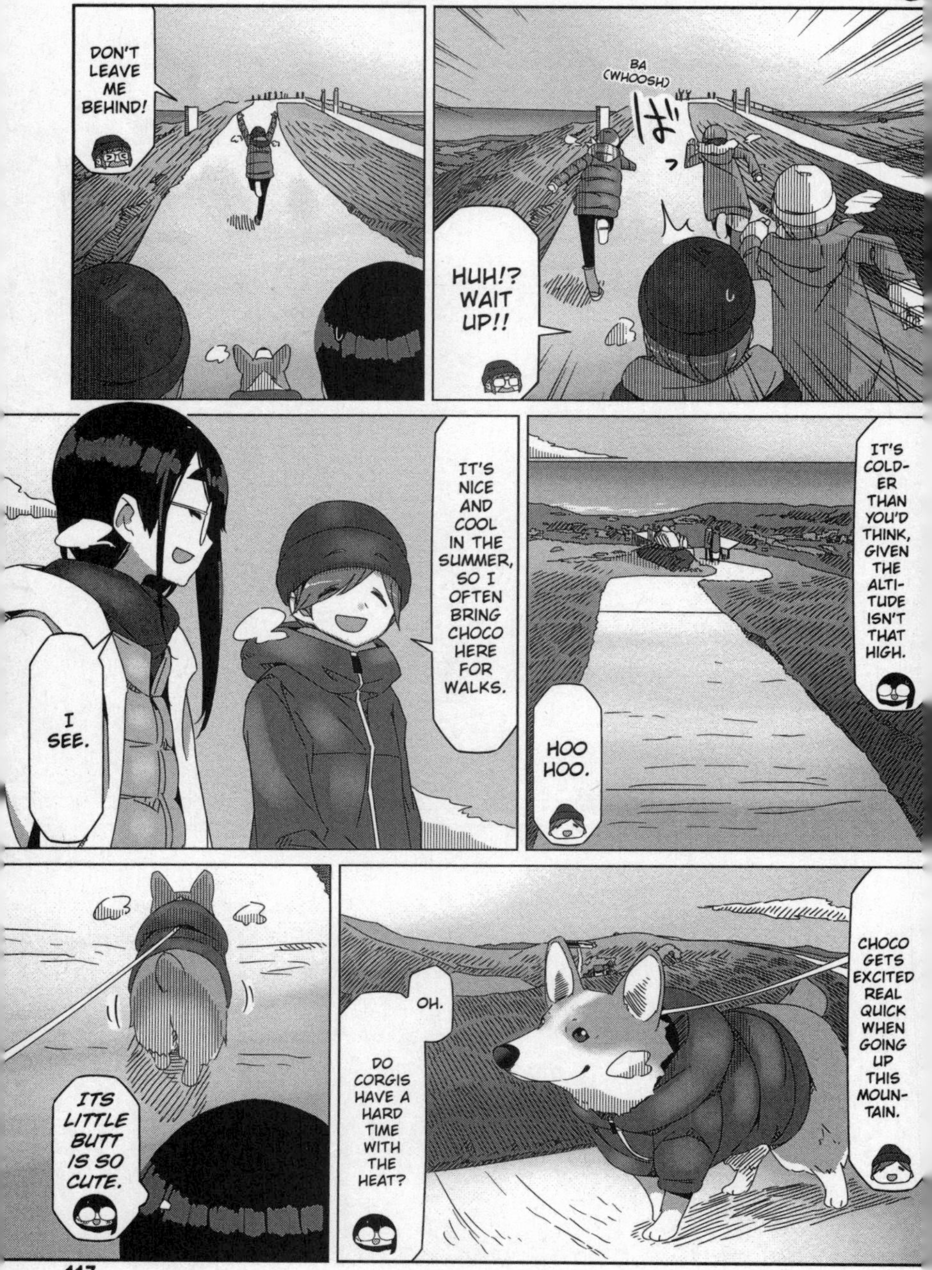
BA (WHOOSH)
ばっ
HUH!? WAIT UP!!
DON'T LEAVE ME BEHIND!
IT'S COLDER THAN YOU'D THINK, GIVEN THE ALTITUDE ISN'T THAT HIGH.
HOO HOO.
IT'S NICE AND COOL IN THE SUMMER, SO I OFTEN BRING CHOCO HERE FOR WALKS.
I SEE.
CHOCO GETS EXCITED REAL QUICK WHEN GOING UP THIS MOUNTAIN.
OH.
DO CORGIS HAVE A HARD TIME WITH THE HEAT?
ITS LITTLE BUTT IS SO CUTE.

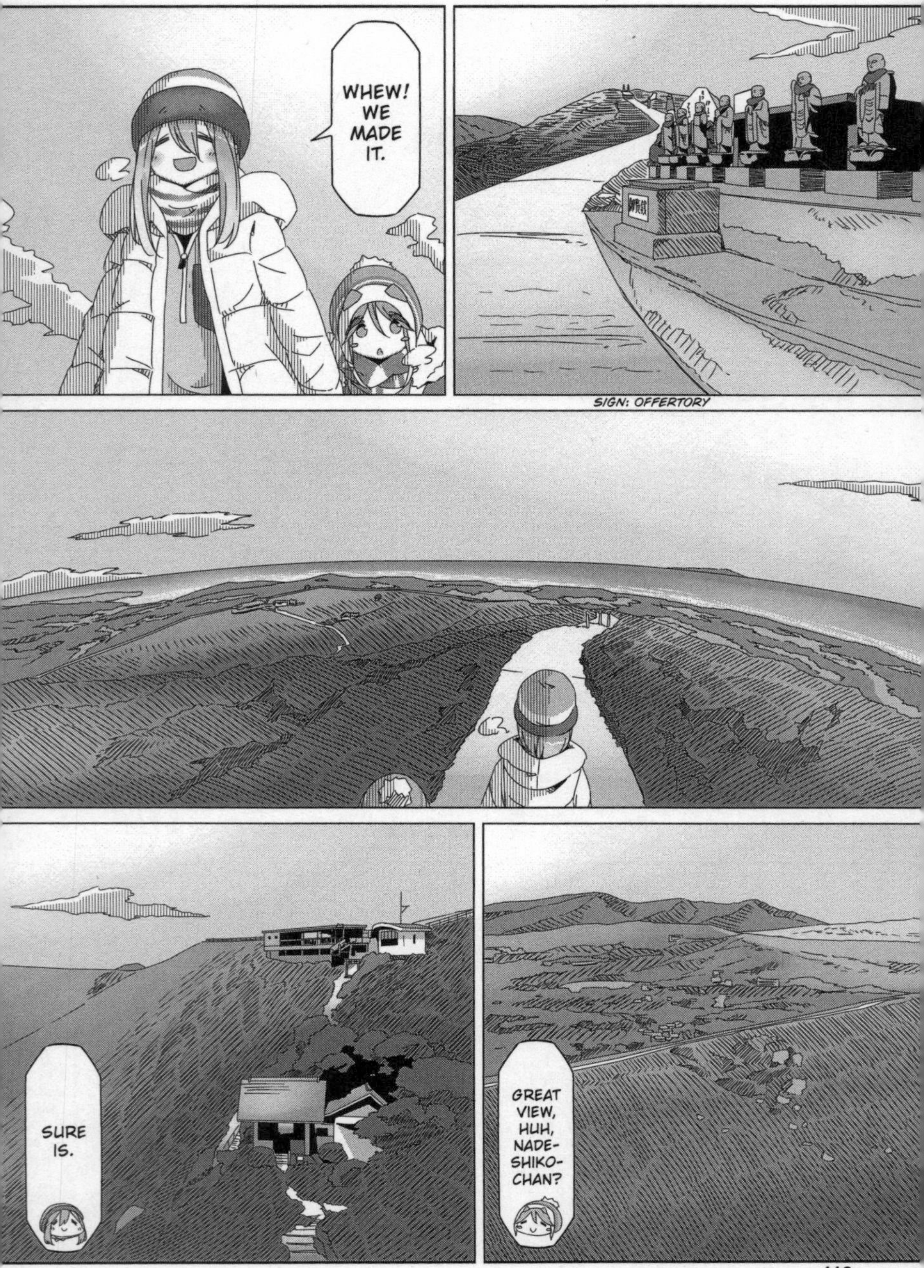
SIGN: OFFERTORY
WHEW! WE MADE IT.
GREAT VIEW, HUH, NADESHIKO-CHAN?
SURE IS.

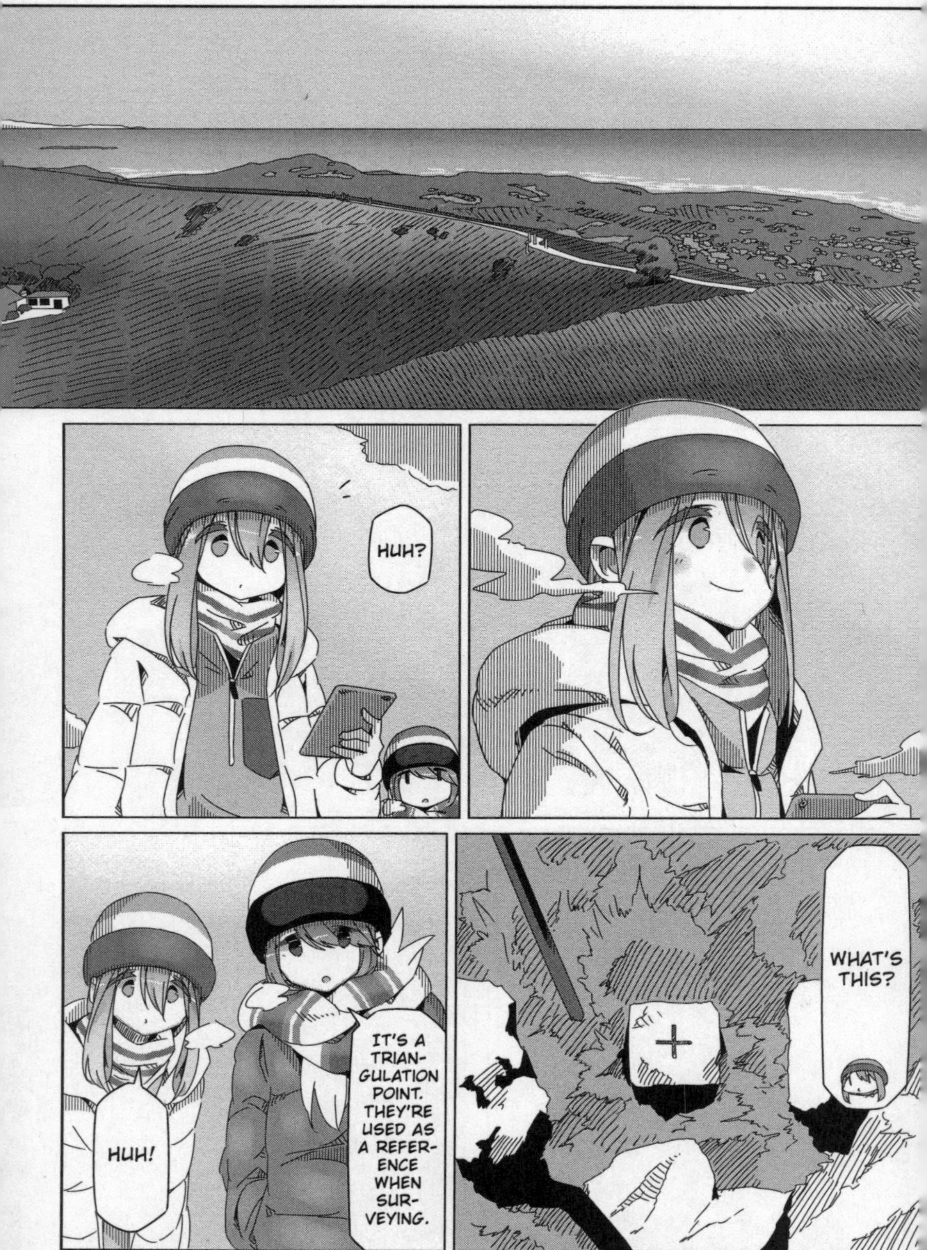
HUH?
WHAT'S THIS?
IT'S A TRIAN-GULATION POINT. THEY'RE USED AS A REFER-ENCE WHEN SUR-VEYING.
HUH!

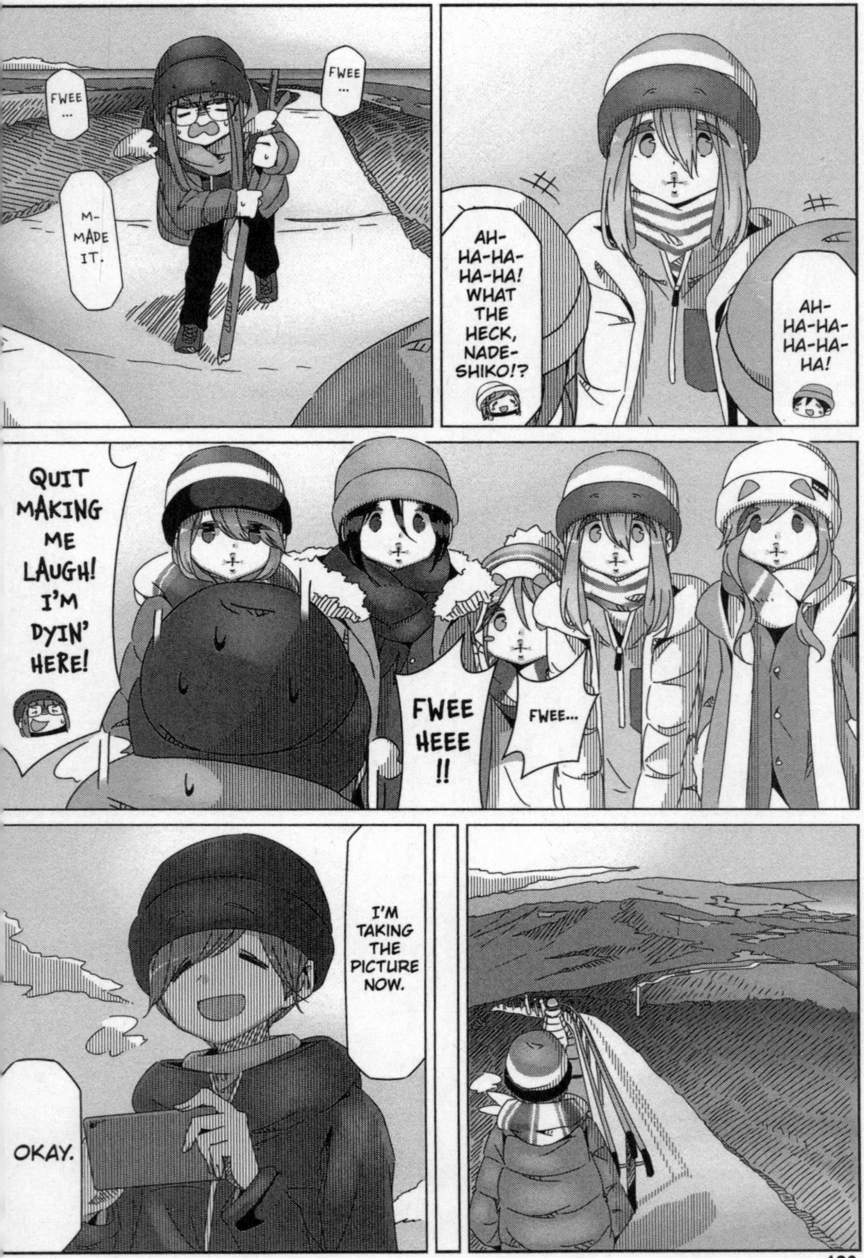
AH-HA-HA-HA-HA-HA!
AH-HA-HA-HA-HA! WHAT THE HECK, NADESHIKO!?
FWEE...
FWEE...
M-MADE IT.
FWEE...
FWEE HEEE!!
QUIT MAKING ME LAUGH! I'M DYIN' HERE!
I'M TAKING THE PICTURE NOW.
OKAY.

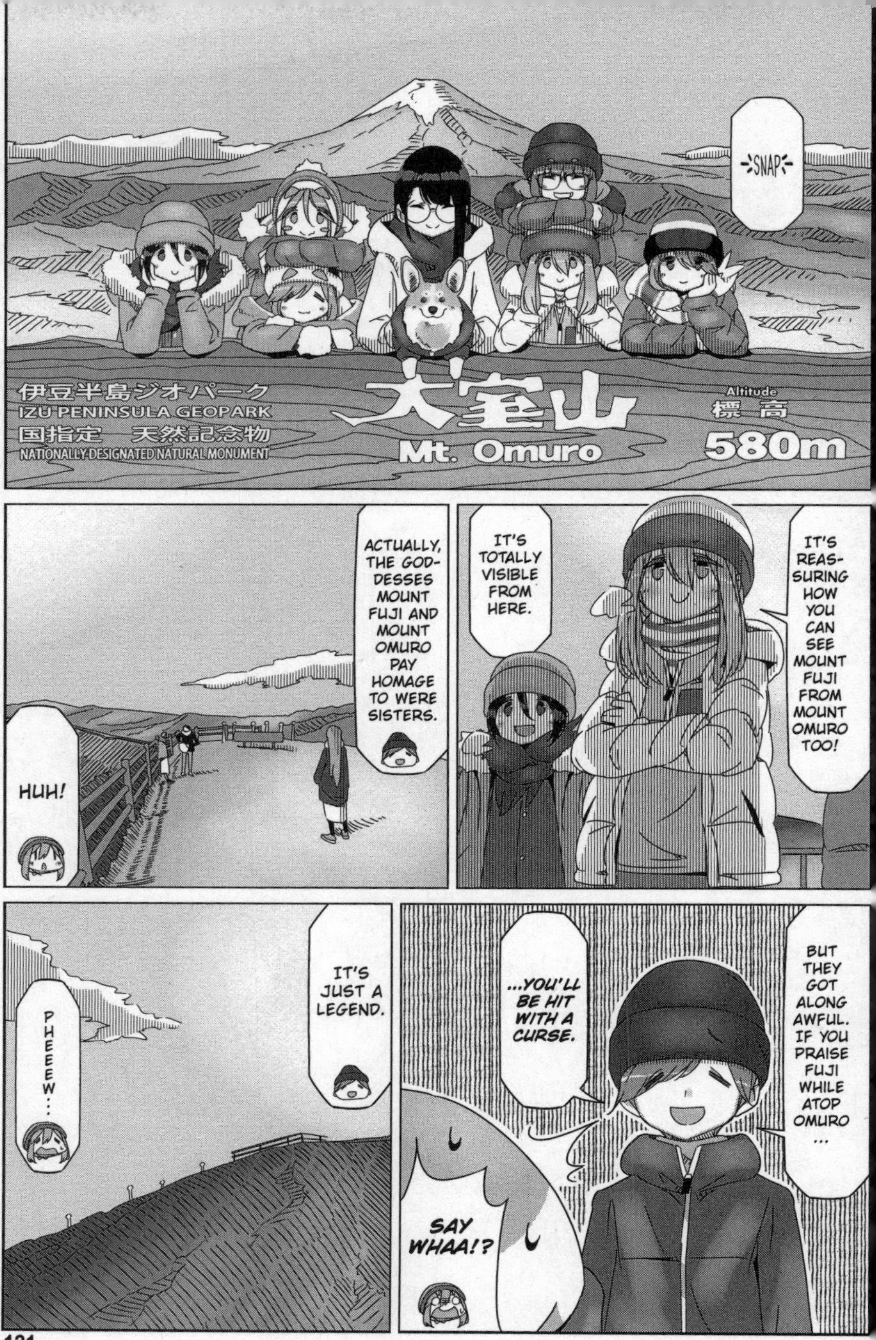
SNAP
伊豆半島ジオパーク
IZU PENINSULA GEOPARK
国指定 天然記念物
NATIONALLY-DESIGNATED NATURAL MONUMENT
大室山
Mt. Omuro
Altitude
標高
580m
IT'S REASSURING HOW YOU CAN SEE MOUNT FUJI FROM MOUNT OMURO TOO!
IT'S TOTALLY VISIBLE FROM HERE.
ACTUALLY, THE GODDESSES MOUNT FUJI AND MOUNT OMURO PAY HOMAGE TO WERE SISTERS.
HUH!
BUT THEY GOT ALONG AWFUL. IF YOU PRAISE FUJI WHILE ATOP OMURO...
...YOU'LL BE HIT WITH A CURSE.
SAY WHAA!?
IT'S JUST A LEGEND.
PHEEEW...

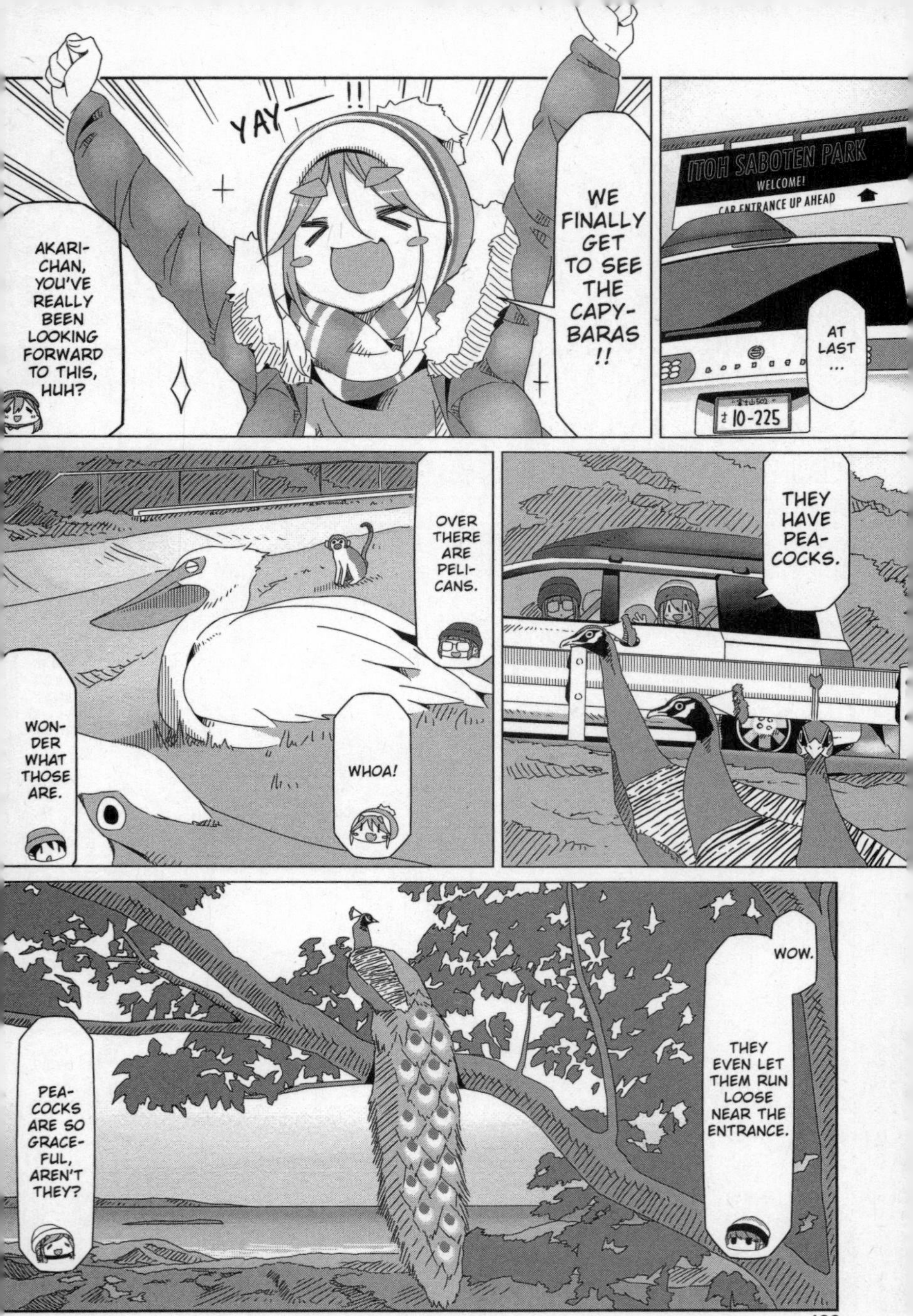
ITOH SABOTEN PARK
WELCOME!
CAR ENTRANCE UP AHEAD
AT LAST ...
10-225
YAY— !!
WE FINALLY GET TO SEE THE CAPY-BARAS !!
AKARI-CHAN, YOU'VE REALLY BEEN LOOKING FORWARD TO THIS, HUH?
THEY HAVE PEA-COCKS.
OVER THERE ARE PELI-CANS.
WHOA!
WON-DER WHAT THOSE ARE.
WOW.
THEY EVEN LET THEM RUN LOOSE NEAR THE ENTRANCE.
PEA-COCKS ARE SO GRACE-FUL, AREN'T THEY?

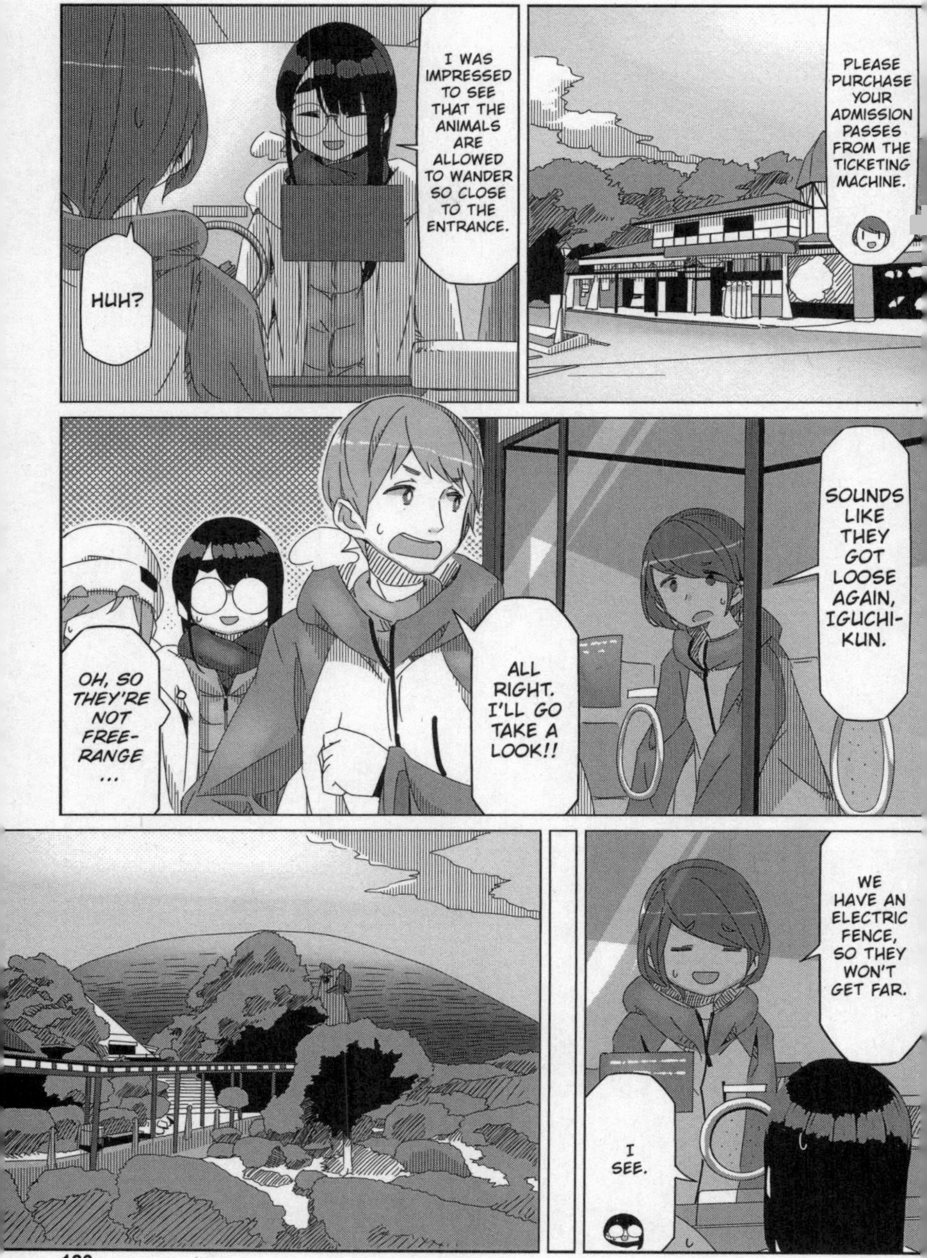
PLEASE PURCHASE YOUR ADMISSION PASSES FROM THE TICKETING MACHINE.
I WAS IMPRESSED TO SEE THAT THE ANIMALS ARE ALLOWED TO WANDER SO CLOSE TO THE ENTRANCE.
HUH?
SOUNDS LIKE THEY GOT LOOSE AGAIN, IGUCHI-KUN.
ALL RIGHT. I'LL GO TAKE A LOOK!!
OH, SO THEY'RE NOT FREE-RANGE ...
WE HAVE AN ELECTRIC FENCE, SO THEY WON'T GET FAR.
I SEE.

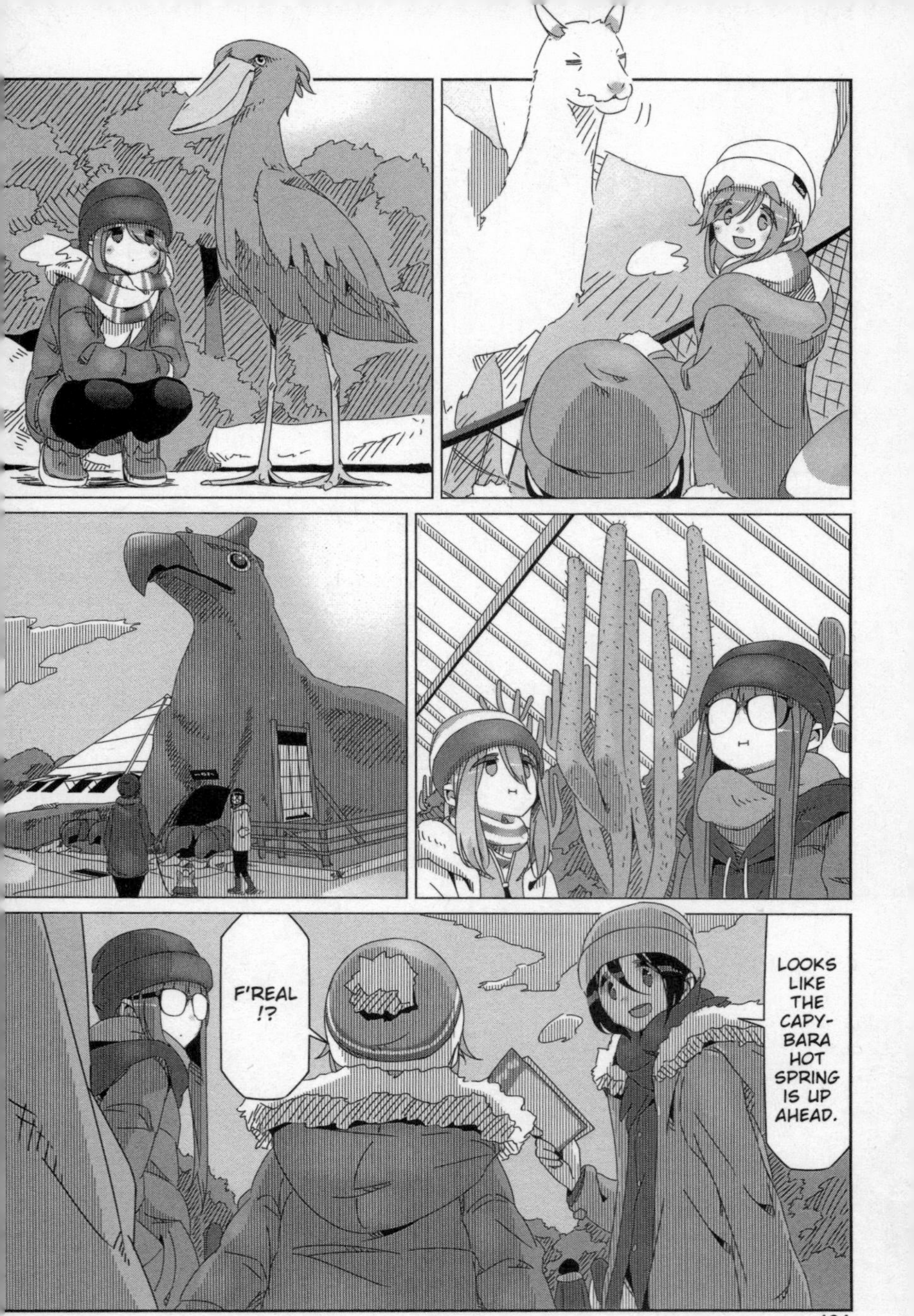
LOOKS LIKE THE CAPY-BARA HOT SPRING IS UP AHEAD.
F'REAL !?

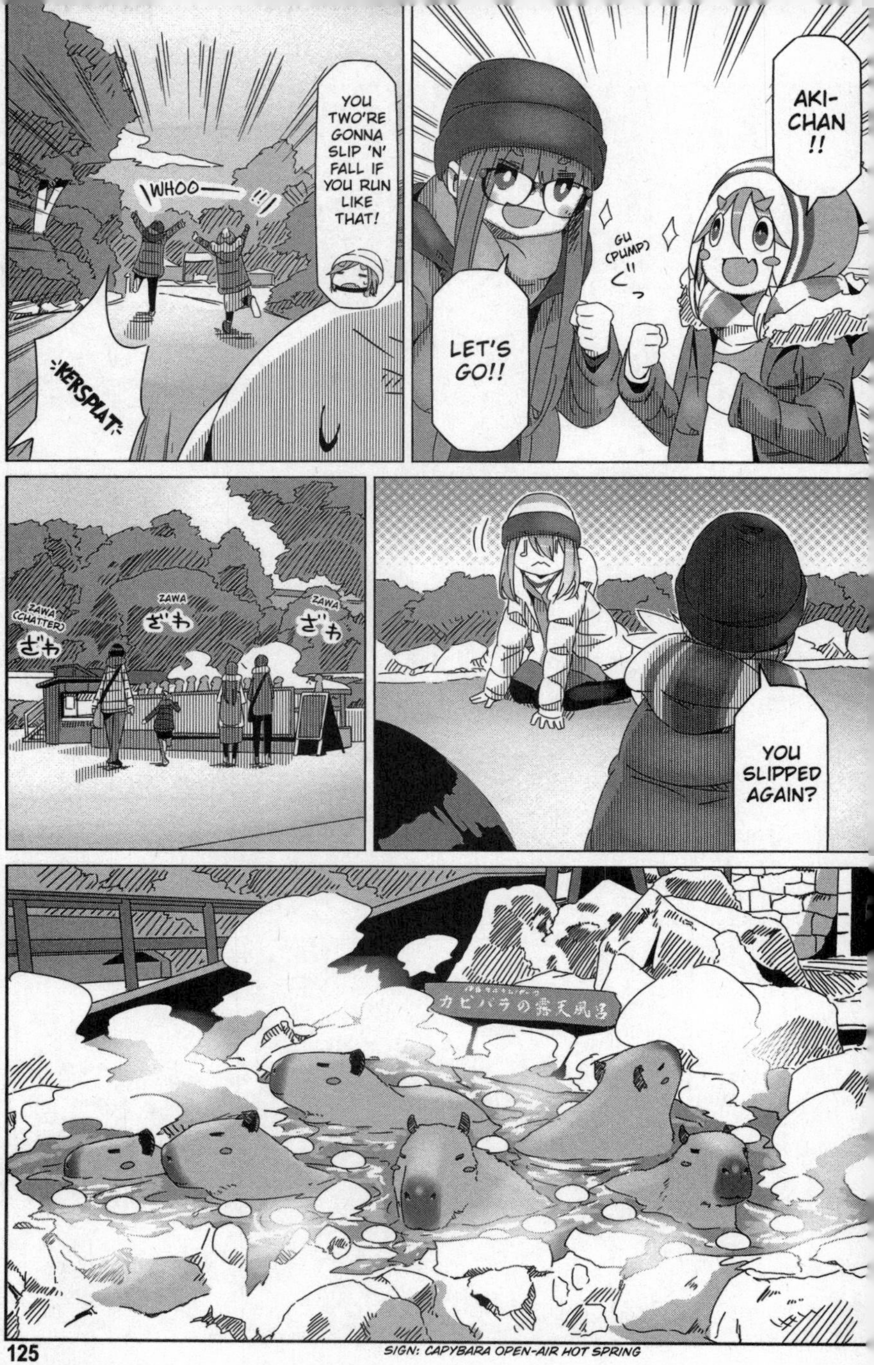
AKI-CHAN!!
GU (PUMP)
LET'S GO!!
YOU TWO'RE GONNA SLIP 'N' FALL IF YOU RUN LIKE THAT!
WHOO—!!
KERSPLAT
YOU SLIPPED AGAIN?
ZAWA
ZAWA
ZAWA (CHATTER)
ざわ
ざわ
ざわ
カピバラの露天風呂

SIGN: CAPYBARA OPEN-AIR HOT SPRING

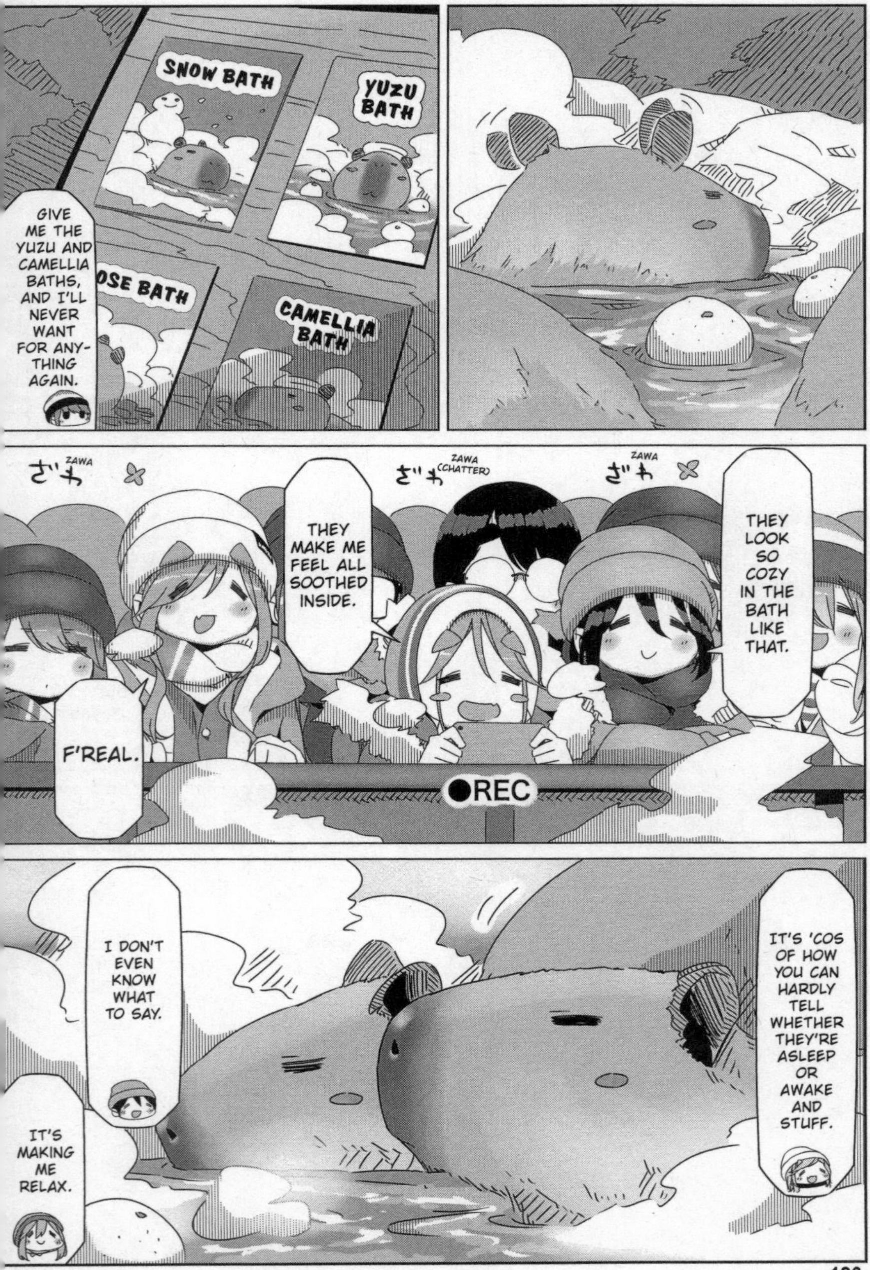
SNOW BATH
YUZU BATH
OSE BATH
CAMELLIA BATH
GIVE ME THE YUZU AND CAMELLIA BATHS, AND I'LL NEVER WANT FOR ANYTHING AGAIN.
ざわ ZAWA
THEY LOOK SO COZY IN THE BATH LIKE THAT.
ざわ ZAWA (CHATTER)
THEY MAKE ME FEEL ALL SOOTHED INSIDE.
ざわ ZAWA
F'REAL.
●REC
IT'S 'COS OF HOW YOU CAN HARDLY TELL WHETHER THEY'RE ASLEEP OR AWAKE AND STUFF.
I DON'T EVEN KNOW WHAT TO SAY.
IT'S MAKING ME RELAX.

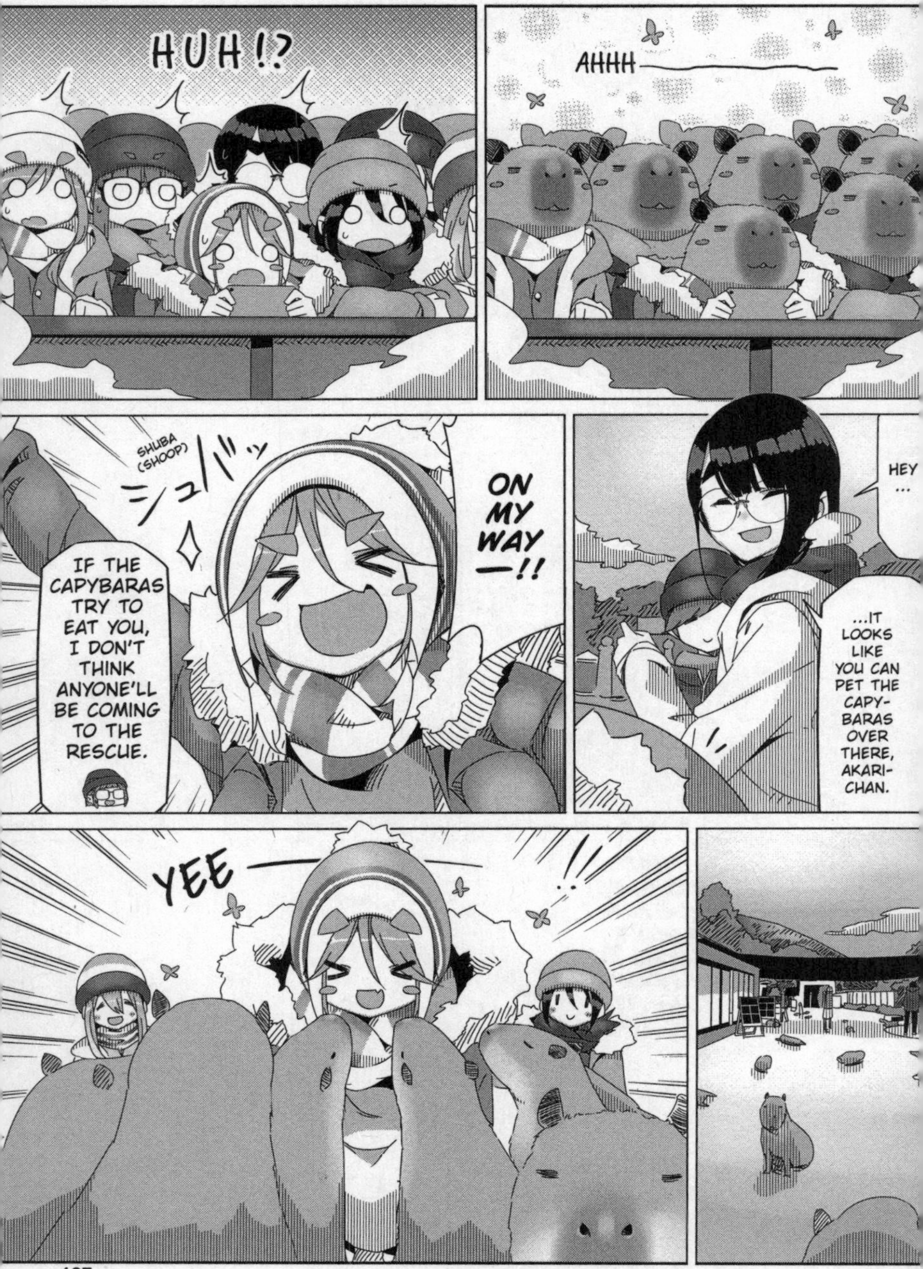
AHHH——
HUH!?
HEY ...
...IT LOOKS LIKE YOU CAN PET THE CAPY-BARAS OVER THERE, AKARI-CHAN.
ON MY WAY—!!
SHUBA (SHOOP)
シュバッ
IF THE CAPYBARAS TRY TO EAT YOU, I DON'T THINK ANYONE'LL BE COMING TO THE RESCUE.
YEE—

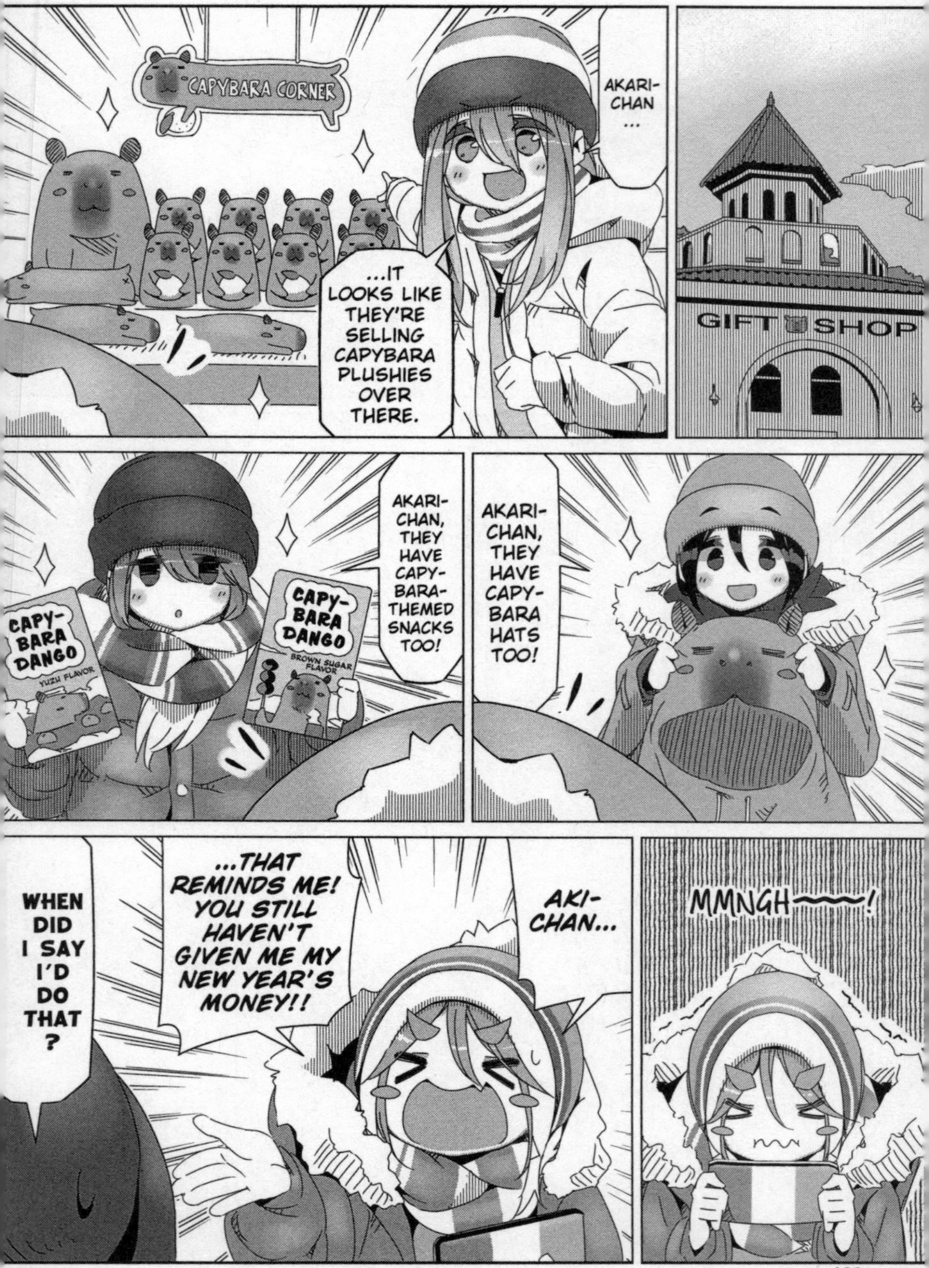
GIFT SHOP
AKARI-CHAN ...
CAPYBARA CORNER
...IT LOOKS LIKE THEY'RE SELLING CAPYBARA PLUSHIES OVER THERE.
AKARI-CHAN, THEY HAVE CAPY-BARA HATS TOO!
AKARI-CHAN, THEY HAVE CAPY-BARA-THEMED SNACKS TOO!
CAPY-BARA DANGO BROWN SUGAR FLAVOR
CAPY-BARA DANGO YUZU FLAVOR
MMNGH——!
AKI-CHAN...
...THAT REMINDS ME! YOU STILL HAVEN'T GIVEN ME MY NEW YEAR'S MONEY!!
WHEN DID I SAY I'D DO THAT?

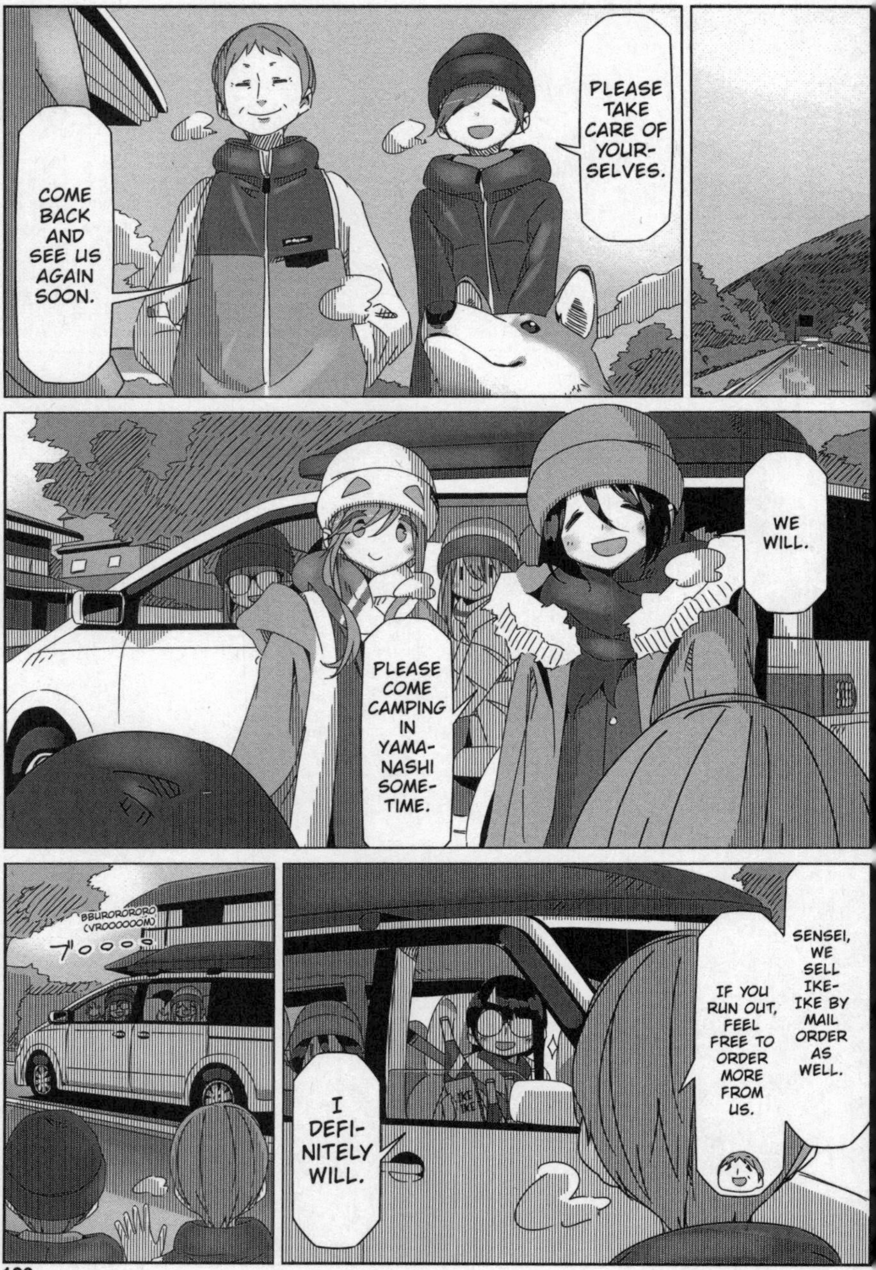
PLEASE TAKE CARE OF YOURSELVES.
COME BACK AND SEE US AGAIN SOON.
WE WILL.
PLEASE COME CAMPING IN YAMANASHI SOMETIME.
SENSEI, WE SELL IKE-IKE BY MAIL ORDER AS WELL.
IF YOU RUN OUT, FEEL FREE TO ORDER MORE FROM US.
I DEFINITELY WILL.
BBURORORORO (VROOOOOOM)

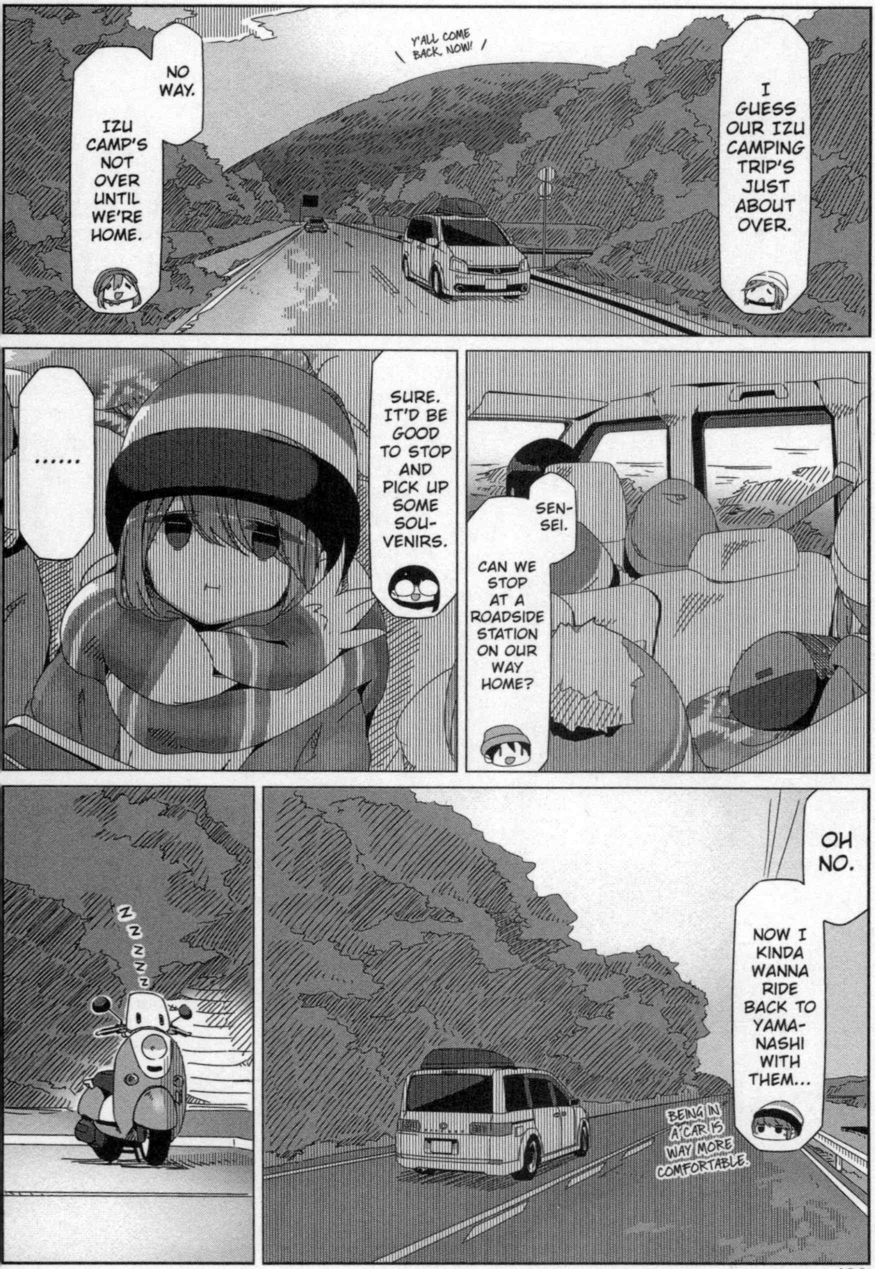
I GUESS OUR IZU CAMPING TRIP'S JUST ABOUT OVER.
Y'ALL COME BACK, NOW!
NO WAY.
IZU CAMP'S NOT OVER UNTIL WE'RE HOME.
SEN-SEI.
CAN WE STOP AT A ROADSIDE STATION ON OUR WAY HOME?
SURE. IT'D BE GOOD TO STOP AND PICK UP SOME SOU-VENIRS.
......
OH NO.
NOW I KINDA WANNA RIDE BACK TO YAMA-NASHI WITH THEM...
BEING IN A CAR IS WAY MORE COMFORTABLE.
Z Z Z Z Z

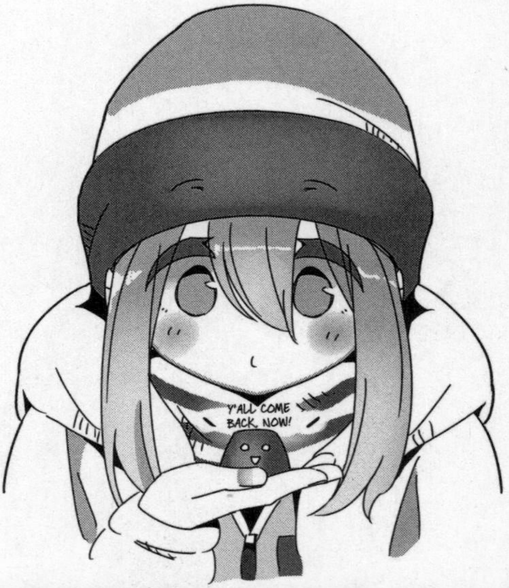
Y'ALL COME BACK, NOW!

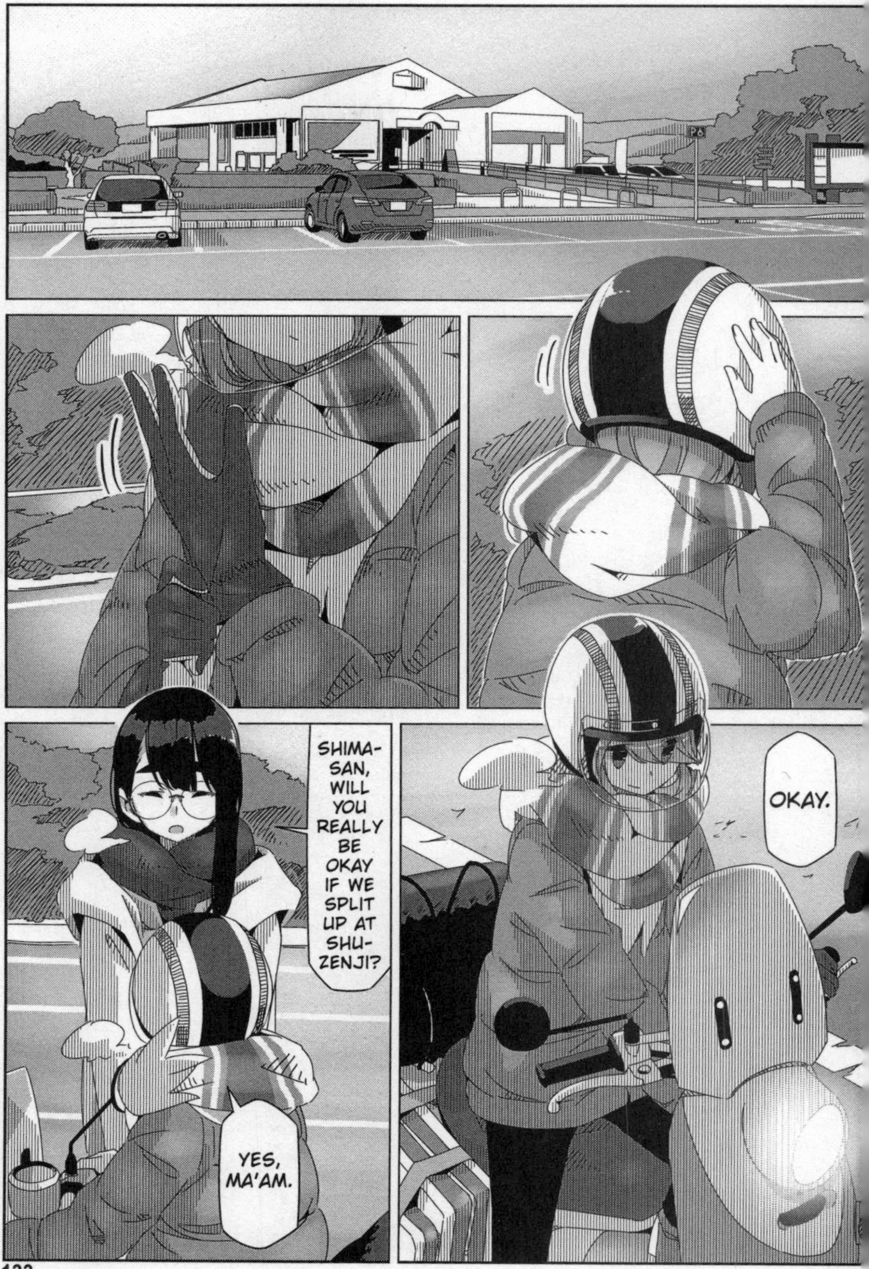
OKAY.
SHIMA-SAN, WILL YOU REALLY BE OKAY IF WE SPLIT UP AT SHUZENJI?
YES, MA'AM.

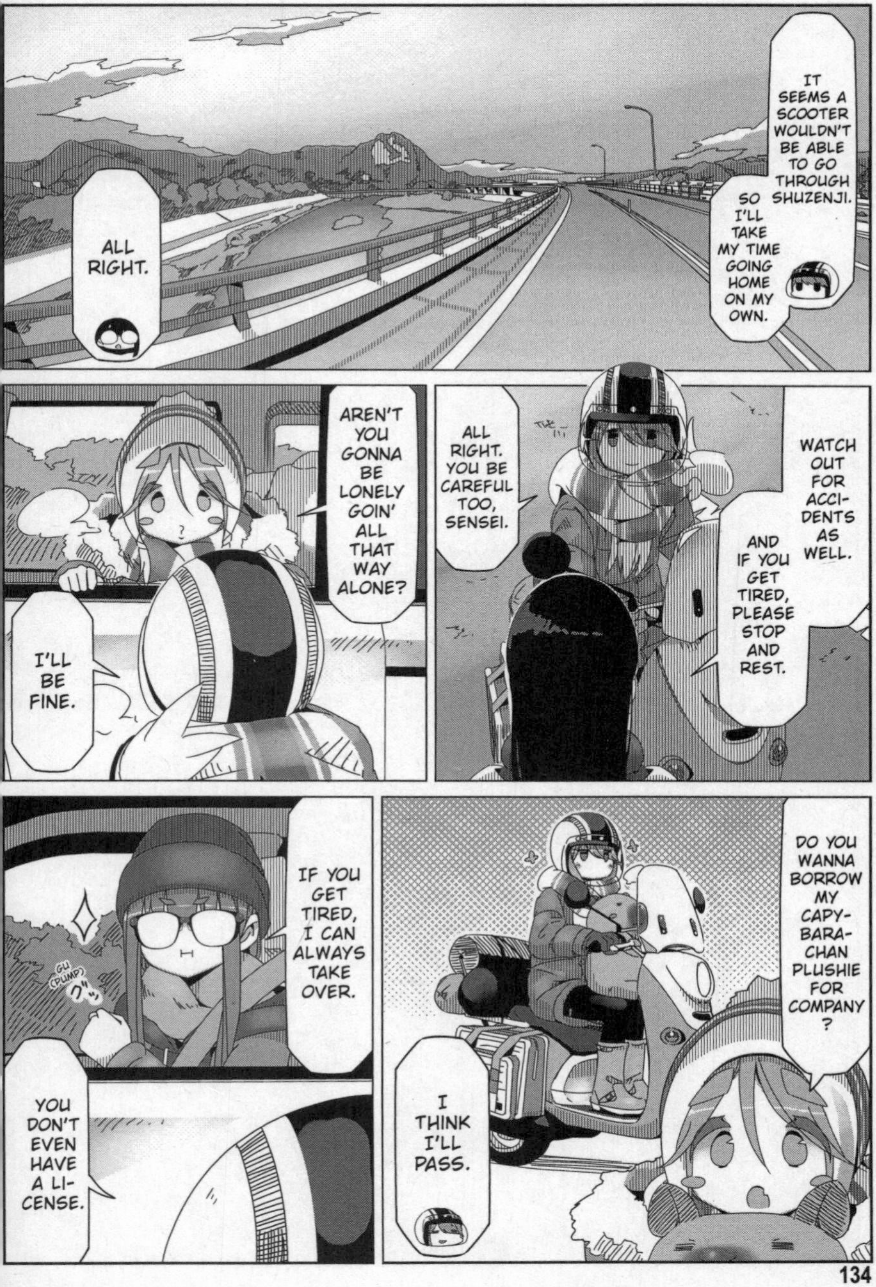
IT SEEMS A SCOOTER WOULDN'T BE ABLE TO GO THROUGH SHUZENJI.
SO I'LL TAKE MY TIME GOING HOME ON MY OWN.
ALL RIGHT.
WATCH OUT FOR ACCI-DENTS AS WELL.
AND IF YOU GET TIRED, PLEASE STOP AND REST.
ALL RIGHT. YOU BE CAREFUL TOO, SENSEI.
AREN'T YOU GONNA BE LONELY GOIN' ALL THAT WAY ALONE?
I'LL BE FINE.
DO YOU WANNA BORROW MY CAPY-BARA-CHAN PLUSHIE FOR COMPANY?
I THINK I'LL PASS.
IF YOU GET TIRED, I CAN ALWAYS TAKE OVER.
GU (PUMP)
YOU DON'T EVEN HAVE A LI-CENSE.

CHAPTER 52 TO A JOURNEY'S END

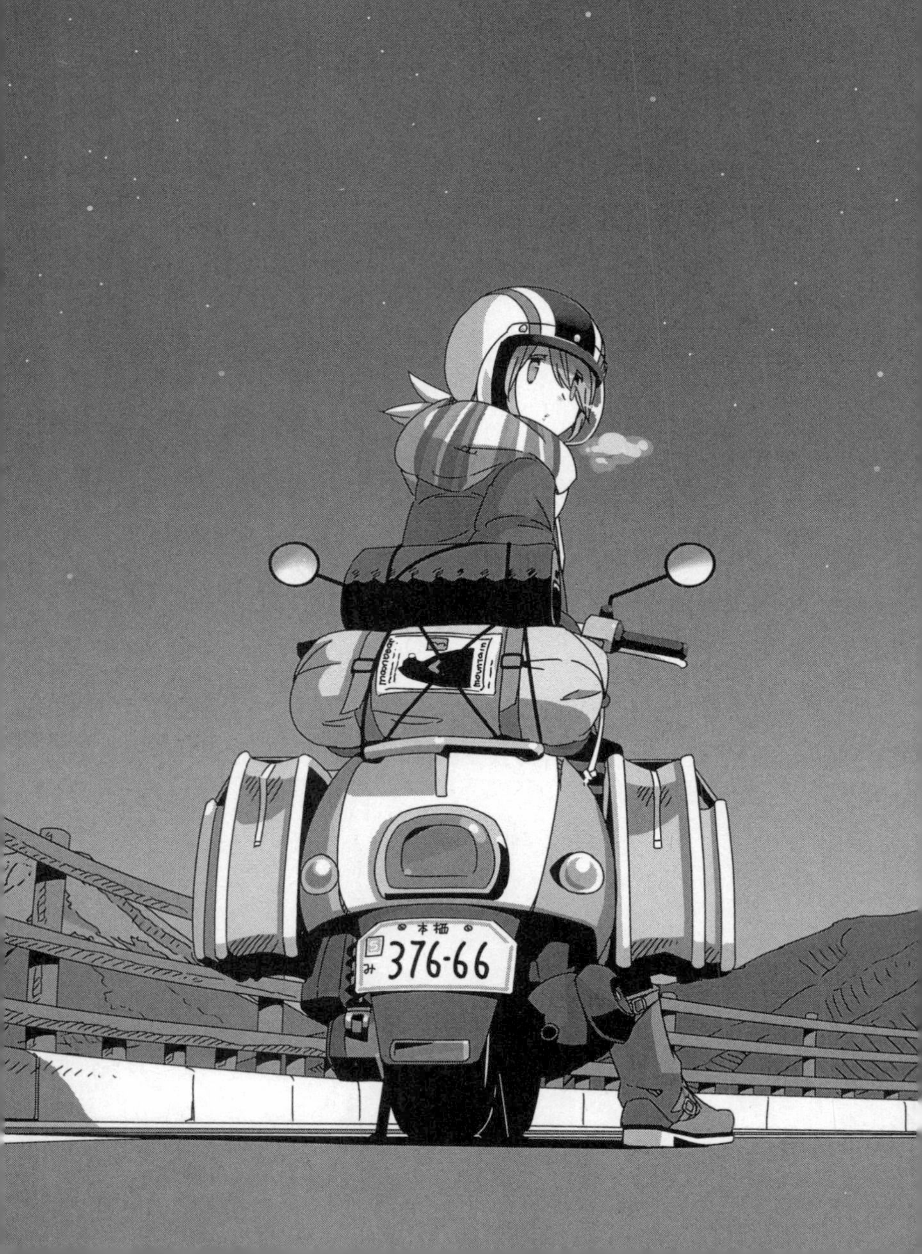
本栖
み 376-66

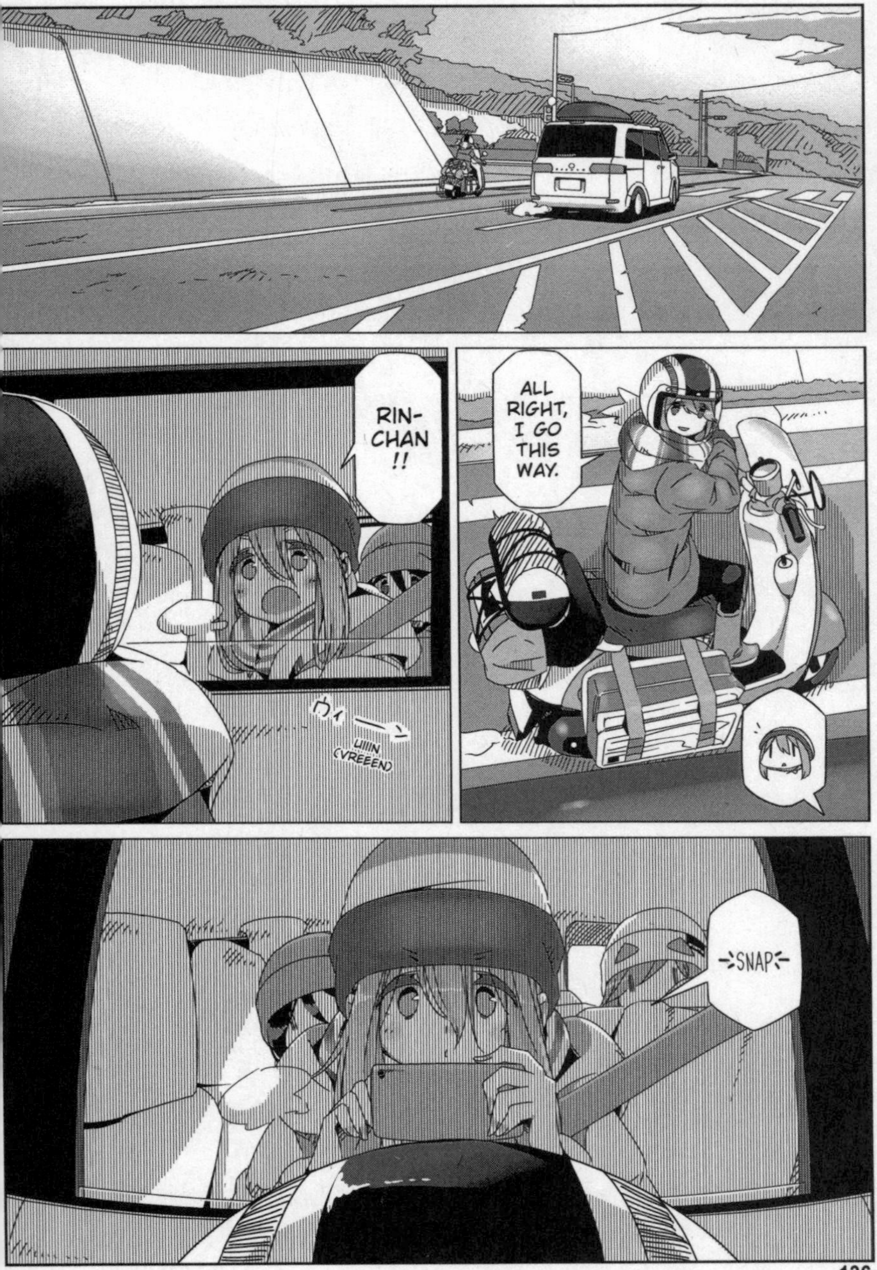
ALL RIGHT, I GO THIS WAY.
RIN-CHAN!!
UIIIN (VREEEN)
SNAP

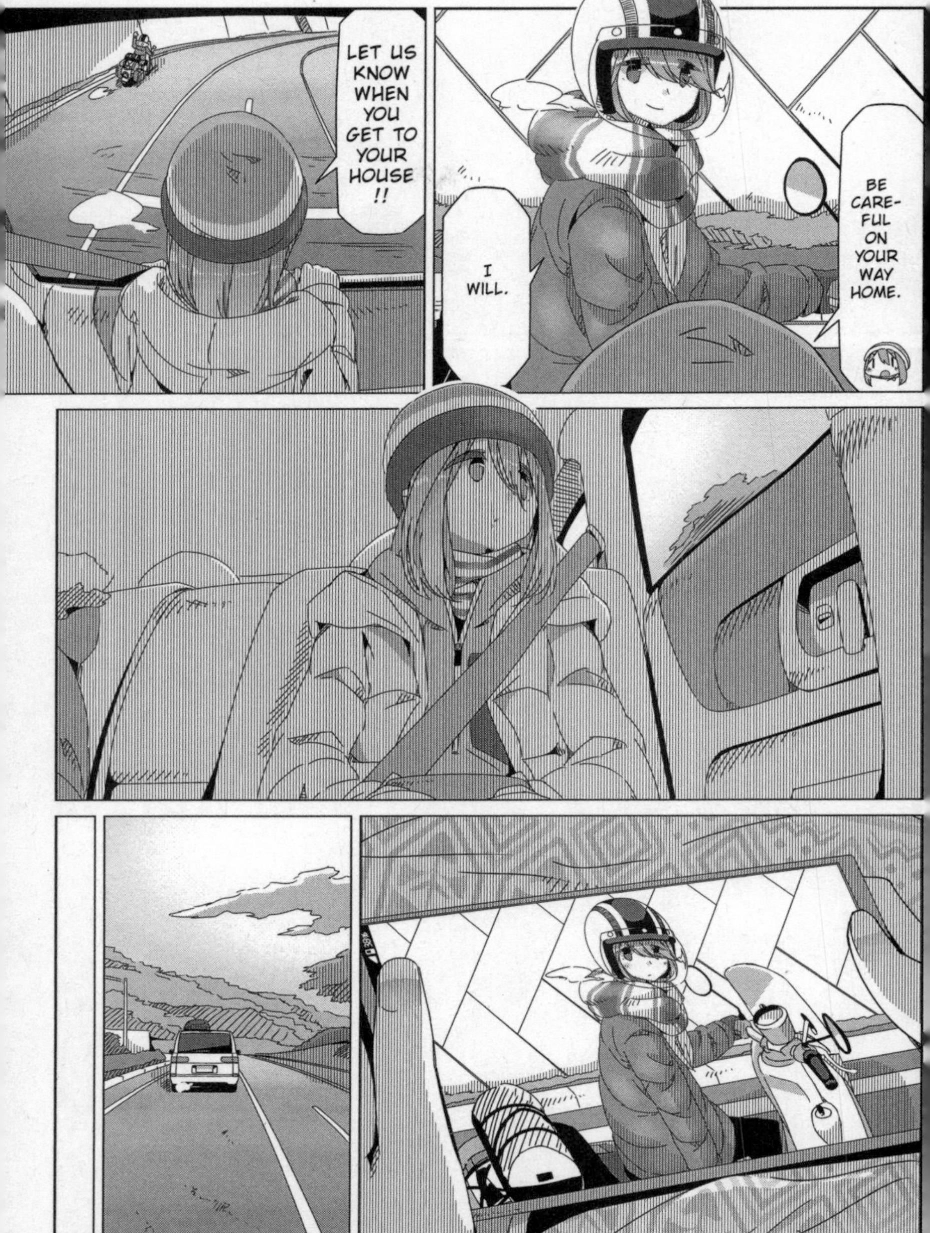
BE CARE-FUL ON YOUR WAY HOME.
I WILL.
LET US KNOW WHEN YOU GET TO YOUR HOUSE !!

SIGN: NO PARKING ON SHOULDER

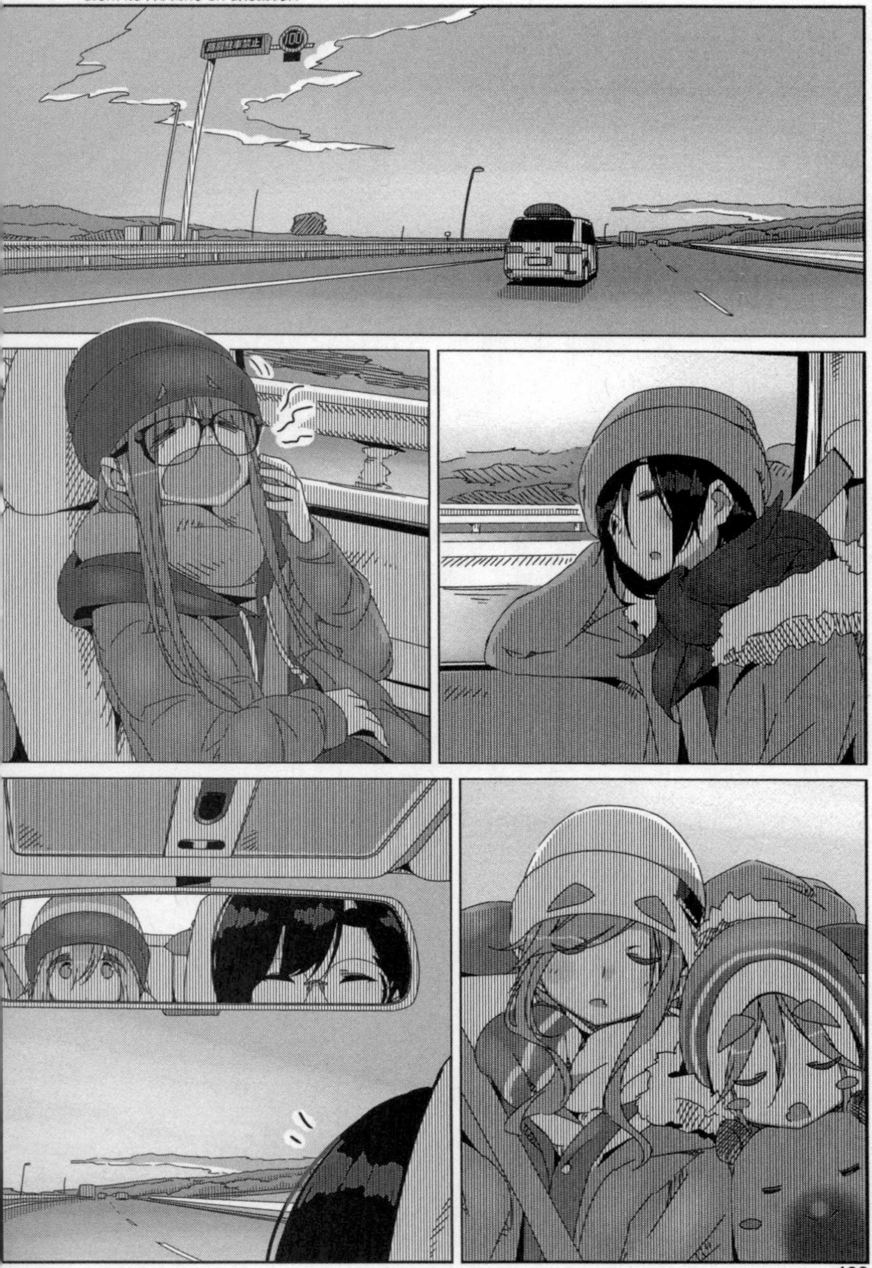

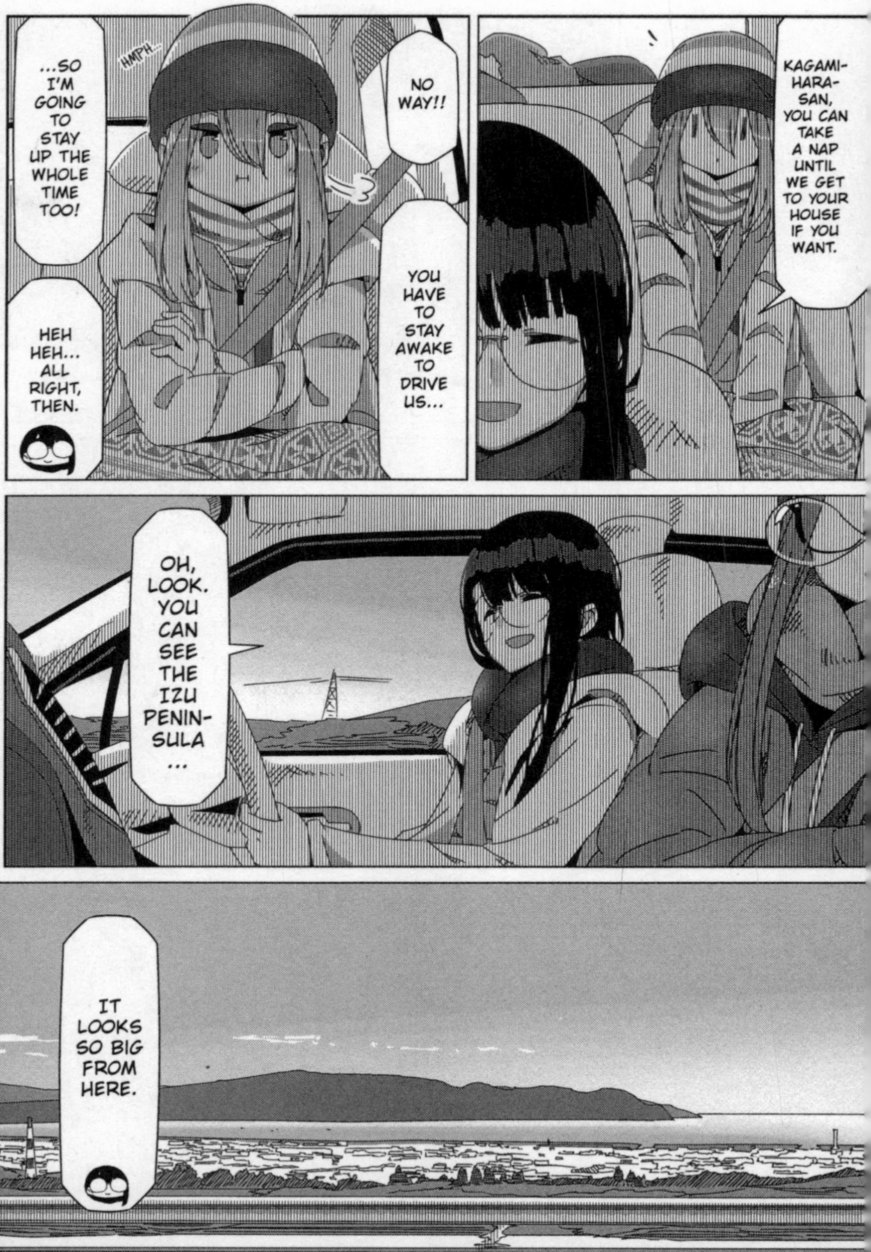
!
KAGAMI-HARA-SAN, YOU CAN TAKE A NAP UNTIL WE GET TO YOUR HOUSE IF YOU WANT.
NO WAY!!
YOU HAVE TO STAY AWAKE TO DRIVE US...
HMPH...
...SO I'M GOING TO STAY UP THE WHOLE TIME TOO!
HEH HEH... ALL RIGHT, THEN.
OH, LOOK. YOU CAN SEE THE IZU PENIN-SULA ...
IT LOOKS SO BIG FROM HERE.

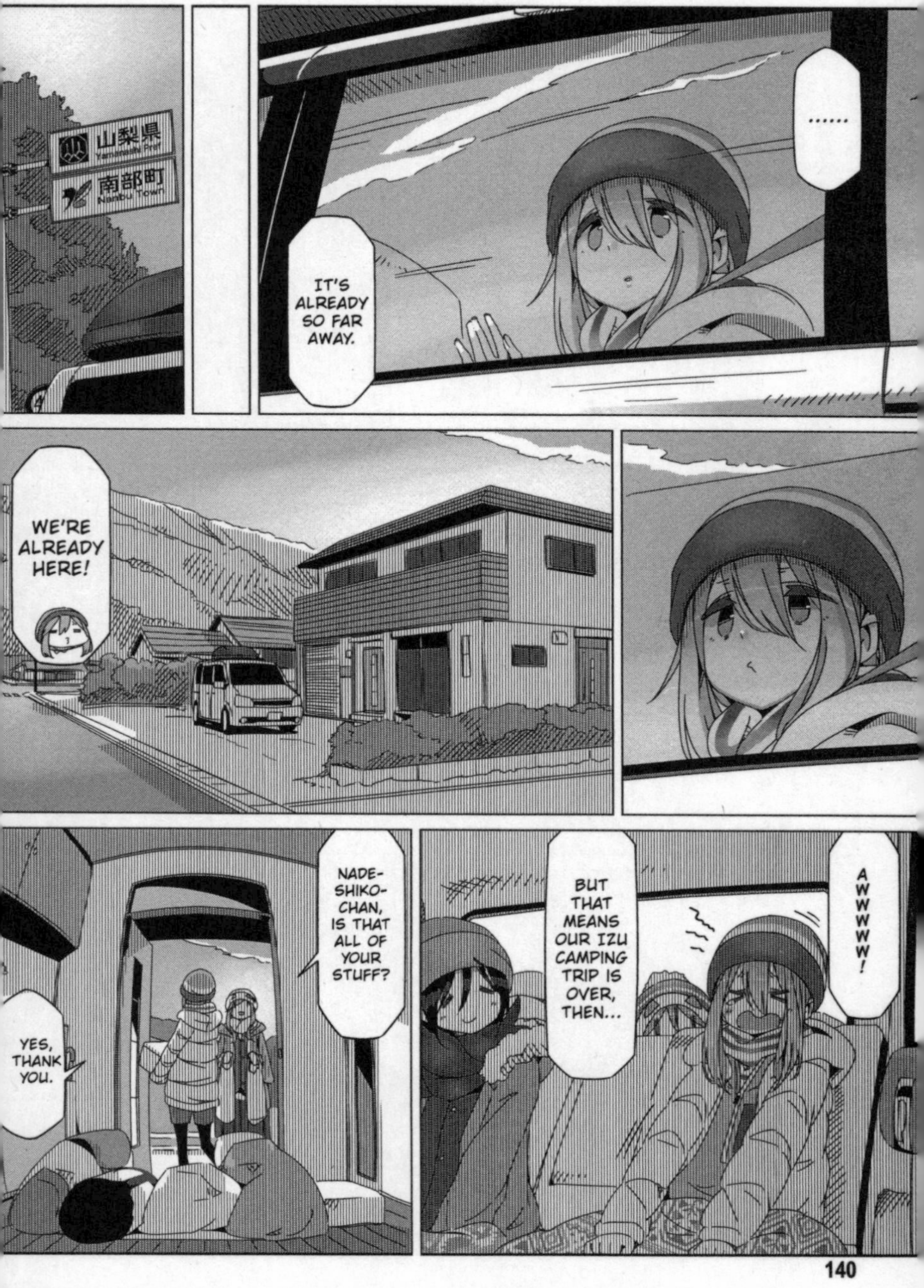
......
IT'S ALREADY SO FAR AWAY.
山梨県
Yamanashi Pref.
南部町
Nanbu Town
WE'RE ALREADY HERE!
AWWWWWW!
BUT THAT MEANS OUR IZU CAMPING TRIP IS OVER, THEN...
NADE-SHIKO-CHAN, IS THAT ALL OF YOUR STUFF?
YES, THANK YOU.

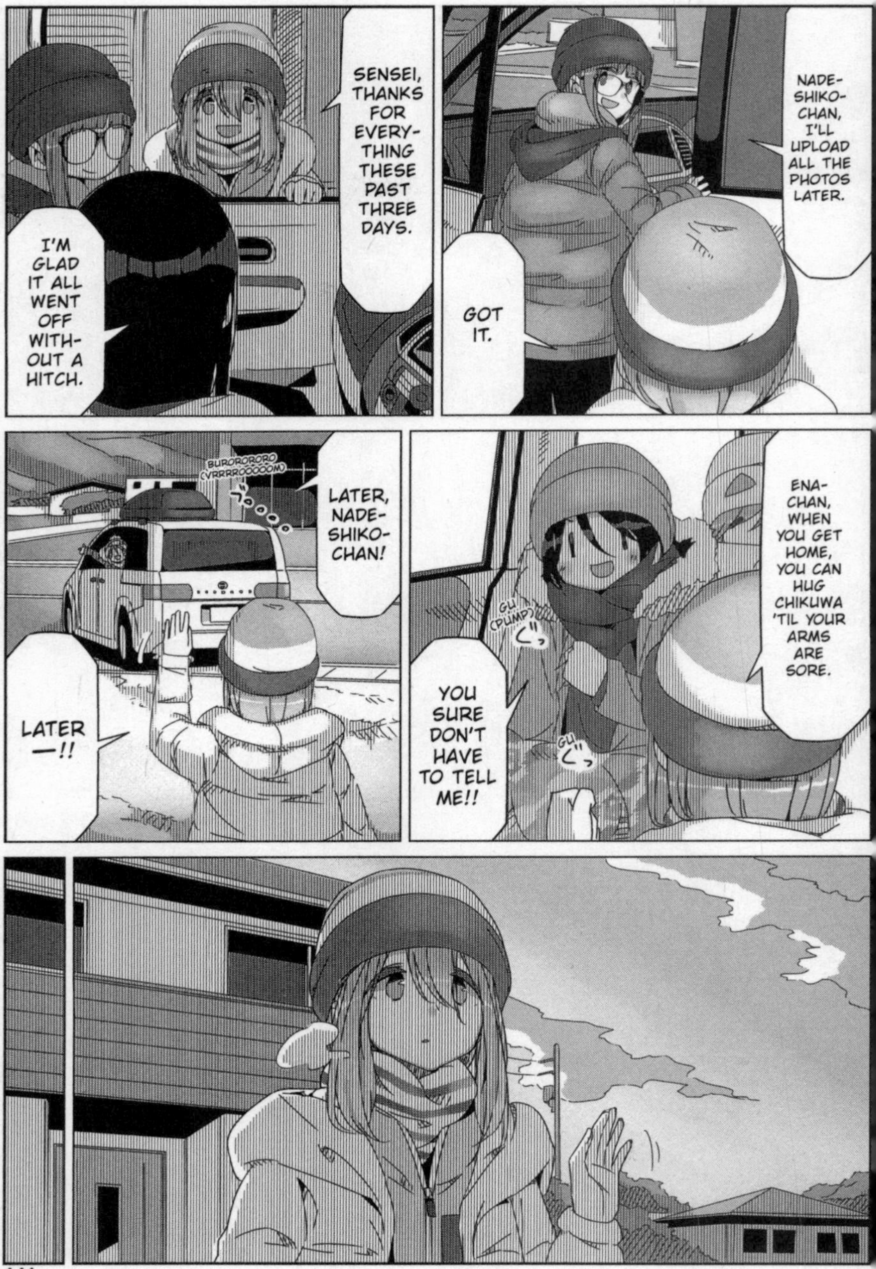
NADE-SHIKO-CHAN, I'LL UPLOAD ALL THE PHOTOS LATER.
GOT IT.
SENSEI, THANKS FOR EVERY-THING THESE PAST THREE DAYS.
I'M GLAD IT ALL WENT OFF WITH-OUT A HITCH.
ENA-CHAN, WHEN YOU GET HOME, YOU CAN HUG CHIKUWA 'TIL YOUR ARMS ARE SORE.
GU (PUMP)
GU
YOU SURE DON'T HAVE TO TELL ME!!
BURORORORO (VRRRROOOOOM)
LATER, NADE-SHIKO-CHAN!
LATER—!!

LOOKS LIKE I MADE IT JUST IN TIME FOR EVENING RUSH HOUR.

(353) 富士宮 10km
Fujinomiya

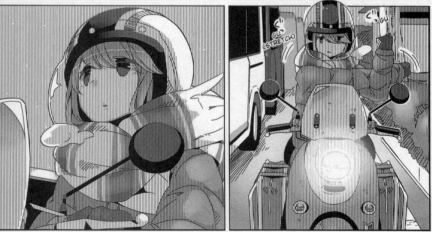

GU
(STRETCH)

GU

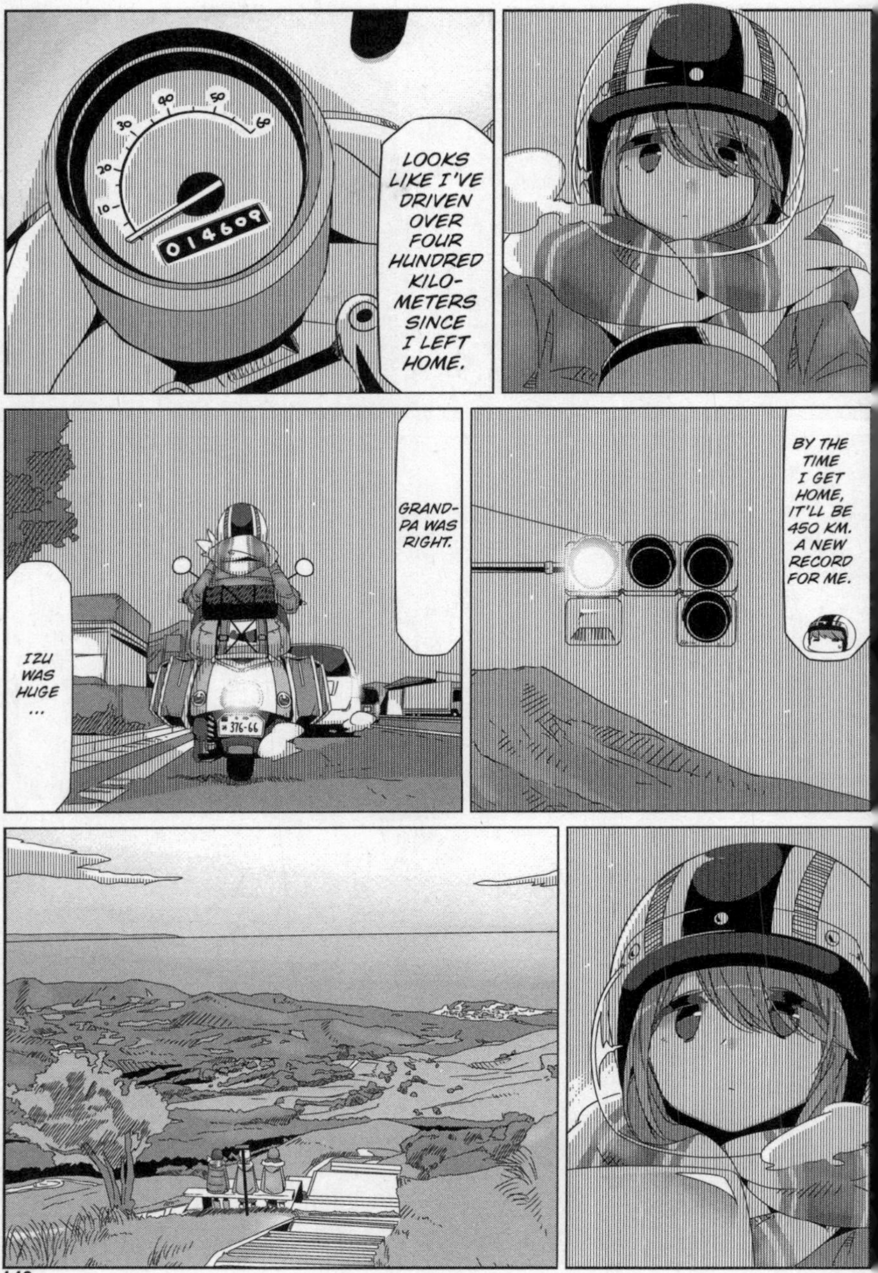
LOOKS LIKE I'VE DRIVEN OVER FOUR HUNDRED KILO-METERS SINCE I LEFT HOME.
BY THE TIME I GET HOME, IT'LL BE 450 KM. A NEW RECORD FOR ME.
GRAND-PA WAS RIGHT.
IZU WAS HUGE ...

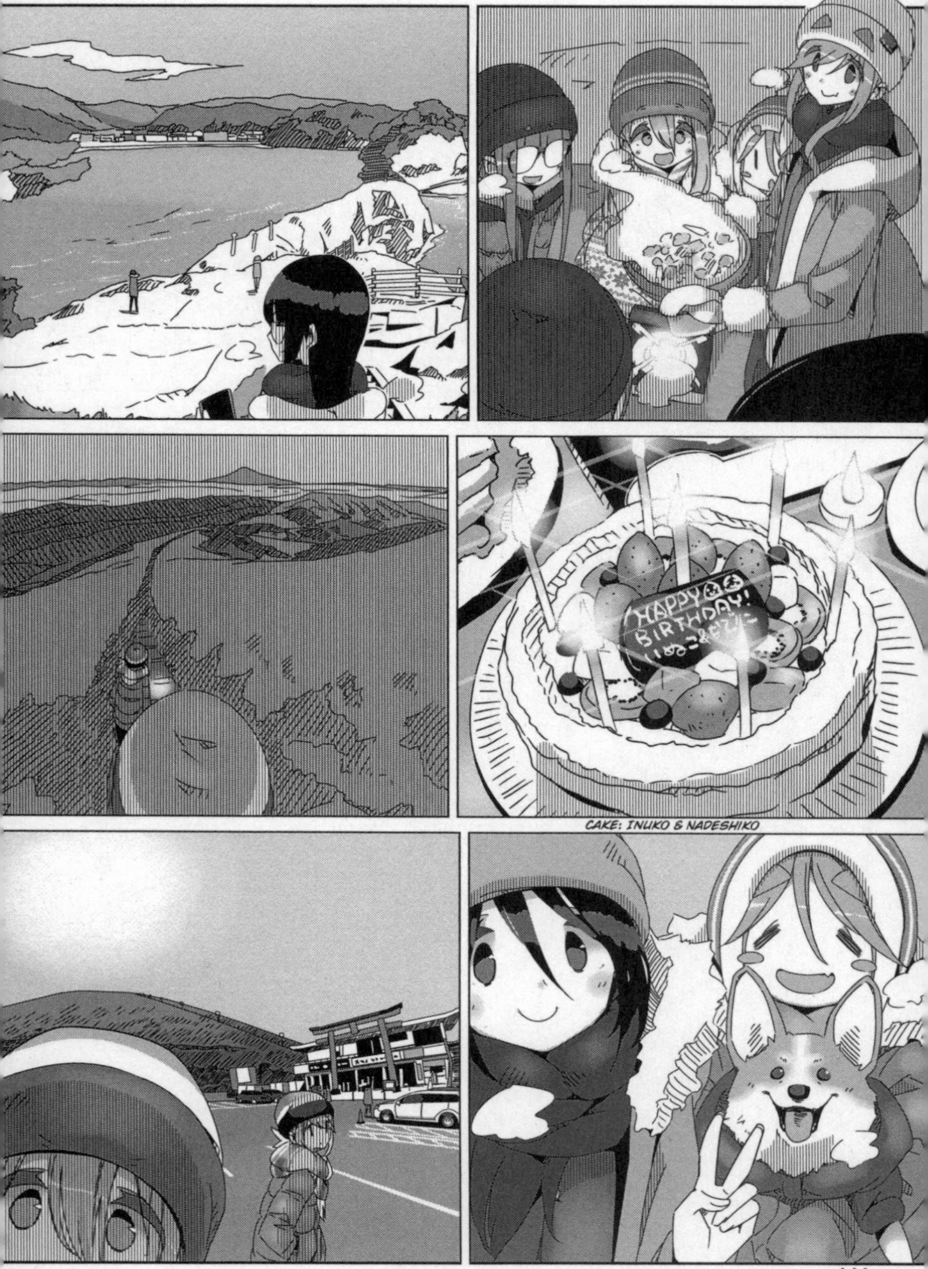
HAPPY
BIRTHDAY!
CAKE: INUKO & NADESHIKO

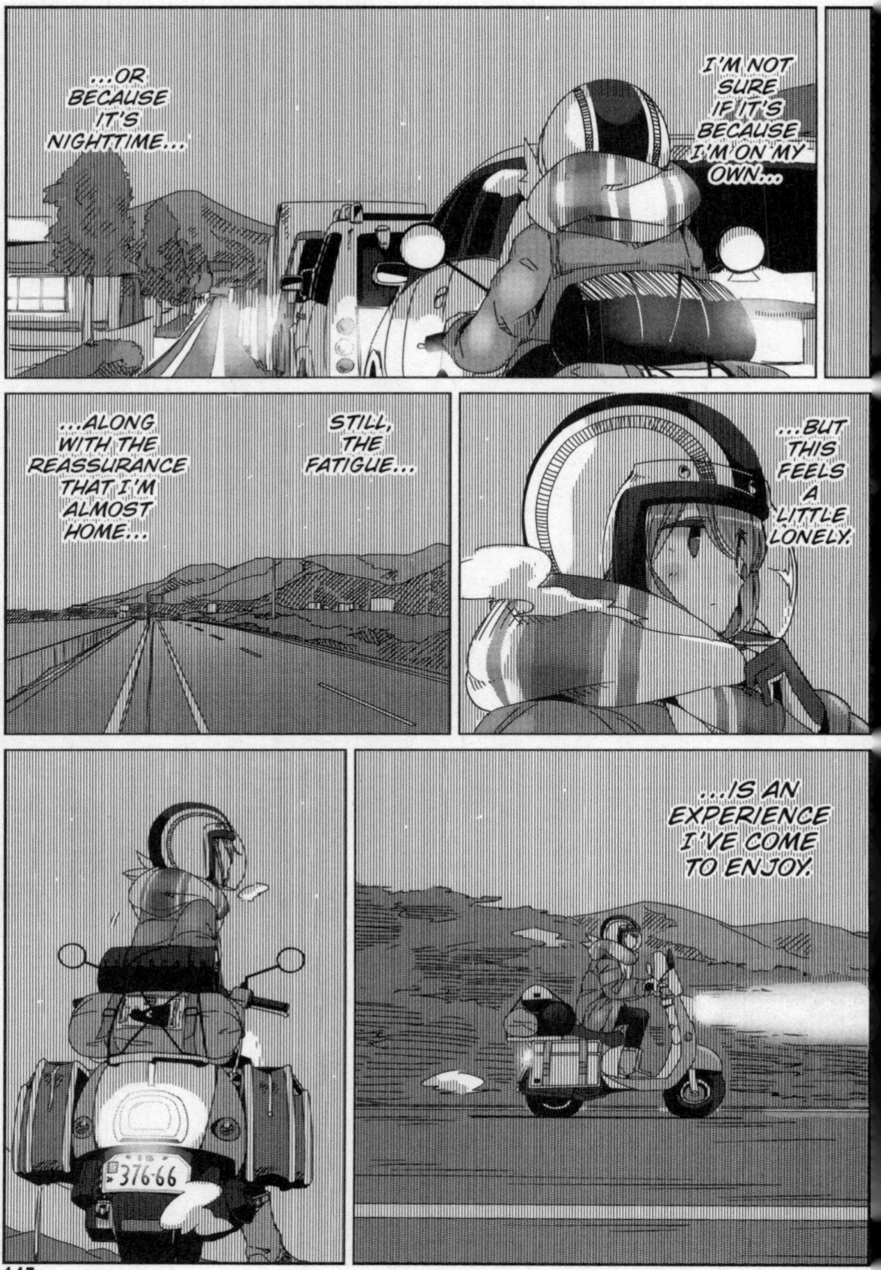
I'M NOT SURE IF IT'S BECAUSE I'M ON MY OWN...
...OR BECAUSE IT'S NIGHTTIME...
...BUT THIS FEELS A LITTLE LONELY.
STILL, THE FATIGUE...
...ALONG WITH THE REASSURANCE THAT I'M ALMOST HOME...
...IS AN EXPERIENCE I'VE COME TO ENJOY.
376-66

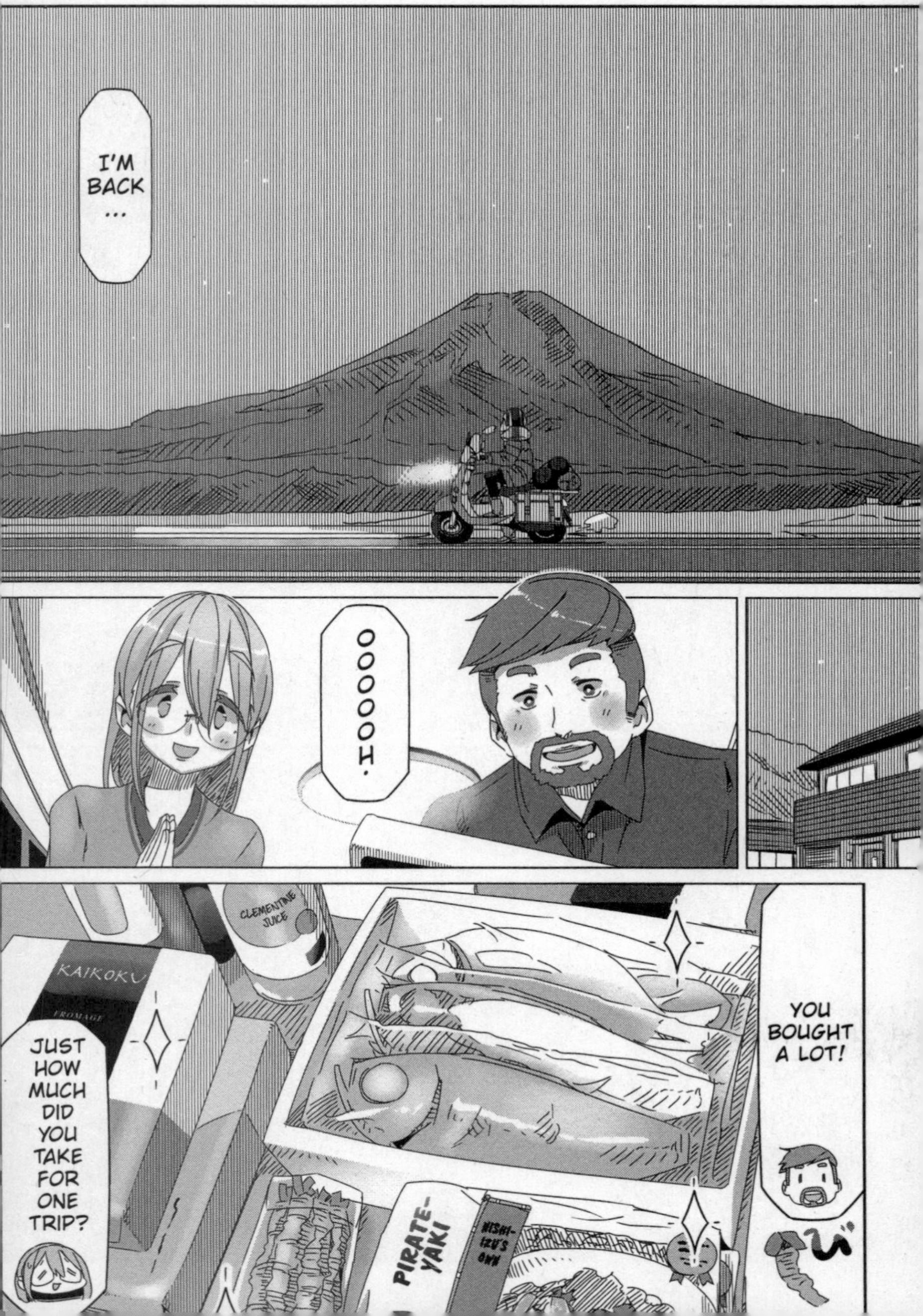
I'M BACK ...
OOOOOH.
YOU BOUGHT A LOT!
CLEMENTINE JUICE
KAIKOKU
FROMAGE
NISHI-IZU'S OWN
PIRATE-YAKI
JUST HOW MUCH DID YOU TAKE FOR ONE TRIP?

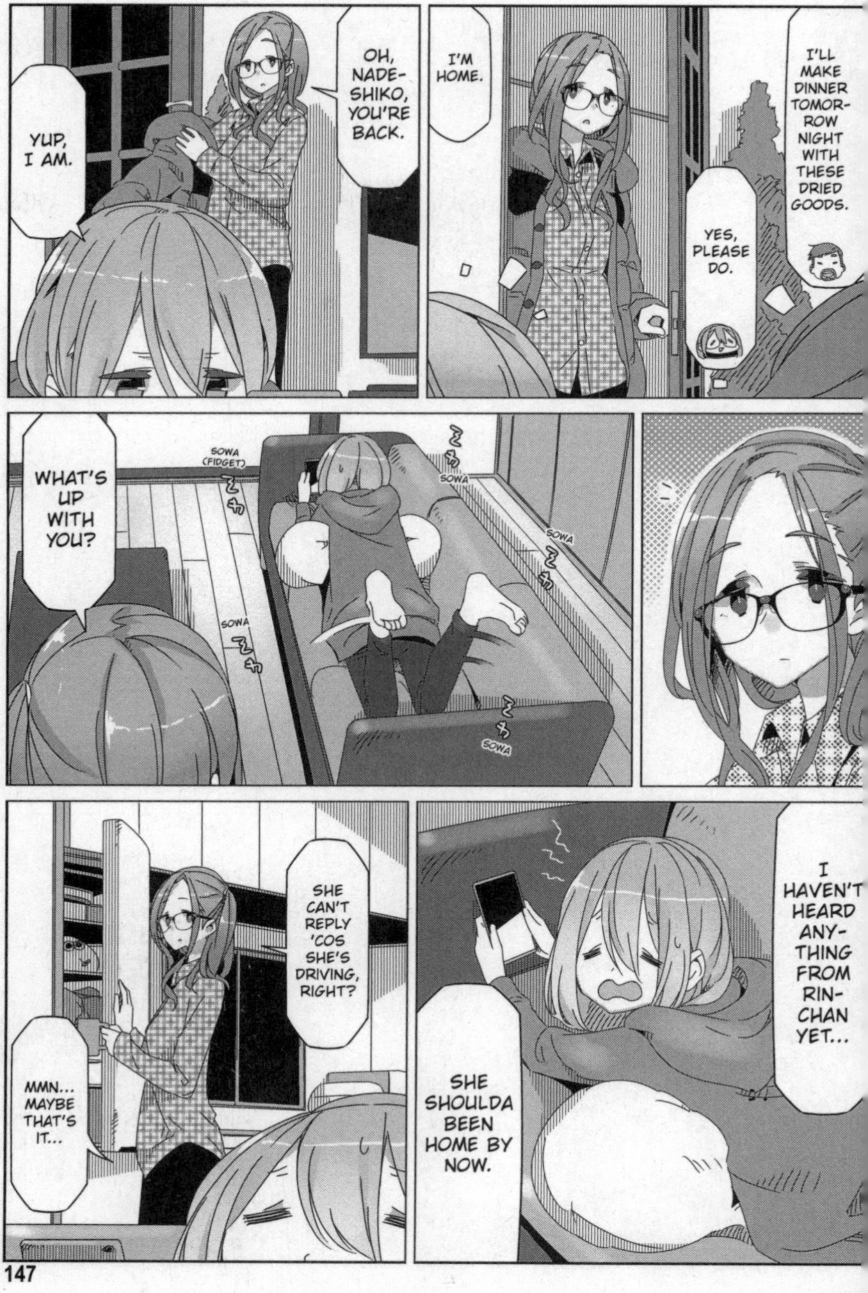
I'M HOME.
I'LL MAKE DINNER TOMORROW NIGHT WITH THESE DRIED GOODS.
YES, PLEASE DO.
OH, NADESHIKO, YOU'RE BACK.
YUP, I AM.
SOWA
SOWA
SOWA (FIDGET)
WHAT'S UP WITH YOU?
SOWA
SOWA
I HAVEN'T HEARD ANYTHING FROM RIN-CHAN YET...
SHE SHOULDA BEEN HOME BY NOW.
SHE CAN'T REPLY 'COS SHE'S DRIVING, RIGHT?
MMN... MAYBE THAT'S IT...

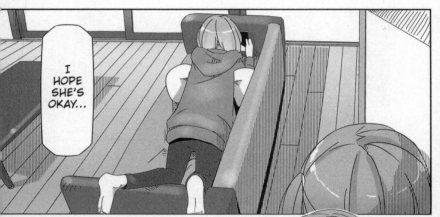

I HOPE SHE'S OKAY...
SIGH...
IT'S SO COLD HERE.
山梨県
Yamanashi Prefecture
身延町
Minobu Town
MADE IT TO MINO-BU!
BIIIN (VREEEN)
ビイーーン

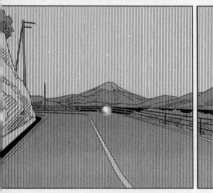

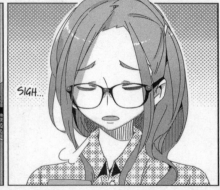

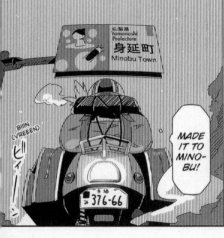

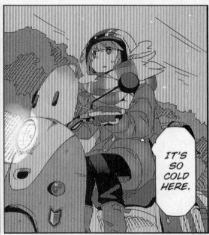

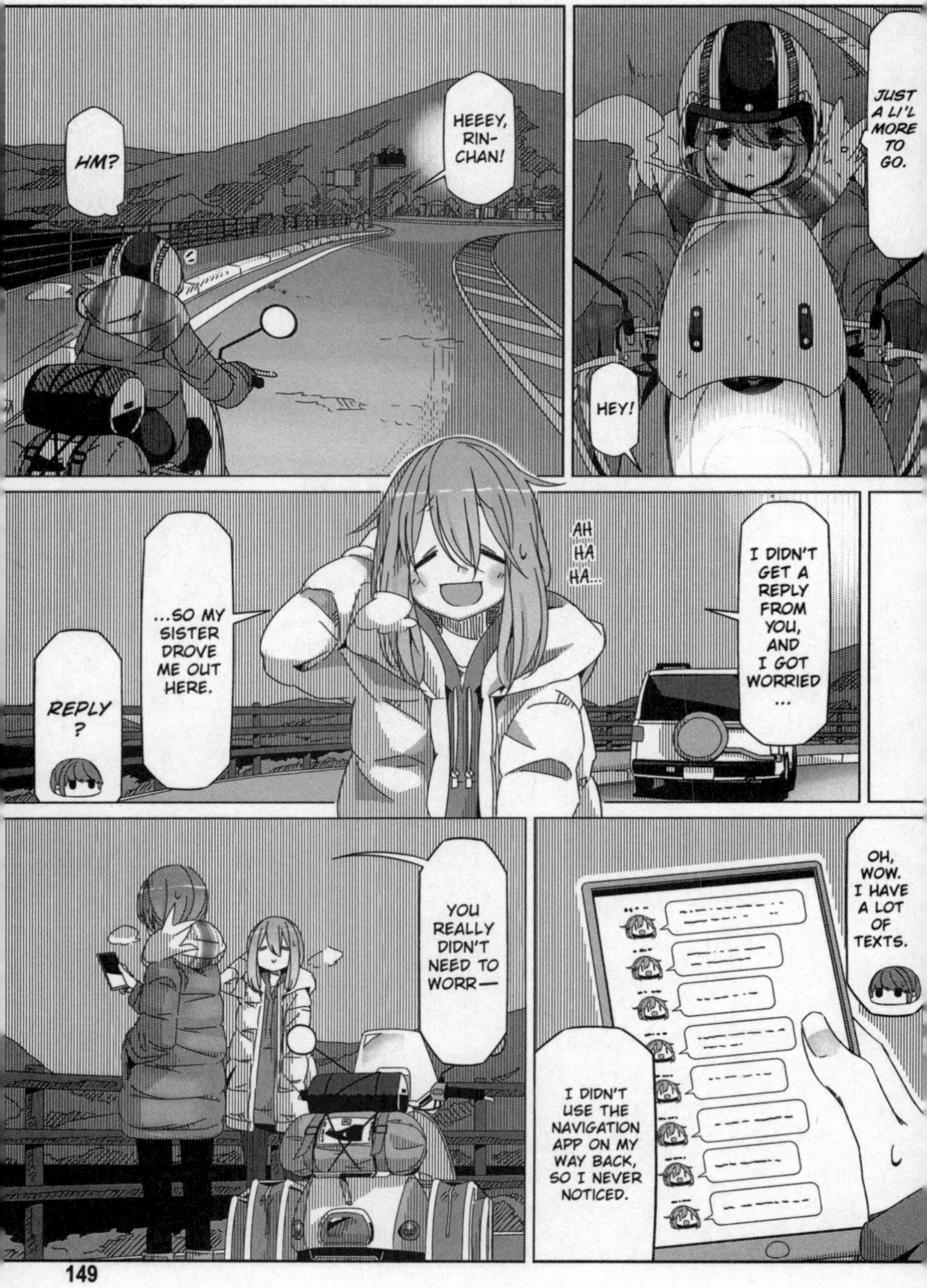
JUST A LI'L MORE TO GO.
HEY!
HEEEY, RIN-CHAN!
HM?
I DIDN'T GET A REPLY FROM YOU, AND I GOT WORRIED...
AH HA HA...
...SO MY SISTER DROVE ME OUT HERE.
REPLY?
OH, WOW. I HAVE A LOT OF TEXTS.
I DIDN'T USE THE NAVIGATION APP ON MY WAY BACK, SO I NEVER NOTICED.
YOU REALLY DIDN'T NEED TO WORR—

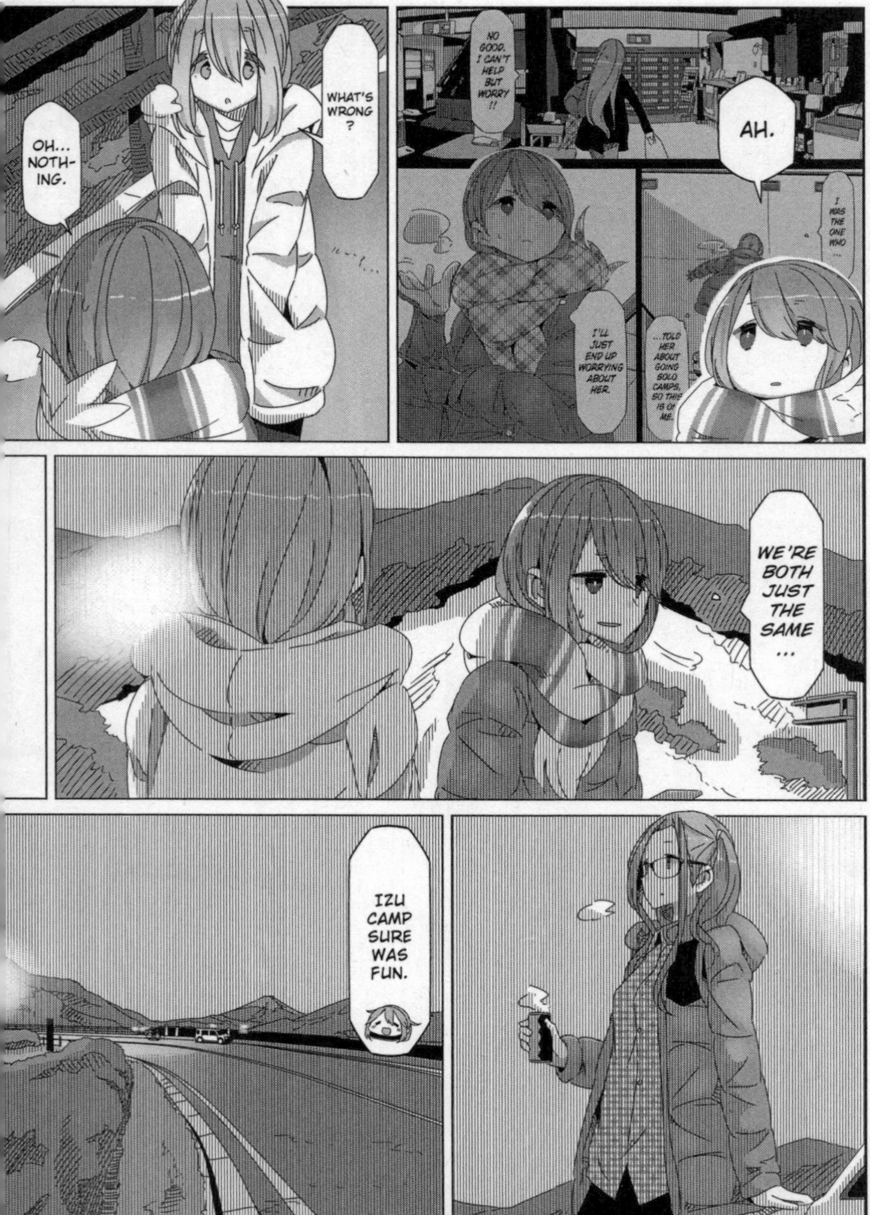
NO GOOD. I CAN'T HELP BUT WORRY!!
AH.
I WAS THE ONE WHO...
...TOLD HER ABOUT GOING SOLO CAMPS, SO THIS IS ON ME.
I'LL JUST END UP WORRYING ABOUT HER.
WHAT'S WRONG?
OH... NOTHING.
WE'RE BOTH JUST THE SAME...
IZU CAMP SURE WAS FUN.

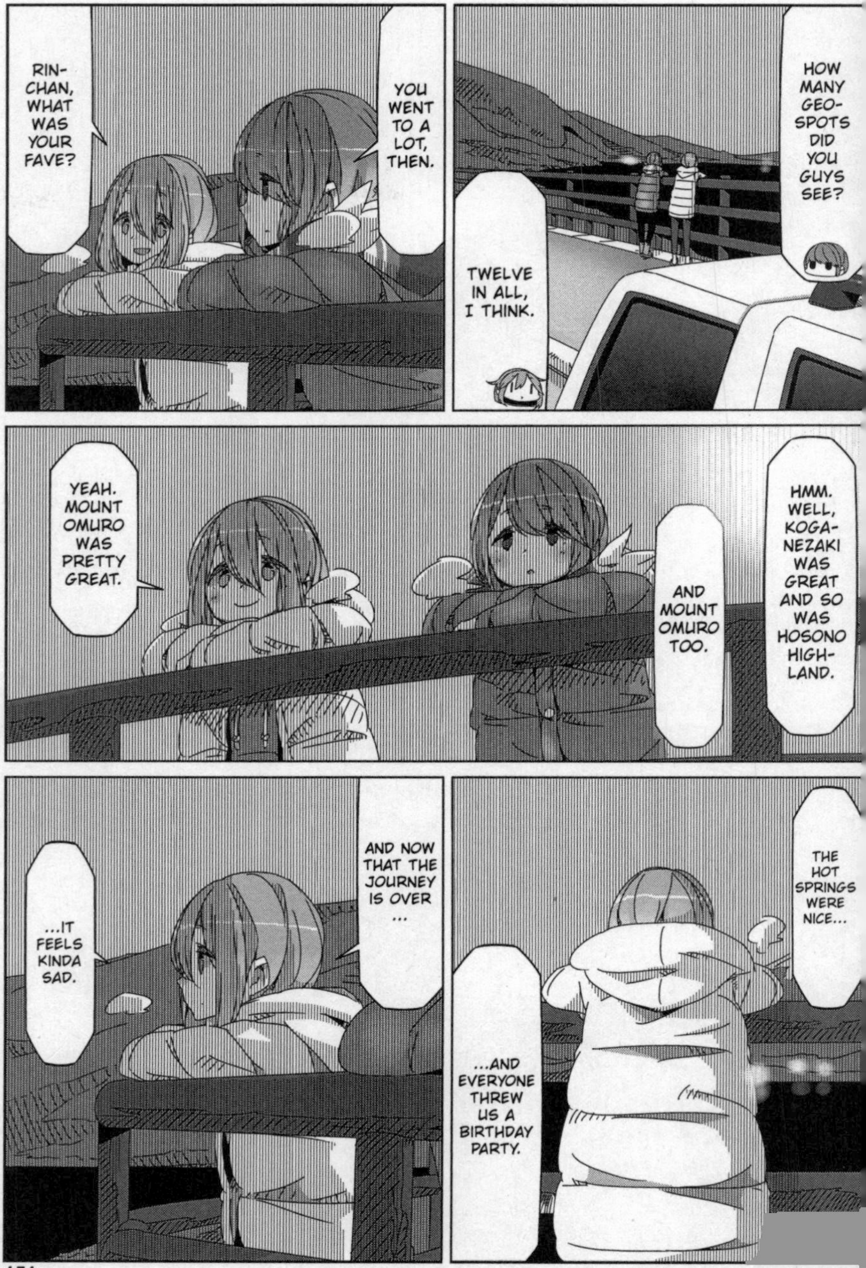
HOW MANY GEO-SPOTS DID YOU GUYS SEE?
TWELVE IN ALL, I THINK.
YOU WENT TO A LOT, THEN.
RIN-CHAN, WHAT WAS YOUR FAVE?
HMM. WELL, KOGA-NEZAKI WAS GREAT AND SO WAS HOSONO HIGH-LAND.
AND MOUNT OMURO TOO.
YEAH. MOUNT OMURO WAS PRETTY GREAT.
THE HOT SPRINGS WERE NICE...
...AND EVERYONE THREW US A BIRTHDAY PARTY.
AND NOW THAT THE JOURNEY IS OVER...
...IT FEELS KINDA SAD.

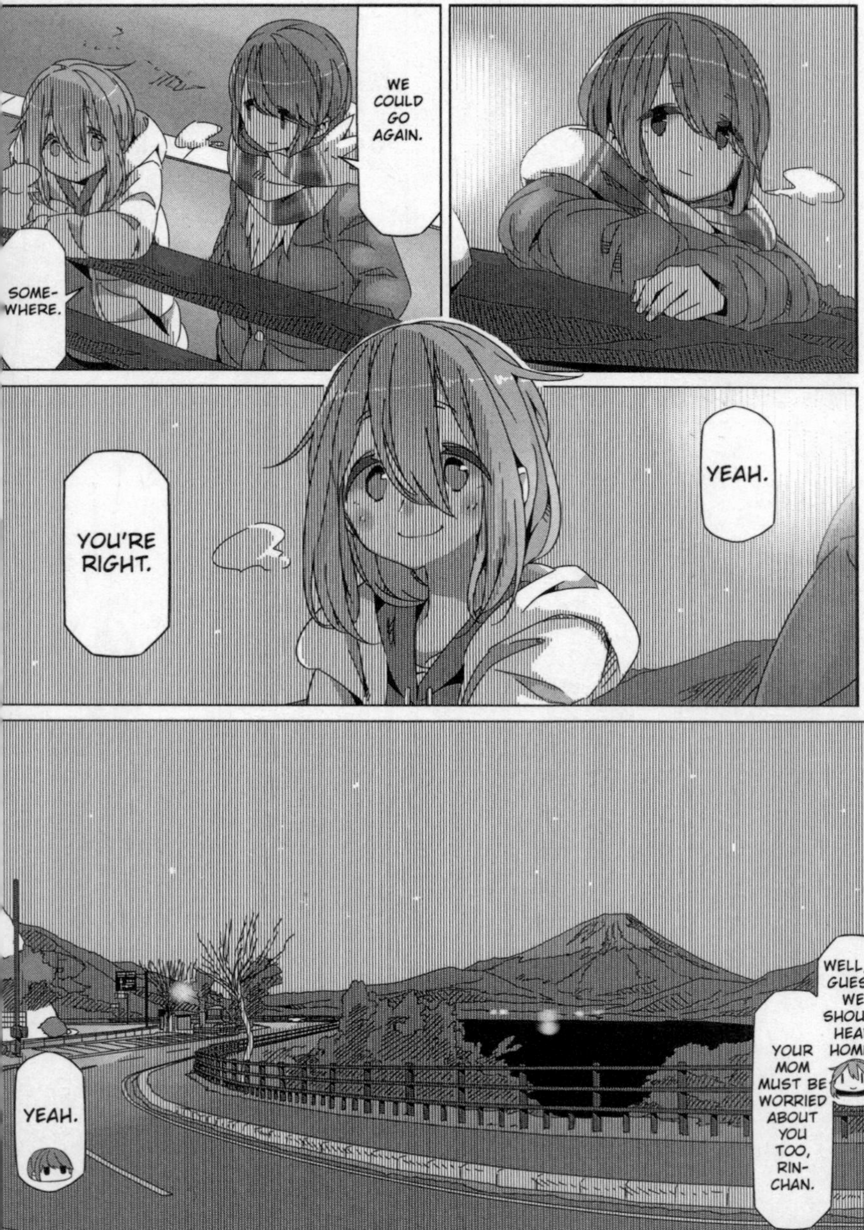
WE COULD GO AGAIN.
SOME-WHERE.
YEAH.
YOU'RE RIGHT.
WELL, I GUESS WE SHOULD HEAD HOME.
YOUR MOM MUST BE WORRIED ABOUT YOU TOO, RIN-CHAN.
YEAH.

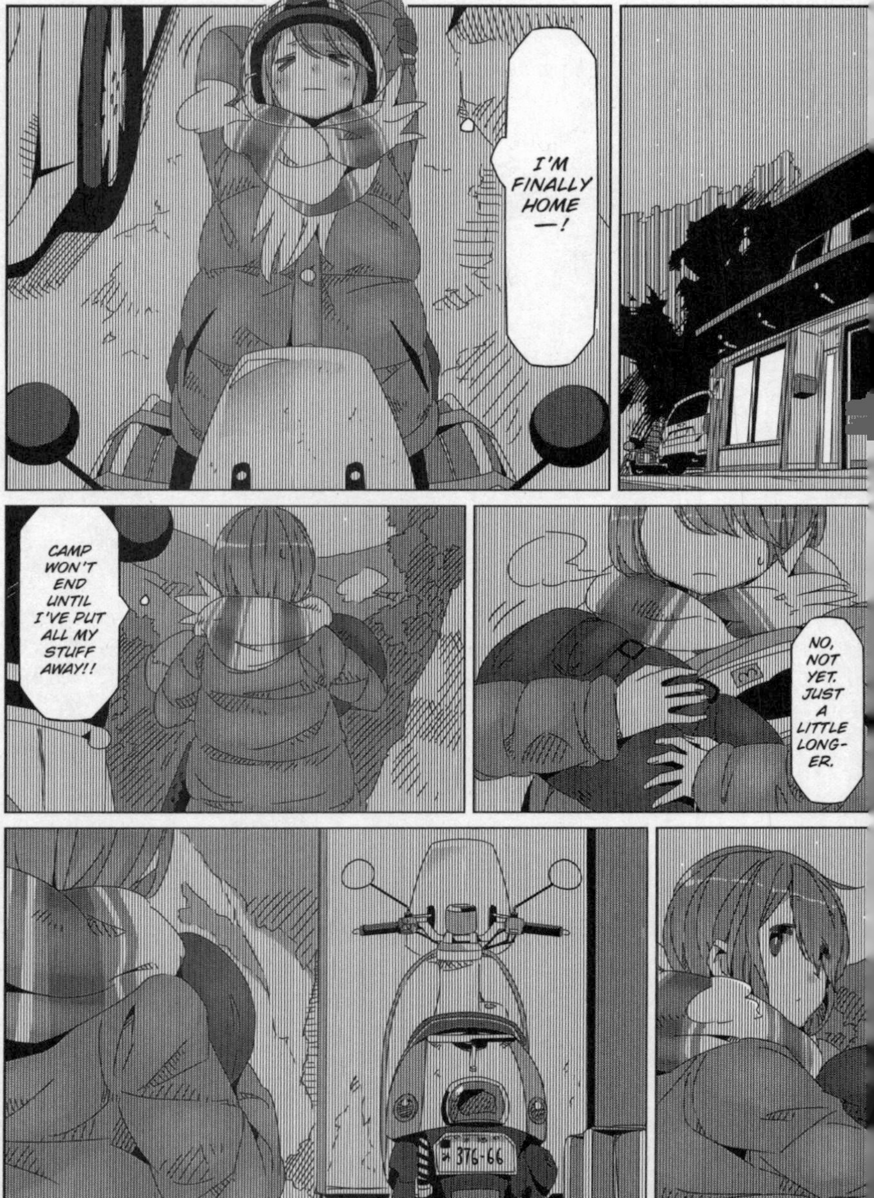
I'M FINALLY HOME—!
NO, NOT YET. JUST A LITTLE LONGER.
CAMP WON'T END UNTIL I'VE PUT ALL MY STUFF AWAY!!
376-66

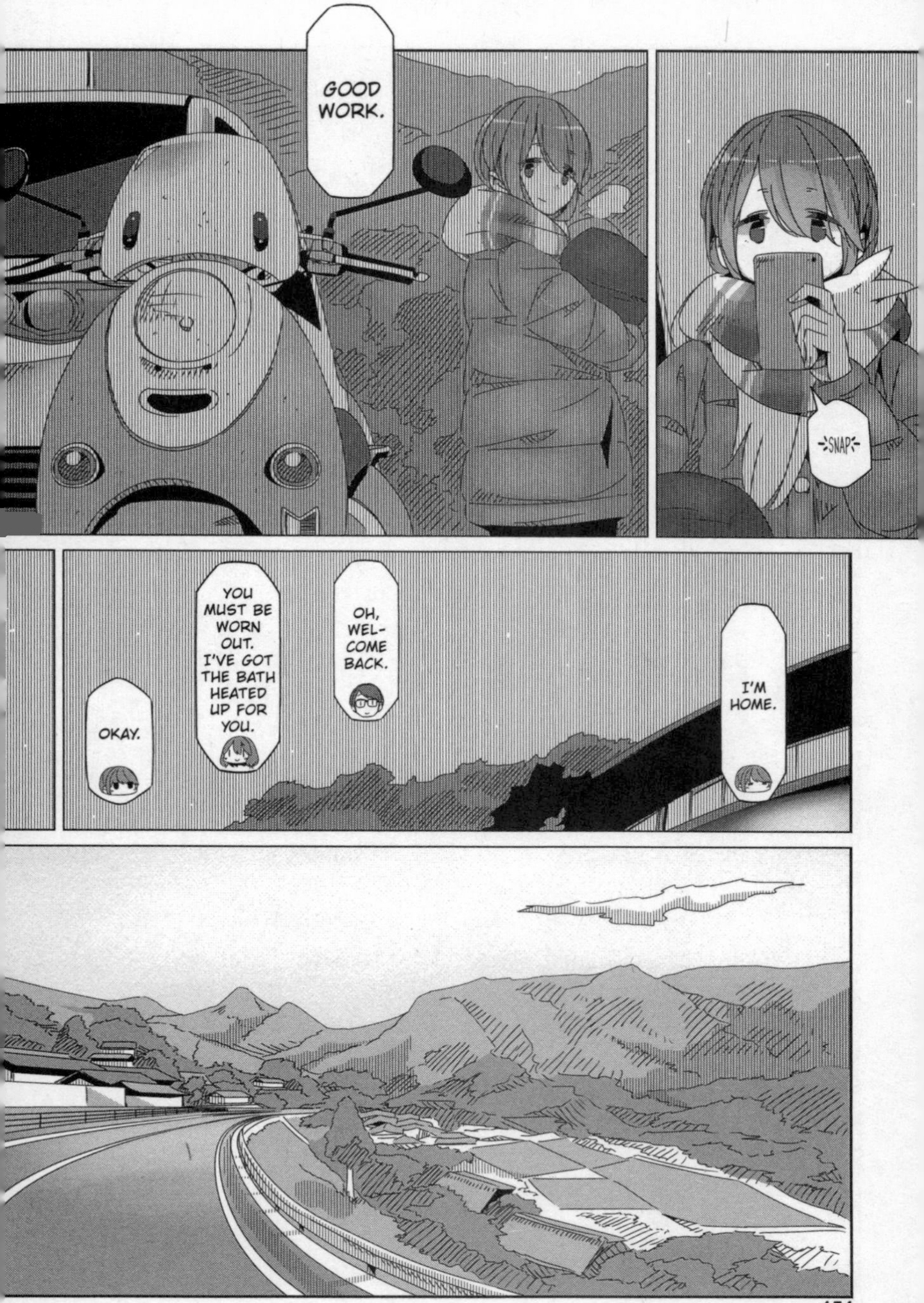

SNAP
GOOD WORK.
I'M HOME.
OH, WEL-COME BACK.
YOU MUST BE WORN OUT. I'VE GOT THE BATH HEATED UP FOR YOU.
OKAY.

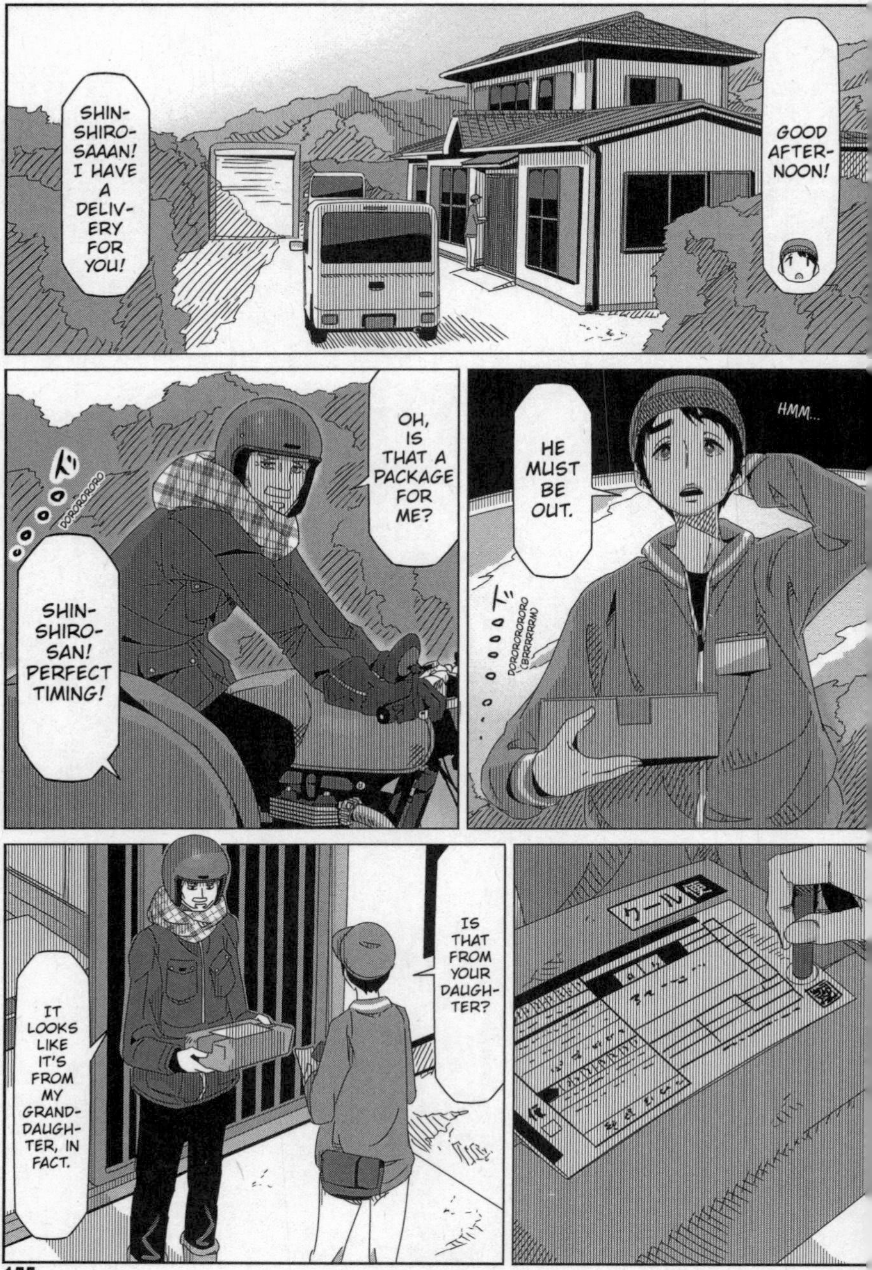
GOOD AFTERNOON!
SHINSHIRO-SAAAN! I HAVE A DELIVERY FOR YOU!
HMM...
HE MUST BE OUT.
ド DORORORORORO (BRRRRRM)
OH, IS THAT A PACKAGE FOR ME?
ド DORORORO
SHINSHIRO-SAN! PERFECT TIMING!
クール
IS THAT FROM YOUR DAUGHTER?
IT LOOKS LIKE IT'S FROM MY GRANDDAUGHTER, IN FACT.

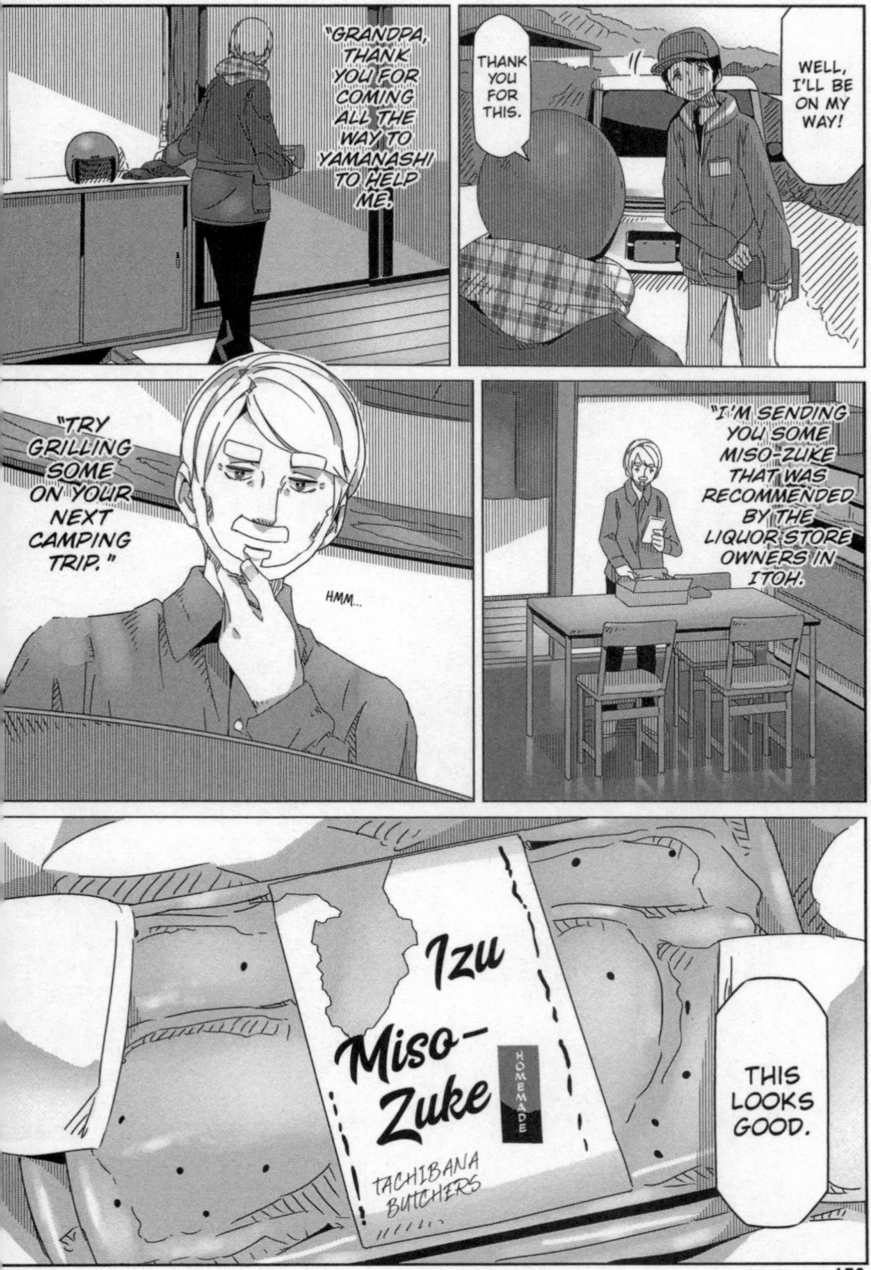
WELL, I'LL BE ON MY WAY!
THANK YOU FOR THIS.
"GRANDPA, THANK YOU FOR COMING ALL THE WAY TO YAMANASHI TO HELP ME.
"I'M SENDING YOU SOME MISO-ZUKE THAT WAS RECOMMENDED BY THE LIQUOR STORE OWNERS IN ITOH.
"TRY GRILLING SOME ON YOUR NEXT CAMPING TRIP."
HMM...
THIS LOOKS GOOD.
Izu Miso-Zuke
HOMEMADE
TACHIBANA BUTCHERS

TRANSLATION NOTES

COMMON HONORIFICS

no honorific: Indicates familiarity or closeness; if used without permission or reason, addressing someone in this manner would constitute an insult.
-san: The Japanese equivalent of Mr./Mrs./Miss. If a situation calls for politeness, this is the fail-safe honorific.
-kun: Used most often when referring to boys, this indicates affection or familiarity. Occasionally used by older men among their peers, but it may also be used by anyone referring to a person of lower standing.
-chan: An affectionate honorific indicating familiarity used mostly in reference to girls; also used in reference to cute persons or animals of either gender.
-sensei: A respectful term for teachers, artists, or high-level professionals.

(o)nee: Japanese equivalent to "older sis."
(o)nii: Japanese equivalent to "older bro."

100 yen is approximately 1 USD.
1 centimeter is approximately 0.39 inches. 1 kilometer is approximately 0.621 miles.

PAGE 7
Ajillo: Originally referring to a condiment made from *guajillo* chili and garlic, in Japan, it's the name of the specific dish shown here. The Japanese pronunciation is *ahiijo*, implying Latin American influence.

Spiny lobster: A crustacean that resembles but is not technically a lobster, the Japanese spiny lobster (featured here) is considered a fairly expensive food item.

PAGE 8
Mizobashiri: A parody of a type of first-run *sake* called *arabashiri*.

PAGE 12
"Ah-heeee": The "j" in *ajillo* is pronounced with the English "h" sound.

PAGE 20
Midnight Black Tea: A spoof on a brand of milk tea called Gogo no Koucha ("Afternoon Black Tea").

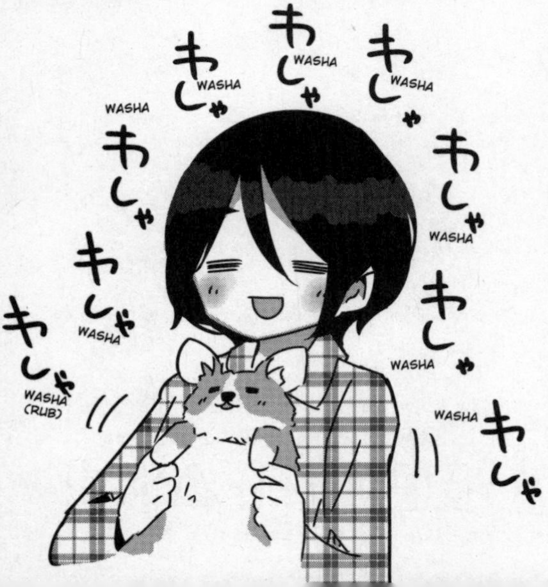
わしゃ WASHA
わしゃ WASHA
わしゃ WASHA
わしゃ WASHA
わしゃ WASHA
わしゃ WASHA
わしゃ WASHA
わしゃ WASHA (RUB)
わしゃ WASHA

PAGE 22
Driver's licenses in Japan: The legal ages are eighteen for cars and sixteen for mopeds. Schools do not offer driver's ed programs, so obtaining a license requires a specialized driving school.

PAGE 29
Nishi-Izu: Also known as Nishiizu or West Izu.

PAGE 30
Koganezaki park bust: The statue shown here is of Izu-no-Isaburou, an Izu native who was the captain of the Japanese military vessel Asahimaru.

PAGE 38
"Hopelessly stupid": Rin is paraphrasing a line from the Hans Christian Andersen tale "The Emperor's New Clothes."

TRANSLATION NOTES (continued)

PAGE 44
Rinlaxing: In Japanese, this is "Sapparin-chan," a portmanteau of the word *sappari* ("refreshed") and "Rin-chan."

PAGE 45
Tokoroten: A gelatinous food made from red-algae seaweed, it is often cut into noodle-like strips.

PAGE 62
Zojima: Literally "Elephant Island" in Japanese, its name refers to how the island resembles an elephant's body with the revealed *tombolo* as its "nose."

PAGE 81
Heda: A village in Numazu, Shizuoka. The Heda monument shown can be found at Deai-misaki, a cape and popular tourist spot.

PAGE 90–91
Shellfish: The Japanese term used here, *ebi*, is a little more specific. It can refer to shrimp, prawns, lobsters, and spiny lobsters. Thus, they're eating *ebi* sauce on top of *ebi*, which is why it's so overwhelming.

PAGE 106
→↘↓↙← + P: Meaning "move the joystick a half circle back and then punch," Nadeshiko's attack references Dhalsim's "Yoga Flame" from *Street Fighter II*, which utilizes a similar half-circle-forward input.

PAGE 111
Ike-Ike: A parody of an actual brand of *sake* called Ike.

PAGE 114
Laid-back mascot: *Yurukyara* in Japanese, the term refers to a kind of mascot often used for promotional purposes throughout Japan. It's the same *yuru* as in *Yurucamp*, the Japanese title of this manga!

***Matcha, hojicha,* coffee jelly**: A type of powdered green tea, a roasted green tea, and a gelatin-like dessert flavored with coffee and sugar, respectively.

PAGE 116
***Chibi* Inuko**: This nickname basically means "Mini Inuko."

PAGE 122
Itoh Saboten Park: Based on a real zoo named Izu Shaboten Zoo that has actual hot-spring capybaras.

PAGE 126
Yuzu: A type of Japanese citrus fruit.

PAGE 146
Pirate-*yaki*: *Kaizokuyaki* in Japanese, it's a special kind of squid-ink fried noodles found in Shizuoka.

PAGE 162
Altar: The altar in front of Aki consists of a spirit tablet and the wooden fish she's hitting, both of which are involved in rituals honoring the dead.

PAGE 173
"Only September": In Japanese convenience stores, meat buns are a seasonal item brought out in the colder months as a warm snack for customers.

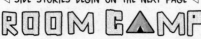

PAGE 176
Hamburg steak: A hamburger-like meat patty closer in consistency to meat loaf or Salisbury steak.

◁ SIDE STORIES BEGIN ON THE NEXT PAGE ◁

ROOM CAMP

AFTER-SCHOOL 70 WEARABLE TENT

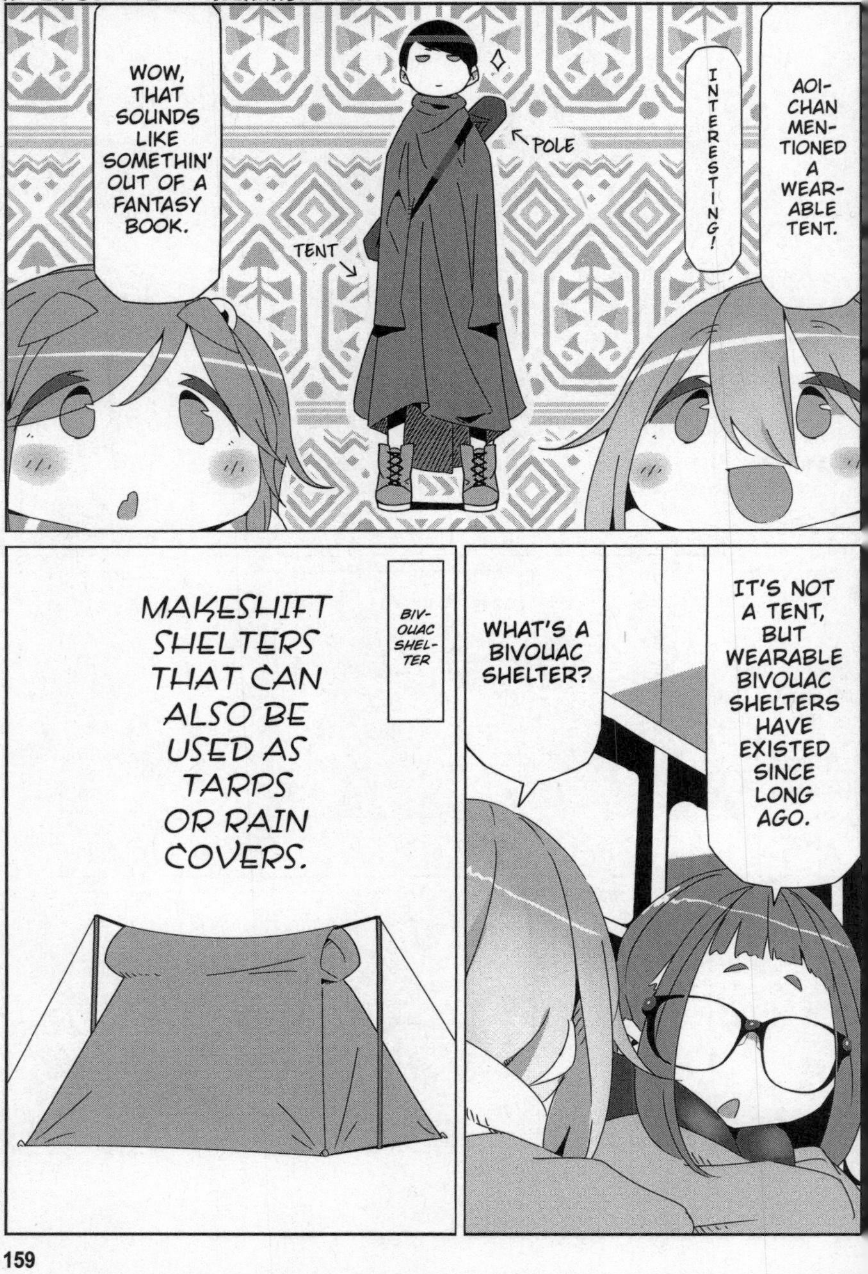

AOI-CHAN MENTIONED A WEARABLE TENT.
INTERESTING!
POLE
TENT
WOW, THAT SOUNDS LIKE SOMETHIN' OUT OF A FANTASY BOOK.
IT'S NOT A TENT, BUT WEARABLE BIVOUAC SHELTERS HAVE EXISTED SINCE LONG AGO.
WHAT'S A BIVOUAC SHELTER?
BIVOUAC SHELTER
MAKESHIFT SHELTERS THAT CAN ALSO BE USED AS TARPS OR RAIN COVERS.

USES
AS A SHEET
AS A PONCHO
WOW, THERE ARE SO MANY DIFFERENT USES.
AS A TARP
A SHELTER FOR TWO
WOW, WHAT'S THAT? LOOKS FUN.
THIS IS ONE OF ITS EMERGENCY USES.
A FOUR-PERSON SHELTER
SO I GUESS THIS IS WHAT IT'D BE LIKE WITH FOUR PEOPLE.
THAT'S RIGHT.
A SIXTEEN-PERSON SHELTER
WOW —!
WHAT PENALTY GAME IS THIS?

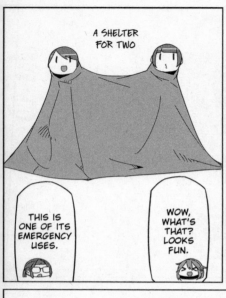

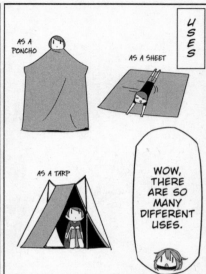

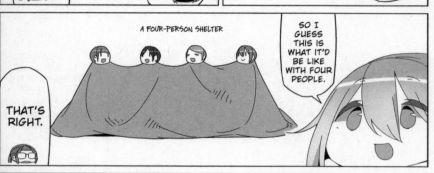

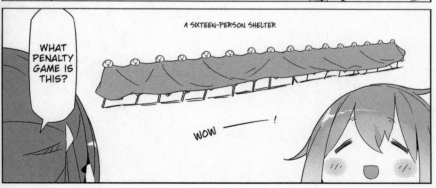

AFTER-SCHOOL 71 THE OEC (ACTUALLY JUST CHIAKI), SIXTY YEARS FROM NOW

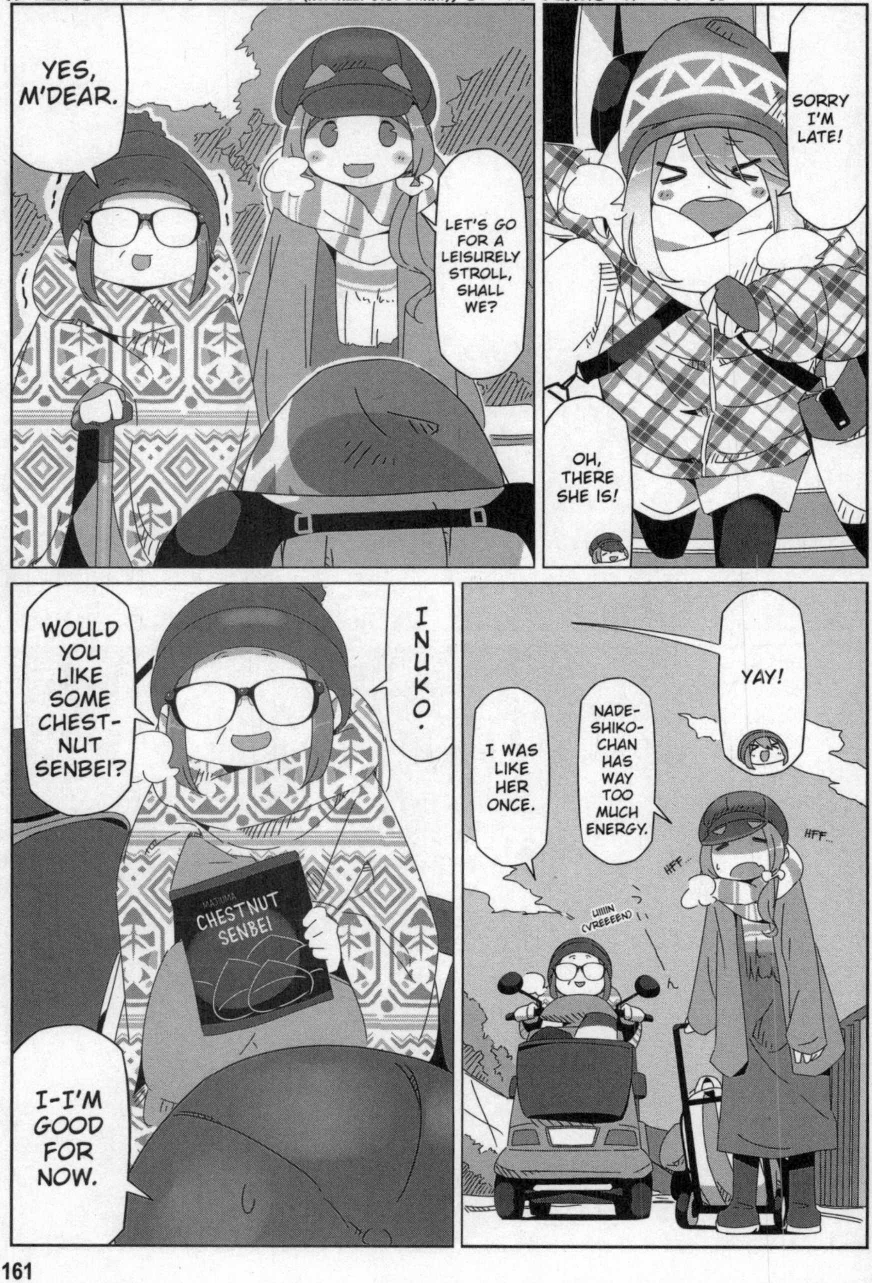

SORRY I'M LATE!
OH, THERE SHE IS!
LET'S GO FOR A LEISURELY STROLL, SHALL WE?
YES, M'DEAR.
YAY!
NADESHIKO-CHAN HAS WAY TOO MUCH ENERGY.
I WAS LIKE HER ONCE.
HFF... HFF...
UIIIIN (VREEEEN)
INUKO.
WOULD YOU LIKE SOME CHESTNUT SENBEI?
CHESTNUT SENBEI
I-I'M GOOD FOR NOW.

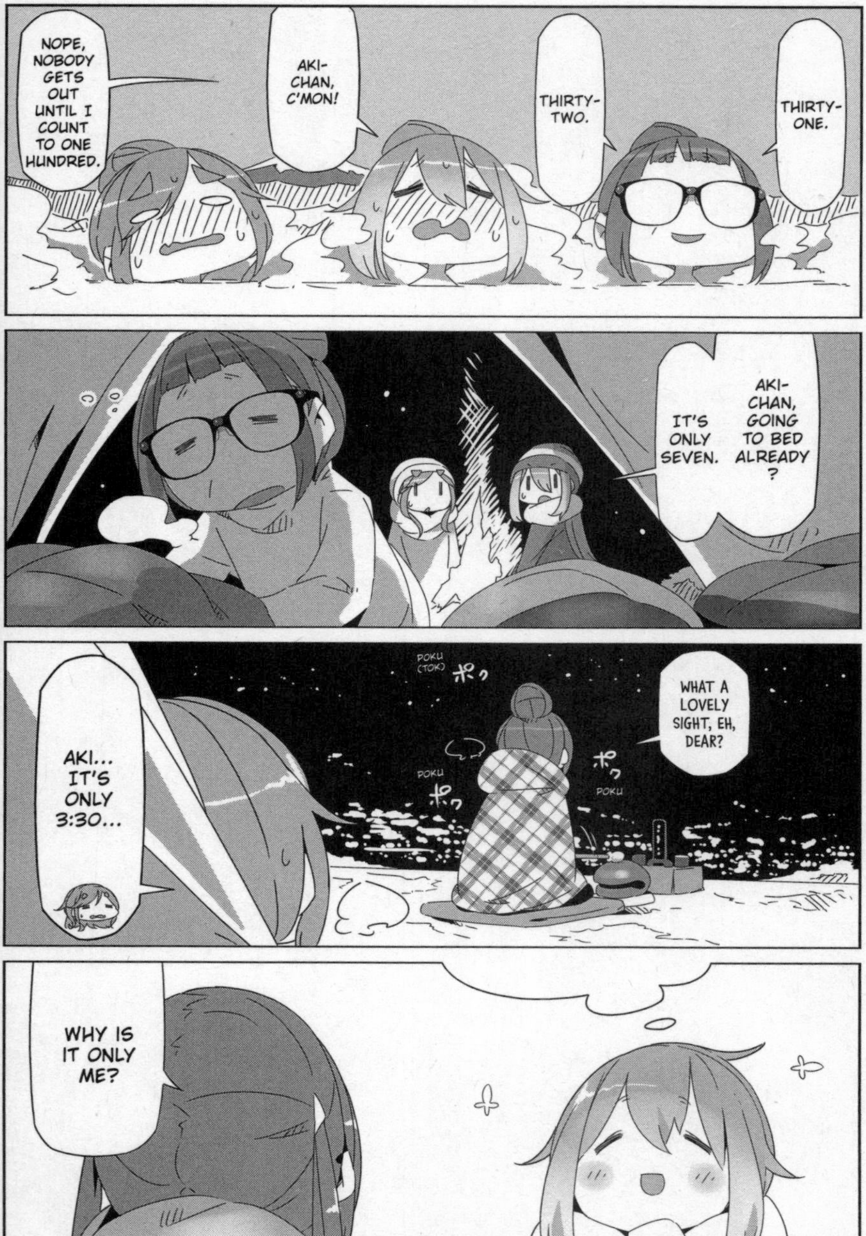
THIRTY-ONE.
THIRTY-TWO.
AKI-CHAN, C'MON!
NOPE, NOBODY GETS OUT UNTIL I COUNT TO ONE HUNDRED.
AKI-CHAN, GOING TO BED ALREADY?
IT'S ONLY SEVEN.
WHAT A LOVELY SIGHT, EH, DEAR?
POKU
POKU (TOK)
POKU
AKI... IT'S ONLY 3:30...
WHY IS IT ONLY ME?

AFTER-SCHOOL 72 KNITTING GAFFE

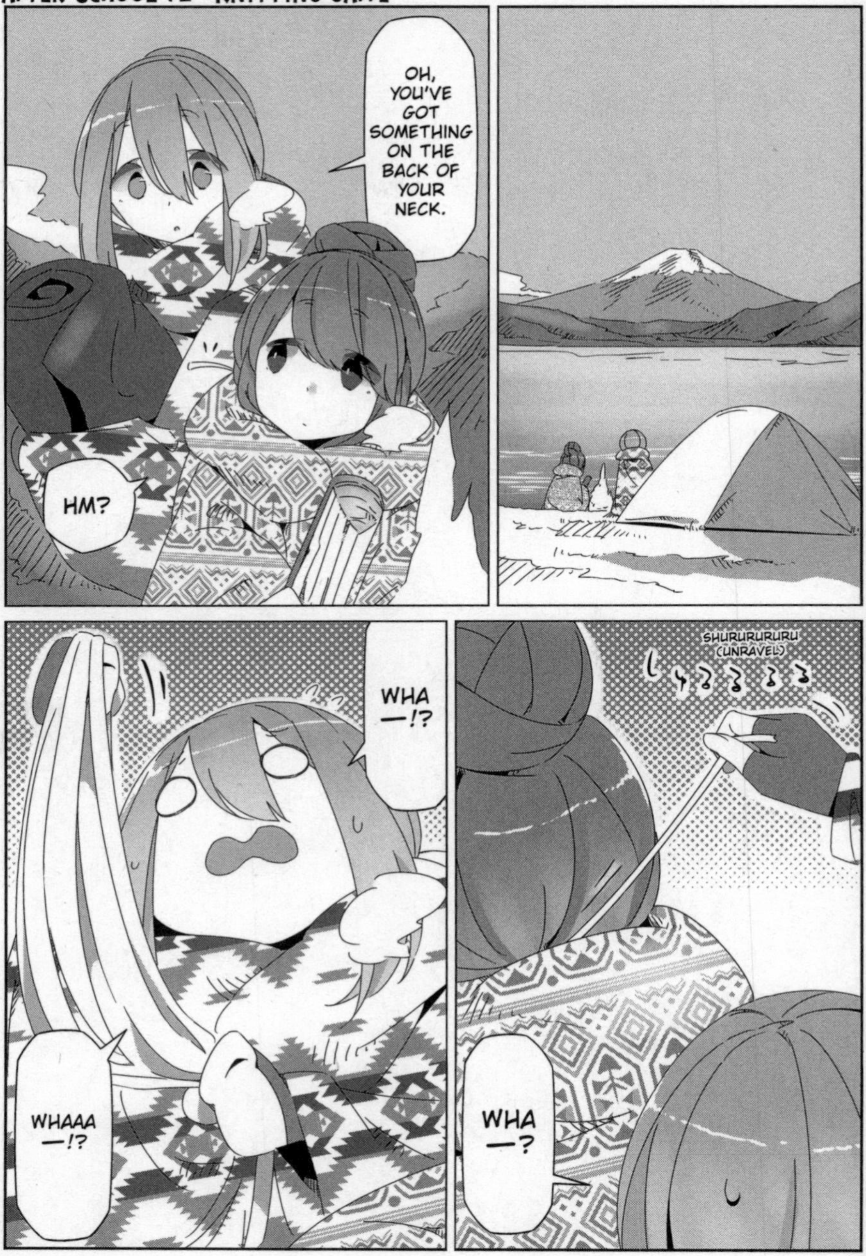

OH, YOU'VE GOT SOMETHING ON THE BACK OF YOUR NECK.
HM?
SHURURURURU (UNRAVEL)
しゅるるるるる
WHA—?
WHA—!?
WHAAA—!?

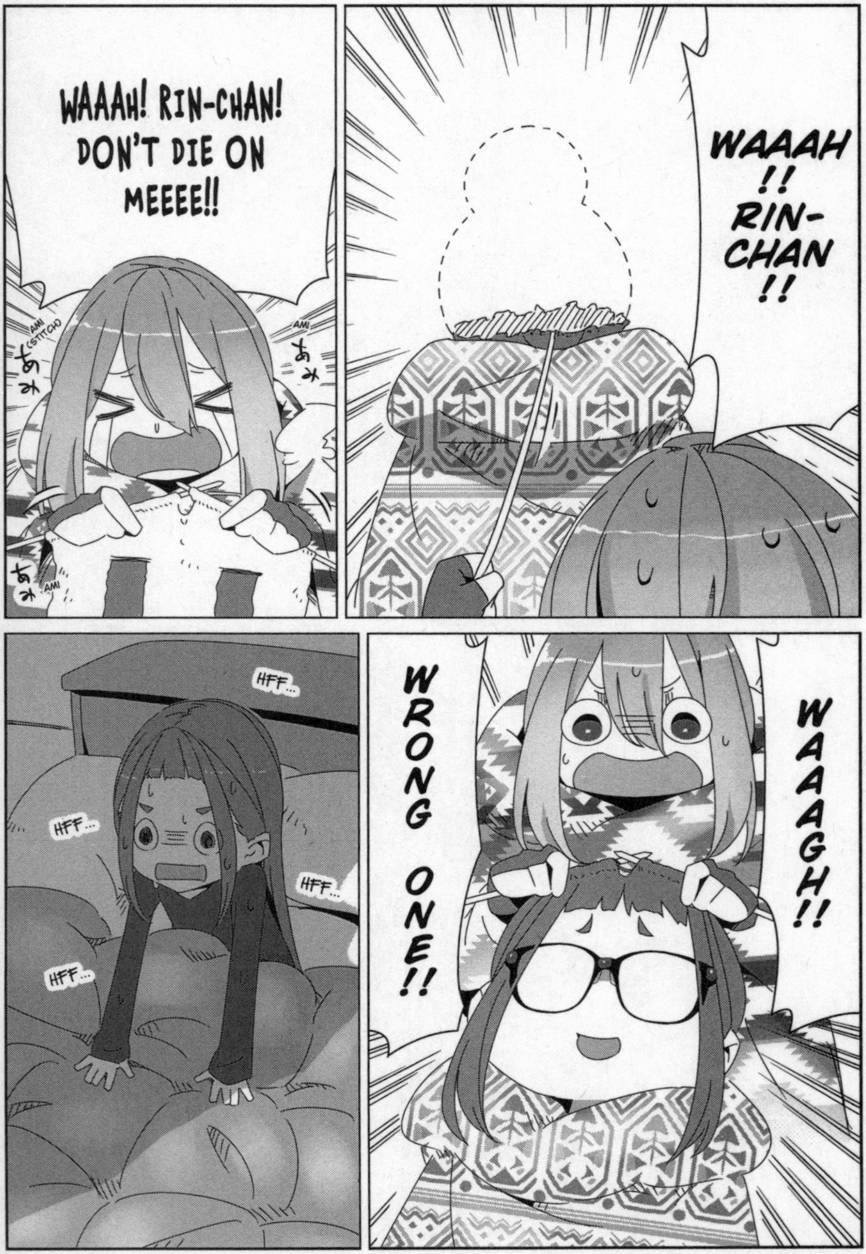
WAAAH!! RIN-CHAN!!
WAAAH! RIN-CHAN! DON'T DIE ON MEEEE!!
AMI (STITCH)
あみ
AMI
あみ
あみ
AMI
WAAAAGH!!
WRONG ONE!!
HFF...
HFF...
HFF...
HFF...

AFTER-SCHOOL 73 THE KAGAMIHARA CONUNDRUM

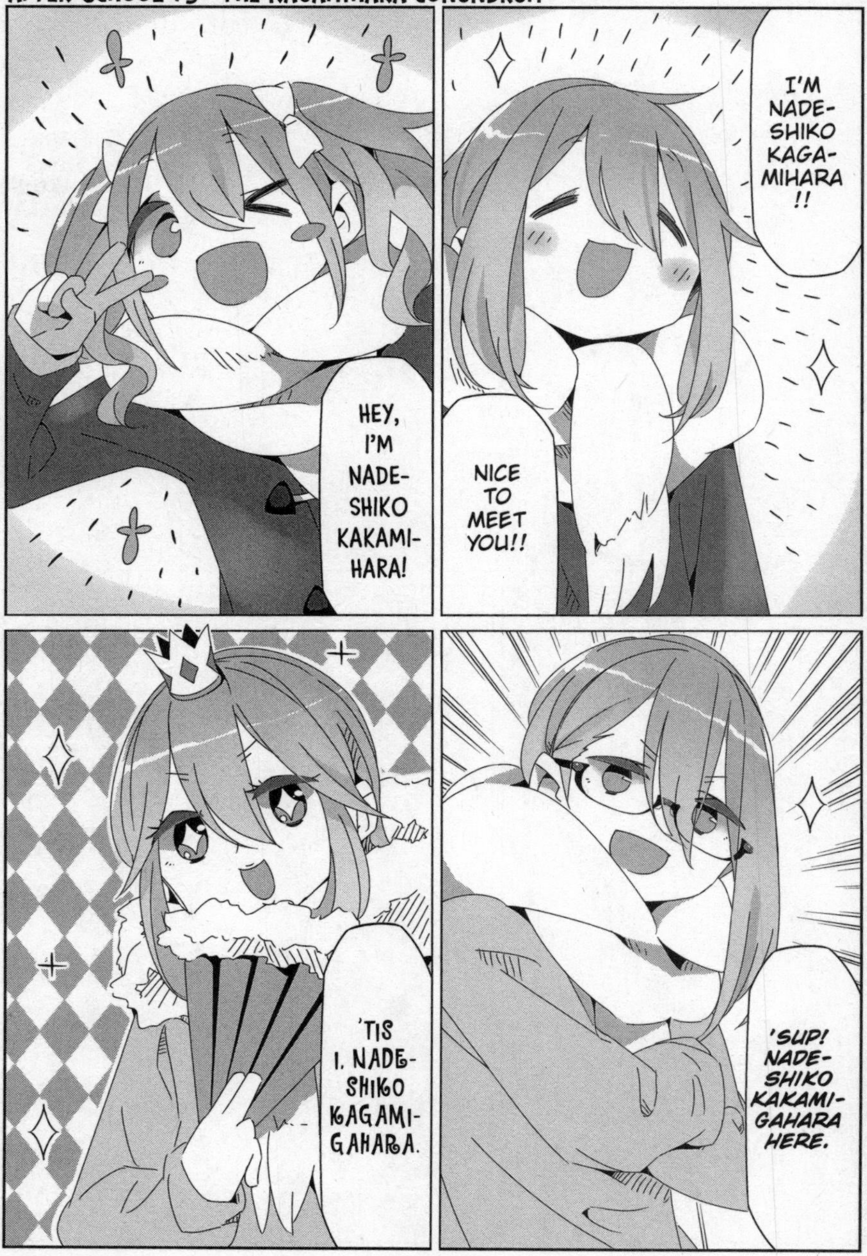
I'M NADESHIKO KAGAMIHARA!!
NICE TO MEET YOU!!
HEY, I'M NADESHIKO KAKAMIHARA!
'SUP! NADESHIKO KAKAMIGAHARA HERE.
'TIS I, NADESHIKO KAGAMIGAHARA.

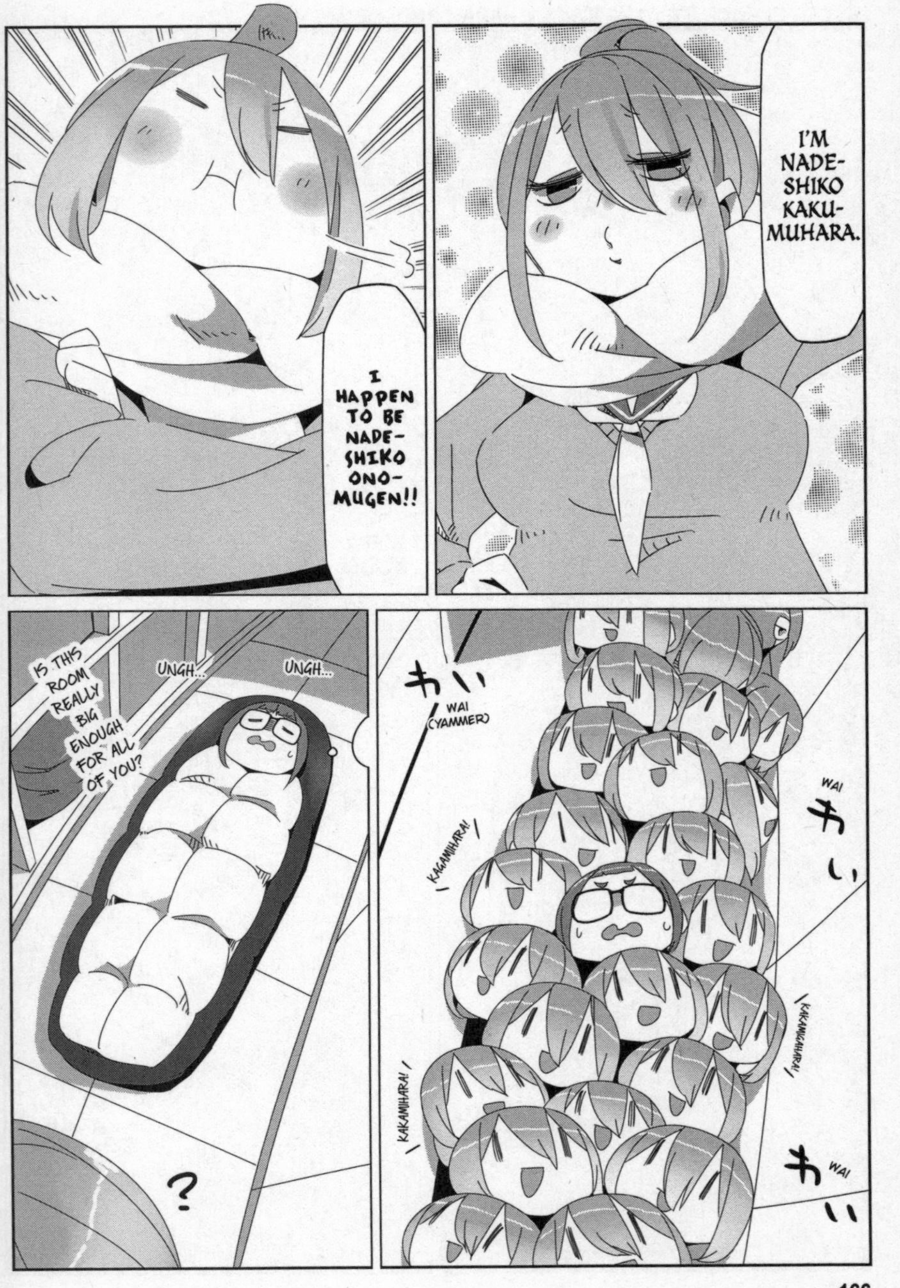
I'M NADE-SHIKO KAKU-MUHARA.
I HAPPEN TO BE NADE-SHIKO ONO-MUGEN!!
わい
WAI (YAMMER)
WAI
わい
WAI
わい
KAGAMIHARA!
KAKAMIGAHARA!
KAKAMIHARA!
UNGH...
UNGH...
IS THIS ROOM REALLY BIG ENOUGH FOR ALL OF YOU?
?

AFTER-SCHOOL 74 ONE CARIBOU-KUN PER HOUSEHOLD

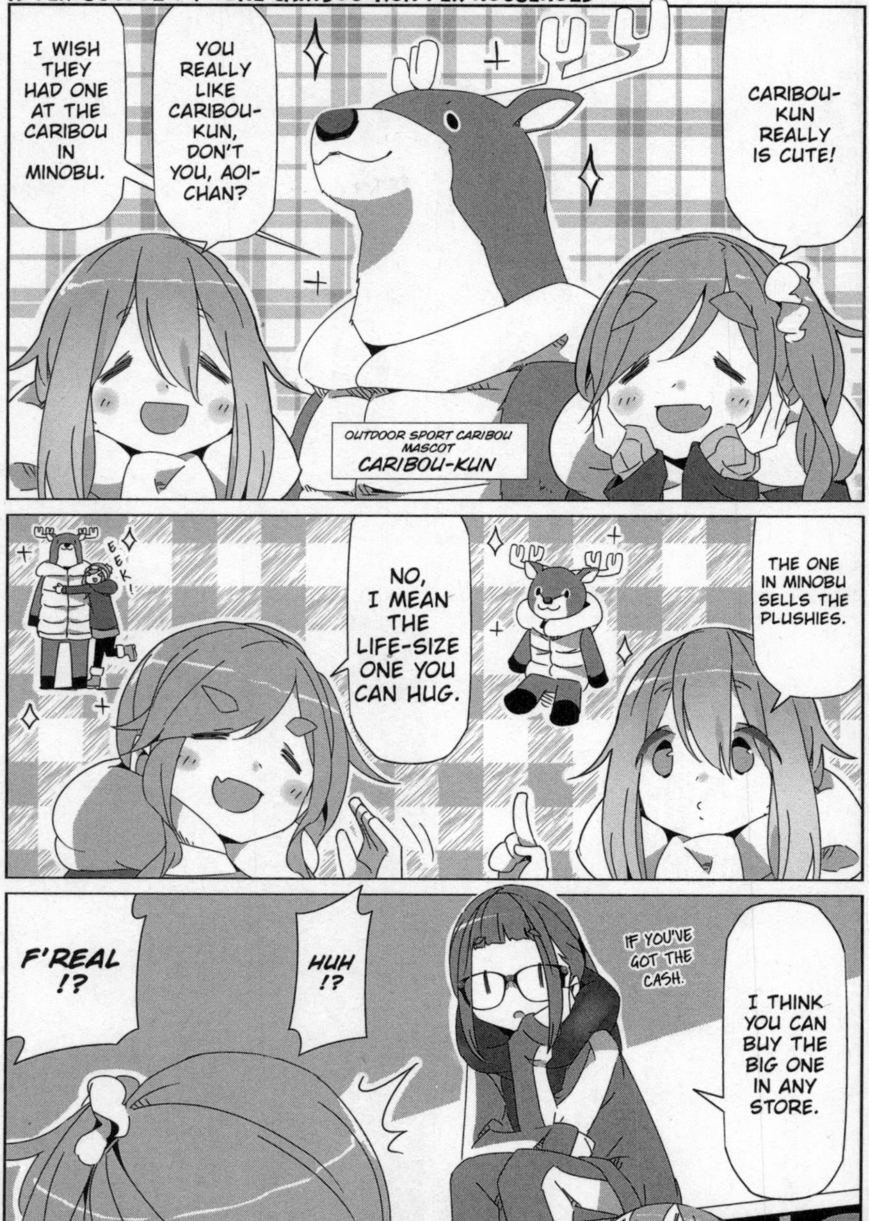
CARIBOU-KUN REALLY IS CUTE!
YOU REALLY LIKE CARIBOU-KUN, DON'T YOU, AOI-CHAN?
I WISH THEY HAD ONE AT THE CARIBOU IN MINOBU.
OUTDOOR SPORT CARIBOU MASCOT CARIBOU-KUN
THE ONE IN MINOBU SELLS THE PLUSHIES.
NO, I MEAN THE LIFE-SIZE ONE YOU CAN HUG.
EEK!
I THINK YOU CAN BUY THE BIG ONE IN ANY STORE.
IF YOU'VE GOT THE CASH.
HUH!?
F'REAL!?

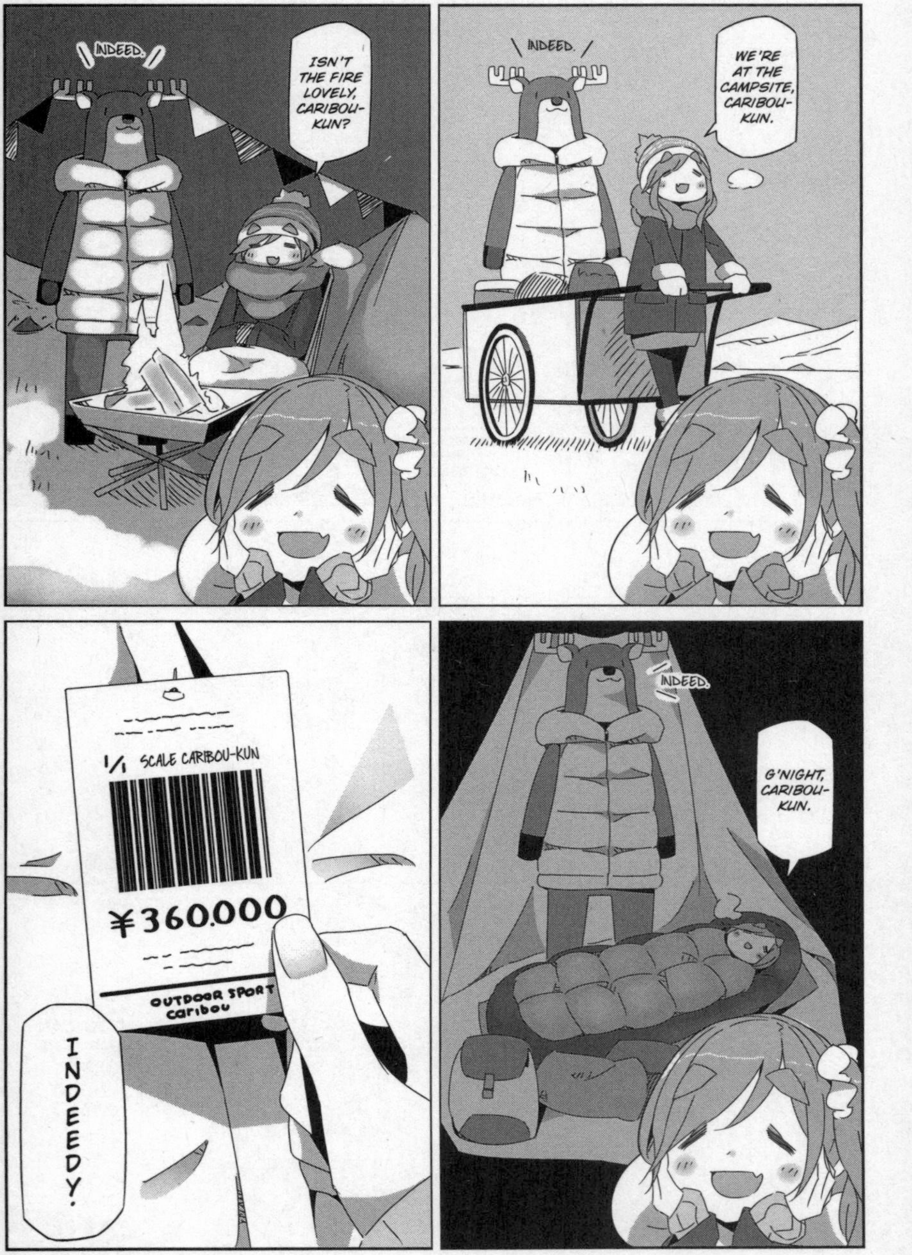
WE'RE AT THE CAMPSITE, CARIBOU-KUN.
INDEED.
ISN'T THE FIRE LOVELY, CARIBOU-KUN?
INDEED.
G'NIGHT, CARIBOU-KUN.
INDEED.
1/1 SCALE CARIBOU-KUN
¥360.000
OUTDOOR SPORT caribou
INDEEDY.

AFTER-SCHOOL 75 MINIATURE CAMP

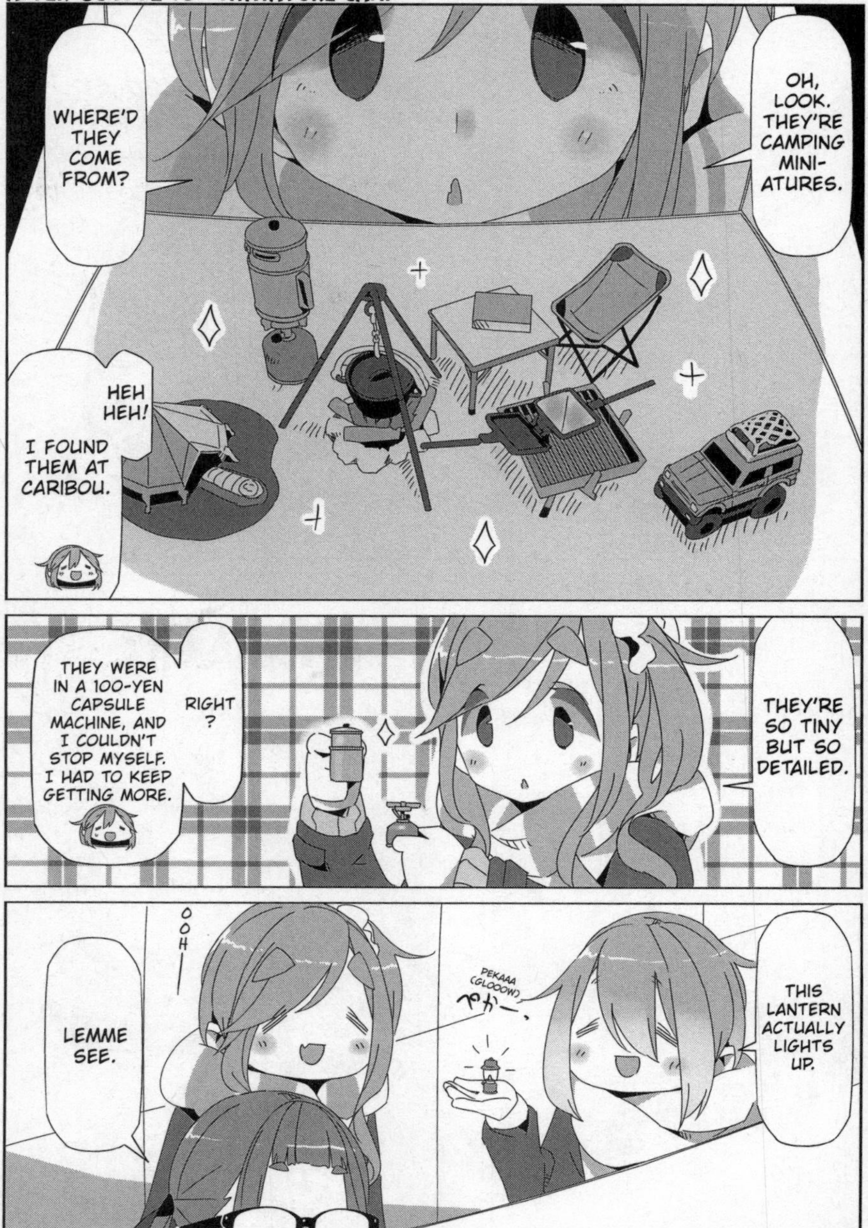
OH, LOOK. THEY'RE CAMPING MINI-ATURES.
WHERE'D THEY COME FROM?
HEH HEH!
I FOUND THEM AT CARIBOU.
THEY'RE SO TINY BUT SO DETAILED.
RIGHT?
THEY WERE IN A 100-YEN CAPSULE MACHINE, AND I COULDN'T STOP MYSELF. I HAD TO KEEP GETTING MORE.
THIS LANTERN ACTUALLY LIGHTS UP.
PEKAAA (GLOOOW)
OOH—
LEMME SEE.

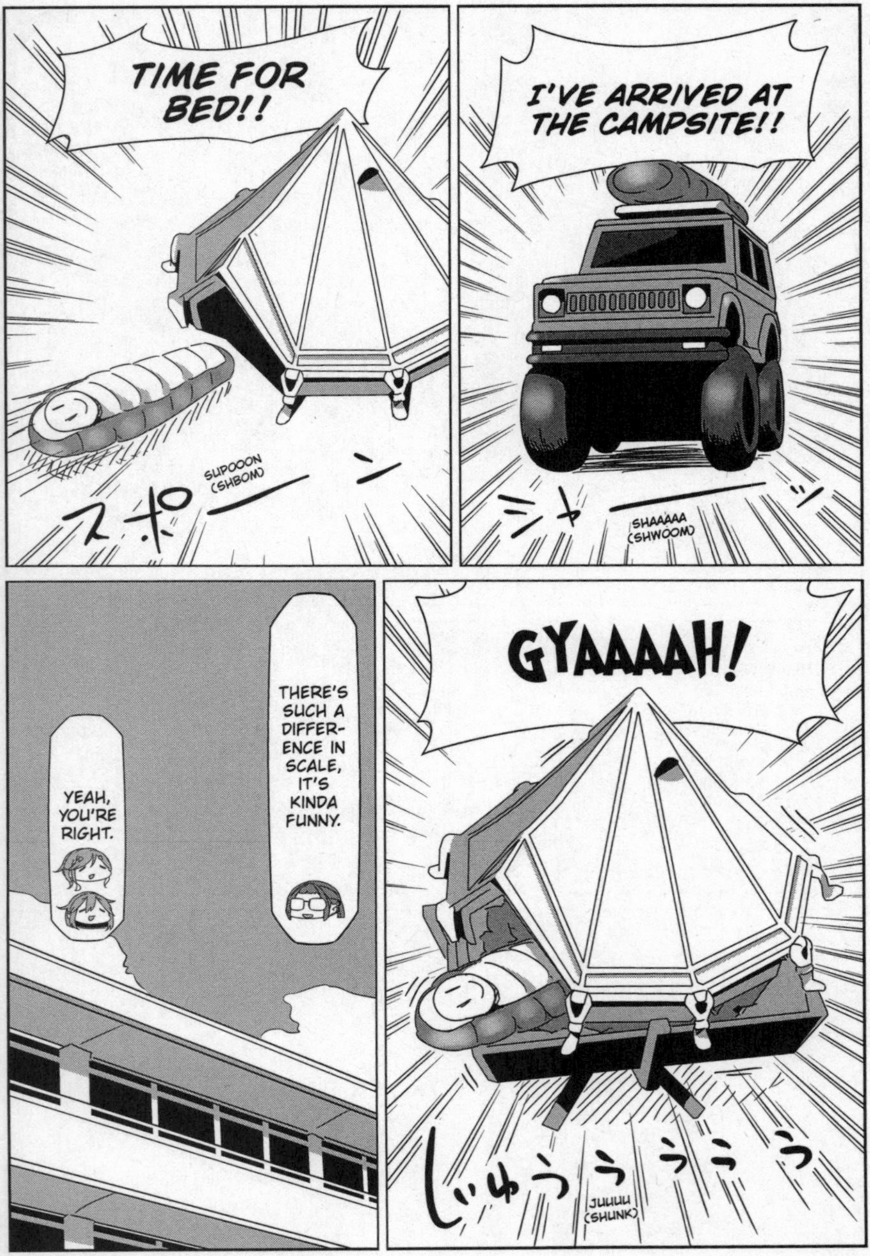
I'VE ARRIVED AT THE CAMPSITE!!
シャーーーッ
SHAAAAA (SHWOOM)
TIME FOR BED!!
スポーーーン
SUPOOON (SHBOM)
GYAAAAH!
じゅううううう
JUUUU (SHUNK)
THERE'S SUCH A DIFFERENCE IN SCALE, IT'S KINDA FUNNY.
YEAH, YOU'RE RIGHT.

AFTER-SCHOOL 76 BURNING POWER

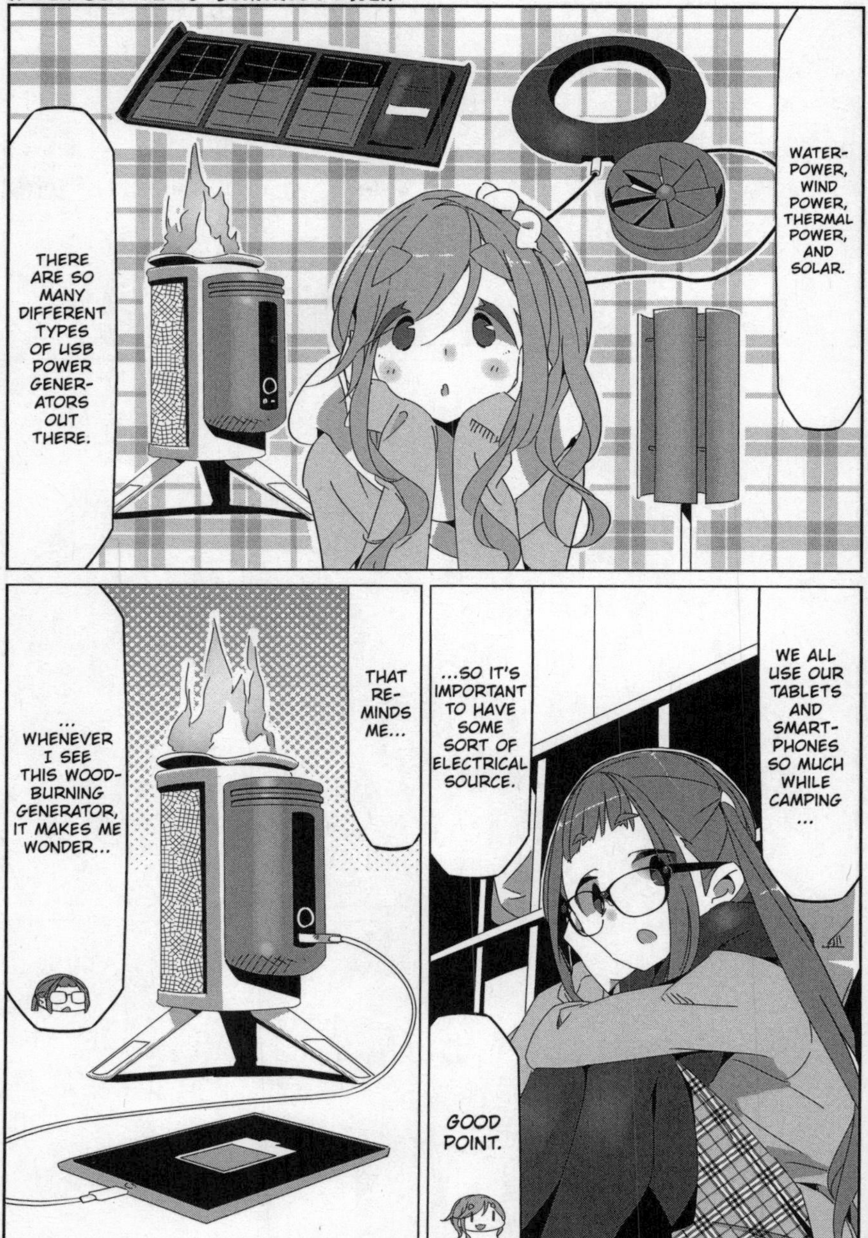
WATER-POWER, WIND POWER, THERMAL POWER, AND SOLAR.
THERE ARE SO MANY DIFFERENT TYPES OF USB POWER GENERATORS OUT THERE.
WE ALL USE OUR TABLETS AND SMARTPHONES SO MUCH WHILE CAMPING...
...SO IT'S IMPORTANT TO HAVE SOME SORT OF ELECTRICAL SOURCE.
GOOD POINT.
THAT REMINDS ME...
...WHENEVER I SEE THIS WOOD-BURNING GENERATOR, IT MAKES ME WONDER...

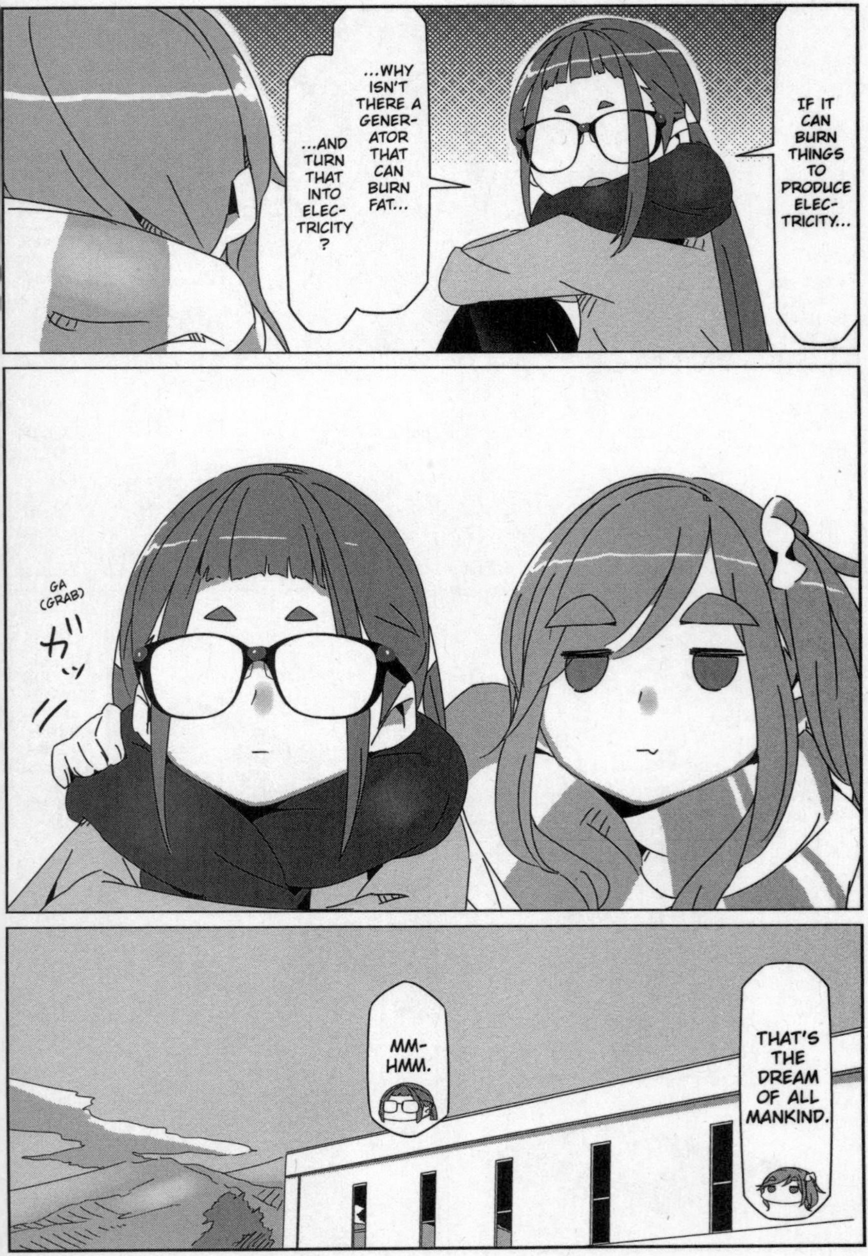
IF IT CAN BURN THINGS TO PRODUCE ELECTRICITY...
...WHY ISN'T THERE A GENERATOR THAT CAN BURN FAT...
...AND TURN THAT INTO ELECTRICITY?
GA (GRAB)
ガッ
THAT'S THE DREAM OF ALL MANKIND.
MM-HMM.

AFTER-SCHOOL 77 THOSE WHO SMOOSH

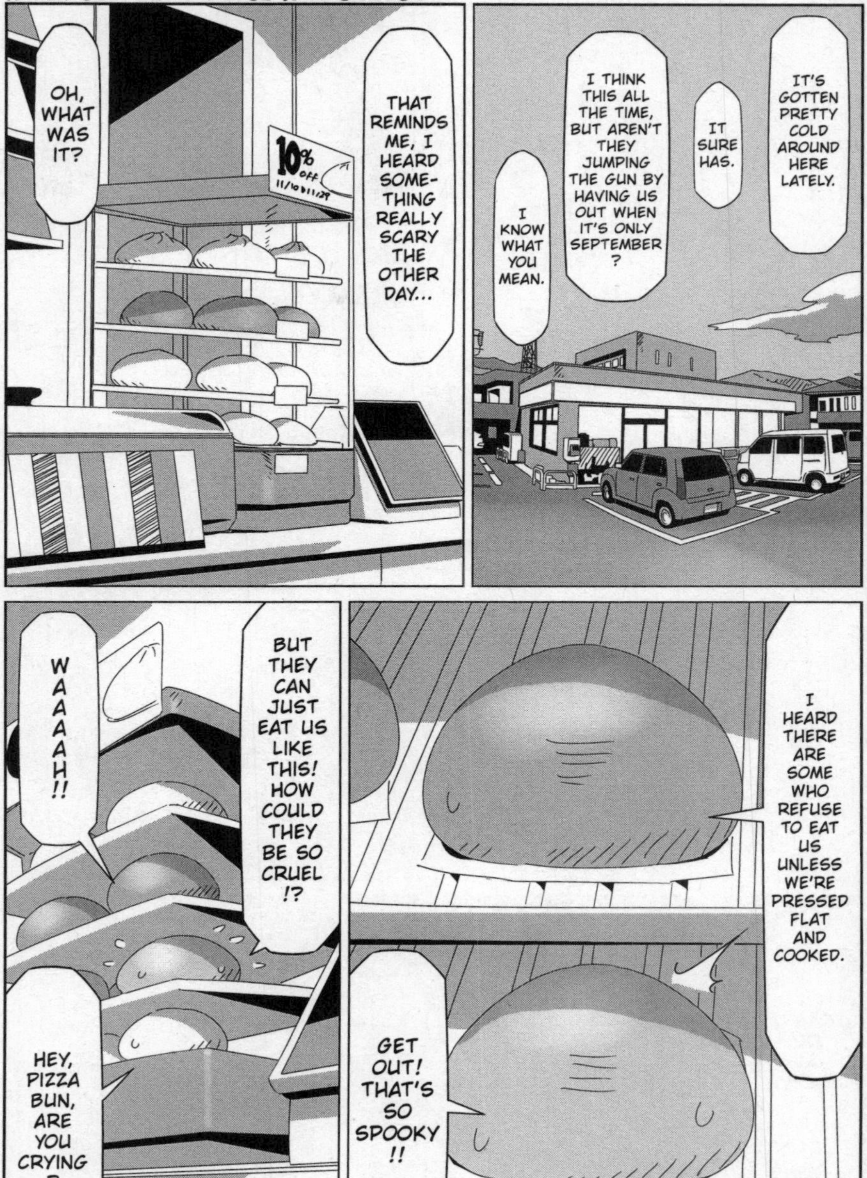

IT'S GOTTEN PRETTY COLD AROUND HERE LATELY.
IT SURE HAS.
I THINK THIS ALL THE TIME, BUT AREN'T THEY JUMPING THE GUN BY HAVING US OUT WHEN IT'S ONLY SEPTEMBER?
I KNOW WHAT YOU MEAN.
THAT REMINDS ME, I HEARD SOMETHING REALLY SCARY THE OTHER DAY...
OH, WHAT WAS IT?
10% off
I HEARD THERE ARE SOME WHO REFUSE TO EAT US UNLESS WE'RE PRESSED FLAT AND COOKED.
GET OUT! THAT'S SO SPOOKY!!
BUT THEY CAN JUST EAT US LIKE THIS! HOW COULD THEY BE SO CRUEL!?
WAAAAAH!!
HEY, PIZZA BUN, ARE YOU CRYING?

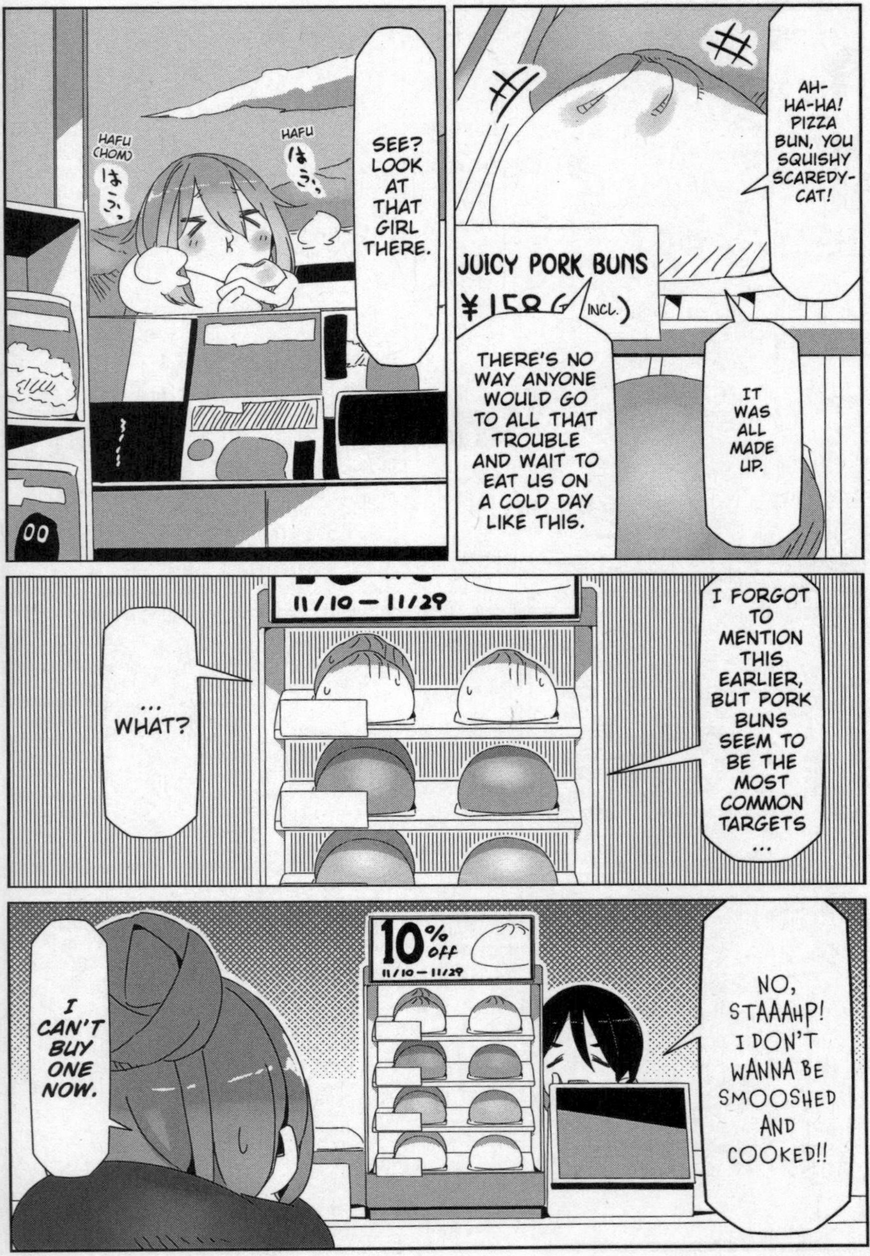

AH-HA-HA! PIZZA BUN, YOU SQUISHY SCAREDY-CAT!
IT WAS ALL MADE UP.
THERE'S NO WAY ANYONE WOULD GO TO ALL THAT TROUBLE AND WAIT TO EAT US ON A COLD DAY LIKE THIS.
JUICY PORK BUNS
¥158 (
INCL.)
SEE? LOOK AT THAT GIRL THERE.
HAFU
HAFU (CHOM)
I FORGOT TO MENTION THIS EARLIER, BUT PORK BUNS SEEM TO BE THE MOST COMMON TARGETS...
... WHAT?
11/10 – 11/29
NO, STAAAHP! I DON'T WANNA BE SMOOSHED AND COOKED!!
10% OFF
11/10 – 11/29
I CAN'T BUY ONE NOW.

AFTER-SCHOOL 78 SANDWICH SHENANIGANS

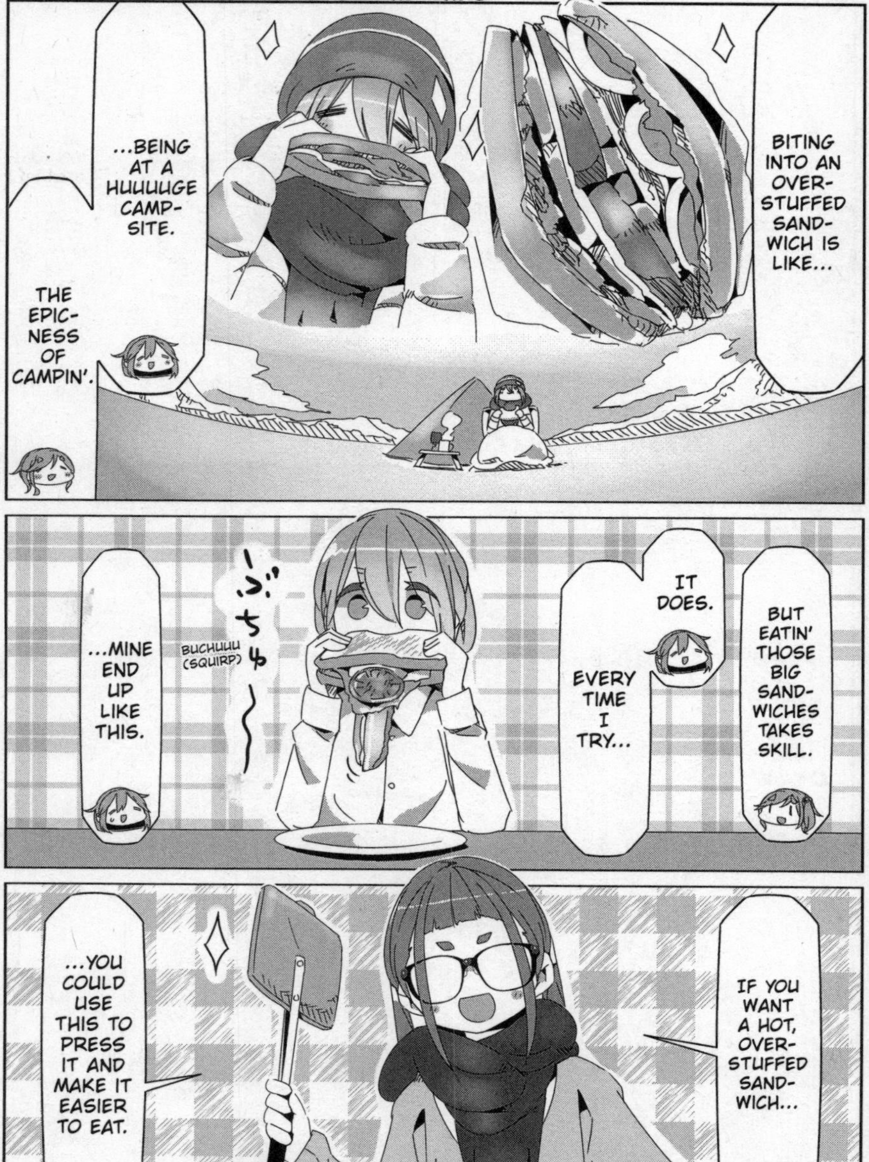
BITING INTO AN OVER-STUFFED SAND-WICH IS LIKE...
...BEING AT A HUUUUGE CAMP-SITE.
THE EPIC-NESS OF CAMPIN'.
BUT EATIN' THOSE BIG SAND-WICHES TAKES SKILL.
IT DOES.
EVERY TIME I TRY...
ぶちゅ〜
BUCHUUU (SQUIRP)
...MINE END UP LIKE THIS.
IF YOU WANT A HOT, OVER-STUFFED SAND-WICH...
...YOU COULD USE THIS TO PRESS IT AND MAKE IT EASIER TO EAT.

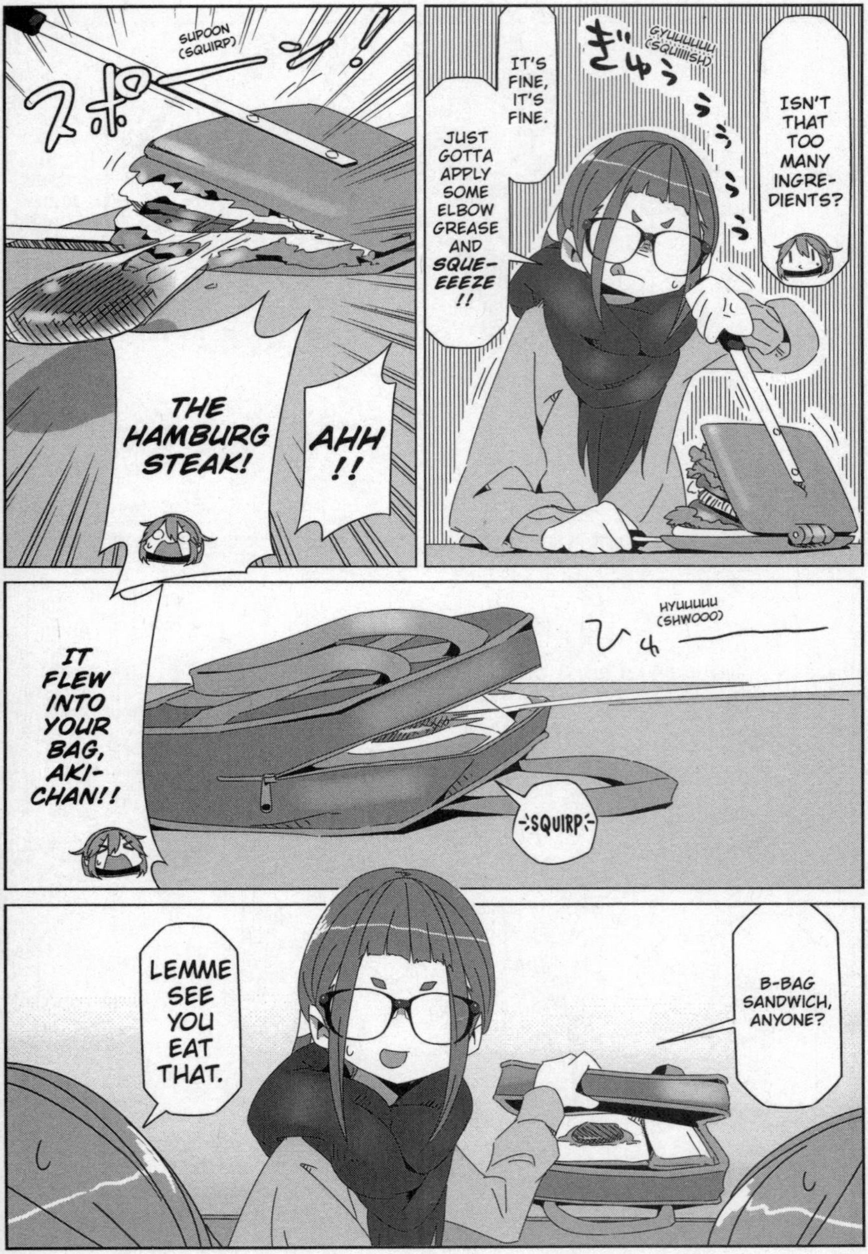
ISN'T THAT TOO MANY INGREDIENTS?
GYUUUUUU (SQUIIIISH)
IT'S FINE, IT'S FINE.
JUST GOTTA APPLY SOME ELBOW GREASE AND SQUEE-EEEZE!!
SUPOON (SQUIRP)
AHH!!
THE HAMBURG STEAK!
HYUUUUU (SHWOOO)
SQUIRP
IT FLEW INTO YOUR BAG, AKI-CHAN!!
B-BAG SANDWICH, ANYONE?
LEMME SEE YOU EAT THAT.